Other books by **Gary B. Boyd**

HUMANITY'S VESSEL

GARY B. BOYD

authorHOUSE

AuthorHouse™
1663 Liberty Drive
Bloomington, IN 47403
www.authorhouse.com
Phone: 833-262-8899

Published by AuthorHouse 10/08/2020

ISBN: 978-1-6655-0358-7 (sc)
ISBN: 978-1-6655-0400-3 (e)

Library of Congress Control Number: 2020919965

Print information available on the last page.

This book is printed on acid-free paper.

CONTENTS

PREFACE

It is human destiny to expand - knowledge, population, territorial dominance. The need is ingrained in the psyche of humanity. Every major religion expresses human expansion as a core value. We will expand, pushing the edges of our existence further and farther. We will become more tomorrow than we are today ... or we will cease to exist as humans. That is our nature.

Human expansion, human growth, comes at a cost. Natural resources, physical and metaphysical, are taxed to support the development of a sentient species.

Metaphysically, religions — the legitimization of all that is valued as social norms — fall into disfavor because the axioms and tenets no longer support the expanded humanity's need to grow, eventually posing impenetrable barriers to expansion and growth. New religions are 'discovered' to supplant the passé dogmatic doctrines. But ... religions represent core believes, core values, essential guides, and boundaries; without religion in some form, human expansion would cease, withering beneath the sharp light of exposure to sociological turmoil. Without boundaries, without rules of engagement, humans fall back on their base nature. They become no different than other forms of life bound only by the survival of the fittest, purposefully selfish to one's own needs. Growth cannot exist without religion to frame it; religion cannot exist without growth to sustain it.

Physically, resources are limited. The earth provides a finite amount of sustenance, breathable air, water, food, raw materials for the tools of expansion and growth, and energy.

Of those, the least limited is energy. Human growth involves discovery of newly available energy sources, some of which are virtually and practically unlimited ... accessibility notwithstanding. New, accessible energy sources will fuel human expansion to the point of exceeding the ability of the planet to provide food, water, and raw materials for tools.

And when that day comes, the ecosystem collapses.

What will humans do when that day comes?

Become extinct? Withdraw into a religion that advocates basic survival rather than continual expansion? Devolve?

Earth, the planet of our ancestors, has often been cited as a mere step along the way for humanity. Authors and pundits have written volumes hypothesizing the 'seeding' of humans on Earth to further the expansion of an ever-growing population of sentient beings in the Milky Way galaxy, or the salvation of human cultures that have exceeded their limits on other planets.

Regardless of ones subscribed belief regarding the role of humanity in the universe, the cold hard truth is that humans will either overpopulate and destroy the planet Earth, or the planet Earth will revolt and expel humanity from its mantle. Humanity must have a plan for survival.

Reach for the stars. The only option available to support expansion and growth is space flight, to be that species described by Eric von Daniken in *Chariots of the Gods*. But ... how will that transpire? Will humanity set off on a journey through the void of space to preselected worlds to supplant indigenous populations? Will humanity seek unsettled worlds to terraform and use for expansion?

Or will humanity take a shot in the dark in hopes of finding salvation at the end of a desperate journey for survival.

Such an endeavor will not just happen. Such an endeavor will require monumental planning. Such an endeavor will require vast resources. Such an endeavor will require sacrifice.

Humanity One, one of humanity's desperate attempts to survive the results of generations of excess expansion and growth, stretched human capabilities by ignoring science... the science of human behavior. It is human destiny to expand because it is humanity's need to question the status quo. One can only hope it is humanity's destiny to survive.

CHAPTER 1

CESAR

Cesar Er Yi shifted his position in the Captain's Chair. The role of Captain was not hereditary, not by design. His sire, August Yi, was the first Captain of Humanity One. Chosen by the Innovators before Humanity One was launched from the dark side of Earth's moon, Captain August Yi was charged with a responsibility unlike any human had experienced since the species became bipedal.

August Yi knew the survival of the human species depended on the successful completion of Humanity One's Mission. He knew the tremendous responsibility he shouldered. He never forgot the magnitude of his obligations for a single moment. He brooded, always fearful of a singular failure, a human error by any one of the Crew Members — even more so, fearful of an error by himself - that would jeopardize the Mission. The intricacies of Humanity One were far greater and more complex than anything previously created by human beings. It was a one of a kind spaceship with a lot of untested technology, technology that must not fail. Complete testing would have exposed the project to public view. That could not happen. An aware public would have derailed the project because too few would benefit personally. The very nature of the Mission dictated almost diametrically opposed conditions: extreme attention to detail and a minimal Crew to attend to those details. To assure future generations of Crew Members did not inadvertently fail, every detail of the voyage across lightyears of seemingly empty space was defined in a voluminous body of Standard Operating Procedures called the Mission Guidance Rules. Of all people aboard Humanity One, August was most keen on strict adherence to the MGR. After all, the Innovators knew what was required to make the Mission a success. He knew the Innovators; they were his contemporaries.

Cesar contemplated his sire, his father, August. His singular memory was of a dark man with a permanently furrowed brow and piercing brown, almost black, eyes that could make as much impact as one of his open hands. August sat in the Chair more than anything else, always there in the event of an emergency. August believed that only the Captain, only he, could prevent mission failure. His presence was a requirement ... if nothing more than for the sake of morale, as assurance that everything was as it should be. Cesar considered the reason he was selected to be Captain as August's replacement. It was simple. August did not trust anyone other than his own offspring with the responsibility of saving Mankind and preserving the technologies accumulated over millennia of human development. August trained Cesar himself, beginning when Cesar was barely more than three-years old. Being Captain was all Cesar knew. It was all he needed to know. Being Captain was his life ... and the life of the vessel. And he knew how to captain based upon August's teachings and the example set by August.

Cesar shifted again. The pain caused by his arthritic spine was unrelenting. He was aging in the Chair. August died when Cesar was twenty. August was fifty-five, a short life. His heart failed. The Chief Medical Officer said it was stress. Stress caused by the duties of Captain and by the physiological stress of space flight. The human body was evolved to thrive on Earth, with its radiation, with its atmosphere, with its gravity. Cesar's role as Captain was in its thirty-fifth year. He was now the same age as August when the First Captain died. The Crew was already in its fourth generation. The Gen 4s were fast approaching adulthood – amended adulthood. When Cesar assumed command of Humanity One, he was only two years into adulthood at the time. Twenty years old. Not mature enough for the awesome responsibilities foisted upon him, though he did not realize it at the time. Nor would he admit it. At that age, he was convinced he knew everything that needed to be known. That belief changed quickly once he was in the Chair. He imitated August's every gesture and facial expression in hopes those physical acts would bring him the judicious skills required to push Humanity One toward its destination. The act worked; the Crew did not detect his self-doubts. Even until the current day, no one suspected Cesar's internal conflicts.

Barely three years after taking command, the Chief Medical Officer, Doctor Ajay Shi, warned the Premier and Captain Cesar about the first detected Mission risk.

The MGR did not dictate societal norms. There was no body of laws written into them that demanded a certain set of behaviors. Apparently, the Innovators expected the Crew to conduct themselves in a manner supportive of the Mission, dedicated to the survival of humans as a species and of human technology. The only dictates were regarding procreation and genetic viability. The Earth custom of family names was eschewed for a more direct method of identifying genetic lines, to help prevent inbreeding. Each original pair was assigned a trailing number. Future generations would contain a generational number and the combination of numbers associated with lineage. To allay some of the coldness of being known by a number, the numbers were chosen from an Earth language, Chinese. Since the chosen language to be used by the Crew was English, the sing-song cadence of the Chinese numbers would add a sense of poetry to the names. Other than that, the MGR provided guidance on the operation of Humanity One as a biosphere, as a space craft, and the information required to assure the success of the Mission. The Mission's success for Humanity One would be measured against safe arrival in orbit around Earth Two. Humanity's success as a species would be measured by generations far beyond the scope of Humanity One and its planned eight generations.

Doctor Shi introduced knowledge of a risk to Humanity One, to the Mission and to humankind. A potentially terminal risk not covered by the MGR. The steadfast guide that the young Captain believed would always provide answers failed them. Doctor Shi showed the Premier and Cesar undeniable evidence that the human life span was less aboard Humanity One than it was on Earth. The possibility was real that it could decline further in future generations. He explained the effects of space radiation as well as the lack of full gravity on the human body. Increased mutations, weakened hearts, atrophied muscles to name a few of the more obvious and easily predicted. The Innovators understood the potential for damage to the chromosome telomeres, and the possibility of cellular senescence. The potential for shortened lifespans was known, but not understood and definitely not addressed by the MGR, other than in passing for the Medical Officers. The Gen 1s were passing earlier than expected at an alarming rate. In some instances where the couples delayed procreation, they died without fully training their replacements. Gen 2s were being forced into service too soon. The lack of training would lead to Mission failure if steps were not taken immediately.

When Doctor Shi laid out the facts, Cesar felt the impact of the statement regarding not being fully trained, or at least not being fully prepared. He had often thought about failure on his part resulting in the failure of the Mission. His memory of the conversation with the Chief Medical Officer made him uncomfortable in multiple ways, just as it had more than thirty years earlier. At the time, he asked Doctor

Shi for recommendations. In his youth and within his MGR guided training, he had no ideas of his own to address human life expectancy. He knew the Chief Medical Officer was a key component to the power triad on Humanity One.

The solution seemed fairly simple. Lower the achievement of adulthood and the acceptable age for procreation to sixteen. If most births occurred before age twenty, the opportunities to train would not be lost even if life spans were shorter. Training would start at an earlier age so the sixteen-year-old adults would be ready to perform their duties. The resulting training might be enhanced because – in theory – the newly trained would have a few years of apprenticeship in preparation for the demise of their trainers. Doctor Shi did not expect, or predict, significant further decline in life expectancy. That was good.

Doctor Shi was right in his initial warning. Gen 2s were destined to be gone by the time they reached fifty, except for a few. Cesar, even with his arthritis, was one of the lucky ones. Only four other Gen 2s still lived, far past their prime.

Premier Paul Er Ling was fifty-seven. Cesar trusted the Premier, largely because Paul often deferred complicated decisions to him. That made it easier, not having to debate the value of one option over another. Paul, like Cesar, became Premier because of his parent's status as the first Premier. Paul accepted the status but was reluctant to make unpopular decisions. His sire and Trainer relied upon consensus rather than edict. It was something Paul was taught to value, but he never learned the fine art of consensus building. Decisions often had to be made sooner rather than later. Cesar was willing to accept responsibility; the primary reason Paul deferred many decisions to the Captain.

Chief Scientist Robert Er Ershiyi-Ershisi was 56, Like Cesar, he was true to the MGR. Most of his duties required MGR references on a routine basis. If the MGR was wrong, if the Innovators were wrong in any way, his whole orderly world of science would be thrown into disarray. Constants were a necessity for the science to work. He was immensely comfortable with constants, and equally uncomfortable with unknowns.

The Chief Stasis Engineer, Deanna Er Jiushi-Jiusan, was the first baby born on Humanity One. She was 60. She relied upon the MGR to ensure the stasis vessels, whose formal nomenclature was Transport Stasis Vessels, were protected. All the faces in the TSVs were visible for visual observation, for inspection to ensure each vessel's telemetry was directionally correct if not exact. If the people in the vessels were resurrected during her lifetime, she would recognize and know them all by name – or, at least, she believed she would.

The Chief Medical Officer, Doctor Katherine Er Shiyi-Shisan was 58. The MGR provided genetics protocols to be administered by the Medical Officer. Procreation was strictly monitored, per MGR, because the original Crew consisted of only one-hundred married pairs. To avoid incestuous line breeding, the Chief Medical Officer approved all mating. Ancestral lines were carefully monitored by the Chief Medical Officer through use of the trailing numbers. Avoiding excess population was also critical to the Mission's success. Humanity One had finite resources. With one-hundred-percent recycling, the vessel could support no more than four-hundred-twenty individuals comfortably. The Innovators, through their MGR, were insistent that the population be controlled at that level at all costs. Katherine had no offspring of her own, choosing to allow an additional birth among her peers to replace her life. It was not a selfless act. She simply had no time for procreation and its responsibilities. She would never be accused of nepotism. It was rumored that her mate may have sired a child, but that was not captured in her records.

Doctor Shi was also wrong. He did not live long enough to see that Gen 3s were not going to live as long as their parents, but Cesar did. The concern among the current Medical Doctors was that the declination of life expectancy might extend into Gen 4s and beyond. Adulthood could not be reduced much further without problems as yet unknown. Cesar knew that calling someone an adult did not make it so. Mental and emotional maturity came with experience and age. It could not be trained. He was reasonably certain that he was not an adult when the captaincy was thrust upon him.

Cesar recognized that his continued existence was a curse to Joseph San Jiu-Er, his son and Captain Trainee. That thought bothered him at times. Like his sire before him, Cesar only trusted his own offspring to be dedicated enough to follow him in the Chair, to become Captain. Joseph was astute. His bearing was right for the job. Cesar even supposed Joseph might be a better Captain than he was. Joseph definitely had more time to train and mature in preparation for the task. Jana Si Yi-Liu was Cesar's grandchild. She was more than a year from achieving adulthood. She would not be able to sit in the Trainee Chair until Joseph sat in the Captain's chair. That would not happen as long as Cesar was viable. Her prospects of becoming Captain before she was past her prime were not good. Which meant that she was not viable by strict adherence to the MGR description. And she was petulant and petty. Impatient to be Captain. In a feudal time of Earth's past, she would probably be inclined to lead a coup to depose him so she could gain the Chair.

Thoughts of Earth's past led Cesar to think of the purpose of the Mission, something he knew better than anyone needed to know. As far as his duties were concerned, the knowledge was nothing more than a distraction. He tried to not dwell on the matter too much. Earth was quickly approaching a hyperthermal interglacial epoch. Heat would replace habitable temperate conditions across all but the extreme polar regions of the planet. Humans would survive, probably … maybe. In small pockets under austere conditions. Subsistence existence. The species had survived glacial and interglacial epochs more than once. Small groups of each episode struggled their way through Earth's unyielding evolution. Their civilizations did not survive. Each swing of temperature extremes pushed many species, humans included, to near extinction and into survival mode. Food and shelter – and desperate procreation - were the only valued amenities. Gathering those things would become the only technology in their lives. Sufficient populations to support scientific technology were lost. Even the memories of lost technologies were lost. A magnificent conundrum: more people could have sustained the technology and the technology could have supported more people. It did not matter. Planet Earth was stronger than Humankind and its technology. Earth would recycle and survive.

Humanity's dilemma was foreseen, though generally ignored by the population. Fortunately, Earth's human scientific leaders' voices were heard, at least by one another and a few forward-looking political leaders. Unproven technology existed to seek shelter from a failing world, to retain the technology for future generations, and to shorten the recovery period between near extinction episodes. In a selfish world, an amalgamation of selfless scientists and world leaders rose to save the species and its technology. The world at large was not aware of the effort. In general, the haves and have-nots renewed their age-old struggles in a vain attempt to prepare for an unknown future. Only twenty-five thousand selectively educated adult souls would be able to escape the doom that was approaching. Selection was done in secret. Most of those would have to trust cryogenics to save them so they could ... in turn ... save humanity and civilization. Put into stasis vessels for the predicted eight-generation voyage across soundless voids to a singular dot in space that scientists identified as Earth-like and suitable. Two-hundred other souls and their progeny would pilot a spaceship with the hopes and dreams of humankind, the vessel called Humanity One, across that empty space.

The Innovators who watched Humanity One depart accepted one truth: their progeny on Earth would revert to hunter-gatherers – if they survived – and *maybe* would achieve a civilization of some kind, likely based upon a religion as yet unfounded, after the climate moderated. But that would be thousands of years in the future. The hope was that the descendants of the souls on Humanity One would thrive and return with knowledge that could be used to restore humans to their former glory. Humanity One was not just about Earth Two. It was about Earth One as well.

Humanity One was built on the dark side of the Moon, away from prying eyes. The vessel was a self-sufficient world – a biosphere - for the Crew, the brave two-hundred, and their subsequent generations. Eight generations in all. Humanity One's course was set, preestablished using advances in space observation and mathematics, and vast amounts of computer memory. The plan was so detailed that the Crew would not be required to make navigational changes to reach Earth Two. As a matter of fact, any changes to the established course were prohibited. A minor change could snowball into a major Mission ending trajectory error. The Captain's training and knowledge included that fact. Cesar's first physical reinforcement of the MGR by August's hand was in response to persistently asking "*Why?*" at the curious age of ten.

Any deviation, even a fraction of a fraction of a degree, would doom the Mission to failure. That was the unyielding mantra. Humanity One would slip quietly past the planet identified as Earth Two and its solar system. Humanity One would miss the neutral zone where it could orbit without expending energy, held in place in that sweet spot with a lack of gravitational pull from Earth Two or its two moons – a perfect alignment of the three bodies to cradle Humanity One. From that vantage point, more precise evaluations of the planet could be made, and the vessel leaders of the day could utilize the Innovators' "final-phase knowledge" held within the minds of the humans in Stasis to develop shuttles for transport to the surface. Until then, the Crew would maintain - plain and simple. Nothing of the plan would work, the Mission itself would fail, if Humanity One did not arrive on time.

The humans in Stasis were educated. Beyond the standard education elements of math, arts and all the sciences known to Man, they were educated to know what to do to establish themselves in their new world. Not just how to survive, but how to thrive and facilitate faster than normal development. All the Earth's accumulated knowledge was saved in computer files aboard Humanity One, in archives. The Innovators were wise enough to know that simply having access to knowledge would not guarantee Mission success. How to use that knowledge to reestablish human civilization and technology was in those valued minds. Those humans would not start from scratch. Earth Two would thrive and be able to return to Earth as saviors in less than five-thousand years – if Earth was ready to be saved.

Psychological profiles were determined to ensure everyone aboard the vessel, Humanity One, was selfless, dedicated to the success of the Mission. That included TSV occupants and the Crew. Selection of the two-hundred Crew Members was particularly intense. Those people knew they would live out their lives inside an artificial container, as would their children and grandchildren for a total of eight generations. Some of the Crew knew that the Eighth generation would carry the burden of assuring humanity thrived at an accelerated pace. Cesar knew. The Premier knew. The Chief Medical Officer knew. No one else needed to know until the Eighth Generation was being born. Until then, it was superfluous information and a probable distraction from the journey. Distractions that could easily result in Mission failure. It was the duty of the Chief Officers to avoid distractions within their areas.

Cesar also knew that the location and identification of a human civilization sustaining planet required decades of intense work by the true Innovators, the people who initiated the mission. Humanity One was not built by one generation of Innovators. Three generations were required. The planets in the solar system were known well enough to determine that their value to humans was as raw material resources and small colonies to mine them. They were not suitable as a permanent home. They could not support human life without heroic intervention from humans on Earth. For human-developed civilization to survive, another solar system would have to provide an anchor planet that would be climatically stable for at least thirty thousand years. That planet was found. The distance stretched the creative minds of the Innovators as they struggled to develop a propulsion system that would not require a vast store, and consumption, of fuel. Stopping for resource replenishment along the way was not within their technology. Stopping was not an option. The vessel that carried the hopes of humanity had to be self-sufficient and self-sustaining.

Stellar engines and solar sails were the answer to making the journey. Solar energy captured by the stellar engines provided propulsion and electrical power for Humanity One. Solar sails captured solar winds, always present even in the void between solar systems. The solar winds provided pressure differentiation propulsion – like a sail on a boat, and also provided fuel for a proton propulsion system that could be used to assist the sails during planned direction changes. From afar, Humanity One looked like a budding flower, its petals not yet fully unfurled. And its appearance changed as the vessel's computers tracked the optimum angle and direction for every solar sail and for the stellar engine parasol. The changes were made automatically by the vessel's navigational computers - with confirming input from Chief Robert's Science and Engineering Technicians - to capture the most energy possible from the not so empty void through which it traveled.

Cesar thought about the humans who remained behind. He wondered if those based on Earth's moon were returned to Earth where they could live out their days. He suspected that the Earth was still supportive of human civilization ... even more than six decades later ... though slowly failing to support the dense population his sire often mentioned as unsustainable. He wondered if they knew their civilization was doomed, soon to be rendered moot by an ever-changing planet that did not care whether humans lived or died. At least, the souls on Humanity One knew their collective future was good – if the Mission did not fail.

As a Gen 2, Cesar only knew life inside the multi-plied hull of a space vessel. No one currently aboard, except those in Stasis, had ever experienced Earth gravity on their bodies or natural sunlight on their skin. But, the selflessness of the Innovators, the first Generation, was instilled into the Second Generation. The Third Generation, the Gen 3s, was also comprised of mostly dedicated Crew members. Cesar wondered about the Gen 4s. They were young and inquisitive, seemingly more focused on their curiosity than their duties. Maybe life was made too easy for them.

August was stern when training Cesar. Harsh and unrelenting. The Gen 1 Captain pounded the importance of every line of the MGR into his son so that it was second nature. Cesar did not complain, or grouse to his Gen 2 friends. He accepted the fact that the success of the Mission superseded his personal feelings or preferences. The Innovators were clear about what was required for the Mission to succeed, it was the duty of every Crew Member to do what was required every moment until his or her life ended. The Gen 4s seemed less concerned about duty, except as it provided privileges ... personal rewards. Like Jana, they sulked as they waited their turn to follow in the footsteps of their parents, the Gen 3s – even though both generations were granted adulthood and viability at an earlier age than originally planned. And the Gen 3s tried to appease their offspring with praise and sweet words of encouragement. Cesar remembered more than once when he lost focus and August's brown hand lashed out to remind him that focus was critical.

Cesar was hard on Joseph. He knew that a new Captain had to be ready to assume command with more training and maturity than he had when he assumed the Chair. He was not sure if he would have been ready to assume command as young as he did if August had not been harsh. But Cesar was not as harsh with Joseph. He kept Joseph in check and on task without August's corporal reinforcements. Joseph was even less strict on Jana. Part of that was because they all knew Jana would be years achieving the Chair, if at all. He wondered if the softening with each generation would lead to Mission failure. That wondering could easily lead to a distracting fear - if he allowed it to do so.

Words Cesar once read that addressed the value of training, of imparting knowledge and skills, were attributed to a long-gone teacher of practical management and statistics, W. Edwards Deming. He considered the truth of an often-repeated phrase Dr. Deming used to disparage improper training between generations of employees, *"Off we go to the Milky Way!"* In essence, Deming was describing what Cesar saw happening on Humanity One. The Gen 4s were wavering between their commitment to defined Crew duties and their personal preferences. Inappropriate, or misdirected, curiosity kept them from focusing on the Mission. It was as if they failed to understand that if they failed, they would expire along with the Mission. The survival of humanity and its current civilization depended on Gen 4s and their progeny. Life in Humanity One was not about any living person's today; it was only about humankind's tomorrow.

Cesar shifted again and grimaced in pain. Doctor Shiyi-Shisan's powders were not working. Only she knew the severity of his condition. No need to disrupt the Crew with information that would only serve to feed the rumor mill and distract them from their duties.

Besides, it did not interfere with his ability to remain viable sitting in the Captain's Chair. He just had to locate the right spot where the pain was less intense. Others, younger, had more severe issues with which to contend. And that knowledge concerned him when nothing else occupied his mind.

CHAPTER 2

JANA

Jana Si Yi-Liu's brow was knitted by her frown. Her normally noble bearing was gone. Her pale-brown eyes gave character to her ashy-brown skin. As a Gen 4, her genetics yielded to blending and possibly the environment. With her face lowered so it was not obvious, she glared toward the Chair, glared at Cesar Er Yi, her grandsire. Captain Cesar was Gen 2, barely removed from the Innovators themselves. In fact, his parents were of the Innovators. Cesar was among the first generation to be born on Humanity One. He followed in his sire's footsteps. They were called "fathers" back then. She had heard that somewhere from someone.

Jana was taller than her Gen 4 peer females, and many of the males. That particular sequence of her double helix strands remained true, inherited from Cesar's lineage. At fourteen, almost fifteen, her life was good. At least it started good. She was in the line of Crew members destined to be true leaders. Against the developing tradition, her parents opted to allow her sire to train her to be his replacement as Captain. Higher status was afforded by that variation. From birth, she was destined for greatness. To sit at the helm of Humanity One. To guide, lead, coax and charm the vessel across the vastness of space to a tiny spot many lightyears from Earth. To establish humanity on another planet in another star system. To Earth Two. She liked the status her role afforded and quickly grasped the basics of her future responsibilities, eager and ready to fulfill her destiny, even though she was still more than a year from adulthood – and two lifetimes away from becoming Captain, those of Cesar and Joseph.

Unlike most Crew Member functions, Captain training began at a very early age. Mentored by her sire, Jana essentially had no childhood. Her behaviors were conditioned toward being a strong, selfless, singularly focused leader beginning the moment her parents made the decision to train her to be Captain. Watching her sire, Joseph San Jui-Er, sit in the chair to the right of the Captain, in the Trainee chair, became unbearable as time passed. She was driven ... by training, by nature ... to be in charge, to be engaged in the role chosen for her. Cesar still lived and still sat in the Captain's Chair. That fact was not lost on Jana. She recognized the incongruity of her position. She was being trained by someone who had not yet proven his viability in the job. She was training for a position that would not be available to her until two prior generations of her lineage recycled.

Second-in-Command Juan San Er-Qi sat in the Chair when Cesar went to his quarters for his rest period. Not Joseph. Joseph was Cesar's heir apparent. The son would assume the role of Captain, not Second-in-Command. Until that day came, Joseph shadowed Cesar. Juan and his Trainee knew that any crisis required the Captain to be summoned to the bridge, regardless of time. Sitting in the Trainee chair with Second Officer Juan was not an option for Jana. She had asked several months earlier when it became apparent to her that Cesar's recycle day was not fast approaching. She was denied and lectured about her place in the hierarchy, about her brazen attempt to take away opportunity for the Second-in-Command Trainee, a fellow Gen 4.

Born to lead but with no chair. Jana wandered the Control System Room, a shadowy presence, watching every person, every activity.

Her waking life was in that room. Everything she knew was in that room. When ... if ... she achieved Captain, even her sleeping life would be connected to that room. She often wondered if she could choose another function, learn something different. Protocol would not allow it. Not after completing Captain training. Her bearing of leadership, her demeanor of control, the role of Captain was too deeply ingrained for her to fit compatibly into a lesser role, to be subservient to anyone. She could not seek lower status.

Jana liked her peers. She admired them in some ways. She envied them for the certainties of their futures. As the prospects of her achieving the Captain's chair anytime soon paled, she found solace in her friends. Trainees, not yet adults. She joined a small group in the mess hall. They laughed. They joked. They respected her, deferred to her, unaware of her fears that she might never sit in the Captain's chair. They accepted her as their future Captain without question. She was in her element when she was with her friends. A leader. And some of them were as unhappy as she.

Rex Si Wu-Wushisi piqued her interest emotionally. Throughout her training, Jana was conditioned to avoid emotional entanglements. The responsibilities of Captain were too important to allow distractions. When she was able to sit across the table from Rex, Jana watched his every move while he ate, when he spoke. She knew her observation skills were better than most. Observation was a key element of Captain training. Observation affects outcomes. What is seen and considered by the observer. What is perceived and feared by the one observed. A practiced observer can guide the outcome without overt interference simply by watching. Rex was not easily affected. He was focused. Whenever he noticed her watching him, he simply smiled. His deep-blue eyes sparkled when he smiled. So did his teeth, even while eating spinach. But it was just a smile of friendship and acknowledgement. He was cordial but seemingly disinterested. That drew her to him more.

Another prize just out of her reach. He was more than a year older than her and would be an adult before she was. He would be mated before she was allowed to take a mate. He was beautiful, and he was in control, as elusive as the Captain Chair.

The Control System Technicians were always busy, focused on their screens and alarm lights. Jana strolled and watched. She understood every function in the Control Room, every necessary decision required by the Con-Sys Techs. She knew what specific ship functions were represented by the wide array of screens and consoles. The panels were arranged so primary functions were in a specific area. Della San Qi was generally accountable for atmosphere in the Hydroponics part of the ship. Hydroponics scrubbed the air that was breathed by the Crew. It was a critical function. Maddison Si Wu-Qi, Maddie to her friends, was training to learn that function. Della and the other Con-Sys Techs were cross-trained to monitor any atmospheric anomalies and direct required corrections or repairs with simple keyboard commands. The system was not automatic, but it was smart, smart enough to offer suggestions to the humans in control. In truth, any qualified adult Con-Sys Tech could adequately function at any of the consoles.

The Captain was never required to intervene – at least not since Cesar became Captain, to hear him tell it. Jana heard that mantra again and again. *"Never interfere. No matter how much you think you know, the Technicians know more. Let them perform their duties."* But - and there was always a "but" - *"Be ready to provide guidance and encouragement during times of crisis."* In other words, know what to do, even if it was never required of you. Observing and asking questions was more effective than routinely thinking for everyone.

Jana was looking forward to the day when Maddie, and even skinny Sean Si San-Si, were allowed into the Con-Sys Trainee chairs. She would have someone with whom she could connect on a routine basis, someone to break through the boredom of not even having a Trainee chair. They would think she was special because she was not confined to a chair. They would not know the true reason she wandered. She heard Cesar's voice in the background. She did not hear his exact words, but she knew what was said. She stepped toward the Captain's chair, turned to face the control consoles, alert and anticipating what would happen next. It was part of the routine, but it was a break from the regular monotony … though at times a monotony of its own.

Joseph nodded affirmation. His instructions were clear. Cesar allowed him to call for the updates from the Con-Sys Techs. It was part of the training, something that Jana could just as easily do. "Status, Stellar engine."

It was not a statement. It was a command in the form of a question. It was spoken aloud rather than using the imbedded Communicators that offered more intimate and expressive communications. It was done according to MGR. It was a physical activity in a room full of mostly mental activities. The small array of screens, alarms and switches that monitored the Stellar engine was staffed by only one Con-Sys. He stood and responded, "All normal."

No one expected anything different. If something were not normal, an alarm would have informed the Con-Sys who would have, in turn, informed the Captain. Depending on the severity, everyone in the Control System Room would probably know, plus any pertinent Crew Members outside the Control System Room. Every functional system Technician responded in turn with those same two words, "All normal." The exercise was part of being Captain. *Inspect what you expect.* The art of observation. By reiterating the importance of the ship's various functions, all of them, with an hourly update, every Con-Sys Tech was reminded of the critical nature of his/her function. A single failure could result in Mission failure … and death to the inhabitants of the vessel, Humanity One. The status update also provided a necessary physical break. Technicians would stand to deliver those all-important words, "All normal."

"Thank you. Captain, control status reports *all normal*," Joseph reiterated loud enough for everyone to hear, as if they might not have heard their peers declare *all normal* – or to ensure his voice became familiar to them.

"Duly noted. Continue on the Mission."

Jana listened to the monotonous status reports. As boring as the routine was, she knew its importance. She also knew the importance of being attentive. She knew what to do if any report was not *all normal*. She had that knowledge, though she had never seen the actual need for the skill during her eleven years and eleven months of training.

CHAPTER 3

MADDIE

A blue light flashed on Maddie's console. First day solo. She was on her own. Her heart rate quickened slightly. Blue equals atmosphere. After a five second delay, a soft alarm joined the blue warning light. She knew from her training that the alarm's intensity would increase the longer the warning went unanswered.

Maddie, formally named Maddison Si Wu-Qi to incorporate the numerical trailers that defined her lineage, was thin and agile. Wiry was the word used to define her physically. She was a maturing female with all the physical attributes that demonstrated her gender, but slim – which was generally unnoticeable among the normally slender Crew. Her deep blue eyes stood in stark contrast to her sun-starved complexion, Maddie's skin tone was best described as alabaster white. Smooth and flawless like Pentelic marble, finely sculpted by a master artist. Her blonde hair draped below her shoulders, her chosen form of rebellion among her peers. And, in her mind, there were ample reasons for rebellion. At times, the long hair tickled her breasts, especially when it draped forward and played side-to-side when she bobbed her head and talked animatedly. Aesthetically, she carried her mother's beauty properly combined with her sire's physical genetics.

Maddie's fingers flew across the computer's virtual command

board, inputting a query to determine the source and severity of the atmospheric alarm. *Hydroponics, Tier 2, Garden Room 20. CO2 level elevated, 15.2%.* A quick mental review of the needs of plants versus humans guided her fingers as she evaluated the situation. The plants did not care. They thrived in high CO_2 environments. In many instances, the higher the better. Humans do not do as well, hence the alarm. She did not really have to remember any of that. Thinking was not always necessary. A white bordered scroll across the bottom of the screen told her what the ideal parameters were, and a red bordered scroll declared the danger readings. She input a recall code to activate a warning beacon inside the Hydroponics section affected. The beacon should have automatically begun signaling the impending danger to any humans inside the room, but her action was protocol to ensure they were properly warned. The CO_2 level was not high enough to warrant a rescue. Room 20 occupants, if there were any, should be physically capable of exiting on their own – if they knew to do so. That was the reason for the beacon. With another quick series of keystrokes and tapped touch-screen icons, Maddie activated venting fans for Room 20. She directed the CO_2 laden air toward another Hydroponics room with a much lower CO_2 level. That action allowed air with less CO_2 to flow into Room 20. Within seconds of the initial alarm, the CO_2 level in Room 20 was within human acceptable parameters. The plants in Room 20 were young, a new crop recently planted. They were not yet capable of using all the carbon dioxide heavy air that was recirculated through Hydroponics to be scrubbed.

"Very good, but you hesitated before you sent the recall." Della San Qi, from her position standing behind Maddie's chair, reached across Maddie's body. Her fingers were a blur as she made a few keystrokes. She pointed to the screen when it filled with the data she had requested. It was three minutes of history for the console, every alarm, system communication, along with every keystroke and input by Maddie. "See. There was a six second pause. If that had been an oxygen depletion situation, rescue might be required – or recovery. What were you thinking?"

Maddie's face clouded as she responded petulantly, "I didn't pause. I was moving as fast as humanly possible. I was evaluating the situation. I didn't make any mistakes."

With a mother's firmness, Della looked into her fifteen-year-old daughter's angry eyes. "Don't respond to me that way. The duties that you will be responsible for in the Control System Room are too critical. If you respond that way to Cesar, your privileges will be revoked."

"Well, this isn't the Control Room and you aren't Cesar." Maddie's feelings were hurt that Della found an insignificant pause in the data analysis and made a point of mentioning it. It was no big deal as far as Maddie was concerned, but her mother saw it in real time, without the aid of the computer tracking data. The young Trainee knew that was the difference between an experienced Con-Sys Technician and a novice, but she did not want to admit it out loud. "You're just nitpicking. Besides, this training is so repetitive that it's a bore."

Della's blue eyes, every bit as bright as Maddie's, darkened. Her face showed her age, more so at the end of a long day. Even so, normally it was barely lined. That changed dramatically when she reacted to her daughter's resistance. Heavy creases expressed her dissatisfaction and anger. She spoke deliberately and emphatically. "And you will continue to train until you are capable of responding to everything on this console and the entire control array in your sleep. This is the first phase of your final qualifications as a Control System Tech. If you can't do this, you can't go into the Control Room. The real control board is much larger and involves more than just Hydroponics. It involves every life on Humanity One. Do you understand me?"

Maddie knew she had pushed Della too far. Mother or trainer, Della was not willing to allow Maddie to fail. Failure was not an option.

Recycling was a very real option for anyone who failed to measure up to the standards required to maintain Humanity One and all its inhabitants. The standards were tough and clearly defined. The Innovators provided Mission Guidance Rules for every phase of existence on the massive vessel. Her mother was not yet too old to birth and train another Con-Sys Tech as a replacement before her expected life cycle ended, though Maddie doubted her mother wanted to go through the process again. Maddie hung her head. Her long blonde strands brushed unnoticed across her breasts. "Aye, Ma'am. I understand. I was recalling the parameters so I wouldn't make a mistake. I will learn to react faster."

Della stepped to the side of Maddie's chair, wrapped one arm around Maddie's shoulder, and protectively pulled the girl's blonde-haired head against her bare belly. "I know you will. You are fully capable. Now, let me initiate another scenario ... and pay attention to the screen. You delayed because you tried to remember something that does not require memory. Allow the computer to guide you. You don't have time to remember details. The computer will do that. Your job is to make decisions based upon the system data. It's all in the MGR. Just follow the MGR."

After the scolding, Maddie devoted her attention to her console and responded well to every scenario that Della presented, up to and including a full hull breach. She could not repair or circumvent every permutation from her virtual keyboard – nor was she expected to, but she responded appropriately with actions that were designed to reduce loss of vessel viability and save as many lives as possible. Alerting repair crews, medical teams, rescue teams, whoever was necessary to ameliorate the damage. More than four-hundred living, breathing humans relied upon each other to not make mistakes or mental errors. The qualifications were relatively easy for her. She would turn sixteen in three months. Adulthood by definition, by ship's law. As an adult, her privileges would increase. She would also be assigned a shift in the Control System Room as a Con-Sys Tech. She would be responsible for a control console with an array of screens and affiliated sensors, a console that was not in training mode. Qualification and adulthood were essential to be accepted as a viable member of the Crew. There was no life other than being a Crew member ... a viable Crew member. Anything else was a burden - an unbearable burden - on the resources of Humanity One. The last fact was not foreign to Maddie. There was no other option.

Maddie dismissed all thoughts and let her subconscious mind control her fingers as her conscious mind watched the screen for anomalies. She felt her self-confidence increase with every success. Her training began when she was eight. For nearly half her days since birth, she had sat in front of simulated control panels, tapping and watching, watching and tapping. She was ready for the real thing, even though Della told her that training would encompass much more than reality. The difference was that reality came with potential consequences for Humanity One, whereas training did not. Maddie foresaw the boredom that would become her life.

Maddie's contemporaries were busy learning their Crew skills in other areas. As a Gen 4, she gravitated toward the other Gen 4s, people near her age. People from whom she would choose a mate and, eventually, join in Recycling. She was part of a small clique with a half dozen or so Gen 4s, mostly from other disciplines. It was a multifunctional group with a singular purpose – preservation of the Mission. She thought of herself as its leader, though some of the others might claim the same title. To Maddie, it was titillating to talk about something other than the Control Room. It broke the boredom. She sometimes envied her friends for their assignments, until she realized they felt the same way. Apparently, no matter what you did, life was a series of boring moments ... which slowly evolved into days and weeks and a lifetime.

Crew members' assignments were generally along familial lines, following in the footsteps of one parent or the other. Della was a Con-Sys Technician. So was Maddie's sire, Len San Wu. He monitored the hull integrity console, though all Control System Technicians could handle any function in the Control System Room. Female parents trained daughters. Male parents trained sons. There was no rational reason for that configuration, but it became the norm by the Fourth generation on the space vessel. For everyone except Jana. She was being trained by her sire to become Captain.

Della beamed with delight. Her smile creases enhanced her mature beauty. Her hair was blonde, but much shorter than Maddie's. At the outer edge of normal length. Barely three inches long with spunky bangs. Easy to maintain. More importantly - it was sanitary. Shed strands of hair were a housekeeper's bane inside the confined spaces of Humanity One. Notably, everyone was a housekeeper. Della's three-holed waistcloth fit well. It was cinched at her waist with a two-inch wide obi. The cotton cloth followed and clung to the contours of her belly and her buttocks until it truncated with two leg opening below the vee at the bottom of her torso. "You got everything right. The hull breach response could have been better if the first call were sent to Mechanical rather than Science Engineering, but they both needed to know before anything could be done." Science Engineering normally calculated repair needs for Mechanical, but Mechanical had to provide the parameters of the repairs based upon their capabilities.

Maddie adjusted her waistcloth at the crotch. She did not realize she was twisting in her chair in reaction to her actions on the control console. The movements caused the cloth to bunch. She understood why her mother wore hers tighter. The cloth could not move independent of her body as easily if it was tight against the skin. Maddie was still growing. Size would come to her soon enough. Soft Fabrication produced the three-holed, cotton waistcloths in a variety of sizes and one color – natural, unbleached creamy white. It was easier to recycle and maintain cloth without dyes. It was also one less resource required inside the closed system of Humanity One. It was up to the wearer to choose a comfortable size. Not bunching or binding in the crotch was a good measure of proper sizing.

All the Crew members wore waistcloths, no footwear. Standard uniform for all but job safety required coverings, such as in the Hard Fabrication shop. The temperature inside the vessel was a constant seventy-two degrees Fahrenheit, with exceptions for need, such as certain Hydroponics rooms for specific crops or the Stasis rooms in general. Comfortable, especially if one was accustomed to it. The Innovators realized that fabric for full body clothing was a luxury that could not be afforded on Humanity One as it made its non-stop, eight-generation journey to Earth Two. There would be no resupply opportunities, no resource fulfillment stops along the way. With finite resources and capacity, amenities were few. Covering genitalia prevented inappropriate distractions and provided sanitary cover. Unplanned defecation and urination, usually by the very young and the very old, were contained by the utilitarian coverings. Menstrual cycles required additional containment, also produced by Soft Fabrication.

Artificial gravity was barely thirty percent of Earth normal – though the living Crew had no experience with anything outside Humanity One.

"When can I sit with you in the Control Room? I want to see a real display. Experience real situations. It's time for my OJT, to learn real stuff."

Della laughed. "I think you are ready. Though, as I've warned you, it's not nearly as exciting as training. Not nearly as many scenarios. I'll talk with Connie." Constance San Jiu was Della's alternate-shift Technician. Shifts were twelve hours except when trained novice adults were available. At that point, the parent generation could lessen their work schedule to accommodate health concerns that increased with aging. "Maybe we can arrange to overlap your OJT so you can work with two Techs. Connie doesn't have a Trainee. Her son is learning Hard Fabrication with his sire."

Maddie winced at the word. Even though it was the word used to describe one's paternal contributor, it seemed cold and mechanical, like the vessel that carried them through the expanses of space between star systems. She was not yet an adult, but she knew the paternal contribution was not made coldly and mechanically. She knew how it happened. At one time in human history ... pre-Humanity One ... the paternal contributor was called *father*. She liked that word. When she had her child, she wanted the baby to be *fathered*, not *sired* - by the mate she chose ... assuming Medical allowed her choice to stand. She thought she knew who she wanted her mate to be. And she wanted a girl so she could train her child. There was no steadfast rule, the Mission Guidance Rules, the MGR, did not cover the subject, it did not define which parent should train which gender, but traditions quickly developed that sires trained sons and mothers trained daughters. Eyebrows were often raised if that minor tradition was ignored unless the training was to a higher status role. But Maddie was prepared to ignore all that if her child was a boy. Traditions were for old people.

"Good. I like Connie." Connie's soft brown eyes always smiled. Maddie wondered how the woman could always be cheerful. She was in her thirties and it was rumored that her mate was less than faithful. But that was rumor, overheard from murmuring adults in the Mess Hall. Connie's age was not a rumor, the same age as Della.

CHAPTER 4

SEAN AND MARLY

Sean Si San-Si beamed. It was not often that he got to sit side-by-side with Marly Si Shiyi-SanShier, though he did so as often as possible. He was fourteen and a month. Almost two years from being an adult, but he understood adult things. He dreamed of adult things. He dreamed about Marly when he dreamed those things. Marly was beautiful – and soft. He shifted closer to Marly on the table bench. He felt the warmth of her thigh against his. He lost focus on his chow. He automatically shoved it into his maw and gulped, only thinking of Marly's warmth combined with his. Maddie was talking to Rex and Jana. He smiled goofily, pretending to hear more than the blood rushing in his ears. Pretending to care about the conversation of his friends. He only cared about Marly and the potentially embarassing discomfort inside his waistcloth.

Sean's hair was short. Almost shaved. He preferred it that way. That was the way of the Crew. Some females wore longer hair, two – three – even four inches. Only Maddie wore her hair really long. It teased her breasts when it was flung forward, and her head bobbed. Her head moved a lot when she talked. He liked watching Maddie when he was not preoccupied with Marly. Maddie was a rebel. She sometimes complained about the fact that no one ever asked her what she would prefer to do as an adult. Sometimes she said she would rather do what Kendra did, work in Hydroponics, where she could smell the fresh air every day. Other times she said she would like to learn how to be Captain like Jana … or maybe learn mathematics and be assigned to Sci-Eng like Rex. Sometimes, Sean worried about Maddie. She was only a few months away from adulthood. If she allowed her mind to wander as an adult, she might lose viability as a Con-Sys Tech. It concerned him but it did not distract him from the promise of Marly.

"Did you prove yourself today?"

Sean gulped, almost choked on a spoonful of soy soup. He looked at Marly, shocked that she had spoken directly to him while a table conversation was underway. Not that she did not speak to him regularly. He was sure she liked him as much as he liked her. She had proven it with warm kisses on the cheeks more than once. Even a secret kiss or two on the lips, moist and head bursting kisses. His pale skin turned beet red from the top of his head to just below his nipple line. His hairless chest lacked the definition of Rex's … or any other Gen 4 his age. He was thin, lanky, skinny. That was why he ate extra portions of soy soup. He hoped the protein would provide bulk to his frail frame. Marly was well developed, and she was only thirteen. She would not be an adult for almost three more years. In reality, all his lust of the moment was wasted. She was petite but she appeared more physically mature than Maddie. Decidedly more mature than him. His pale blue eyes teared from the heat of his face. He blinked and choked on his chow. "What?"

Marly smiled the prettiest smile on the ship, bar none. "Silly. Don't choke to death. I'll be forced to give you mouth-to-mouth and CPR."

Sean reddened further as the others at the table laughed at Marly's words. They all knew the pair of Gen 4s were destined to be mates – if the two of them had anything to say about it.

"Did you prove yourself today? How is your training progressing?"

His waistcloth discomfort disappeared in an instant. Sean grinned sheepishly, "It went well. I think Baker is impressed with how quickly I learn." Baker San Liu was his sire and trainer. Baker was a Gen 3 Con-Sys Technician. Sean's mother, Shelley San Jiuer, was a Hydroponic Technician, a Hy-Tech. If Sean had been born female, he – or she – would have probably been trained for Hydroponics. The idea was not bad … learning Hydroponics rather than Control … as long as he could still be a male. He would not want to miss the opportunity to mate with Marly. The thoughts of it drove him to distraction at times – too many times. "How is your training progressing?"

Marly was precocious in nearly every sense of the word. An impetuous child in an adult body, she kept her dark hair barely one-half inch long. Any more than that and it curled too tightly. Her soft brown skin contrasted with the off-white waistcloth. The color contrast was eye catching and attractive. Her dark-brown eyes sparkled when she spoke with Sean. She was attracted to him – a lot. She liked to press against him and watch his face tighten and turn red. She did it every chance she got, in the narrow, dimly lit passageways, in the food line, whenever they were together, anytime anywhere.

Marly's mother was her trainer. Her mother, Pamela San Shiwu-Shisi was being mentored to become a Medical Doctor. Pamela was a late bloomer, choosing to dedicate herself to becoming a Medical Doctor after serving a few years as a Med-Tech Nurse and Pharmacist. Most Medical Doctors achieved that status before thirty because they chose early. Pamela was exactly thirty and very close to achieving her Doctor's status. Mother and daughter would likely qualify within a year, though Marly would be closely monitored as an apprentice until she achieved adulthood.

Marly's sire, Dexter San Shiyi-Shier was also thirty and a Med-Tech. He was a Radiology Technician and a Surgical Nurse. At thirty, he had proven himself to be adept at providing excellent medical aid in areas other than diagnostics.

"Pamela and Doctor Katherine both say I will become the youngest Doctor ever. The first Gen 4 Medical Doctor." Marly smiled proudly as she spoke. "Today, I was allowed to assist with surgery. Doctor Aaron removed a small tumor from a Crew member. Dexter assisted as well. He said I'm a natural."

Sean put his right hand on Marly's left forearm, an opportunity presented by the conversation. "That is wonderful. I'd like for you to doctor me." His words hung in the air momentarily as his friends paused what they were doing and allowed him time to hear what he had said. They burst out laughing when realization hit him. He blushed, grinned, shrugged and sheepishly commented, "Well ..."

Marly grinned. Her feelings for Sean were muddled. Sean was sweet. Sean was attentive. His blushing face expressed his admiration every time he was around her. He was warm – physically. She felt the heat from his thin thighs against hers. The heat attracted her. Despite his lankiness, Sean had full lips that felt compatible with hers. She delighted in the taste of him every time they kissed - kisses initiated by her because of his bumbling shyness. Sean's genetics indicated that he should develop into a more suitable specimen as he matured. The extra protein in the soy soup was probably not necessary, but she opted to not mention it. She liked to see him blush, but she did not want him to be self-conscious. Too self-conscious and he would not respond as she desired. Rex Si Wu-Wushisi was already physically attractive. He was almost an adult, fifteen years and eleven months, and his body showed it. Her every fiber sensed the sexuality he naturally exuded. Rex ignored hers and other young women's signals, their instinctive advances. He was more interested in achieving his objective as a Sci-Eng Trainee. He was focused. Marly admired Rex, but she knew he was too focused to be interested in her. She was too young. In the scheme of things, Rex would be mated before she achieved adulthood. Sean would be a perfect mate, loving and attentive and always available. That did not mean Rex could not sire her child when the time came, especially if he mated with Maddie. Maddie's lack of commitment could render her nonviable, and Rex would be alone again, prime for extra-marital mating.

CHAPTER 5

KENDRA

Kendra Si Sanshiyi-Sanshier deftly placed the tiny seeds among the granules, evenly spaced as she had been trained to do. Carefully, so as not to disturb the spacing, she used her fingertips to lightly cover each seed with the vermiculite and perlite mixture. After the seeds were planted, the fifteen-year-old girl carefully adjusted the misting system that would keep the seeds moist, but not too wet, until they sprouted. She did not want the seeds to drown and rot. She *could not* do that. Wasting seeds and losing growing time for replanting would result in a major failure.

Kendra exhaled a satisfied sigh. Even though she was not yet an adult, she already had personal responsibilities within Hydroponics. She knew she was mature for her age, both physically and emotionally. She was an adult without the formality of age to afford her the privileges. She had proven herself to be highly capable in her upcoming role as a Hydroponics Technician, Hy-Tech. Carrots, beets and turnips. The narrow rows of Room 17 that she had just completed planting would produce enough of those three root crops to feed the Crew for more than a week, as side dishes of boiled, stir-fried or steamed vegetables plus leafy greens from the beets and turnips. The carrot tops would make a tasty pesto sauce. Once harvested, she would replant. This would be her third solo crop. She was a veteran root crop grower. She also grew radishes and rutabagas in her assigned room. All nutrient packed and entirely edible from root tip to leafy top. She was ready to accept a second room as soon as the need arose. She wanted to be responsible for the soybean room. Soybeans were a big responsibility. She felt pride in her function as a Hy-Tech. Because of her proven maturity, she was seldom bothered by her Trainer, her mother, Jean San Sanshier.

Her function was extremely important to the Crew - and more importantly, to the Mission. Kendra might not be an adult with adult privileges, but she was already viable with responsibilities. She saw the smiling reflection of her freckled face in the stainless-steel cleaning table where she would rinse away any clinging medium from the harvested chow and separate the greens from the roots. Anything not consumable or immediately reusable in the growth of more vegetables would be placed into a recycle bin and sent to Sanitary Recycling. Not much went to Recycling from her crops. Most of what she grew went straight to Food Processing.

Kendra recorded her planting activities in the Hydroponics computer log. Earth date. Earth time. Root vegetable variety. Number of seeds. Row number. Each hydroponic "row" was capable of producing a specific number of plants. If the number of seeds was more than one percent different from the designed capability, the screen reddened. She smiled. All green. Once again, she excelled. She wondered if the green screens were the reason for the gardener's accolade of *Green Thumb*.

Kendra noticed the back of her hands as she input the data. They were freckled. In fact, her whole body, except that part covered by her waistcloth, was pink and freckled. Jean San Sanshier was also freckled. She knew it would happen. Red-haired and fair-skinned, the UV lights would either give her a robust tan or cause freckles. All the Hydroponics workers were tanned, much darker than their counterparts from other areas. She and her mother freckled instead. Kendra wondered if her offspring would inherit the same skin tone.

She inhaled deeply. The maturing plants in the rotational rows were heavy with green leaves that released water vapor and oxygen into the atmosphere. The oxygen content in parts of Hydroponics were often higher than elsewhere on the ship. The oxygenated air felt good in Kendra's lungs. Fresher than the mechanical smell of the air in other parts of the ship. All the air in the ship flowed through Hydroponics as well as chemo-mechanical scrubbers to keep the mixture right for humans. She knew the odor of the ship's air was more than simple metal contact with circulating air molecules. For the better part of four generations, the same gases had circulated throughout Humanity One, sustaining plant and human lives. The other occupants of the ship did not notice the odor of the air. Only Hy-Techs had a point of reference to notice the difference. The most noticeable problem was the methane. A special scrubber captured human methane and incorporated it into the plant nutrient system. Without the plants, the humans would eventually die – and not just because of the lack of chow.

Kendra's daily root crop duties were completed. The next harvest and planting in her root crop room was not scheduled for at least a week. That was the cycle she was scheduled to maintain. Stay a few days ahead of the need in case of a crop failure. Crop failures in one row or another did occur from time to time. An equipment malfunction or a human error. Not usually a complete loss, just an occasional sizeable reduction in output. But careful planning avoided a single row or bed failure from causing serious issues, such as an entire room failure would cause. Maybe a missed or reduced serving of one's favorite vegetable for a week. Nothing more. The fact she only had one room assigned to her did not mean she was without use now that her primary duties were completed. The Technicians in the grain rooms, leafy vegetable rooms, bean rooms, and all the other rooms stacked into five tiers of Humanity One were always in need of assistance – and a friendly visit. Chow was always being harvested and processed. Hy-Techs were not expected to process the vegetables after harvest. That required a specific set of skills and knowledge that was not part of the normal Hy-Tech training cycle. That did not mean Kendra could not go help in Food Processing. She could go learn the skills.

Kendra smiled at Tiffany San Sanshiwu. The mechanical sounds of processing equipment filled the air with a steady whirring hum and with the aroma of freshly sliced carrots – her carrots.

"Hello, Carrot Top," Tiffany said with her familiar greeting for Kendra.

"Hi, Tiff. Mind if I watch?" Kendra knew the reference was to her three-inch red-orange hair, not her vegetables. It was what made her different.

"Of course, you can. It's your crop. Nice carrots you sent in this morning. Very sweet. You should be proud. Want to taste one?" Tiffany spoke short sentences in rapid fire fashion. She took a carrot slice from a small conveyor that carried the carrot coins into a large pot and offered it to Kendra.

Kendra grinned at the compliment and accepted the bright orange goodie. She chewed it and nodded agreement with the older woman. She did not bother telling Tiffany that she had already eaten a whole carrot, lacey top and all, while harvesting her crops. A perk afforded Hy-Techs, just like eating morsels was a perk of Food Processing and Preparation. "Good. Not too bad for a non-adult, if I do say so myself," she laughed.

"Carrot Top, you are the best. Maybe someday, you'll be Hydroponics Chief."

Kendra blushed. She had never spoken her pipedream aloud,

but at that moment she wondered if Tiffany could read her mind, hear her inner most thoughts, if her Communicator was accidentally linked. Some of her thoughts were not fitting for a non-adult. She did not want Tiffany, or anyone else, to know them. *Chief* would suit her desired life position. "I'm just doing what Jean taught me. Besides, you are better positioned to be Hydroponics Chief."

Tiffany laughed. "Not me. I still have Seelie to train." Seelie Si Ershiba-Sanshiwu was Tiffany's ten-year-old daughter. The thirty-five-year-old woman bore her child later than most. She had no formal mate. Seelie's sire was mated to another female who was a Sci-Eng like he was. The ship was like a small town with lots of "secrets" that everyone whispered. An imbalance of females in Gen 3 created the opportunities for "secrets." "I need to make sure she's trained before I lose viability."

Kendra frowned. She did not like to hear Gen 3s talk about losing viability. She thought of her mother and sire, both Gen 3. Both seemed healthy and viable. They were a few years younger than Tiffany. Most of the Gen 3s were in their thirties. She blushed as she thought about one of the few notable exceptions. Tiffany's face was lined more than some, but her body was firm and supple. She was pale, her skin untouched by UV lights that created the tanned glow of the Hydroponics Technicians. Food Processing and Preparation did not require the high energy lighting that fed photosynthesis in the growing rooms. "You will be viable for many more years."

Tiffany smiled demurely. "You say the sweetest things. We know our days are precious few. Best spent accomplishing the Mission. All for the sake of humanity."

"We are humanity," Kendra protested. "We are the reason for the Mission. It's not just about the future. It's about the present as well."

Tiffany paused and saw the fire in the striking topaz eyes that were framed by a redder, freckled face. "I used to think that was true.

Life has taught me differently. Each of us has a role to play. A life to live. And it's all in support of the Mission." She reached and touched Kendra's forearm as she spoke. "But," she turned back to her duties of watching the processing machine chop the carrots into coins, "that doesn't mean we give up our dreams. We don't abandon our own happiness. Find it everywhere you can."

Kendra realized the conversation had drifted into an area of human frailty where neither of them could profit from discussing. Pathos was not her schtick. She quickly shifted to a cheerful smile, "I do. I want to be remembered as someone who lived life to the fullest." Her heart smiled as unspoken thoughts filtered into her conscious mind.

Tiffany nodded. "And I think you will be. No doubt, you got the best atoms available when you were formed. Hey. I'm about ready to process the turnips. You want to watch?" She hoped for the company but feared the direction the initial conversation had taken.

"No. I think I should go help in the grain room. It's almost harvest time for the wheat."

"Yes. Wheat is on the schedule. I'll be drying kernels and grinding flour next week."

Kendra walked from the processing room into a narrow hallway, a mere passageway. The passageway was wide enough for two people to pass without rubbing too tightly against one another. Lighted arrows overhead indicated that traffic could pass both directions. The Hydroponics' hallways were designed as a conduit for harvested produce. When a wheeled box of crops was being transported to Processing, a single arrow indicated the direction that was allowed. Pedestrians diverted through doorways and walked through grow rooms along the way. There was not a lot of pedestrian traffic in the hallways. Most Hy-Techs used the grow rooms as passageways because it allowed them opportunity to visit with fellow Hy-Techs as they went about their duties.

Room 34, a grain room, was amber filled. The stalks of wheat were drooped with heavy grain heads. Tiffany's schedule was right. The grass was in the final process of drying in place. Watering was basically stopped, and the lighting intensified. Even from her limited experience with grains, Kendra knew the room was offering a bumper crop. She also knew it was the result of an experimental crossbreeding exercise. It was a gamble not taken lightly by the Hydroponics Chief and the scientists who supported Hydroponics. The gamble required approval of the Vessel Leadership Team. If it had failed, that room would have yielded much less, if any at all, and the humans on the ship would have suffered a shortage of bread and other wheat-flour based foods until the next crop ripened. At least a month.

Kendra was curious enough to listen and quietly observe as the experiment progressed. She knew the Mission Guideline Rules, the MGR, all but forbid any kind of alteration or manipulation of anything during the journey. The Innovators were very precise in their planning, down to the chow on the table and the recycling of all things. Nothing was left to chance. But the Hydroponics Chief put her viability on the line in support of the wheat experiment. From what Kendra was able to learn through rumor and eavesdropping – and properly asked questions – the experiment was spawned by an anomalous section of a wheat crop in a single grow room four years earlier.

An unexpected mutation within a single stalk produced extra-large grains, grains larger than corn kernels. Unnatural curiosity drove the Hydroponics Chief and the Grain Room Hy-Tech to selectively crossbreed the plants created by those seed with other, heavy stalked mutations. The big grains would require stouter support stems if they were to succeed. After a few generations, enough seed was collected to dedicate an entire room to the progeny of that single wheat plant. The result was a room full of bloated and vibrant grain heads.

An unexpected boon for the humans on board Humanity One if it produced as promised.

Kendra marveled at the prospects of chow production improvements that could be made through selective breeding. Maybe carrots could be made fat like a turnip or radish leaves could be made sweet like beet leaves. And in her private thoughts, she wondered if people could be made smarter and more consistently beautiful if mating was properly done. Those thoughts made her shudder. Medical Technology was already involved in mating, granting or denying approval based upon some selection criteria within the MGR. The prospect that the Innovators were intentionally denying human genetic advancement came to mind, just like their MGR tried to limit chow production.

Kendra pushed the questions from her mind. Too often, she wondered if the imbedded Communicators could read her thoughts. The Communicators were thought activated and required practice to access and use properly. Communicators were not embedded until after the age of twelve. No need for them prior to that level of training. The Communicators were linked to the ship's computers. Every communication process through the computer and was recorded. The devices were not for general communication, only for duty specific uses. Personal use was not restricted, but at risk of wider broadcast if the user was inexperienced. No one intentionally monitored those communications, but they were there for review if necessary. Mechanical Technicians, Mech-Techs, making hull repairs while in environmental suits could link to one another without the radiation driven static that affected electronics, such as two-way radios, and their Communications could be reviewed if something went awry. Kendra and her fellow Hy-Techs frequently connected while working alone in their assigned rooms. They could summons help or offer the same without leaving their posts. The Communications could be for all Hy-Techs or for specific individuals. All one needed was the code for each Communicator in the ship and a private conversation could be had anywhere with anyone at any time.

That was how she often contacted Kevin San JiuJiu-Jiushi when she wanted to hear his voice in her head. In her heart flush, she forgot about recorded Communicator conversations, not that it would have stopped her. Some of their illicit conversations could be in the computer archives.

The Communicators were better than vocalized communications because ideas and concepts and visuals were expressed more clearly and without the clutter of misunderstood words. Kendra often wondered why the Crew even bothered to talk aloud once they had their Communicators implanted. Of course, she also understood that poorly controlled Communicators communicated raw emotions – hatred, undisguised anger, jealousy, envy, even lust – or especially lust.

CHAPTER 6

REX

Gen 4 Science Engineering Trainee, Rex Si Wu-Ershiliu, was fifteen. Just four weeks and three days away from adulthood. He was imprisoned. Not by bars and walls, but by the limitations of his training. He was brilliant, born with a gift for seeing what others could not even imagine ... or choose not to imagine. The calculations that defined his craft, his Sci-Eng status, came easily to him. Even as a Trainee, his trainer, his male parent Stan San Wuwu, engaged him in calculations required to maintain the massive structure that was Humanity One. The calculations were not challenging, but the value of the outcomes pacified him to a certain degree.

Stan was understanding and giving, and at times - forgiving. Barely five-feet six-inches tall, Stan kept his dark hair longer than most males. His skull was lumpy, covered with moles that prevented cutting his hair too closely for fear of slicing into one. He loved Rex's mother, Melba San Ershiliu, unconditionally. They were 36 and 32, respectively.

Any number of routine events, planned and unplanned, created the need for adjustments or repairs to the space vessel that carried the hope of humankind in its bowels. The planned events were specifically described in the MGR, with provisions for recalculations to ensure the original math was correct. The unplanned definitively required use of the mathematics and science that built the vessel in the first place, but the unplanned did not happen. The Innovators thought of every eventuality. Minor adjustments were required for the stellar engines. Nothing significant. Angle of the sails mostly. Like a giant schooner of days of yore, the solar winds required constant measurement and the sails had to be adjusted to capture the emanations from far flung stars the same way the schooners captured air currents. Between the solar winds and the energy captured and converted to propulsion by the stellar engines, the giant vessel plied the seas of space at a speed and trajectory calculated to rendezvous with a tiny spot in a distant star system, a planet visualized as a duplicate of Earth orbiting a solar mass similar in size and energy to the Sun. The timing was critical so that Humanity One would come together with Earth Two and become its third satellite, eased into a gravity-neutral spot amongst the planet and its two moons. The journey was calculated to take eight generations to complete. The course was preset, established by the best Earth minds using the best Earth computers available to the Innovators. That preset course did not require recalculation, only the gathering of energy to complete the Mission – and reaffirmation of the original math used. The math always proved correct. The amount of energy available for capture from stars passed was the only variable, sometimes less, sometimes more, always exactly enough – even if occasional sacrifices were necessary to protect the integrity of the Mission.

Humanity One required massive amounts of energy to sustain itself and the human population within its multi-ply hull. Heat. Lights. Electricity to power complex and essential systems from hydroponics to stasis to computers to cooking chow and, just as importantly, for recycling waste so no molecules were ever wasted. Sustaining a human population of more than four-hundred individuals while hurtling through space toward an object that was not big enough to even be a dot to the human eye required precise calculations, accurate calculations to the thirtieth decimal. Nothing was left to chance. Use and reuse of all available resources. Gathering and metering the use of the available energy in the space beyond the obvious influence of star systems was a deeply involved science, one that most minds could not easily grasp. Rex could.

Rex liked the precision. The logic of mathematic and the beauty of stellar science embraced him like a mother's arms. But he wanted more. He wanted more involvement in the actions that were led by Chief Scientist Robert Er Ershiyi-Ershisi. He suspected the brilliance of the elderly man was limited by a lack of creativity. Neither mathematics nor science can survive without creativity, the search for something new. Rex knew the stellar engines were shackled by old thinking. When he mentioned his thoughts to Stan, Stan immediately and harshly quieted him. Some of Stan's not-so-forgiving moments. Some thoughts were considered heresy; any thoughts that varied from the MGR even a little bit.

Rex was taller than most males his age, and many of the adult males, especially Stan. Not toweringly so, but taller. And erect. He stood his height, unashamed. He was not arrogant, though his physique with his blond hair, blue eyes and clear skin would have given him cause. Genetically, he favored his sire. His physical maturity attracted the attention of several of the pre-adult females. He generally ignored them. He liked to talk with Maddie. She was comfortable, even when she was in one of her suspicious, conspiratorial moods – which seemed to sprout from her boredom at more and more frequent intervals. Their personalities were compatible without sexual tension. They were close friends.

Rex did not like tension. His one weakness was that he understood the value of the MGR, even while he questioned the strict adherence to them by Robert. The Gen 2 Chief Scientist was set in his ways, inflexible and unwilling to entertain any view that was not one-hundred-percent compliant, the result of being trained by a Gen 1 Chief Scientist. Knowing Robert's penchant for the MGR created tension in Rex's mind. What he knew from his own private calculations ... his heresy ... could not be put to use with Robert as Chief Scientist.

Early in his training, Rex outpaced Stan's ability to teach. After several requests and deliberate consideration, Robert acquiesced and allowed Rex to use the ship's science computers to access the archives. Within those archives, the dusty library of accumulated human knowledge, Rex was able to further his understanding of the ship and all the science associated with its construction and function. Fortunately, the MGR supported aggressive training, even while they demanded adherence. It was not heresy to read the archives. Rex absorbed the electronically preserved knowledge easily. And he used it. Not just to support the routine calculations required for his life's duties as a viable Sci-Eng Technician aboard Humanity One, but also to expand his understanding of the science used by the creators of the vessel, the Innovators. He seemed to be the only one on board who cared about Humanity One's origins. The rest of the Crew were content to uncritically follow the MGR; the MGR kept everything in equilibrium.

The Innovators were not infallible, as some might want to believe. As everyone in power wanted their followers to believe. The Gen 2 and Gen 3 leaders and trainers were adamant that the MGR was the way, the only way. They did not read the archives to see the history of the failures that led to the development of Humanity One and the Mission. From the basis of historical understanding, Rex saw another way. The stellar engines, as mighty as they were, were capable of much more without taxing the system, without increasing the risk of failure or diminishing the life expectancy of the individual Crew members. More energy could be captured. More power could be generated. With more power, more people could be supported by Humanity One's systems. The birthrate would not be as worrisome as it had been for four generations. Not a doubling, but more people to help maintain the ship and its inhabitants. As he drew closer to adulthood, Rex increased his pressure on Stan to allow him to speak candidly with Chief Robert and the Gen 3 Sci-Eng Techs, to explain what he knew to be true.

"Rex," Stan's voice was high pitched normally, even more so when stressed or angry. The too-often broached subject stressed him. Rex's heresy stressed him. "We've had this discussion. Chief Scientist Robert cannot tolerate anyone in his ranks who is unwilling to accept what we all know as truth. The math proves the Innovators knew what they were doing. For three generations, we have followed their rules to a "T", and they have not failed us. We are precisely where their calculations have said we would be."

"But we could be better. We could be further. We could be more than we are," Rex argued.

"And we could be dead, the Mission failed, ended by impetuous thoughts and actions. Rex, you are young, not yet an adult. You will learn the truth is as simple as following the MGR as the Innovators directed."

"But Stan...,"

"No buts. For one last time, don't further involve yourself in quackery. It is not taken lightly. Heretic thoughts could deem you unviable." Stan lowered his head so he could peer upward as if over reading glasses. It did not work. The height difference was too great. He had to tilt his head back to look up at his taller son.

Rex fumed momentarily. He knew Stan's reason for shutting him down was right. Stan was trying to protect him. He knew Stan's protection was invaluable. Every human on Humanity One had to be viable – and perceived as viable. There was no other choice. Resources demanded complete viability. Additional resources would not change that same demand. "Very well. I will hold my peace until I am Chief Scientist." Rex smiled disarmingly. He would never lose his desire to implement what he knew to be true, but he knew he had to bide his time. A hard thing for a pre-adult to do. He wished Stan were a freer thinker, like his mother Melba San Wushisi. It was difficult to gather support for changes when the status quo served everyone's purposes comfortably.

CHAPTER 7

ZACK

Zack Si Jiushiliu-Jiushiqi gazed into the crystalline enclosure. The face inside was long familiar. As a Gen 4 Stasis Technician Trainee, Sta-Tech, Zack was coming to know each of the faces he saw by name. "Hi Zhou." That was the simple name of the tank, or box, or pod, or whatever it could be called. The MGR applied the nomenclature of *transport support vessel* to each of the units. That moniker seemed cold and impersonal to Zack, but it probably was – for sure - cold. The seemingly sleeping face was mature, but not as aged as most Gen 3s. Even in the dim lighting of the Stasis unit where he trained, he could tell the skin tone was darker, healthier, not frail and pale. Much darker than his own ashy skin.

As a trainee of fourteen, soon to be fifteen, Zack was assigned to a small Stasis room. The room was specifically designed for Trainees. Only twelve support vessels were in the room. They were crowded together, abutted in pairs, with barely enough room to squeeze between the sets of pairs. Zack was small for his age. Thin and easily able to navigate the otherwise tight quarters. He had seen the larger Stasis rooms. The vessels there were stacked one atop the other, crammed into the space as efficiently as humanly possible. A sliding library ladder was used to monitor each vessel's telemetry and to visually audit its occupant, a precautionary measure to audit the veracity of the computerized monitoring system. Nothing was – or could be – left to chance.

The dim lighting in Stasis was difficult to adapt to in the beginning of his training. He learned early that the people in the support vessels were not affected by the light, or sounds, or the cold that kept them lifeless in their tubular beds. The lights were dim because they were generally unnecessary for monitoring the support vessels. Too much light was a waste of energy, a valuable resource better used elsewhere. A small, lighted panel on each support vessel reported the condition of its inhabitant. It was his duty to routinely and periodically check each panel to ensure it was functioning properly. A failure meant a death, and, ultimately, a transfer to Sanitary Recycling – for the occupant, if not also the Sta-Tech. Worse, it meant the loss of a valuable part of Humanity One's Mission, a part that could result in Mission failure.

In slightly over one year, Zack would reach adulthood. A prized benchmark. First, within his technology, he would advance from the training room to one of the larger rooms that held hundreds, if not thousands, of support vessels. There were almost twenty-five thousand vessels in all, every one of them home to an occupant, a human being. The small training room, though important, required attention but not a lot of physical activity. He thought and wondered. A lot. He had time to wonder about many things. For the next three-hundred-seventy plus days, that small room would be his life routine for as much as eight hours per day. With only twelve support vessels to monitor, he would be fighting boredom daily. That was part of the training. Learn to manage boredom. For the rest of his natural life, he could not allow boredom to distract him from the importance of his job. The primary Mission of the space vessel Humanity One was to deliver those transport support vessels to Earth Two – with occupants safe and sound.

Zack had no idea how those people would come into being, how they would step out of their vessels as viable human beings. For over sixty years, they had lain in those vessels without moving, eating, breathing, or going to the bathroom. Supposedly, the Innovators provided knowledge that would be used when the time came to revive the people in the vessels. He would be long gone, recycled and his atoms used by someone else when that happened. That thought gave him some comfort. The atoms that combined to make him would still be in use when the mission was completed. His atoms would enjoy Earth Two even if he did not.

His charges did nothing. Just exist, if being inside the support vessels could be called existence. Zack wondered why only one person per vessel. Why not two? Husband and wife. Mother and child. There were no children in the training room vessels. His training told him that there were only adults in all of Stasis. No support vessel was used for anyone who was not a fully educated and trained adult. Each vessel contained not just a person, but also valuable knowledge and the necessary skills to use it. All that knowledge and skill was frozen behind those placid faces. All the support vessels were over six feet long. He did not know very many people who were six feet tall. Only Cesar. Maybe Robert the Scientist was when he was younger - when his back was straighter. They were both old, from Gen 2. Gen 2 people were generally taller. The people in the vessels must be the same as Gen 1, close to the same age when the Mission began. They were undoubtedly of the same generation as many of the Innovators. They were from among the Innovators. Interesting to consider that they *were* the Innovators. Zack wondered if they knew everything about the ship, about the Mission, about Earth Two. Even more, he wondered if they knew about Earth One, if they knew the real reason Humanity One was sent on its Mission to Earth Two. He ultimately wondered if they were the Innovators, the humans who built Humanity One to save themselves from whatever was to befall Earth One.

Zack wondered if the people in the vessels would be able to procreate when they were revived. Would they even want to after all those years? Would they wonder where they were, awakened in a strange place, lightyears from the only home they had ever known? Would they be frightened, afraid to crawl from their vessels, fearful of the Gen 8s? He was sure the Gen 8 Sta-Techs would know what to do. The Premier of that time, or the Captain, would release the passcodes that would unlock the final-phase knowledge in the Stasis computers. That knowledge would provide all the answers about which Zack could only wonder and speculate. Other than satisfying his curiosity, there was nothing to be gained by knowing. There was nothing to be gained by wondering, but it kept him from dozing. Maddie thought they should know all the knowledge. He admired Maddie but feared her intensity.

Zack carefully performed his routine check of each support vessel's control panel for anomalies, there were none. His mind did not fail him by wandering away in the boredom. So, he wondered. Maddie was beautiful. A year older, a year wiser, friendly, and just as curious as he was. She was the only person aboard Humanity One with long hair, except some of the females in the Stasis TSVs. Silky, long blond hair that drove him to distraction when he was near her in the dining hall. He tried to be near her, at least at the same table. Several Gen 4s congregated there. That was their social life – his social life. She made him uncomfortable in a good way. His waistcloth was normally loose fitting, but not when she was around. It bound. He wondered if Maddie was taken, or even being pursued. He did notice an attraction between her and Rex, the Sci-Eng Trainee. All the females were attracted to Rex. Even some of the Gen 3 females. They would glance at Rex and smile softly, wantingly, when their mates were not looking. Rex could have his pick of any female on the ship. Why couldn't he just leave Maddie alone? Zack would give anything to be Maddie's mate.

Zack's heart stopped. He gulped. A number was not right. TSV 00009 was not right. The temperature was up point zero-zero-two degrees Fahrenheit. Not a big change, but he had never noted a change before. That was a lot of variation for the hour since his last inspection. That rate of increase would accumulate to almost five hundredths of a degree in a twenty-four-hour day. Beyond that, who knew how high it would go.

Zack hurried to the main control console and queried TSV 00009. The data stream poured faster than he could read it. He hit refresh and paused the download. Slowly, he allowed data to stream across and down the screen. If he remembered the code correctly, the crux of the defect was in an errant code copy on line seventy-five. He had no idea why the code copied wrong. He was sure that he recalled what the code should be. Even so, he wondered if his memory was right. If he was wrong and made the change ... the correction, there was no telling what harm might befall the occupant of TSV 00009. The thought passed through his mind to contact his sire, his trainer. He could not afford to make a mistake.

Zack once again wondered about those twelve vessels, those twelve people. Did they volunteer to be the guinea pigs for Trainees? Was their worth so insignificant that losing one or all of them to a rookie mistake would have no deleterious effect on the total Mission? Sad to think that those twelve were simply not viable except as training dummies. It did not matter. He had to correct the problem as he determined it. He could not show hesitation or fear of failure. If he were wrong, he was sure his sire would rush in and correct the problem. Nothing ventured, nothing gained. He input the correction and waited, half expecting to hear an alarm, a claxon that was designed to wake the dead – or the long frozen, and tell the entire ship that Zack made a fatal error.

His fix worked. The problem was not in the vessel's control system code. It was in the monitoring code. It was a false reading. Zack smiled when he heard a voice inside his head.

"Excellent work," said Matt San Jiushiba, Zack's sire and trainer. "I'm pleased you were able to catch the code error as quickly as you did. I only input it ten minutes ago."

Zack signed relief and returned to his reverie. He was sure his charges in those twelve TSVs were non-viable. There was no other reason their lives would be considered expendable. Or maybe they were already dead, simply brought along to help train, cadavers with computer regulated TSV monitoring data. The others, in the big rooms, the twenty-five thousand, were afforded extra care. Protected from any danger every moment of their lives – if that was the correct term for their condition. Even the Premier was not afforded the same level of care and respect. In essence, those twenty-five thousand humans *were* the Mission.

Still Zack wondered. Twenty-five thousand people is a lot of people, but if their mission were to terraform Earth Two, they were not that many. It would require generations of procreation to achieve a population capable of establishing an Earthlike civilization on a new planet. He wondered if there was something more, some secret knowledge held by a select few. Maddie seemed to think so. She was suspicious, angry and at times – paranoid about the Vessel Leadership Team's actions.

CHAPTER 8

THE GROUP

The Mess Hall served chow at regular intervals, intervals designed to afford everyone awake the opportunity to gather and enjoy the company of others without jeopardizing the control of the vessel. The chow was nutritious and good. The success of Hydroponics Technicians and the skills of Food Preparation Technicians determined the quality and flavors.

The VLT, Vessel Leadership Team, who normally dined at the same time, chose a quiet table against a back wall of the Mess Hall, isolated by respectful Gen 3 Techs. The level of interaction, or at least the volume, increased as the distance across the Mess Hall from the VLT table increased. The Gen 4 Trainees, not yet adults, sat together at two or three tables, depending on the number of them in the hall, closest to the serving lines. They did not seek quiet. They sought tension release through socialization. They sought to be noticed and heard by their peers. Youth always has something to prove, something to show, something to be heard.

Rex looked up from his plate and smiled greeting to Maddie. Maddie brushed her long hair away from her chin and pushed it behind her shoulders after she placed her full plate on the table next to Rex. She did not want the hair in her chow. Across the table from Rex, Zack almost swallowed his tongue when Maddie moved her hair. He wanted to touch her hair, feel its silkiness slide between his fingers. He was disappointed that Maddie did not sit next to him instead of Rex – the Golden One. She frequently tossed her head, which sent her hair into a cascade, often touching the shoulder or arms of anyone close enough. He shivered at the thought of any part of Maddie touching his skin.

Red faced, Zack blurted out, "Hi, Maddie. Your hair is as beautiful as ever." It was all he could think to say.

Maddie laughed appreciatively. She liked the attention and the public recognition. She saw others at nearby tables turn their heads at Zack's words. A few approving nods from Gen 4 Trainees, but more Gen 3 heads shaken in disapproval. "Thank you, Zack. Kendra, your carrots look delicious."

Kendra's freckled face burst into a self-conscious grin, pulled away from her glance toward a table of Gen 3s. "Thank you, Maddie. They are sweeter than normal. I don't know if the strain has changed or if the nutrient mixture was different. It could be as simple as better lighting. Photosynthesis creates sugars." Her previous distraction caused her to ramble. She knew no one really cared about the growing process, only that it was working as it should. And Maddie was just being polite.

Sean spoke after he swallowed a mouth full of soy protein soup. He held a pale arm out for emphasis. "I think we could all use a little photosynthesis."

The Group laughed and added minor comments of agreement, and a few words regarding the lack of sufficient UV lighting outside of Hydroponics. They all knew UV was essential to creating and processing some vitamins. The Mess Hall did have some UV lighting, but not enough to bronze skin – or even cause freckles. Barely enough to synthesis vitamin D from cholesterol.

Marly familiarly patted Sean's offered arm. "Now Sean, your skin is beautiful. Smooth and unmarked by wrinkles."

Sean blushed. The smooth reference made him look at Rex's textured musculature. "I meant we need some color like Kendra."

Jana held out her arm, "I have color."

"True," Sean replied, "but think of how deep and luxurious that color would be if you were a Hy-Tech like Kendra."

Kendra nervously laughed. "I just freckle, like my mother. Some others darken. Not me."

Maddie replied, "I think your freckles are becoming. We could all do with a few freckles. But," her tone became serious, "what did you mean when you said the strain may have changed?"

Kendra wanted to glance toward the Gen 3 table that screamed for her attention. A singular voice caressed her ears. She wanted to see the face, the mouth that formed the sounds. "Oddities occur occasionally," she responded dismissively, not really wanting to belabor the thought. "Sometimes it's good. Sometimes it's bad."

"You mean like evolution?" Maddie queried.

Marly interjected, "Or mutation." She sat erect with her thigh pressed against Sean's and waited while everyone processed her comment – and for a returned press by Sean.

"Why would carrots mutate?" Jana asked.

"Everything can mutate, especially if it's exposed to some forms of radiation."

"Where would the radiation come from, inside Humanity One?" Sean asked.

"Space. Radiation is everywhere," Rex answered succinctly.

Rex's comment required a few moments to process. Maddie asked, "I thought the hull stopped space radiation?" The thought concerned her. If Kendra's comments were accurate, then Rex's comment created cause for deep concern.

"To some degree, but some radiation either can't be stopped or it requires specialized barriers."

Kendra slowly responded, "That may be why we have a new strain of wheat. Bigger grains, almost as big as corn kernels. We will soon harvest the first room with that wheat strain."

"Where did it come from?" Sean asked, amazed.

"A single stalk a few years ago. Hydroponics Chief Kellie approved experimentation. They crossbred it with other varieties until it had the characteristics she wanted to try. We have a whole room of grain ready for harvest in a week. It will provide twice as much wheat using the same resources as the standard strain. Maybe even more."

Jana leaned toward the Group and softly replied, "I'm fairly sure that is against the MGR. The Chief may be in violation."

"Surely she got approval from the Premier and the VLT," Maddie whispered cautiously, almost questioningly.

Jana snorted a bit louder than she intended, "The Gen 2s would never approve any change. They've lost touch."

A moment of quiet at the Gen 4 table followed Jana's words, with several sets of eyes looking to see if she was overheard. The noise level in the room did not vary.

Rex spoke softly, "She's not wrong. How many times have we seen opportunities presented that could improve our lives, enhance our resources, and be told the MGR is absolute and unquestionable by the Gen 2s in charge?"

Jana nodded vigorously. "Exactly. The Gen 2s are holding us back, keeping us from reaching our potential."

Marly spoke pedantically, less softly, "Chief Stasis Engineer, Deanna Er Jiushi-Jiusan, is a Gen 2. She's over sixty. Medical science says that is far older than standard. There are only five Gen 2s still alive." The young girl was proud to demonstrate her medical knowledge.

Jana replied angrily, still louder than the conversation merited, "Exactly. And every one of them is impeding progress, keeping someone younger and more energetic from accomplishing great things."

Kendra, recoiling back slightly, retorted, "What would you suggest we do? Recycle them?"

Maddie answered, "Maybe. Maybe just let them live out their days until recycle."

"If someone is not viable, they pose more harm than good. They use resources that could be used to support new births. We are limited, you know," replied Zack. He tried to sound mature and knowledgeable. "We have to utilize our resources to ensure the viability of the Mission. That means continuation of the humans on board Humanity One - through procreation." He glanced toward Maddie, hoping she was listening, understanding his awkward recitation of indoctrination. She may have heard his words, but she did not react to his subtle insinuation. To Zack's dismay, Maddie turned toward Rex.

"Rex, Chief Scientist Robert Er Ershiyi-Ershisi is a Gen 2. Do you see issues with his viability?"

Rex moiled the question while the others waited for his response. "Some. I'm not sure how old he actually is, but ..."

"Fifty-six," Marly interjected.

Rex nodded, "Fifty-six. Okay. Robert is fifty-six. Adulthood was changed from eighteen to sixteen for the Gen 3s, and us. Why was that? I'll tell you why. Because to continue procreation at a replacement pace and be able to train the offspring while the propagating generation is still viable, we had to start earlier."

"True," Marly replied. "The life span of Gen 2s averages near fifty Earth years. All the living Gen 2s have exceeded that statistical average."

"And," Rex continued, "those five are artificially pushing that average higher with each passing day. If we took the outliers out of the equation, that average is nearer forty-five."

"What does that mean?" Maddie asked, puzzled by the conversation's turn.

Jana responded, just as angry but softer, seething more, "It means we don't have as many Gen 4s as we should have because the Gen 2s are using resources that could be utilized for the future instead of the past."

"She's not wrong," Rex said. "The MGR supports maintaining the ship's population at twice the number of original Gen 1s. There were two hundred. Am I right, Marly? You're in Medical. You probably know that better than the rest of us." Rex was adept at involving others to enhance the merits of his words.

"True. There were two hundred. Their life averages were just under sixty Earth years. On Earth One, the average was reckoned at more than seventy years."

"Why would the life average change that drastically?" Rex asked. "There has to be a medical reason for the average to drop from seventy to sixty and then to fifty."

"I don't know that," Marly responded apologetically. "I learned what I do know by reading the Medical files, some of them outside of my training directives."

"Can you find out more? Will the Gen 3s be forty and Gen 4s be thirty? Gen 7 will have to procreate before they're old enough to walk if Gen 8 is to reach Earth Two."

"That can't happen," Kendra said incredulously. "Procreation requires maturity."

Rex chuckled, "I was exaggerating, but something is happening – has happened. Maybe your new strain of wheat is part of the answer to what."

"Well, whatever the answer, the Gen 2's are taking up resources that could be better used," Jana reiterated emphatically.

The subject was one that the Gen 4s often discussed, though with less detail. The few with access to historical data - Marly, Jana and Rex - slowly delved into areas beyond their normal training. Knowledge was generally compartmentalized to support the different functions. MGR suggested that unnecessary knowledge would only detract from the different functional duties. The suggestion made sense on the surface. Except to the Group, Maddie's group. Curiosity demanded that they know more; Maddie wanted to know more. Maddie wanted to know not just *the what* and *the how*; she wanted to know *the why. The whys* were buried. Youthful curiosity is hard to contain, especially for the young.

"Then, we need to gather more information. The day will eventually come when we will be in positions like the Gen 2s and Gen 3s. If we have the knowledge, we can change the status quo. We have to be prepared." Rex was pragmatic. It would be nice if his process to increase energy production could be implemented. The additional resource would enhance life aboard the ship and prove to everyone that change was acceptable, not an anathema to the Innovators, or a danger to the Mission.

"I don't plan to wait that long," retorted Jana. "I won't become an adult for more than a year. I plan to use the power of knowledge to change the status quo. Viability should come with knowledge, not age." Her situation was markedly different than the others. Her peers did not fully realize her concerns.

CHAPTER 9

ROGUE

A limited Communication filled Cesar's head. It broke him from his reminiscences, his distractions. Voices become strained during crisis. Thoughts do too, but not with sudden octave shifts like audible utterings. Thought Communication was sometimes jumbled with highly descriptive imagery as the stress level of the person communicating increased. One of the Con-Sys Techs offered a description that was more than Cesar had ever encountered, and her tension was obvious. The subdural Communicators were useful in a lot of ways, beginning with enhanced idea expression that was not constrained by vocabulary. Visual images accompanied the verbal patterns. Colors were real, as precise as each individual's visual acuity allowed.

Unnoticed on the "front windshield", a large viewer that projected a computer-generated image of space in front of Humanity One, a tiny speck of light represented a heavenly body moving steadfastly along its course. No different than thousands of larger and smaller specks. Nothing about the visible speck predicted harm, or danger – or appeared unusual. Without other means of observation and tracking, that tiny dot would have gone unnoticed. The Communicator helped Cesar locate it on the screen whereas words would have required the use of a physical pointer.

The voice in Cesar's head advised that the object was on a course that predicted intersection with that of Humanity One's. Cesar used the imbedded Communicator to ask, "Time to intersection?"

"Less than three days."

"How much less?" Cesar wanted precise answers, usable information. August would have it no other way. August passed, lost viability, in a sudden moment. There was no formal parting. Gone from life, passed to Recycling without fanfare. There was no time for anything different. Cesar was pressed into service, called to duty immediately – frightened and resolved to never fail. His quest for precision was unrelenting ... especially in crisis.

A flurry of disoriented thoughts slowly coalesced into an answer. "Two ... rather, sixty-six hours – if the computer's calculations are correct."

"Is there any reason to suspect they are not correct?" Cesar allowed his impatience to be Communicated to the Con-Sys Tech. The situation required a focused, and probably urgent, response. Estimation and hesitation would not suffice.

"Not that I know. I rely on the computer for such things."

The thoughts expressed frustration. Cesar knew he had pushed the Con-Sys Tech to her limit of capability. "Thank you, Con-Sys Tech Winn. And thank you for using a single connection to me. It might be better if we study this before we speak of it openly." He knew the information would be spread soon enough, but he preferred there was more data available to alleviate concern. An unexpected event like the object might create panic and a loss of focus with the Crew. It would be unacceptable for him to allow that to happen.

Mentally, Cesar switched his Communicator to Chief Scientist Robert. "Robert, I need an immediate calculation. A rogue object has been detected by System. Projected contact – *as in collision* – is sixty-six hours. Verify and offer options." Con-Sys Tech Winn seemed certain of the intersection, of the potential for contact, but Cesar needed confirmation. Everything depended on knowing for sure.

Robert acknowledged receipt and understanding of the assignment. The Communication did not close until Cesar had imparted all the details of the Con-Sys Tech's data stream, how to interface with the live data and the brief historical record of the rogue object.

Cesar waited. Even though Con-Sys Tech Winn seemed alarmed, he was not ready to become alarmed yet. That might come later. He used his Communicator to reassure the observant Con-Sys Tech that Chief Robert would resolve the issue. The Innovators set the course of Humanity One in as straight a line as possible, shortest distance between two points, but that yielded to commonsense. More than once, only noticed by him and course tracking Con-Sys Technicians, Humanity One altered its course for one reason or another. The Innovators knew every object along Humanity One's reckoned path. The course changed to avoid predicted collisions. The course also changed to get more thrust from solar winds as predicted by the Innovators' observations of space and the objects within it. The course changed to avoid the gravity of large masses or to utilize the slingshot effects of those masses to push Humanity One further along its course and feed into the velocity calculation. All course changes were part of the preset navigational plan, part of the mission protocol. The course was not changed beyond those that were part of the plan. The Sci-Eng Techs were called upon to verify each planned change, nothing more.

Robert's response finally came. "Sixty-five hours and forty-two minutes. The object is not much larger than Humanity One, moving slightly slower."

"Doesn't matter how big it is. I don't want it to hit our vessel. That would end the Mission in failure. Do you predict it will intersect and collide with Humanity One?"

A flustered pause preceded Chief Robert's response. "Yes. The calculations predict collision."

"Options?"

"None that I can offer."

"Did the Innovators miss this one? It *is* relatively small, in the scheme of things."

Robert's thoughts expressed his shock that Cesar would suggest a mistake by the Innovators, an error by the Infallible. "They've predicted and set course to avoid smaller objects. There's no reason to believe this is any different."

"Well, Robert, it's there - on a collision course. It is definitely different," Cesar challenged sarcastically.

Robert's thoughts tried to assimilate the unthinkable. "Are you sure? Maybe it's not what it seems. Maybe it only appears to be on collision course. The Innovators can't be wrong."

Cesar suppressed his inclination to physically laugh out loud. He successfully prevented thoughts filled with laughter from transmitting to Robert. Robert did not respond well to anyone or anything that questioned his capabilities as a scientist, or the authority of the MGR. And he lacked a sense of humor. Even so, it was less frustrating to Communicate with the deliberate scientist via the Communicators than verbally. The man's thoughts were less hesitant. They flowed freely. Robert's speaking voice was slow and deliberate, irritatingly so. "Robert, *you* confirmed the data. If the System and your calculations are correct, the Innovators got this one wrong."

"That can't be."

"Robert." Cesar felt Robert's mind filling with uncertainty, losing control of the moment. "Calculate again if you have doubts. Otherwise, we need a plan to avoid the rogue."

Cesar was concerned. Chief Robert was wavering, fearful of the new uncertainty the rogue represented. He allowed Robert to understand the emotional side of his concern before he cut Communication. The methodical Chief Scientist needed to set aside his ingrained reverence for the Innovators and focus on the problem. He shifted in The Chair. The pain in his back was momentarily muted by the impending crisis. Radically changing Humanity One's course was not an easy option. Not just because it went against the MGR, but because the Innovators did not install a positive steering system. By their reckoning and according to their plan, a robust steering system was not necessary. All moves, all deviations from a straight line, were preplanned and those course changes were made gradually over a period of days, even weeks, by adjusting the solar sails. The proton propulsion system, a typical rocketry system that used the energetic discharge of streamed protons, could make the changes more quickly, but even that was not immediate. Proton propulsion came at great expense, lots of protons were required. Any unplanned use – such as what seemed to be the logical option to the rogue's trajectory - would tap into meager reserves needed for routine course maintenance. Inertia played a big role in steering and propulsion. Humanity One was a cannonball hurtling through space at a speed as near that of light as was humanly possible, almost half.

In the front of Cesar's mind, his looming concern, was the fact that if the Innovators were erroneous about objects only six decades into the Mission, the potentially devastating errors that might exist in the future could easily doom the Mission – if Humanity One survived the rogue. In reality, failure was now an option.

As Stan's Trainee and a respected student, Rex was privy to an emergency Communication from Chief Scientist Robert. Or it was a mistake on Chief Robert's part. He felt the urgency of the Chief's mental Communication. He also sensed frustration, even fear. He followed his sire, Stan, to a designated Focus Room within the Science and Engineering section.

Robert appeared haggard. His age showed more than normal. The gravity of the situation, whatever it was, pulled his shoulder toward the deck, something the vessel's low gravity could not do with force. The low gravity did contribute to the weakened bones that were manifested in everyone older than thirty. He spoke softly, hesitantly, almost fearful that his vocalized words would not flow properly or be in the right order. That was the way he always spoke. "I called this meeting, this small group, to evaluate a problem." He blinked apprehensively and leaned forward slightly as he formed his next sentence. "We are the only ones who need to be aware. A ..." he paused, lost in his search for words, "rogue object appears to be on a collision course with Humanity One." He paused again and waited until everyone nodded and grimaced acknowledgement. "We must determine how to avoid it. Time is of the essence." His frail hand touched the work computer that was dedicated to that Focus Room. The situation was critical and unfettered knowledge of it could create a distraction among the Crew. "Everything we know is already loaded."

Gen 3 Scientist Gail San Ershisan-Sishiba, heir apparent to the role of Chief spoke confidently, "We will have the answer within half an hour." She moved close to the computer and said with authority, "Science One, I will lead." The command was to the computer. The five other people in the small room noticed but did not react to Gail's behavior. They all knew the assignment was of high importance because of their segregation from the rest of the Sci-Eng Team.

"Science One awaits, Gail." The computer's voice was female and sounded flawless. It recognized Gail's voice. It recognized all adult voices in Science and Engineering.

Rex knew to remain silent, at least until he was fully apprised of the situation. His role was to observe and learn – if his invitation was intentional. As a Trainee, he would be asked if his input were desired – and that input would be expected to be parroting of previous lessons learned. The only reason he was there was because Stan was needed – and because Chief Scientist Robert liked him ... or forgot to not include him. He observed, not totally surprised that Gail all but physically shoved Chief Scientist Robert away from the computer.

"Re-evaluate the trajectory of an object identified as Rogue One. Compare that trajectory to Humanity One's course. Define the outcome of doing nothing." Gail looked at the computer, oblivious to the others in the small room. She had her own thoughts.

Within seconds, the screen displayed a visual representation of the rogue's calculated path with a red line. Humanity One's path was represented by a yellow line. A large orange burst represented the intersection point. "Rogue One will impact Humanity One with catastrophic results for both objects in precisely sixty-five hours, thirty-four minutes and seventeen seconds."

Everyone reacted to the impact representation. It was sudden and startling. "This does not bode well," Stan exclaimed, barely loud enough to be heard.

Gail scowled toward Stan, "Ya think? Mission failure in one cataclysmic moment. Humanity lost. No. It does *not* bode well. We must alter course immediately."

Robert's face reddened with angry determination. "That is not an option," he snapped at Gail, his sentence blurted faster than his normal cadence.

"Then we die," Gail retorted with matched anger.

"The option is to reroute the rogue." Robert stood fast in his resolve to abide by the MGR. At that moment, he was prepared to battle with Gail for control of the group. He was growing weary of her increasingly bold attempts to ignore his leadership authority. He was keenly aware of his diminishing ability to remain viable. His age, his health, his weariness affected his energy and focus. He knew it. The time for his life to end was near. Even so, he did not intend to surrender it or his authority easily. He was not completely selfless. "We cannot alter the course of Humanity One. The Innovators, the MGR, expressly forbid it."

Gail shook her head in disbelief. The thirty-eight-year-old was not going to allow the moment to pass without a challenge. She had no faith in Robert as a crisis leader. To her, he was too slow, too hesitant, too staid for crisis management. In fact, this was the first real crisis Humanity One had ever experienced and the old man was relying on the only source he understood – the MGR and the infallibility of the Innovators. As far as she was concerned, he was incapable of leading during crisis. Too steeped in tradition and adamantly inflexible. The problem was outside all predicted parameters. Apparently, even the Innovators missed it; but that did not mean they left no means to address an occurrence of that sort. "The Innovators put humans on Humanity One because they expected us to do the necessary to save the Mission from failure, even if it comes to deviating from the MGR. We are here to think."

"They did not!" Robert barked; his eyes suddenly filled with a long-lost spark; his words firm and clear. He knew he had to win if he and the Mission were to remain viable. "We will not change course. Cesar and the Premier won't allow it."

Stan remained calmly apart from the angry exchange, as did Bella, Rex, Bard and Lela. He did not remain silent, though. Arguments and posturing were not going to solve the problem. The clock was ticking. Whatever action was chosen, time might prevent its implementation anyway, but they had to try. He asked in as calm a tone as he could muster. "How do we alter the course of the rogue? I'm unaware of any of the ship's systems that allow that option."

"Exactly," Gail said with a crooked smile of appreciation, not an unexpected reaction from her.

Robert's hands shook and he balanced himself by leaning on the computer table. The action made it appear that he was preparing to physically displace Gail from the command position. The others watched warily as he slowly formed his response and spoke in his halting style. His words came so slowly that his listeners were leaning forward, anticipating what the next word would – or should – be. "The proton propulsion rockets can be directed in any direction. A strong stream of protons on its leading edge should alter the rogue's course enough to avoid collision. We only need to nudge it." His statement, though haltingly made, was made with conviction.

"Opposite and equal," Stan said calmly, with as few words as practical so he did not appear to be choosing sides. He was unwilling to allow Robert and Gail to engage in a pissing contest while the fate of Humanity One was at stake.

"What?" Robert blinked.

Gail replied condescendingly, "If we fire the proton propulsion rockets to alter the rogue's course, our own course will be altered. The effect will be exactly what you refuse to accept as the proper action – without predictability or assurances of success. Altering Humanity One's course is the only viable option, the only solution with absolute predictability." She paused and gave a meaningful look toward the others before she added, "And viability is the key to the success of our Mission."

Rex understood the underlying meaning of Gail's words. She wanted the Chief Scientist position sooner rather than later. She was no longer willing to accept a strong second-in-command role. He cringed inside. The battle was a distraction. It made him nervous. The fate of Humanity One was hinged on the outcome of that battle. Gail's face briefly became placid, imperceptibly so to anyone who was not attentive. Rex recognized the expression as the result of the mental effort required to activate the Communicator. Gail's Communication did not include him.

Robert's reddened face paled around his lips as he pursed them tightly in thought. With measured speech, he replied, "Science One, calculate the angle and power required of our proton propulsion to displace the rogue sufficiently enough to alter its course to avoid collision with Humanity One." His eyes dared Gail to challenge him further. He spoke directly to her without blinking, "We will abide by MGR and not alter our course."

Gail stared at her superior with unseeing eyes for more than a minute, a quiet lapse that built tension within the select group. "We shall see," she replied dismissively as she continued to stare without flinching. Another minute passed. The only sounds outside of the background noises of the vessel, were nervously cleared throats and bare feet shuffling on the cool floor. Finally, she pulled herself to her full height, appearing as tall as Chief Scientist Robert because of his stooped back. She spoke in an even voice with an authoritative tone, "Chief Scientist Robert Er Ershiyi-Ershisi, for failing to remain viable in the performance of your duties, I am hereby executing the authority afforded me by the MGR to replace you as Chief Scientist."

Before Robert could respond with anything more than a shocked look, before the others fully comprehended the turn of events, two able-bodied Security Officers briskly entered the room, grasped Robert's upper arms, and turned him toward the doorway. There was no doubt that her Communication was with people outside the room.

Rex watched with widened eyes as Chief Scientist Robert was led away without further incident.

Gail spoke before Robert was out of sight, "Science One, belay the command issued by former Chief Scientist Robert. Calculate a course correction for Humanity One that will avoid the rogue. Detail all actions required and the timing of execution that will provide the greatest chance of success."

"Calculating," was the simply response.

CHAPTER 10

METEOR

Cesar was involved in the Communication initiated by Gail. As a matter of fact, he was the primary contact. He should not have been. The Premier, or even the Chief Medical Officer, should have been the initial contact. He allowed his discomfort with the coup to be known. He liked Robert. They were friends. They were of the same generation. They experienced the settlement years, the years during which Gen 1s had children and settled into their routines. More strikingly, the years when the Gen 1s accepted their fate. Gen 1s willfully sacrificed their lives to the Mission, knowingly forfeited their futures and that of their progeny. Gen 2s experienced the harsh training of their dour parents, people so intensely dedicated to the Mission, to the MGR, that all else was unnecessary. Gen 2s and Gen 3s never considered that life was any different than life inside Humanity One. They had no choice. They had no benchmark outside of the vessel against which to measure life. Even so, Gen 3s could never appreciate the hardships of those settlement years. They did not experience any of that struggle firsthand. Cesar's generation softened when training their children, though not as much as the Gen 3s did with their offspring. He included Paul in the Communication. Gail was remiss by not contacting the Premier with her request for ascension to Chief Scientist. Ascensions were normally less dramatic. A sudden loss of viability through death or infirmity. The assumed heir simply ascended into the role. No fanfare. No grand entrance. A ship's bell intoned a three-note indication of a human passed to recycling. That was the entirety of death and replacement. It was better not to belabor the pain of loss of loved ones in the small group of humans.

Cesar knew the Earth-bound humans placed greater symbolism on the passing of a life, of a loved one's death. They had the luxury of relationships. Funerals and memorials were standard, steeped in religious rituals as the remains were returned to the earth, dust to dust, ashes to ashes, by burial or cremation. His parents mentioned it at some point in somber conversation following the death of a fellow Gen 1 Crew member whose body was transferred to Recycling. Inside Humanity One, a body could not be "buried," hidden away for eternity in a memorial garden. Cremation required massive amounts of thermal energy, energy that could not be spared. Nor could a body be dumped into space, littering the void with a seven-generation trail of fallen heroes. The success of the Mission required the use and reuse of every single atom that was loaded onto Humanity One before it left the Solar System. He knew that he would be required to order the intonation, the knell, before the end of the day. It had to be done. The danger was real. The calculation to save Humanity One had to be done without consideration of conventional constraints – and friendships. He and the Premier would decide whether to implement the suggested course of action. Both actions. It would not fall on anyone else's shoulders.

Cesar listened as Gail's Communicator shared her observations while Robert was replaced. His friend knew and accepted the inevitable. After Robert was escorted from the Focus Room, Cesar encouraged Gail to complete the calculations without further comment. He then cut the link. He had a greater issue to address.

The Innovators had access to visual and sensory telescopes

positioned throughout the Solar System. They could detect objects even smaller than Humanity One along the path chosen as the course to Earth Two. They observed and measured the actions of every object they saw, precisely calculated each object's path. They left nothing to chance. They could not. That was the reason the rogue's presence was a surprise to Cesar, even a shock. Without the steadfast belief that every eventuality regarding the position of space objects was accurately plotted, the remainder of the journey, the next five generations of the Mission, would be stress-filled as generations of Captains worried hourly about the next missed object hurtling through space on a collision course with Humanity One. Calm days were gone, not that the days aboard Humanity One were truly calm, mostly just boring.

Until the rogue appeared, the greatest concern was that small, undetectable objects would strike Humanity One. Humanity One was ingeniously constructed to bolster hull integrity, to protect its occupants. To ameliorate the catastrophic potential of such an impact, the hull was multi-plied. The outer hull extended around the vessel entirely. It was a hard, nearly unyielding titanium alloy that could easily support the solar sails, stellar engines, and proton propulsion rockets. The second layer, set nearly one meter inside the titanium hull, also covered the entirety of the vessel. It was a metallic fabric that, like a knight's mail armor, was almost impenetrable. It was designed and installed with a framework that allowed it to flex and absorb the impact of any object that penetrated the outer hull. The flexible inner hull could comfortably stop most objects up to half a meter in diameter. Anything smaller was hardly a match for the outer hull. Anything larger was predicted and avoided. Another, less impact resistant inner hull encased the vessel two feet below the flexible layer. It was a sheathing attached to the uppermost ceiling of the habitable area of Humanity One. Its sole purpose was to ameliorate the radiation that constantly bombarded all objects in space. Without that layer, that tertiary shield, Gen 1 would have died of radiation poisoning long before Gen 2 could be born. Even if they were born, Gen 2 would have suffered the consequences of unpredictable mutations.

Two areas of the vessel were provided extra protection from exotic radiation that filled the universe, spewed from exploding stars and unpredictable nebulae. The Mission was doomed if anything went wrong in those areas. Hydroponics and Stasis. Especially Stasis. The humans inside the TSVs had to be protected from long term exposure to errant radiation, because they had to survive eight human generations in space. Loosely calculated, they would suffer exposure for more than two centuries.

Hydroponics had an extra layer of radiation protection. The ceilings, floors and walls were constructed using lead enhanced materials. The added protection was to prevent the crops from suffering from mutating radiation. Plant generations were far shorter than that of humans. Each species of consumable was genetically modified to retain its characteristics and to produce viable seeds that would sprout true to the parent plant. Even with GMO status, through intensive gardening techniques, some plant varieties had to thrive for as many as a thousand generations. Cesar knew the reasoning that only some areas of the vessel were lead-lined. The extra weight required to cover the entire living compartment also meant extra mass. Mass affected speed and energy resources. A few minor mutations among the Crew could be ameliorated better than uncontrolled mutations in the food source. The food sources would eventually be transferred to Earth Two. Unpredicted mutations within the food supply could jeopardize the survival of humans on Earth Two, they could jeopardize the Mission itself.

Stasis was lined with lead as was Hydroponics, but it also had added protection using a layer of specialized paper. The primary difference, the most substantial difference between Stasis and everywhere else, was that the outer walls, lowest floor, and uppermost ceiling of Stasis was constructed with an inner compartment filled with water. Even the doors were water filled. Most importantly, Stasis was nearer the center of the vessel, which provided additional protection from some types of radiation. The more barriers, the better.

Few of the current Crew members were aware of the disparity of protection between the active humans and the stasis humans. It was knowledge that served no purpose for their duties and the completion of the Mission. It simply had to be that way for the long-term survival of the species.

For the second time within two hours, shortly after an "All Normal" review, Cesar's head filled with sounds and visions. Con-Sys Tech Della San Qi communicated a hull breach. The breach was detected above Hydroponics, seemingly restricted to the outer hull. Della had already notified Mech-Techs of the breach. Standard procedure per the MGR.

"Is there venting?"

"None detected," Della responded via the Communicator. "The Mech-Techs will clear it."

"Understood. Continue to monitor. I will take it from here. We may be in a meteor shower. Be alert." Cesar knew he did not have to tell Della, or any Con-Sys Tech, those two words. He switched his Communicator to those of Premier Paul and the Chief Mechanic of Hard Fabrication, Donald San Sishiqi-Qishijui. "Chief Donald, I take it you have a team assigned to a hull breach above Hydroponics." The thought wavered between a statement of fact and a query.

"Aye, Captain. The alert was just received. The team is almost suited. It will require a few minutes to get to the breach zone. Indications are that the object did not penetrate beyond that zone. Routine event," Chief Donald added the last with a mental shrug.

Environmental suits were required to access the areas outside the living compartment. Atmosphere was not wasted in those areas that were exposed to potential breaches. The loss of a single atom might be enough to put the Mission at risk.

"Probably another meteor. The timing is bad, but that's my worry." Cesar clouded his mind, so thoughts of the rogue did not bleed through into his Communication. The Communicators were tricky at times. Without discipline, the wrong thoughts could join the basic message. Secrets do not keep well in Communicator mode. There was no need for excess information at that moment. "Let me know as soon as your team identifies the extent of the damage and repair time. I can't over-emphasis the gravity of a breach in Hydroponics."

"Aye, Captain. We're on top of it. We've patched a lot of those holes." Donald chuckled. "We keep a few repair kits of different sizes on hand. The Team will carry four different kits to make sure they have the right one. They'll have it repaired before they leave the affected zone."

"Thank you."

As soon as the Chief Mechanic was cleared of the Communicator, Paul asked Cesar, "Have you gotten anything more on the rogue?" His concern was real. The rogue was the first real crisis of his lifetime, of Humanity One's lifetime. Until that moment, the flight had been uneventful, even boring if one could ignore the high stakes of the Mission. The rogue could abruptly end the Mission. He did not want history to reflect that Mission failure occurred during his term – not that there would be anyone to record the event in the annals.

"Not yet. Ro … Gail is leading it and being creative."

A wave of sadness swept across the Communicator from Paul when he caught the Captain's near error of identification. "I hate the loss of Robert. He is a good Scientist … and friend." The sadness passed. "I don't like creativity. There should be something in the Science Engineering section of the MGR that provides solutions to the problem, to all problems – even rogues. I'm surprised Robert didn't present it to thwart Gail's actions."

"If it's there, the Sci-Engs will find it. Relax. We will resolve this soon." Cesar had the same thoughts. Robert knew the MGR inside and out. He, more than all people, was a disciple of the Innovators. If there was something, Robert would have referenced it to save himself. Apparently, there was nothing ... or the aging Chief Scientist actually lost mental viability. Cesar leaned back in his chair, aware that Joseph was expectantly watching him. He needed to let Joseph know what was happening. If Humanity One survived, the Captain-In-Waiting would need every bit of information from this incident to prepare himself for similar incidents in the future. There was no doubt the Innovators missed the rogue. That meant there could be hundreds of unplanned rogues out there, waiting to end humanity in one explosive burst – or a catastrophic venting through a breached hull. He motioned Joseph to approach The Chair. Jana followed, curious and with nothing better to do. He said in a hushed voice. "Joseph, a rogue object has been detected on an intersecting course with Humanity One. Sci-Engs are calculating options for avoidance."

Jana blurted, "I thought the Innovators planned for all large objects."

Cesar scowled at his granddaughter, "They may have missed one. The MGR will provide our course of action. Be patient and learn." He wished he had dismissed her before he spoke, or used the Communicator instead. The young ones talk too much, often about things that are sometime imprudent to mention. "Chief Scientist Robert has lost viability. Chief Scientist Gail San Ershisan-Sishiba has replaced him. She is calculating our options. Joseph, I want you to stick close to me for the next sixty-five hours as we work through this. There may be new learning for our future Captains."

"I'll stay close," Jana replied, her emotions between eagerness and indignation. Cesar was always curt with her, even when he did not have to be.

Joseph patted his daughter's shoulder and replied perfunctorily, "Aye, Captain. Is there anything more we can do?" He intentionally included Jana.

Cesar eyed the two and twisted his lips tightly. "Observe and learn."

❧

Gen 3 Mech-Tech Chi San Sishiliu-Ershier ascended the ladder that led to an airlock hatch. His 15-year-old trainee son Ying Si Sishiliu-Sishiba followed close behind. Chi's partner on the assignment was Gen 3 Mech-Tech Ballard San Sishiqi-Shisan who followed behind Ying. It was Ying's first time on a hull repair assignment. Chi was proud of his son. The boy was extremely dedicated to training as a Mech-Tech. At times, the dedication was worrisome. Chi encouraged Ying to sit with the Gen 4s in the Mess Hall. The young adult had to learn to socialize, to learn from his peers about other duties, to be ready to sire a Gen 5. Ying could not do that by following Gen 3s all the time. The young pre-adult was exceptionally good at mechanical repairs, capable of crafting any number of parts using the equipment in the Hard Fabrication shop. The boy was true to his name which means "*clever*" in one of the Earth languages not used on Humanity One. It was time to test him on the hull.

The access points between the three primary hull levels were complicated airlocks, barely capable of holding three suited bodies. Normally, two-person teams went on hull repair assignments. That configuration was for normal repairs, such as the assignment that faced the team.

"Ying, pull in tighter against me and the wall so Ballard can squeeze in. We don't want to have to make two separate entries between each ply."

"Sorry," Ying replied via the Communicator. "I couldn't tell I wasn't already squeezed in."

Ballard laughed, "The suits take time to learn. Maybe someday, someone will figure out how to make them sense things like a second skin."

Chi laughed in return, "And then everyone would complain about the cold." The reference was to the extreme coldness outside the living compartment of the vessel. Without attenuated atmosphere, the space between the three primary layers of hull were no different than the vastness of space – with one notable exception, it was cave black between the layers of hull. There were no tiny points of light to help with orientation. Small lamps built into the forehead of the suit helmets provided light and a dizzying interpretation of the space between the two hulls.

Ying would have to learn to turn his head the right direction to see his work. Without atmospheric particles, the beam of light was not diffused and scattered to provide peripheral lighting. It went in a straight line from the source to where it was pointed, relentlessly focused, though not laser like. As the team made their way across the space between the two outermost plies, he was scolded more than once for pointing his light directly into the face plates of the other two when they spoke.

"Ying, we're using Communicators. Pretend we are in different rooms. You don't need to look at my face to understand me," Chi said after the third bright light incident.

"Aye Sir. Sorry." Ying's contrition was sincere.

The team crawled single file toward the zone identified as the point of the breach. The inside of the outer hull was gridded with reflective lines and numbers. The gridding corresponded to the Control System's computer hull monitoring program. Their assignment was in Grid 5437. The Innovators were very astute for providing the grid system rather than relying on longitude and latitude. Inside, cramped between the hull layers on all fours, the grid numbering system was simpler for orientation.

They were not crawling along the outside of a balloon, though it seemed that way in the pitch blackness. Struts and support beams between the hull plies created gridworks of their own, causing one to wonder if the outer hull was solid and the struts were there to hold the inner hull in place, dangled below; or if the struts were there like beams to hold the outer hull above the flexible layer. In truth, they were there because neither hull could be allowed to float freely. The struts were the only way to maintain proper spacing.

"Ahead," Chi said. "We are almost there. Go slow and search the flex hull for an object. There was no indication of its size. We only know it didn't penetrate the flex hull, but it was big enough to burst through the solid hull." Chi was in charge of that particular mission, but his instructions were not intended for Ballard. Ballard knew the routine. The Communication was for Ying, for his Trainee.

"What will it look like?" Ying asked.

"Round. Flat. Square. Short. Long. Black. White. Who knows? Search carefully. Chief Mech Donald will want to see it – or the scattered pieces."

"Hopefully, it's iron or nickel and in one piece. Recycle will add it to our resources," Ballard said.

"Really?" Ying was amazed by Ballard's Communication that added visuals of a small lump of metal being processed into a flat bar of iron capable of being transformed into something useful. He was new to learning how effective thought transference was for visualizations of ideas and concepts. For the novice, the volume of information that came from the Communicators was almost overwhelming.

Chi chuckled. "See, you didn't realize how important our jobs are. We are viable in more ways than most people give us credit for."

"I see a dip," Ballard said. "Left about two body lengths." The distance was hard to estimate in the darkness, but Ballard had enough experience that his guess was only a third off. He picked the projectile up in his gloved hand and looked straight above, searching for the breach in the metal hull. He found it almost directly above.

"Wow!" Chi exclaimed. "That's tiny. A lot smaller than I expected it to be. Barely bigger than my thumb – and I don't have big thumbs. I'm surprised it got through the outer hull."

"It was lodged in the flex hull. I had to pry it loose."

"Really? It almost penetrated? I didn't bring a repair kit for that."

"I have one," Ballard replied. "You never know."

"True, but I've never heard of a meteor penetrating the flex hull. It's supposed to flex enough to reduce the energy to zero. Once, I found one that bounced out of the flex and landed several meters from the impact site."

Ying stared at the object in Ballard's hand. It was small compared to the suit glove. He was inexplicably disappointed. Ballard's earlier Communicator visions of large chunks of rock did not fit what they found. He glanced up at the breach. The object hit with tremendous force. The exit edges of the hole were splayed inward as the kinetic energy of the meteor was initially reduced.

Chi silently studied the damage. His primary goal was to determine what size repair kit to use. The titanium of the hull was tough. The hole required work, so the patch would lie flat when it was welded in place with heat activated adhesive. A small battery powered heating unit specifically designed for outer hull patches was on his tool belt. All three of them carried the same tools. While Communicating his thoughts, he reached for a cleaning cloth in his belt and carefully rubbed and daubed the inside of the hole. A dark smudge on the cloth was folded toward the middle to protect it before he stuffed the cloth back into his belt. "Search the area for every small bit. It may have shattered. We don't want to waste anything." Even though the projectile opened a clean hole, tiny bits of titanium might have been shed. "Also, we need to relax the pit in the flex hull." The flex hull was indented deeper than he had ever seen, almost enough to create a hole. He marveled at the ingenious design that kept the flex hull intact. Part of the repair process was to return the flex hull to its normal shape, ready for the next breach. He had never seen an object that small penetrate the outer hull, but he had not seen them all. Again, his Communication was more for Trainee Ying than the experienced Ballard. Chi moved his helmet close to the breach and moved his head in several directions.

"What are you doing?" Ying asked his sire.

"Recording the breach with my helmet camera. Chief Donald and the Sci-Engs will study it. They claim they can calculate the speed the object was moving from the shape of the hole and the damage. They can even tell from which direction it came. Direct hit or tangential blow."

"What difference does all that make?"

Ballard laughed, "It gives them something to do."

Ying laughed along with the two older men, unsure why it was funny. Everyone was viable. If not, they were recycled. *Something to do* was not a viable occupation. Another question crossed his mind, fed into the Communicator.

"Black with points of light," Chi responded.

"What?" Ying asked.

"You were wondering what it looks like through the breach. It's black with points of light. If we're close enough to a star system, the points are much bigger, but it's still black. This hole is too small to peer through from inside a helmet."

"Oh." Ying was disappointed with the answer and with his inability to completely control his Communicator.

The repair made, the threesome returned to the repair embarkation room and removed their suits. Chi took the recovered projectile, a few small shavings of metal and the cleaning cloth to Chief Mech-Tech Donald. The photos and videos he had taken were already captured by the Mechanical and Sci-Eng computers. As far as he knew, someone was already evaluating the damage and making calculations. That was not his worry. He rolled the object across his palms. Aside from being smaller, it was different from all the other meteors he had recovered during his time, but most of them were different from each other. Each unique in size and general shape. Never had he found one that was conically cylindrical and flat on one end. The explanation of what or why was not his concern. He was a worker who repaired things to ensure the Mission was a success. He would not allow mechanical failure to risk the Mission as long as he lived. He would allow the Scientists to determine what they could about the object. He did know the kit he used, the smallest he had, was much larger than it needed to be. He would recommend a few smaller kits in case they encountered other breaches that small. They would waste less material, fewer resources.

⁓❧⁓

Chief Donald rolled the projectile in his hand, touching every square millimeter of it with his fingertips. Chi's assessment that it was different was accurate. It was smoother than any he had seen. He examined it under a magnifying light. It had marks and striations that did not make sense to him. He activated his Communicator and hailed the Captain. "Captain, I have the cause of our hull breach. I think you should look at it."

Cesar held his thoughts in check. His mind was still fretting over the delayed response from Chief Gail. He did not have time to look at a meteor, nor did he care to do so. But Chief Donald had never called the Captain to look at a meteor. Something of great significance caused the man to make the request. Cesar offered to meet Donald in the Premier's Decision Room. With an almost instantaneous mental maneuver, he extended his Communicator to include everyone in the Control System Room. "Joseph, take the Chair while I tend to personal business." He saw Jana's face light up. He winked at his granddaughter. He knew she would fill the Trainee Chair as soon as his back was turned. She seldom got to do that. Her petulance aside, she had potential.

Cesar contacted Premier Paul on his way to the Decision Room located within a few steps of Paul's private quarters. It was the Premier's *control room*, where he commanded meetings with the Vessel Leadership Team and evaluated information for decision making. The VLT meetings were regular, but seldom yielded more than an opportunity to coordinate routine activities, to verify that everything on the vessel was functioning properly, much like Cesar's Control System status updates. Chief Donald arrived at the same time as Paul. "What do you have, Donald?" Cesar held out his hand.

"Something I've never seen before. What do you think?" The Mechanical Chief replied as he put the object in Cesar's hand.

The Premier stared at the projectile in Cesar's big hand; consternation furrowed his forehead.

Cesar turned the object in his hands, tactilely studying ever bit of it. "Meteors are outside my purview. What kind of meteor is this? It's smooth. I thought meteors were rough and randomly shaped."

"They normally are. If they are rock – and penetrate the titanium, we normally find bits and pieces scattered around the flex hull beneath the impact breach. Iron or nickel meteors generally remain intact and are captured by a deep indentation in the flex hull. And normally much more than this."

"Is this all of it? It feels like metal. Did you Mech-Tech's miss some of it?" Cesar handed the object to Paul whose anticipation was palpable. "What do you think, Paul?"

Donald answered, "That's all of it. There were no shattered pieces. A few fragments of the hull were scattered, but not much."

"Meteors this size don't normally penetrate the outer hull, do they?" The Premier asked.

"I've never seen one this small get through. The projectile was traveling at a much greater velocity than normal."

"How do you know that?"

"The inward splaying of the breach point."

"Is that natural? Are we entering a part of space where objects travel faster than normal?"

"Not that I'm aware. The Sci-Engs will have to answer that question," Donald replied to the Premier as he looked at Cesar.

"What are those spiral markings?" Cesar asked.

Donald raised his eyebrows. "If I didn't know better, I would suggest they were rifling marks."

"Rifling? You mean like an expanded-gas weapon barrel?" Cesar asked incredulously.

"I've never seen one, but when I compared it to pictures in the archives, that was the closest thing I could find. This is not a natural meteor. This is crafted."

"By whom?" The Premier challenged. The idea went against everything he knew and believed.

Donald was not fazed by the Premier's tone. "I can't answer that. I'm only offering an opinion. It's not a natural object. It was going faster than I would anticipate a natural object could travel. It came from somewhere."

Before the Premier could challenge further, Cesar waved his hand. "I will take the object to Gail. I need to speak with her. She can put her people on it. Maybe they can sort it out." He desperately needed to know if Humanity One's course could be altered in time to avoid a collision with the rogue asteroid. He had zero time or energy for speculation on any other subject. If course change was impossible, nothing else would matter. "It is Gail's to worry about. Understood?"

"Aye, Captain," Donald said with a shrug. His duty was done.

CHAPTER 11

OPTIONS

Cesar used his Communicator to hail Gail as he walked along the dimly lit, narrow hall that would lead him to the Control System Room. His back hurt. Standing and walking were painful. Sitting too long was worse. He fought the urge to hunch his back to find a comfortable spot. He knew that was how Robert managed his back pain. He had to remain erect. He could not appear defeated. "Chief Gail, status." A flurry of thoughts not his own quickly filled Cesar's mind before Gail settled on a response. Like every new Chief, she thought the position brought her status beyond that of normal duties. She would learn.

"Captain, I have a preliminary calculation completed to change our course. I recommend you not implement it until I've recalculated to account for all energy consumption."

Cesar allowed a small chiding thought to transfer before he answered. She needed to adjust her head size and do so quickly, or she would become unviable. He knew there were some bright people in Sci-Eng. Robert often described one young Trainee as a genius. "That decision is not yours. I want … I need options immediately. Give me a complete calculation, not your speculation."

Gail's mind reeled momentarily. "Aye, Captain. I will have them ready within the hour."

"You have five minutes." Cesar was tired of waiting. Three hours had already elapsed since the rogue's discovery. If there was a solution that required a course change, a deviation from the MGR, the decision to do so would not come easily or quickly. Calculation time was not time well spent as far as he was concerned. Humanity One was a mere sixty-two hours from collision. "Transfer the data to the Decision Room computer, DR-ComX."

"I know the address," Gail's thought response was laden with frustration and a note of sarcasm.

"Come to the Decision Room after you transfer the data. I have something else for you." Cesar waited for confirmation then switched his Communicator to Joseph. "I will be a bit longer."

Cesar returned to the Decision Room and found momentary comfort in his normal chair. He summonsed Paul and they waited for Gail while he stared at the projectile. A shiver passed over his body, pushing the pain of the arthritis upward into his neck.

"Does Gail have a solution?" Paul asked aloud, biding time more than anything else.

"She thinks she does. But we may have bigger issues than we thought." Cesar exhaled impatiently. Barely three minutes had passed, but he was unaccustomed to waiting. He stared at the cylindrical object until Gail walked into the room.

"Greeting, Premier. Hello, Captain. I hurried as fast as I could." Gail moved directly to the computer. "If you will allow me, I will open the data feed." She placed a small packet with a piece of cloth on the conference table while she opened the data. "As you can see, if we initiate within the next hour, we can execute a maneuver to the right that will move us out of the rogue's trajectory."

"Why to the right?" Cesar asked.

Gail looked shocked. "Uh, mm, ah ... because that will put us behind the rogue quicker if it stays on its course. If we go left, we will miss colliding with it, but it does put us in front of it for a period of time."

"Directly?" Cesar knew the answer. Gail still needed to understand her role and focus only on mission required duties. He wanted options from the Chief Scientist, not decisions.

Gail scowled. "No. Of course not. Because of the rogue's tangential angle, to the left, we will cross the rogue's predicted course many hours before it reaches us. It will pass behind us from our right."

"So, we are seeing it front-on all the way if we go right, but it will be behind us if we go left."

"What difference does it make?" Paul asked. "Front or back?"

Cesar held his hand to pause the question. He nodded toward the packet Gail brought. "What do you have there?"

Gail was flustered by the sudden subject switch. "That? Something Chief Donald asked me to analyze."

"Did you?"

"Yes. One of the Sci-Eng Techs ran it through the mass spectrometer as soon as we got it."

"And?"

Gail's face skewed. She glanced from Cesar to Paul and back. "What difference does it make?"

Cesar rolled the projectile toward Gail. "It and this may make the difference in whether we go right or left."

Gail paused as she stopped the rolling projectile with one hand, unsure if Cesar was serious. "The cloth was a swab of the entry hole made by the latest meteor impact. Standard procedure. It's just powdered titanium."

"Powdered by the impact?"

"I suppose. Chief Donald said the entry hole and the projectile were odd." Gail glanced at the projectile as she spoke.

"Have you ever seen an entry hole swab with powdered titanium?"

Gail thought a moment. "I haven't seen very many of the impact swabs. Robert generally assigned that to lesser Techs. I can look it up on the Sci-Eng system if you like."

Cesar nodded. "I like." He drummed his fingers on the table while he waited.

Cesar's drumming did not go unnoticed by the novice Chief Scientist. Gail studied data from the computer as she scrolled a list. Her face was questioning when she turned back to Cesar. "That's odd. All the data indicates various types of rock, iron, and nickel. Never titanium. What does that mean?"

"You're the Chief Scientist. You tell me." Cesar glared at Gail.

Gail was flustered. She studied the computer screen then picked up the projectile and studied it. Cesar had connected the object to her data with his comment. "What is this?"

"That's what made the impact hole in the hull."

"That's the meteor? It doesn't look like any meteor I've ever seen." Seamlessly, Gail used the computer to open a file that catalogued every hull breach meteor retrieved during Humanity One's flight. "See. Nothing even close."

Cesar did not flinch. "Explain your analysis of the swab."

Gail was again taken aback by the Captain's sudden focus shift. "Simple. We put scrapings from the cloth ..."

Cesar shook his head impatiently. "Not your analytical process. What does the titanium powder indicate?"

"I really don't want to answer without further analysis of the repair team's data stream and an analysis to this piece."

"You don't have time. I need an answer now. You're a Scientist – Chief Scientist. Be scientific. Use what you know."

Gail's eyes focused on the projectile while her mind chased an answer. Finally, she leaned forward and met Cesar's eyes, fighting against the power of them, suddenly aware of the power of them.

"Apparently, this meteor hit with enough force to powder our titanium alloy hull, yet ... from the looks of it, the meteor is unfazed. That could be because it carried tremendous speed, more speed than we could naturally anticipate; but I would add that it is probably made of harder material than our titanium alloy hull. What are your thoughts?"

Cesar adjusted his back. Muscle tension tugged at every vertebra in an attempt to pull each one from his spine. "I have to assume it is connected to our rogue. I think we go to the left. How much will this cost us?"

"We will be short of energy after the maneuver. The proton drives are costly to run at the level required to shift Humanity One enough to guarantee we don't re-encounter the rogue and any potentially dangerous following debris."

"Like a comet?"

"Not really a comet, but a lot of asteroids have space trash trailing in their gravity wake. Small stuff mostly," Gail paused to nod toward the projectile, "but if this is the kind of trash following it, it could be a problem."

Paul cleared his throat. He was uncomfortable with the entirety of the discussion. "Course deviation is not an option. The MGR is clear on matters of the course, and the speed. Am I not correct, Captain?"

Gail started to speak but was cut short by Cesar's raised hand.

"It's very clear, Premier." Cesar waited for Paul to smile victoriously, which was almost instantaneous. "But the MGR is even clearer that Mission success is undeniably the most important ... the only ... critical measure. A collision in the middle of nowhere is an extinction event for humanity."

Cesar watched Paul's face contort as he processed the information, as he reconciled what he knew had to be done as compared to his training and to the MGR. Gail sat impatiently watching the Premier, yearning to speak her mind.

95

Paul's shoulders slumped, "I suppose you are correct. What is the danger of those trailing meteors? Should we be prepared to make more hull repairs? That requires a lot of resources, necessary as it may be. With the loss of all our energy reserve, we will have to take amelioration measures."

"If we go left, there will be no issues with trailing trash," Gail answered enthusiastically, startlingly aware of the brilliance of Cesar's thought processes.

Cesar pursed his lips. "I don't think there is any trailing trash. Chief Gail, we need to know the composition of that projectile. How soon can we get that? My final decision will be based on what we learn."

"It may take half an hour. Maybe longer if it's a rare element. It may have some odd ingredients. The stuff that is ejected by exploding stars and large body collisions can be rather exotic."

"If your course correction calculation anticipates that implementation must be done within an hour of the start of this meeting, you better hurry," Cesar replied evenly.

"Aye, Captain." Gail hurried away with the projectile and a new understanding of Cesar's impatience.

Paul asked as soon as Gail was gone, "What are your thoughts, Cesar? I'm still hesitant to go against MGR."

"My thoughts? That we have a bigger issue than whether the MGR must be followed blindly. What does the MGR say about sentient beings along the course?"

"Nothing. Well, it addresses that subject by advising us that there have never been any such beings detected. They are not calculated to be an issue. A greater issue is the deviation from our planned course. How do we regain the proper trajectory? And the time we will lose? And the energy resource losses? I'd say aliens are a non-issue."

"Unless they are responsible for the hull breach."

Paul's lips moved without sound as he contemplated Cesar's

words. Finally, softly - painfully aware of the implications - he asked, "Do you think the rogue asteroid is in fact an alien craft that fired upon us? We're not prepared ..." The Premier's voice trailed off.

"Chief Gail's analysis will tell us if the object is natural or manmade."

The Premier leaned forward, eyes wide. "Do you think they are human?"

"Let me rephrase – sentient-being made. I don't know what to think other than the rogue appeared on our tracking system and a short time later we are hit by an unusual object, too small to explain the hull tear, too hard to be damaged by the impact with the hull. Gail's information will carry more weight than she can imagine."

Paul's face slacked. "Tell me again why Gail is Chief of Science Engineering. Why did Robert have to be replaced?"

Cesar looked squarely in Paul's weary eyes. "Can you imagine where we would be in this discussion if Robert were still Chief? The argument would be stalled at whether we should even engage in the discussion about changing course."

"Is she the right person?" Paul tried to rationalize his previous question.

"Premier, Robert thought she was. If we value Robert's knowledge and opinion, we have to believe Gail is currently the best among the Sci-Eng Techs."

"She's too quick to ignore years of facts."

Cesar cocked his head meaningfully, "Or years of tradition based upon questionable beliefs."

"Do you no longer believe the MGR?" Paul was visibly stunned, eyes darting as if afraid of being overheard.

"I believe a knowledgeable set of guidelines supports success. Success sometimes comes from creative thinking. The Innovators made a decision that there were no sentient beings other than the humans on Earth. That was their belief, one of many that are the foundation for the MGR. If we find that belief to be wrong, it is up to us to make decisions that will assure the success of the Mission. That is why Humanity One was not put on autopilot and sent on its way. Without the Crew, another fifty-thousand TSVs could have been stowed."

"I don't know." Paul nervously stared at his fingernails and shook his head. He knew Cesar was right. "I just don't know."

"I can't say that I know either, except that I know we will move right or left depending on Gail's findings. I have no desire to carry my faith in the infallibility of the Innovators all the way to a terminal collision."

Paul recovered. "What about the proton drives? Can they be used as a weapon against the rogue? Destroy it?"

"No," Cesar responded without hesitation. He had already considered that option. The Innovators did not provide defense capabilities for Humanity One. Without sentient beings to pose threats to travel or with a prior claim on Earth Two as a human haven, there was no need for major weapons. An armory of what was referred to as "small arms" weaponry was available for use on Earth Two in the event the planet was home to indigenous, non-sentient species that were dangerous to humans. Humans were not crossing space as conquerors. They were space émigrés. "The Innovators did not calculate or plan for any kind of armed conflict to reach or to settle Earth Two. Probably just as well."

Gail interrupted further conversation when she burst into the Decision Room breathlessly. "It's manmade!"

Cesar nodded and rose to his feet, straightening his aching back to achieve his full height, as much as was still within him. "Send the calculations for the port-side course change to the Chair. I will execute as soon as I return to the Control System Room." The tall, wizened man paused and then added, "The projectile is top secret. No further conversation except those who already know. No need to create more distraction. We will have enough anxiety caused by the course change and the loss of certainty for Mission success. Some things can't be kept secret, but some secrets help if they are kept."

CHAPTER 12

PASSCODES

Jana stomped toward the Mess Hall. Her mind roiled with petulant thoughts. As soon as Cesar returned to the Control Room, to reclaim the Chair, she was summarily dismissed without explanation. Sent from the Control System Room as if she did not belong. She seethed. Too often, Trainees are kept in the dark, out of the loop. Not allowed access to all the knowledge. Only adults were considered whole. The admonition that a Trainee's primary focus was ... had to be ... on learning the necessary knowledge and skills to perform their adult duties was just another way to suppress young minds, to keep secrets. The adults did not respect Gen 4s. It was disheartening. Anger causing. Humanity One's Mission success depended on the Trainees' capabilities once they assumed control of the vessel. And that day would come as sure as the human body aged – but only if they were allowed to learn everything they could. Keeping secrets helped no one as far as Jana and her friends were concerned. It only made them feel disrespected – and angry.

The Mess Hall was filled with the warm aroma of chow. Hydroponics grew almost every spice known to humankind. No matter which vegetable, no matter the manner of presentation, the aromas were always inviting. The tastes and textures were worthy of the effort to eat the offerings available. From fresh to further processed, every morsel was relished by someone in the vessel. Not driven by hunger but by habit, Jana moved her tray along the self-serve line, selecting her share of the measured offerings that appealed to her at the moment. She slapped the serving ladles back into the presentation pots and glared at anyone who dared to react disapprovingly.

Sean tried to ignore Jana's behaviors in the serving line. She was angry as often as not. It defined her almost as much as her physical beauty. He chose the soy soup. His reason was not flavor or texture. He wanted to develop muscularity, to look more like Rex and the adult males. He was thin and self-conscious. His greatest fear was that Marly would turn away from him in favor of Rex, or someone as sculpted as the Sci-Tech Trainee. He slurped his soup and waited for the conversation at the Gen 4 table to become interesting. Only one member of the Group was still not seated. He furtively watched Jana approach the table. Her heavy-footed gait made clear her state of mind. The conversation would indeed be interesting.

Zack nervously ate. The gathering of Gen 4s at the table was the normal group. An early arrival already seated; he saw Jana enter the Mess Hall in a huff. Whatever was on her mind would probably drive the talk among the Group. He knew the subject to be discussed would require caution and careful consideration. He was apprehensive, unsure whether he should hurry his chow and leave if the conversation became too loud or too intense – or leave before it began. He was not as old as some of them. Maddie, Rex, and Kendra were almost adults. He was older than Marly and about the same age as Sean. Ying was sitting at their table. He joined from time to time, but his involvement seemed forced and he seldom spoke about anything other than his Trainee duties as Mech-Tech. Zack found himself wanting to be in his

Stasis Training Room. There was never any conflict with the occupants of the TSVs. They simply slept – or whatever it was they did.

Maddy moved her luxurious blonde hair away from her face with one hand as she moved a speared mushroom bit toward her mouth. She did not appear to notice Jana's mood. "Something is happening."

"Like what?" Kendra asked, more than slightly distracted by a nearby table of Gen 3s.

Maddie chewed then replied, "Something ... I'm not sure. Something Della said at the end of her day makes me suspicious that they are keeping more secrets from us."

Marly teasingly pressed her thigh against Sean's and suppressed a smile when his face and neck burned bright red. He almost choked on his soup. "What could she say that makes you think something is happening?" she asked as if nothing was happening unseen beneath the table.

Jana made room on the table for her stacked tray; her face darkened by a scowl. She sat across the table from Kendra, next to Marly, with her back to the rest of the room. Every meal was similar but with variations based on which crops were currently ripened. A few limited quantity crops were offered first come - first served. She did not get any of those, but there was plenty to eat. As if the table conversation was waiting for her arrival, she huffily asked, "Have you heard?"

Ying Si Sishiliu-Sishiba was sitting at the edge of the Group, two spaces away from Maddie on the same side as Kendra, nervously eating and hoping to be recognized as part of the Gen 4 Group. At that moment, with Jana's tone, he questioned his decision to acquiesce to his sire's admonition to hang with his peers. He preferred to sit with the Gen 3 Mech-Techs. He preferred to spend his time learning more from them, more about his duties. Adulthood was almost a year away. He wanted to be ready. His favored choice for meal companions was other Mech-Tech Trainees, or even Elect-Tech Trainees. Their interests were similar to his own and he could always learn from them. Chi insisted that he spend more time with the Gen 4 Group, to develop friendships outside of Mechanical. The Group was multi-disciplined and offered different learning options. They were people he would be obligated to interact with in the future. He smiled at Jana when her eyes momentarily lingered on his. He tried to ignore her obvious anger, her lack of response to his cordiality. He was impressed with her stature and bearing and hoped his friendly overture would lessen her ire, at least toward him. Close to the same age, he had hopes.

"Heard what?" Kendra asked tersely, her freckled brow wrinkled. "What's with you and Maddie and the guessing games? If you have something to tell us, say it. I thought we were against all the secrecy."

Jana leaned forward, an action that encouraged all the others to stop what they were doing and lean toward her. Softly, after a quick look over her shoulder for unwanted ears, she said with whispered anger, "I think we're changing course."

"What does that mean?" Kendra asked. She still was not satisfied. "Everyone knows the vessel makes course adjustments to harvest energy periodically."

Maddie responded, emboldened by Jana's revelation and oblivious to the Captain Trainee's obvious state of agitation, "It means we are doing something that has never been done during Humanity One's voyage. We've all read the MGR. Course changes are not allowed."

"Not unless they are part of the original navigational plot," Rex, across the table from Maddie and between Sean and Zack, corrected matter-of-factly. He wanted to dampen the mood, reduce the conflict that was brewing in the minds of his friends. He feared they might press the issue too far.

Maddie rolled her eyes. She knew Rex would brain-up the subject and make it less interesting. "But this may not be part of the original navigation. Maybe it wasn't calculated by the Innovators. Let's hear what Jana has to say." Her blue eyes dared Rex to refute what she said. The Con-Sys Trainee was sure that something strange was afoot – something they were not being told. Jana probably knew. She wanted to know.

"Cesar has to make the change," Jana said smugly, "to avoid a rogue asteroid." She knew she was not supposed to know all the details, or discuss the matter, but her disgust with Cesar made it easy to ignore any qualms she might have had at the moment.

Kendra shook her head and picked at her food. She refused to be swayed. "I'm with Rex. It's probably part of the MGR. There are parts of it that the rest of us don't need to know. I raise carrots. I don't need to know about the course, and you don't need to know how to coax carrot seeds to grow. There are real secrets more important than a course change." Her tone was dismissive as she forked a carrot coin for emphasis.

"No!" Jana snapped. She did not like Kendra's dismissive attitude toward her news. "I know the Captain MGR – and much more. There is nothing in the course process that required the suddenness of the change. Adjustments are always preplanned. Not hurried. Cesar doesn't think I'm smart enough to figure it out. He sent me away because he thinks that will keep me from knowing what is happening."

Maddie came to Jana's defense. "That's probably what Della was talking about. A course change is a big thing. It could affect our ability to complete the Mission on time. How big is the change?"

Jana accepted the help with an appreciative smile. "I'm not sure. Cesar told me to go to dinner and then take my rest period. He and Joseph didn't leave the Control System Room. He's in the Chair even though Second is there with his Trainee." She paused long enough to sniff a forkful of green, leafy vegetable before she added sarcastically, "At least Second will see how it feels to stand and wait."

Every Group member looked toward the far table where some of the Chiefs were quietly eating their chow. Neither the Captain nor the Premier was there. Chief Robert was missing also. Rex ate quietly, observing the interaction bemusedly.

Sean listened but paid more attention to Marly's pressing warmth and the growing discomfort in his waistcloth. Whispered promises played over in his mind as he responded to the touch of her skin against his. He ate more soup.

Kendra reacted to a sudden burst of laughter from the Gen 3 table she was surreptitiously watching. She smiled at someone and then looked to Jana. "So, the course change has not yet happened?"

"It's happening right now," Jana stated, aggravated by the question that challenged the veracity of her contribution. "Weren't you listening. I was told to leave so they could do it without me knowing. More secrets."

"Why would they not want you to know? Are you sure they are making a course change?"

Jana's dark eyes darkened further. "Yes, I'm sure. I'm telling you; a rogue asteroid is on a collision course with Humanity One. And they don't want me to know because Cesar is still Captain. I'll probably never get to be Captain because he still lives."

Kendra was not sympathetic, slightly distracted by the Gen 3 table occupants. "Cesar isn't the reason you're not Captain. Joseph is."

Rex spoke. His words were timed to interrupt Jana's rebuttal. He saw the anger in the pre-adult's brown eyes. Kendra was emotionally mature, more so than Jana. Jana lacked the control to speak cautiously in the crowded Mess Hall. Kendra often challenged the Captain Trainee, her game to avoid being perceived as subservient. Rex knew that the subject of the day was not for public discussion. There were listeners. He did not – they did not – want to be overheard. An angry Jana could cause that to happen. "The course change is being made to avoid collision with an unpredicted asteroid. If we don't make the change, Humanity One could be destroyed." He filled his mouth with a piece of soy curd that left a greasy feel on his tongue and slowly chewed it while the others considered what he had said.

"So, you know all about the course change?" Jana challenged, visibly upset that she knew less than a Sci-Tech Trainee.

Rex nodded and casually finished chewing before he replied. "Yes. I was on the team Chief Robert called to calculate the course correction required to avoid collision."

A loud, synthesized bell sounded. Everyone sat silently until the third peal echoed into silence. They all knew it meant someone was no longer among the living. Someone had recycled.

Rex nodded toward a speaker built into the ceiling. "Chief Robert became unviable. Our new Chief Scientist is Gail San Ershisan-Sishiba." He chose to not reveal the ascension process. "Chief Gail is former Chief Robert's chosen replacement. He guided her."

Maddie's eyes were wide. "Wow! That was sudden. I didn't even hear that he was ailing."

Rex nodded. "It was a surprise to all of us on the team. He *was* very old, you know. But Chief Robert bravely led us to the very end. He will always be remembered as a good Chief." There was nothing more to say. Gail had what she wanted, and Rex knew how to work with her as Chief.

"I heard an intonation yesterday. Does anyone know who that was?" Maddie asked, the subject changed momentarily.

Marly responded quickly, glad to be able to contribute, "A 12-year-old Gen 4 Recycling Trainee. His heart failed to develop properly." She could have said more, but there was no need. Besides, discussing personal medical issues was in bad taste. No one would trust her as a doctor if she made a habit of gossiping about ailments.

Maddie glowered for a moment, then said what was on her mind. "I think it's wrong that we don't know everything. They could announce the names, like Chief Robert's passing, so we would know. What other secrets are there? They won't even let us know about a rogue asteroid that could cause our doom. What else are they hiding?"

Ying felt compelled to speak. His face reddened slightly. "Why is it necessary to know everything? Would it not be a distraction?"

The vessel was not populated very heavily. Most of the four-hundred-plus humans recognized the faces and the names of all other humans – especially within their own generation. Maddie stared at Ying a moment before she spoke, "Ying, that is just an excuse used by the older people to keep their secrets. A Gen 4 passed, and no one told us." She glared toward Marly before she turned her attention back to Ying.

Ying blushed more, but he maintained eye contact. Maddie was the one among the Gen 4 Group that fascinated him, even aroused him. Even though she was older, he had hopes for her– if she did not choose Rex. "That's possibly true, but shouldn't everyone be allowed secrets?"

"What's that supposed to mean? Someone we knew recycled and we weren't told," Maddie snapped angrily.

"Would knowing make a difference, or would it create a distraction?"

"More of a distraction than this?" Maddie asked sarcastically. "I don't keep secrets. Do you?"

"I have secrets," Ying smiled, hoping to defuse Maddie's anger. "I choose to not share all of them with just anyone. Of those I am willing to share, one need only ask."

Jana was still smarting from her earlier ejection from the Control System Room. She did not like to be shoved aside for the convenience of anyone. She lashed out at Ying. "What kind of secrets could a Mech-Tech Trainee have? Which part is needed to repair a circulation fan?"

Ying was not easily riled, even by Jana's scoffing tone. He smiled coyly, "Well, that is important to know. So is the fact that Humanity One was impacted by an object mid-afternoon. Does anyone care to speculate how the two recent occurrences are connected?"

Maddie replied dismissively, "Humanity One has been impacted by meteors many times. That is one of the things Con-Sys Techs monitor around the clock."

"Monitor, yes. Many times, yes. But does everyone know anything about those meteors. Their composition? Their size? The damage they inflict on our hull? Does everyone need to know?"

"Everyone should be able to know. It shouldn't be a secret."

"Maybe so, Maddie," Ying replied with a smile. "But why does everyone need to know? Sure, Sci-Eng needs to know so they can calculate the accumulated damage to hull integrity. Too many repairs in one zone could create a fatal weakness. And Recycle Sanitation needs to know because they can incorporate those recovered meteors into our resources. Mostly, Mech-Techs needs to know so they can adequately repair the hulls, because those meteors do damage to the two outer plies on a regular basis."

"Why, then, shouldn't everyone know? Why shouldn't Kendra know if a meteor has damaged the hull above Hydroponics.

Ying smiled at Kendra who was particularly attentive because her name was used. He knew she would be mated long before he reached adulthood, but he felt comfortable in her presence. "As a matter of fact, the last meteor impacted above Hydroponics. By knowing such things happen, Kendra might become distracted from her duties. Her crop could fail because she is constantly worried that her ceiling might collapse in on her, that such a collapse could vent her and the vessel's atmosphere into space. It is a fact of life. It is with us every day. No amount of worrying will help."

"Well, it shouldn't be kept secret. If someone wants to know, they should be able to know." Maddie was not pleased with Ying's comments. He was not regularly a part of their ongoing conversation. It was apparent that he did not share the same concerns about secrets.

"I'm not aware of any secrets purposely kept," Ying said. "So, back to my question. Do you want to guess how the rogue asteroid and the meteor impact might be related?"

"Does it matter?" Jana asked.

"It could, if the two are related."

"Related how?"

"It could be that we could not have one without the other." Ying smiled. He was the center of attention. Chi would be proud that he was forming strong relationships with Gen 4s from other areas of the ship. Maddie was sensually beautiful. Jana was alluringly beautiful. Kendra was sultrily beautiful. He wondered if any of them were interested in him. They were all three watching him attentively. He liked it. "The meteor that hit us is unlike anything anyone has ever seen."

The Group waited for Ying to continue. Rex watched pensively. He knew only that Chief Gail's demeanor changed dramatically after she returned from a meeting with Captain Cesar. Maybe she had a secret.

Ying was creative, always searching for answers, for connections and correlations between events and objects. Preventing the need for repairs was better than making repairs. He did not want to be known as a repairer; he wanted to be a preventer. "It could be that the meteor is part of a larger threat created by the rogue." Ying forked another mouthful of vegetables into his mouth, determined to only answer questions rather than make unsolicited statements. If the others wanted to know, they could ask – as he had previously said.

"Pure speculation," Rex broke the silence around the table of Gen 4s. "Ying, I wouldn't repeat that for fear of the consequences of speculative ideation. Continued speculation would definitely be a distraction without merit." He knew the logical progression of Ying's conjecture could lead to a heretic conclusion. There was nothing to be gained and much to be lost by conjuring up unsubstantiated gossip. The Group was concerned about the lack of knowledge, of secrets to understanding everything about Humanity One. That was their focus, the reason for their disquiet. There was no reason that he could fathom, nor could the others, why any knowledge would be kept from them. The more they knew, the better they could perform. Knowledge improved viability. Lack of knowledge created opportunities for speculation – such as Ying offered.

"But, if it's true ..." Maddie protested.

Rex held up his hand and held Maddie's eyes with his own suddenly steely blue irises. He heard Jana gasp at his sudden posture of authority. "Some things are not subject to speculation. This is one of them. What do we gain through speculation? Our greater concern is the secrecy that withholds helpful knowledge."

Maddie did not like to be quieted. Rationally, she knew the discussion of the rogue asteroid and the possibility that small meteors accompanied it through space would yield nothing of value. Even under the best of circumstances, there was absolutely nothing they could do about it. The Group had other subjects that bore greater promise. "That may be true, and maybe the whole subject is speculative and not worth our time to discuss, but we do need to learn the secrets that control our lives."

"Such as?" Kendra asked almost absently. The Gen 3 table occupants were finishing their meal, less engaged in idle gossip and more involved in eating before retiring to their private quarters for earned rest and relaxation. She watched them anxiously.

"Such as why we are under their thumbs, unable to make choices – or be heard. We've had this discussion." Maddie was upset at Kendra's apparent distraction. "Why are we rehashing old conversations? We've all agreed on this before. We're intelligent people, not little children without the ability to think for ourselves." Maddie nodded toward Rex. "Rex may be the most intelligent person in all of Humanity One."

Rex smiled and demurely accepted the aggrandizement from someone he saw as a confidant.

Kendra's eyes and mind were still on the Gen 3 table, which was down to two people – a young man and an older woman. Their shared laughter grated on her, but she could not allow the conversation to go on without her. She looked back at Maddie more attentively. "Understood. As I've said before, we should be able to decide who our mates will be. Why is Medical required to approve every mating – and the number of children we can have? If you love somebody ..." Her voice trailed and her eyes flashed when the two Gen 3s left the Dining Hall at the same time.

Without noticing Kendra's distraction, Marly replied as she adjusted her waistcloth. It had slipped a little while she was intentionally scooting against Sean. She had on an oversized waistcloth that fit very loosely and tended to wad at bunching points. "There are secrets about mating that the Chief Medical Officer knows. Those secrets establish the rules for mating."

"Secrets. Again, they have secrets." Maddie's voice was impatiently angry. "If we knew them, we could understand and not be engaged in this conversation at all. Are the secrets in the Medical MGR? Can you read them?"

"Not specifically. I looked for them, like I promised. All I could find that was remotely related to the subject were discussions of genetics." Marly glanced toward Sean who had finally finished his soy soup and was sitting with one hand in his lap and the other with fingertips "accidentally" touching her thigh where the heat was highest. "I did find Menu items that are passcode protected. I'm not sure if Chief Katherine accesses them. They are not specifically attached to Medical. More like General Access but protected."

Maddie's brow furrowed. "I don't know that we have secrets in Con-Sys. I've never encountered any areas that require a passcode. I've looked, but I only have access to a training computer. All the secrets are out of a Trainee's reach anyway." She looked toward each of the others in turn. "Did everyone else check for secret knowledge protected by passcodes in their data bases?"

Jana smirked. "Lots of secure areas in the Captain MGR. It's like I can never get the truth. I think there are things that we need to know beyond who our mates will be. Things about the Mission that are kept secret."

"Like what?" Kendra asked, still distracted by the Gen 3 table even though it was empty.

"Like, what is the real Mission?"

"I think that's evident," Rex replied. "We are the last hope of an Earth-like civilization because Earth became unlivable."

Jana's voice rose. She was not going to allow anyone else to cut her short. Not that day. Not again. "What's not evident is the manner in which that will happen. How do we save civilization? By piloting a vessel across light years of space? Do you really think four-hundred humans are the answer, are really the Mission?"

Kendra replied, "There are thousands of people in Stasis. They're the core of our Mission. They're the ones who will reestablish Earth's civilization on Earth Two. Right, Zack?"

Zack almost choked on his tongue before he gasped an embarrassed, "Yes."

"Are they? Are they really?" Jana asked, her volume again rising. "Even twenty-five thousand people are not enough to rebuild a civilization. They can only remember it. Computers can do that. What else is their purpose? What is our purpose ... our real purpose? What are our grandchildren supposed to do? If they only learn what we learn, they will not know what to do beyond rote chores. They will only know what we pass on to them in training. Am I not right?" she challenged.

Maddie whispered heavily, "Yes. You're right." She glanced around, "We all know that the answers are in the secret knowledge areas of the computers. How do we get to them?" She was alertly poised on the edge of her seat. She glanced expectantly toward everyone at the table, a look that inspired conspiratorial acquiescence. The subject was finally where she wanted it to be, and even Kendra seemed to be on topic. "Zack, surely there is secret knowledge for Stasis. Did you find anything?"

Zack gulped. He feared the question that he knew would be asked of him. "There could be. Probably is. Like you, I only have access to a training computer. I have tried to connect to the primary Stasis computer." He was afraid to tell Maddie that he did not try very hard for fear of being monitored. Matt frequently monitored Zack's computer entries as part of the training.

"The people most apt to have the passcodes are the Premier and the Captain. I think the Chief Medical Officer's passcodes may be to less inclusive information. It might answer our mating questions, but I doubt it will tell us what the core mission is. Stasis might have something interesting, but it's probably accessed by double passcoding." Rex said thoughtfully. He looked to Marly and Zack for confirmation of his assessment.

Marly was partially distracted by Sean's fingertips on her skin, and her promise. "Uh … yes. I think you're right, Rex. Doctor Katherine is only interested in medical." She nervously reached below the table and took Sean's hand and squeezed it.

"How do we get the passcodes?" Maddie asked quietly. They had their own secret to protect. They had to keep their voices down.

Jana replied excitedly, "I have an idea. Maybe I can gain access to a Con-Sys console." Wistfully, she continued, "I have no real purpose as

Trainee. I can come and go as I please without anyone taking notice. Since Captain Cesar gains most of his access through Con-Sys, his Menu is probably there. Even if I can't guess his passcode, we'll at least know where to go to look."

Maddie nodded agreement. "Rex, can you visit the Premier's quarters? Since Chief Robert has passed, the Premier will be alone. It's his habit to visit every area of Humanity One every day. That's his routine. His quarters will be unattended for a long period of time. You, better than the rest of us, should know where to look for passcodes."

Rex exhaled. Maddie knew how to appeal to his ego. He knew she knew, but he could not help himself. "I'll see what I can do. I'm still a Trainee, like the rest of you." he glanced toward Jana and smiled understanding, "though in some ways, as a Sci-Eng Trainee, I'm like Jana. I have considerable freedom to move without notice." He was glad to see that Jana's anger was abated somewhat. It always helped if there was something to do, something more engaging than emotions. Jana had something to do.

Maddie smiled. "Good. Soon we will know the answers to all the secrets."

Ying tentatively asked, "Has anyone asked for the answers?" He immediately noticed that Maddie was no less beautiful when she scowled.

"The only answer we get is "it's according to the MGR." Do you get every answer to every question?"

"Ah ... maybe ... sometimes ... no." Ying was not sure if he should smile apologetically or keep his mouth shut. The Group was heading toward danger. He felt a sense of dread amid the excitement.

CHAPTER 13

PAUL

Premier Paul Er Ling sat alone in his quarters. The events of the day went against everything he knew. The Innovators did not take the launch of Humanity One lightly. It was a well-planned endeavor to save humankind's technological civilization from extinction. In their assessment of the dangers facing life on Earth, they knew there was no other choice. Through the efforts of thousands of brilliant minds over three generations, all the options were measured and weighed until Humanity One rose to the top as the only viable method of preserving thousands of years of technological development. It was a last-ditch effort with a limited chance of success, but it was the only chance they had.

Paul knew from his father, Premier Gregory Ling, that the Innovators poured their lives into creating Humanity One and the Mission Guidance Rules. The MGR was as important, as worthy of protection as was the vessel Humanity One and its habitants. The MGR was the result of incalculable hours of dedicated work. Within the MGR were the result of calculations that required tremendous amounts of computer memory and time, more than any single project ever undertaken by humankind. What good was technology if it was not capable of saving itself?

The Innovators observed the skies using optical and radio telescopes. Infrared, ultraviolet, radiation, digital visual mirror telescopes were used to find and track star systems, stars, planets, moons, asteroids, comets, and all manner of space detritus. Every discovered body from the largest star system down to asteroids a meter in diameter was tracked and its path calculated. The need to avoid impact was critical for obvious reasons, but the gravitational forces exerted by each body was every bit as valuable as the object was dangerous. Humanity One relied upon those gravitational tugs to provide extra propulsion for the journey. Every minute and meter of the journey was measured and mathematically calculated to thirty or more decimals. Light years are gigantic distances but a single error of speed or distance smaller than could be measured by the human eye would doom the Mission. Mission failure meant Humanity One would not reach Earth Two. Mission failure meant humankind, the rediscovery of human technology and the redevelopment of human civilization, would be left to the random chances of cosmic chaos.

The entirety of Humanity One's Crew through eight generations would not – could not – devote as much time and energy to the project as did the Innovators. The Innovators thought of everything. Iteration after iteration was required to uncover and discover every possible event, every object, every errant behavior that could possibly create Mission failure. Nothing was left to chance. Everything done in preparation for the Mission was precisely accurate. The Innovators were infallible.

Or so it would seem.

And Premier Paul Er Ling, the protector of the MGR, the protector of the vessel that carried humanity's hopes, had given his approval to ignoring the Innovators to avoid a collision with an unplanned asteroid, a space object. He allowed Captain Cesar to alter Humanity One's course. Any damage to the Mission was his responsibility. He was the

Premier. He was accountable. Not that accountability would matter. If the Mission failed, if Earth Two was not reached or if the Gen 8 Crew of Humanity One did not awaken Humanity One's precious cargo from Stasis, his accountability would not matter. Everyone who would know of his failure would be gone. Gone without recycling.

Paul gasped as thoughts of recycling crossed his mind. Finality. His parents' generation often referred to recycling as dying. At some point before he was old enough to fully comprehend the concept, *dead* and *dying* were eschewed for the euphemisms *passed* and *passing*. The tight-knit group that was Gen 1 could not bear the finality of death away from Earth. A few bemoaned a deity that had forsaken them. Paul never fully understood the laments, unaware of the attraction to a spiritual power, but he did understand the concept of becoming unviable. *Passing to recycling* was emotionally more bearable, more palatable than *dying to the unknown*. Gen 2 was the last generation to actually interchange the words. Gen 3 and beyond would forevermore call it recycling.

The thought of recycling was acceptable to the Crew. Within that thought was the understanding that everything physical within Humanity One would remain as long as recycling was done without fail. All the atoms that were stowed inside Humanity One on the day of launch were still within the ship. Despite the many hundreds of outer hull breaches by meteors, no meteor had ever penetrated beyond the flex hull. The Innovators were ingenious. They preplanned course changes to avoid large objects, even use them for propulsion enhancements, and stopped smaller objects with the ingenious hull system. As a result of the Innovators' infallibility, not a single needed atom had ever escaped from Humanity One. Humanity One and its Crew were whole.

Paul did not feel whole. He was weary. Premier Gregory, his father – his sire – served as Premier until Paul was twenty-eight. His sire died.

He remembered the day; the morning Gregory's body was discovered in quarters. Paul's mother awakened to a cold body in the bed next to her. She died within months of that time. Paul often wondered if her passing was the result of a loss of the will to live without her mate. His own mate passed to recycling because of cancer. Shu was a delight. Her life lasted no longer than most other Gen 2s. They knew to expect it. He did not know to expect to live another ten years after she passed. He was lonely. With only four other Crew Members who understood the early struggles, the Settling Years, it was hard to relate to Gen 3s. There was no way to relate to Gen 4s.

The thought struck Paul that there were now only three other Gen 2s aboard the vessel. He closed his eyes and sobbed. Robert was a good friend. They were two lonely men who shared the Premier quarters. Both without mates. Both viable. The use of a dual space by anyone, even the Premier or a Technology Chief, made no sense to Paul. Robert was a good roommate, and he did not snore too badly.

Robert was a good man. A viable man for all his many years. He stood his ground to protect the MGR, to protect the infallibility of the Innovators. A stance not appreciated by some of the Gen 3 Sci-Eng Techs, the brighter more creative ones. He paid with his viability. Gail was quick to use that singular moment when the rogue appeared to declare Robert unviable. The copious writings within the MGR that Robert protected so adamantly included procedures to ensure all Crew members remained viable until recycling, and procedures for declaring a Crew member unviable, if the member became mentally unfit before passing to recycling.

Dying. Passing. Recycling. The words morphed into something less sinister, less fearful. In his lifetime, Paul saw many Crew members face recycling with the same stoic bravery as had Robert. Some chose to recycle rather than continue a life of pain from whatever disease gripped their frail human bodies. It was their choice if a viable replacement was immediately available. And so many suffered pains, pains of ailments and illnesses that they were conditioned to keep to themselves, to avoid the potential of being declared unviable. As Premier, he was responsible for every person. His sire instilled that in him. He, like Gregory, attended recyclings, especially planned ones. The presence of the Premier during Crew members' final moments provided reassurance that their contributions were valued. They all seemed to pass peacefully, painlessly. He wondered if any of them regretted passing.

Paul wondered if his daughter, Mia San Ba-Qi, would use the MGR to declare him unviable. She could. She was trained. She was an adult. She was not involved in the decisions recently made for one reason. Paul wanted to protect her from what he feared could be a decision that might be eventually considered an act of heresy, the reason for Mission failure. Gregory would not have allowed the decision to alter course to be approved. Paul was not as strong as Gregory. He was unable to not allow it.

Paul deferred to Captain Cesar almost from the beginning of his reign as Premier. Cesar's sire passed to recycling at a young age, younger than most. Cesar assumed The Chair barely two years into adulthood. By the time Paul became Premier, Cesar was seasoned. Cesar was a friend, not as close as Robert, but a good friend. Cesar was as dedicated as any Gen 1 Crew Member had ever been, a model for his Gen 2 peers. Cesar believed the Innovators were infallible. Cesar always used the MGR to support and enforce his decisions. Cesar was always firm in his decisions, in his training, in his expectations of other Crew Members. Cesar was not afraid to make a decision. Cesar was heroic in Paul's eyes. The Premier deferred decisions that were his to make to Cesar because he knew Cesar would always make good decisions, decisions that would protect the safety of Humanity One and the success of the Mission. He even allowed Cesar to make the decision to declare Robert unviable. But ... he wondered what had caused Cesar to alter course. He wondered if the indomitable Cesar feared being declared unviable if he stood firm on the MGR like Robert.

Tears streamed down Paul's wrinkled cheeks. He sniffed to keep snot from dripping. It did not work. A clear, viscous string from his nostril separated and spread across his frail thighs. He stared at the wetness through blurred eyes. He absently wondered if viability was all that important at his age. He had walked with Robert to Medical. He could not bear the thought of Robert going alone, or he might have chosen to be with Cesar awaiting the calculations from Science Engineering. Both were important events worthy of the Premier's presence. Robert would have understood. Robert's steps were halting. Paul remembered the coolness of Robert's arm as he pretended to assist his friend along the corridor toward Chief Medical Officer Katherine's medical office. He could not remember if there were other people in the area, or even in the hall. His eyes were focused ahead, unseeing except what needed to be seen, afraid to look at Robert's eyes. His thoughts were on his personal discomfort with the circumstance, not on his friend's plight. When Katherine calmly guided Robert to an examination table and helped him recline on its cool surface, he saw the passivity of Robert's expression. Robert was resigned to his fate. Recycling was natural and orderly. Robert's disciplined mind accepted order above all else.

Robert did not flinch when Katherine injected a few milliliters of bright pink liquid into a blood vessel under the pale skin in the crook of his right elbow. He did smile briefly at Paul before his entire body relaxed then stiffened momentarily before final relaxation.

Just like that, it was over. Paul gingerly patted Robert's forehead with a shaking hand. It broke his heart to watch two Recycle Technicians take Robert's body. He knew where they were going. He knew how the process worked. He had seen it many times. He did not need to see it with his friend. That is why he was sitting silently in his room. The Passing intonation reverberated throughout the vessel, more meaningful to him than it had ever been before – even more than when Shu passed. Doctor Katherine must have notified Captain Cesar as soon as Recycle Sanitation Chief Kara San Luishiyi-Qishiqi completed the recycling process.

As much as he tried to avoid the thoughts, Paul relived Robert's last moments. Effortlessly, it was over. No pained reaction. Robert simply slipped into cold sleep. He wondered if Katherine could provide him the same thing. Mia was ready to be Premier. She was already training her daughter, who was barely seven years old. He stood in the path of both if he remained viable. His mind massaged the value of his continued life, life that he was not sure he still valued.

The Innovators valued life. That was a certainty. Paul learned it listening to the Gen 1s discuss how precious life was. Gen 1s were the same as the Innovators, contemporaries who understood the dynamics of the Mission to save human civilization from extinction. As precious as the Gen 1s declared life to be, anyone observing understood that the reverence for life was for the life of humanity as a whole, not just the individual. Individuals were merely the vessels that carried humanity from one generation to the next. Of all the lives inside Humanity One, the most precious were the ones in Stasis. Without them, the Mission was a failure. The MGR that pertained to Premier training and duties referred to them as the Founders, founders of the new civilization on Earth Two. Even the name "Innovators" evolved from references made by Gen 1 Crew Members to the scientists back on Earth. The term was never used in the MGR.

As Premier, Paul's decisions were focused on protecting the Founders in Stasis and assuring that every single one of them arrived at Earth Two undamaged. Upon arrival, the MGR specified that specific TSV's would be opened and those occupants would be revived first.

The awakened Founders had assigned roles. Within those minds was knowledge, the final Mission plans. Plans inaccessible to the Crew, even the Premier. Plans that the Crew did not need to have as a distraction to their roles in the Mission. Specific knowledge that he and other Humanity One Leaders needed to know were within the MGR and passcode protected for access when the time was right, passcodes set by the original Gen 1 Leaders. He received his passcodes when his ascension was near. It could have been lost, considering the fact that Gregory passed suddenly in his sleep. Paul shuddered to think about losing access to vital information, about Gregory waiting too long to share that part of his training.

Paul knew something that only the triumvirate of the Captain and the Premier and the Chief Medical Officer knew. Each held one third of a passcode that was to be used to open critical Mission knowledge within the computer archives during the Seventh generation. The three of them knew that the knowledge was necessary for the final stages of the Mission but was of no use otherwise. He understood that the knowledge would be superfluous to the Crew, to anyone not of the Seventh generation. A distraction subject to diversionary speculation. Even so, Paul's curiosity sometimes caused him to wonder if Cesar and Katherine were as curious as he was. He wondered if they would join him to read the Seventh-generation knowledge. They could. Knowing the knowledge ahead of time would not risk the Mission; at least he could think of no reason it would. Just a distraction.

But Paul allowed Cesar to alter the course. The success of the Mission was at risk. Paul was to blame. His tears were dried. He sniffed one final time to prevent drippage, more successfully this time. Humanity One was in the process of moving millions of miles off course. He was not a scientist with knowledge of mathematics. He was not a vessel captain with an understanding of ship motion. But he was knowledgeable enough to understand that the deviation and the time lost from Humanity One's original course would result in arrival at a different point in space than the Innovator's planned for and programmed into Humanity One's navigation system. The Mission was already a failure. No one yet knew what that meant for humanity.

Paul allowed it because there was reason to believe the Innovators were fallible. Cesar's heresy was to believe that. His own heresy was not stopping Cesar. But - there was more to it. Cesar believed, or at least strongly suspected, the rogue was not an object missed by the Innovators. The Captain believed it was a sentient-being created vessel. A spaceship carrying aliens across space on a collision course with Humanity One. The Innovators searched the heavens dutifully for generations in search of sentient beings and found nothing to indicate such existed. In particular, they declared that any sentient beings that might exist lacked modern technologies because there were no signs to indicate otherwise. Cesar must have viable reasons to doubt the infallibility of the Innovators, even though he did not want to doubt them. Paul knew that, but it did not make the failure any more bearable. Humanity was lost.

CHAPTER 14

IMMATURITY

Sean's hands shook. He pressed them together, fingers intertwined, to try to stop the trembling. He stared at them; his body flushed with fear. A metallic taste covered his tongue. He was sure he was going to puke. His heart pounded in his ears. He was sure it would burst from his chest at any moment. The chair was uncomfortable for his boney rear, though he barely noticed. His thoughts were on recycling.

Some unwritten rules ... or maybe they were written, just not located where everyone could easily read them ... were drummed into every Crew member's mind from an early age. Mating of Crew members and the processes of procreation are carefully regulated. Sean knew that. Mating without approval by the Chief Medical Officer was forbidden. Procreation could happen outside of mating, but genealogical standards had to be met to avoid dire consequences to future generations. Genealogy guided all mating and procreation decisions. Only Medical could approve mating and procreational activities. The penalty for violating those rules could include recycling. Sean trembled as the concept of recycling ... the possibility of recycling ... kept flooding into his mind.

The Medical Department conference room was small. The conference table was small. The lighting was dim except for an area on one side of the table. There were two chairs on that side, the bright side. Four other chairs ringed the table, dimly lit. Sean was seated in one of the well-lit chairs. The beam of light that illuminated him was intense, directly in his eyes, nearly blinding, and made the dim side even darker. His chair was hard and cold. Metallic with a contoured seat that did not fit all sizes. Sean's smaller butt size was definitely not accommodated well. He squirmed, vainly searching for a better spot, vainly squinting against the light that became painful as time passed.

Sean was not sure how long he sat in the room alone. Or how long he would be required to sit there. He assumed it would be as long as the rest of his life. A Medical Technician, a Nurse whose name his terrified mind could not recall, guided him to the room and told him to sit in the chair ... she made sure he sat in the appropriate chair ... to wait until Doctor Katherine came to speak with him. If the choice had been his, he would have chosen one of the other chairs, chosen the supposed anonymity of the unlit chairs. He desperately wanted to be in one of those chairs. Thoughts of Marly filtered in between the layers of dread that gripped his mind.

Marly was not in the room yet. Sean was not sure where she was at that moment. He was not sure he needed to see her under the circumstances. Nonetheless, he wanted to know ... felt the need to know. He hoped she was alright. When they were caught, Marly sobbed and ran from her bedroom without her waistcloth. He laid on the bed, exposed, scrambling for the blanket, embarrassed, unable to hide what they were attempting to do, what they would have done if Marly's mother had not arrived unannounced. Marly left him to face her mother, Pamela San Shiwu-Shisi, alone. He reckoned Marly would have to face her mother later – also alone. He was in the Chief Medical Officer's meeting room – alone – awaiting whatever fate Doctor Katherine deemed necessary.

Medical Tech, Doctor Trainee, Pamela was Marly's trainer, though

Marly received most of her instructions from Chief Medical Officer Katherine. Doctor Katherine dedicated her time to training potential doctors. Marly may have lost her viability as a doctor. Only thirteen, Marly's emotional maturity did not match her physical development. Her desires were more than Sean could resist. He had desires that a fourteen-year old did not fully understand nor the maturity to control.

Hesitantly, Sean glanced around the room. Without being told the details, he knew Doctor Katherine had demanded he be brought to face the Medical Review Board. He did not know what to expect, or who to expect. He did know the penalties for unapproved procreation. Recycling of one – or both – was well within the realm of possibility. He suspected the MGR provided the procedures Doctor Katherine would follow ... was required to follow, even though he did not know what they would be.

The door opened. A tall figure, indistinguishable against the bright light in his eyes, entered first and sat in a chair on one end of the table, bathed in darkness. Sean was sure it was the Premier. He did not know the Premier was involved in Medical Review Board decisions. It was not a routine matter if the Premier was involved. His hands trembled uncontrollably. His lower lip quivered, and his eyes filled with tears. He tried to convince himself it was because of the bright lights. He did not want to enter recycling with tears of fear on his cheeks.

A smaller figure followed, almost unnoticed at first, behind the Premier – sandwiched between the Premier and another adult. Doctor Katherine's voice commanded the figure to go to the other lit chair. It was Marly. Her eyes were down when Sean glanced toward her. He tried to smile reassurances that he did not feel, that she did not see. Through his blurry eyes, he saw that her normally warm, brown face was pale and slack. She sat with her hands pressed tightly in her lap.

A fourth figure followed Doctor Katherine. That person waited until Doctor Katherine took the chair directly across from the two lit chairs and then sat to her right. Sean was sure he recognized the man as a Medical Technician. His fumbling mind could not coalesce on a name, but he knew the man. Sean focused on not trembling – though it did not work.

Doctor Katherine's voice was harsh. "Do the two of you understand why you are here?" She waited.

Marly barely squeaked, "Yes, Doctor Katherine."

Sean's voice was no better when he acknowledged that he understood, though he knew he did not know the purpose, the anticipated outcome. That was the part that bothered him most.

"I don't think you do - either of you. You have violated one of Humanity One's most sacred laws, the law of procreation." Katherine paused.

Even though blinded by the light, Sean knew Katherine's eyes were boring into this head. If she could, she would lay his mind bare, expose his darkest secrets, his lusts. He felt that he had to say something. He blurted while fighting back tears, "We didn't do anything."

Sarcasm oozed from Katherine's words. "Are you trying to tell me that the two of you were naked together but had no intentions of doing anything?"

Sean felt the accusing scorn, the mockery of the Doctor's words. He did not know how to avoid the inevitable outcome that he feared. At that moment, he wanted his parents there to comfort him. He was not an adult. He felt it – a lot more than he felt it before Pamela burst into Marly's bedroom. All he could do was repeat more forcefully, "We didn't do anything." He looked toward Marly for confirmation.

"Why were you in Marly Shiyi-SanShier's quarters, in Marly's private bed if you weren't there to behave as mates, to fornicate?"

Sean squinted. He knew he had to stand up for himself, for Marly. He had to convince the Medical Review Board that they had not violated the law, the MGR, regardless of their intentions. "We were there to ..." he could not form the word. "But ... Pamela arrived before we did anything."

"You didn't touch Marly?"

"Not like that. No." Sean felt emboldened by a slight shift in Katherine's tone. He thought he saw the Premier lean back, a sign that Paul was disinterested now that the truth was revealed.

"How then?"

Sean glanced toward Marly. He saw her legs tighten together as she continued to stare at her hands in her lap. Whatever happened to Marly before she was brought to the room had demoralized her. He felt sorry for her, but she needed to help him help them. Recycling was a real possibility. "Just touching with hands. Kissing and stuff. You know." He tried to keep his eyes leveled toward where he thought Katherine's eyes should be. The light hurt and made his tear-filled eyes water more.

"No. I don't know. I wasn't there."

"Pamela knows. She saw us. We weren't doing anything – not that thing."

Katherine abruptly asked the Medical Technician, "Bailey, did you examine Marly?"

Sean felt it more than he saw it when Marly drew inward, her thighs and hands pressed tightly in a protective posture. Even her breast seemed to draw toward one another. He wished he had not noticed. Even at that moment, Marly was the prettiest girl he knew. He feared for her safety more than his own.

Bailey cleared his throat, "Yes, Doctor Katherine. I performed several tests to determine her current condition."

"What were your findings?"

Sean knew Doctor Katherine was not hearing her Technician for the first time. She was being formal before she announced her recommendation to the Premier, the man who would decide their fates.

"No sign of recent activity, other than heavy petting."

"No chance of impregnation?"

"None. I took swabs from every inch of her torso, searching for evidence of activity. I even did a pregnancy test to determine if previous activity might have caused pregnancy."

"Was there previous activity?"

"I would not say that factually. There was no evidence of recent activity, which was my primary search parameter."

"Thank you, Bailey. Good work – as always."

Sean thought about Bailey's words. He was horrified for Marly. That was the reason she looked beaten and shocked. A battery of tests like that by a man was humiliating for Marly. There were plenty of female Technicians - even Pamela - who could have done those tests. Doctor Katherine did it for a reason. She was teaching Marly a lesson. She knew what the results would be. Pamela probably told her what she saw. He kept his thoughts to himself. A decision was pending.

Doctor Katherine leaned toward Sean. "Tell me why you thought it was appropriate to do what you did, what you almost did. You and Marly are both minors, not yet adults. There is no secret about our laws against sexual activity outside of formal mating. Tell me."

Sean gulped. He said all he could think of, "We love each other."

"You think being in love is an excuse for your behavior?"

Sean hung his head. The light forced his eyes downward. The tone of Katherine voice pushed his head down. "No, Doctor Katherine. I wasn't thinking clearly."

"You weren't thinking clearly? Is that what we can expect from you when you reach adulthood? That is unviable." Katherine words were harsh, cutting through Sean's weak exterior.

Sean slumped his shoulders and clasped his hands in his lap like

Marly. The words from Doctor Katherine made an impact. Unviable was not a word any Crew member wanted to hear. Recycling was the next word that would be used. "We can think clearly. We are viable." That was all he could think to say.

Katherine's tone did not change. "You're not viable until adulthood. Until that time, you are a drain on resources, irreplaceable resources. For fourteen years, your parents have been preparing you, training you, so you can be viable as a Con-Sys Tech. What would Captain Cesar say about having a Con-Sys Tech whose mind is filled with carnal thoughts rather than being focused on the Control Console? Do you think the Captain wants a Con-Sys Tech who is easily distracted? Do you think he would want someone like you to monitor the systems, to guard the mission of Humanity One?"

"Captain Cesar would not be pleased. I am a good Trainee. We are in love, maybe too young. I am sorry for my behavior and will do better. It is my fault. I'm the oldest." Sean knew contrition was his only hope. He would not turn his back on Marly. He wanted to take her hands in his.

"You may not get the chance to do better," Katherine said abruptly. "Premier Paul, you know Captain Cesar better than most of us. Is he the forgiving kind?"

Paul responded, "Not at all. There can be no room for error on Humanity One. The Captain cannot abide mistakes. It is simply not viable."

Sean sobbed. Marly simply sat and stared at her white knuckles in her lap. Sean waited for the words that would end his life.

"Your genealogy is acceptable for procreation, but you are not yet adults. We have not reached the level of depravity to allow children to breed. If stopping such behaviors among the young could be stopped by recycling *your* atoms and starting anew, I would gladly do it." Katherine's tone was even.

Sean barely heard the words in context. He heard the one word he feared the most. He knew where the words would end. There was little more he could say, nothing more he could do. He wondered if the pain would be unbearable. He knew very little about recycling, except that it was inevitable for everyone.

"Young love ... lust ... is not new to humans, or to Humanity One. You are fortunate that your salacious behaviors were observed by wiser heads. You are fortunate that those wiser heads shared the observations with Pamela. You are fortunate that Pamela is wise enough to rescue you from your immaturity. When you reach adulthood, if the love still exists, petition the Medical Review Board for the right to mate. Premier Paul, do you have more to add?"

Paul was aggravated, angered – and tired. Twelve hours had elapsed since the course correction, not enough time to know the ultimate status of Humanity One. His response was rehearsed prior to the meeting. "We are in the midst of a crisis. Though not widely discussed, the fate of our Mission is in jeopardy; yet I find myself distracted by youthful lust. This is distasteful. I wonder what is wrong with you Gen 4s. Do we need to wrap and bind all of you from head to toe so you are neither tempted nor able to engage in unbecoming activities? This entire episode disgusts me. I'm not averse to recycling, if that is your recommendation, Doctor Katherine. Sometimes examples must be made.

"But ... I will add that you have previously stated Marly is destined to be the youngest doctor ever qualified. If I can be assured that she will no longer engage in lascivious activities prior to adulthood, I can be convinced to set aside my feelings if by so doing the total viability of Humanity One is improved.

"I have less to say about Sean. I think Captain Cesar is less forgiving than you, Doctor Katherine." Premier Paul paused, staring from the dimness toward Sean.

Sean could not keep his entire body from shaking. He struggled to control his bowels and bladder. He could not look up, stare into the darkness and let the fear in his eyes be seen.

Premier Paul sighed loudly, "But ... what is fair for one is fair for the other. I need assurance that these two will not be together without plenty of prying eyes." He finished speaking.

Sean barely heard the Premier's final sentence. All the preceding words were filled with accusations and finality. He was confused. He tried to control his trembling body, to accept his fate with dignity. That was all he had left. He stared at his hands. He was sure he felt dampness in his waistcloth.

"Well?" Katherine's voice challenged from the darkness into the light. "Do I have a response to the Premier's conditions?"

Sean jerked his head and squinted into the light. His eyes moved from side to side, trying to see Doctor Katherine's and Premier Paul's expressions. He could not see anything except the brightness of the light in his blurred eyes. He tried to recall the words that were barely heard and less understood. It dawned on him that Premier Paul had offered a reprieve. "Yes," he blurted.

"Yes what?"

"Yes, we will not be together alone." Sean looked toward Marly, who was still broken. "Won't we, Marly?" Marly did not respond. Sean knew she had to say something. That was their only hope, his only hope. He reached out and touched Marly's shoulder. "Marly, tell them we will not be alone together again. Not until we are adults. Tell them." He was desperate.

Marly drew away from his touch. She cut her eyes toward Sean. Angry and hurt eyes that showed deep distrust. She understood Sean's words. Without looking away from Sean, she replied, "We will."

"I believe you," Katherine replied. "Marly, return to your quarters. Pamela and Dexter are waiting for you. Bailey will escort you."

Marly came alive. She snarled toward the dark form that was Bailey. "I can find my way."

"No," Katherine snapped. "You will not go alone."

Marly shook with anger but said nothing in rebuttal.

"Sean, I will walk you to your quarters. And – I will not remind you again that you cannot be together alone. I have lost all trust in either of you."

CHAPTER 15

COURSE ALTERATION

Cesar's back hurt. Tension added to the sharp, arthritis pains. He felt every muscle in his back gripped tightly, pulling in every direction on his spine and ribs. The Chair had no comfortable spots. He stood and paced in front of it. He tried to avoid becoming a disturbance in the Control System Room. Hard to do.

The Room was not large enough to provide open spaces for anything other than access to the myriad of workspaces, the consoles where every aspect of the vessel's function was monitored. Cesar knew his motion would create tension among the Con-Sys Techs. They would automatically think he was looking over their shoulders. Paranoia among the ranks has value for a leader some of the time. This was not one of those times. He did not need any distractions. The rogue's potential was too chilling. If the projectile was indeed an attempt to disable or destroy Humanity One, the situation could devolve rapidly. Every system required undivided attention. Everyone in the room knew it was time for Cesar to rest. The fact that he and Joseph were there along with Second and his Trainee was distraction enough. The Con-Sys Techs on duty were not accustomed to the Captain's presence.

Even Joseph did not know the entirety of Cesar's concerns. The course alteration was nerve wracking and risky in more ways than Cesar could confidently reckon, more ways than he fully understood. He chose a move to the left because – if the rogue were actually an alien vessel – it would be less menacing than a move to the right, toward the rogue, if misinterpreted. The move left would appear to be a retreat, an evasive move, not an attack.

With unseen effort, Cesar used his Communicator to contact the Con-Sys Tech monitoring the navigational coordinates. He contacted Joseph and Second as well so they would know what was happening. "Is the alteration showing?"

"Aye, Captain. We are veering left on the trajectory provided by Sci-Eng."

"Thank you. Update me immediately if there are any anomalies – even after I yield Con to Second."

"Aye, Captain."

The entire process would require more than eight days. Cesar could not be there every moment, but he could be there during what he perceived as the most critical moments. The start, the apogee of the arc and the return to the original course. The trajectory chosen was a wide swing, an arc several million miles in depth. Cesar, through Gail, wanted to take no chances of miscalculation. Swing as far away from the initially projected collision point as practical to assure no chance of contact. Because of Humanity One's propulsion and steering design, quick course changes were not possible. The arc had to be wide anyway. They could only nudge the vessel off its trajectory and would have to nudge it back on course. If all went as planned, Humanity One would settle back onto the originally plotted course, bound for its meeting with Earth Two and completion of the Mission.

Cesar knew the plan was bad. Before the Mission could be completed successfully, future Captains would have to find a way to get Humanity One back on schedule. The course change would put

Humanity One behind by seventy-five hours and fifteen minutes, more than three days. That time variation meant Humanity One would arrive at its destination too late to slide into the gravity neutral point predicted and planned by the Innovators. A critical part of the Mission was for Humanity One to obtain an orbital presence in the gravity neutral point bounded by Earth Two and its two moons. From there, Humanity One would be able to effortlessly maintain position while the Gen 8s completed revival of the Stasis inhabitants and prepared to descend to their new home. The gravity neutral point varied with the orbits of the three celestial objects, with infrequent juxtaposition that put the three of them the perfect distance apart to support the Innovators' plan. As he paced, Cesar knew the Mission was officially a failure at the moment the course alteration began. Salvaging success was unlikely, even by a future Captain. The name Cesar Er Yi would be associated with Mission failure, not that it would matter.

A quick mental shift contacted the Con-Sys Tech responsible for identifying and tracking objects along the route. "John, is the rogue still tracking and holding course?" The prospect that the rogue was actually another vessel made the course alteration maneuver more tense. The projectile was not natural. As much as Cesar wanted to believe it was just one of nature's oddities, he knew better. If the rogue was a sentient-being controlled vessel, and if they had truly fired upon Humanity One, the collision course might have been an intentional interception for attack. Easily changed by a maneuverable vessel's Captain with offense in mind.

"Aye, Captain. The object has not changed velocity or course."

"Thank you. Alert me if it does." Cesar paced back to the Chair. Too many eyes were diverted from the consoles by his presence on the floor. He settled in the familiar seat and leaned his elbow on a chair arm. He rested his jaw in his hand as he watched and contemplated another scenario. The rogue could be nothing more than an uncharted asteroid, still a hazard but not an ongoing danger. If so, the projectile came from somewhere else. Sci-Eng had not yet confirmed the projectiles point of origin. He contacted Gail by Communicator. "Have you confirmed the projectile's origin?"

Cesar's head filled with unexpected thoughts, images and emotions. Pleasures he no longer enjoyed. Gail accepted his hail before disengaging from her off-duty activities. It was her rest period also. She was with her mate in their quarters.

Gail's response was initiated by surprise and panicked confusion. "It should be ready by tomorrow. The second team is working on it."

Cesar generally ignored Gail's attached emotions, as much as he could. He knew his sense of urgency did not match hers. "Secrecy is critical. You do understand? I don't want undue panic."

"Yes. I put everything in place to guard it."

"First thing tomorrow. Good night." Cesar smiled to himself. Gail allowed her emotions to interfere with her Communicator. He wondered if her mate even noticed that she was distracted for a moment. He missed his mate.

The alteration was taking place according to plan. There was nothing more that Cesar could do ... other than worry. He could do that in the comfort of his quarters. Some of Katherine's powders might ease his pain. Aloud, he said, "Second, the Chair is yours. Joseph and I are bed bound. Alert me if anything happens out of the ordinary." Even though the Technicians observing the space around Humanity One declared the chosen course to be clear of hazards, Cesar knew Humanity One was entering unknown territory. For more than sixty years, the vessel had only passed through predicted and understood space, charted territory. In the new reality, nothing was understood – definitely no longer accurately predicted.

Cesar's quarters were unlit until he arrived. Sensors detected his presence and activated dim lighting, sufficient to prepare himself for bed. His body was ready. Not so much his mind. He wriggled to adjust the bed to his needs. He wanted to relax away the tension. Doctor Katherine's powder was neither fast acting nor narcotic. He had to help it.

After a few minutes, the lights darkened. Cesar's mind was floating in its own light, unable to match the darkness of the room. He wondered what the Captain of the alien vessel was thinking. He wondered if the Captain noticed Humanity One's course change. He wondered if the Captain understood Humanity One was on a peaceful voyage. He wondered what he would do if he was Captain of the alien vessel. He could have asked. He could have hailed the vessel. He could have told them that his was a peaceful vessel merely passing through that section of void on its way to a distant destination. He could have done those things if Humanity One was equipped with broadband communication capabilities. She was not because there was no calculated need. He feared that an attempt to broadcast electromagnetic waves might signify something sinister, threatening.

Cesar cringed. The thought occurred to him that the alien vessel's mission might be patrol. That section of the galaxy might be the alien's territorial waters. Humanity One was there uninvited, an intruder. The Innovators denied the existence of sentient beings. They did not seek permission from someone that – to them – did not exist. Humanity One had no defensive weapons. His only defense was to avoid contact because Humanity One was not designed or equipped for either flight or fight.

Cesar knew he could hail the aliens, use the narrow system available to him, and tell them that he was peaceful and meant no harm. He could say he was sorry. But, Con-Sys reported no electromagnetic transmissions emanating from the alien vessel, no signals to declare Humanity One was not welcome. If the Alien Captain were truly on patrol to protect his territory, it only made sense that he would send out a warning – or question the intruder's purpose. That is what Cesar reckoned he would do if the roles were reversed. Or, maybe electromagnetic transmissions would be perceived as an act of aggression. He had no idea of what kind of reaction a sudden burst of radio waves would elicit. He could find himself on the losing end of a battle for simply trying to apologize.

Humanity One was not designed with robust communication capabilities for several reasons. Primarily, there was no plan for the vessel to remain in contact with Earth. Contact would, by natural design, become less frequent up to complete loss as Humanity One raced away and the generations in both places passed from one into another. The emotional connection between Earth and Humanity One would dissipate after Gen 1 passed. Cesar, as a Gen 2, felt no emotional connection to Earth and its people; no more than what one would feel for ancestors that were only known as pictures or words in a history book. Secondly, there was no reason to squander resources for a system that would not be of use in space that was devoid of sentient beings.

Since unknown alien technology might rely upon some forms of electromagnetic energy waves as weapons. Cesar had no choice but to avoid contact with the limited system he did have. Humanity One's mission was singularly focused – save humanity and its technology. Sentient-being contact was not part of the Mission. As a matter of fact, sentient-being contact – determined by the Innovators to be a nearly zero possibility – was discouraged by the MGR. Any detraction from the Mission because of aliens would cause Mission failure.

Cesar struggled to sleep. The Innovators were right. As of that moment, the Mission was a failure because of alien contact. And – he had no idea whether the contact was ended. Humanity One was still in their territory.

CHAPTER 16

SEARCHING

Jana's mind was on something other than Captain training. She avoided making eye contact with Cesar or Joseph, fearful that they could force the Communicator to reveal everything on her mind. Or maybe she was fearful that her own paranoia would cause her subconscious to activate the Communicator and reveal all her thoughts. The use of the Communicator was as much an art as it was a skill. At least, she was finally allowed back in the Control System Room for her daily training.

Jana noticed that Cesar was intense, more so than normal, almost to the point of distraction. The course change meant more to him than she imagined it would. Apparently, he knew something that no one else knew; probably not even Joseph. The Premier might know, but no one else. Another secret. If Cesar would share his concern with others, maybe whatever was bothering him could be remedied by someone else. A fresh perspective. She was smart. She could help him if he would let her. But – Cesar would not let a Gen 4 help. Like all the other Leaders, he would rather fail than trust someone who was not an adult. An open console was located on the far side of the Con-Sys Room. Jana wanted to know the secrets and was willing to risk the search. She nonchalantly approached the console and slid into the chair.

Before she could log-on, Joseph called for a status update. Startled, Jana leapt to her feet and moved closer to the Captain's chair, to her adopted spot, and stood to watch the Con-Sys Techs deliver their hourly status reports. "All normal" was the response from every position. She wondered why no one mentioned the rogue or the fact Humanity One was on an altered course. She wondered if that information was being suppressed. She activated her Communicator for Joseph, cautious to only connect with him. Curiosity drove her. She could not help but ask. The worst that could happen is a scolding from Joseph. "Why did no one report that we were on a new course?"

Joseph responded, "We are tracking the alternate course as it is plotted, so it is *all normal.*"

It was a simple answer. Jana contained her query about the rogue object. She reckoned her sire's response would be that it was still on its predicted course, so it too was *all normal.* "Thank you. I was just wondering." It grated on her that she was denied access to the same information as the Captain. After all, she was a Captain Trainee. She pushed the angry thoughts from her mind. She would know everything soon enough. She cautiously, gradually, made her way back across the Control Room to the empty console.

The console was a spare. Occasionally, a console would require repair or preventive maintenance. The spare served as the backup, so nothing was missed – not that there was much to miss. Rex had friends who were Elec-Techs. When asked, they told him that no repairs or maintenance was scheduled for the Con-Sys Room. He got the information for Jana. Jana could work undisturbed.

With every fiber of her body on edge, Jana began her search on the console computer. She preferred the touch mode rather than virtual keys. She tried to appear at ease, as if what she was doing was natural and normal activity. It was not uncommon for her to use a console to monitor ongoing activities in the Control Room. The screen was inclined for best visibility for the person in the seat directly in front of it. Even so, it could be seen by the eyes of anyone walking behind her or close on either side of her. Watching for prying eyes made her wary of her posture. Cesar was an expert observer. If she acted guilty, he would detect it. She closed her eyes and slowly exhaled, forced herself to smile and relax. She pointed to the Menu. The Menu was the same Menu that was visible to anyone on any Con-Sys console. Theoretically, anyone with access to the computer could access any Menu item, even if only to find that it required a passcode to open. The only way to test the menu items was to try each one.

Jana was familiar with most of the Menu choices. The routine programs opened instantly when she touched them. Jana recognized each one she opened. The Menu was similar to her training console in function, with one major difference. Every system console within the Con-Sys Room was visible to her from that one computer, that one console. Any console in the Con-Sys Room could be used to monitor every control function – *Review Only,* if that function were already in use. All that was required was to select the appropriate Menu item. She was careful to not attempt to make entries. Even if she did, nothing would happen if the item was already in use, but she feared that the real User could see what she did and become suspicious. She knew how the systems worked, but paranoia prevailed. Finally, she reached Menu items that she did not recognize. They were not on her training computer. Her heart raced with excitement. She had found the secret knowledge files.

The first unfamiliar Menu item turned out to be the Captain's log. It was *Review Only* from that console, no write privileges. She reckoned it was *Review Only* from all consoles. The Captain and Second made log entries throughout the day in the Chair's computer. The Captain had over-write power to amend all entries from his quarters if he so desired. The log was not visible to her on the training computer. It was one of those mysterious learnings that piqued her curiosity. She devoured several days of the log entries before she became discouraged. No secrets. Very routine, inclusive of all status update results, *all normal*. The rogue asteroid was mentioned when it occurred. The course alteration was noted with the exact moment of execution. A little more specific information about those events than she knew, but nothing she thought to be of value. Nothing that ranked as a high secret.

A selection identified as CAP PERS was passcode protected. So was an item named SEVENTH. After reassuring herself that no one was wise to her activities, Jana used the virtual keyboard to enter her grandmother's name and numeric birthdate on the passcode line for CAP PERS. It opened so quickly that her eyes popped. She suppressed a delighted giggle. It was too easy. She knew Cesar idolized his mate, probably the only human he genuinely loved. She was surprised that he had not used the facial recognition feature or a bio-print as the passcode. She did not care. She was in. Her hands trembled as she moved the cursor to access the data.

The folder had multiple sub-files. Each one covered a different subject, ranging from routine duties of the Captain to specific responses to a variety of situations. Every sub-file was identified using alpha-numerics that she recognized as MGR headers. It was the MGR for the Captain, though in more detail than the MGR for the Captain Trainee. Secrets. She found some, but nothing that was ship-shaking. Nothing that satisfied her lust for more information. A file carried the same name as one of the passcode protected items on the Menu - SEVENTH. Jana tapped the screen to open it, half expecting it to require a passcode. More MGR, but slightly more ominous. She carefully read it, embroiled to distraction by the introductory paragraphs.

During Generation 7, prepare the Crew for the production of

Generation 8. Each Generation 7 mated pair shall bear four daughters. In the event a Generation 7 female is barren or fails to bear daughters, her number shall be borne by other females. This directive may cause concerns among the Crew. Resources within the vessel will not support naturally occurring gender distribution to achieve the four-daughter requirement. The Captain must be prepared to support the Chief Medical Officer in ensuring compliance. The methods used to achieve this goal are defined in the Chief Medical Officer's MGR.

When Humanity One has achieved neutral orbit within Earth Two's stellar system - near the end of the 24th decade when Generation 8 is mature - the Captain, the Premier and the Chief Medical Officer shall combine the passcodes each has protected from Generation 1 to open the SEVENTH Menu item. The item is so named because Generation 7 will still be the superior generation in all but the most remote circumstances and will be expected to execute the preparatory tasks for revival of the people in Stasis.

Jana barely blinked as she read the rest of the file. It was guidance for the end of the Mission. References to the Premier, Chief Medical Officer and even the Stasis Chief left her wondering how the entire plan came together. The Captain had specific duties to perform, specific instructions to ensure Gen 7 prepared Gen 8 for the settlement of Earth Two. Gen 8's role for a successful settlement was apparently huge, but as specific as the instructions were, they did not describe exactly what Gen 8 would be required to do – only that their failure to perform would doom the Mission. One final paragraph stated that Keegan Masters would be the President as soon as he was revived from Stasis and he would provide instructions for the timing and order of further revivals.

Jana closed the file and considered what she had read. It was almost time for another status update. She arose and slowly wandered toward Joseph and Cesar. She would dwell on her thoughts until after the *all normal* recital. Apparently, the Menu item SEVENTH required a combination of three passcodes. Hacking that file would require more skills than she possessed. If it were set by the Innovators, it would not be as simple as knowing what passcodes each of the three leaders mentioned might use. All she had learned for sure was that there definitely was a cache of secret knowledge.

⌇⌇⌇

Rex felt moisture under his arms. Nervous sweat. He wondered why he let his ego control him. He was smarter than that. Maddie was probably right about his intelligence in relation to that of all other Crew members, but she was smart enough to guile him into action. He understood things that other Sci-Eng Techs did not seem to be able to grasp. He did not see the final calculations presented to the Captain, but he knew from what parts he saw that the alteration would create more problems. He had the answer, the solution, but Stan cautioned him from saying anything. After all, Rex was still a Trainee, not yet an adult. Stan feared the heresy that Rex's creative ideas represented.

Kendra Communicated to Rex that the Premier was in Hydroponics, destined for Stasis next as he began his routine tour of Humanity One. Kendra's thoughts seemed hesitant, fearful. Even though she had agreed to provide the information, there was a deep sense of reluctance, even fear, in the tone of the Communication. She knew Communicators could easily be monitored. Rex shook his head and focused on his task. The tour would last at least four hours, plenty of time for Rex to go to the Premier's quarters and access his computer. Stan thought he was in quarters alone - training. Rex's dedication to learning provided him his best cover. There was no reason to suspect Rex would be doing anything else.

Personal quarters were not equipped with locks. In the closed society, unwritten privacy rules were followed by all. The lack of locks probably reinforced the need to respect the privacy of others, to avoid unannounced intrusions into personal space. Rex felt guilty for slipping into the Premier's quarters. There was no time for guilt. He was not there to pry into the Premier's personal life, only to access secret knowledge. Rex knew it existed. Surely the Premier had access to most of it, if not all of it.

The Premier's personal computer opened at the Menu, right where the Premier left it before it went to idle. Rex began opening Menu items. If an item opened without a passcode, he closed it and went to the next. Secret knowledge would not be unprotected. Item PRE PERS required a passcode. Rex tried a few combinations of letters and numbers that he thought the Premier might use. None worked. He had only one option.

Rex understood computers better than most Sci-Eng Techs. His friends in Electronic Technology willingly shared their knowledge. Computer technology was not a secret; most people did not care to know how they worked, just that they worked as advertised. He could troubleshoot the software as well as any Elec-Tech. All of Rex's learning had proven that the Innovators were truly ingenious, especially with the computer systems. The software they installed was robust and hardy. It did not fail. Simply coded programs and routines that would repeat unadulterated for hundreds of years, millennia if the hardware it ran on did not fail. It was also accessible to someone who understood it. He knew it. Passcodes were hackable with minimal effort. One only needed time. The more types of symbols used; the more time hacking would require. The Premier was a simple man – in the most obvious way – bound by what he experienced. In all likelihood, the Premier chose an easy to remember combination of either numbers or letters with no more than six characters – the minimum required. Rex wrote his own computer code, a brute force passcode breaker described in the archives. He launched it against the PRE PERS passcode. And waited.

Time passed slowly, or so it seemed in the private quarters of the highest ranking, if not the most powerful, person on Humanity One - in Rex's world. Less than ten minutes actually elapsed before the item opened. Rex eagerly leaned forward and scanned a long list of sub-files. He recognized the MGR identification system. The Premier's MGR was ready to share its secrets. Rex knew a general MGR existed publicly that defined the Premier's duties and powers. None of the sub-files belabored the obvious; they were specific. The first one he opened was slightly unnerving.

As Humanity One approaches the final decades of the mission, successful completion will require a shift in mating and procreation. The Chief Medical Officer will dictate the final pairings for traits described in the Chief Medical Officer's SEVENTH Generation MGR. Anticipate resistance from the Crew and be prepared to enforce the decisions of the Chief Medical Officer.

Direct the Chief Mechanical Technician and the Chief Electronic Technician to execute the vessel changes specified within work instructions PRE.WI.37.4501.067 through PRE.WI.37.4501.301.

When Humanity One has achieved neutral orbit within Earth Two's stellar system - near the end of the 24th decade when Generation 8 is mature – the Captain, the Premier and the Chief Medical Officer shall combine the passcodes each has protected since Generation 1 to open the SEVENTH Menu item. The item is so named because Generation 7 will still be the superior generation in all but the most remote circumstances and will be expected to execute the preparatory tasks for revival of the people in Stasis.

Keegan Masters shall be the first revived and shall be elevated to the position of President. At his command and on his schedule, revivals of the people in Stasis shall begin. The Premier will be responsible for the coordination of Generation 7 and Generation 8 Crew members' activities in support of President Masters and the Captain.

In the event a Stasis failure renders Keegan Masters unrevivable, Corrina Sandoval shall be revived to serve as President.

Rex read every sub-file. Several contained information and instructions that defined the Premier's role, the Chief Medical Officer's role and the Stasis Chief's role. The Captain's role was less well defined, but every reference indicated the Captain's power increased. Hydroponics was instructed to alter the use of growing rooms to accommodate sprouting seeds of trees. The seeds were to be revived from a section of Stasis. Rex was unfamiliar with Stasis, other than the fact that it contained the dormant bodies of Earth humans. He did not know Stasis also held seeds not currently produced as food in Hydroponics. In truth, he did not know what a tree was. He, nor his peers, needed to know.

The Work Instructions designated for Mechanical and Electrical were revealing, though Rex was not entirely sure of what they revealed. Bulkhead walls were to be removed and private quarters were to be combined into barracks that would accommodate twice as many people as current space would allow. Privacy would be all but eliminated. Walls within Hard and Soft Fabrication would be removed to provide more room for a major building project that President Masters would direct. The space within Stasis would be prepped for a major change of use as people were revived. One grow room would be adjusted with a higher ceiling to accommodate "sapling" trees, described as fruit, nut and lumber trees.

Rex could not force the SEVENTH Menu item, not in the time he had available. He tried - he hoped his hack code would stumble on the passcode quickly. Fearful of discovery and further confused by what he had learned, he returned the computer to its found condition — idle on the Menu. Only then did he notice an unassuming string of characters at the bottom of the computer screen. He committed them to memory and slipped away to his quarters to contemplate what he had learned. The indication that the Captain's power would increase was a clue to where more information could be found. He hoped Jana was able to find it.

As revealing as all the information should have been, something disturbed him. He was not sure what it was, but he was sure he had learned more than his conscious mind could process. There was a lot to understand, and more secrets to learn. He especially wanted to learn about a reference to the Chief Medical Officer's 7th Generation MGR and four daughter per female.

The Group met in the Mess Hall with plates filled. Marly sat next to Maddie. Sean sat across the table from her. With a puzzled look, Rex sat next to Sean. Jana sat with Rex, not too close. Kendra smiled meekly and joined Maddie's side of the table. Zack found a place and waited for the conversation to begin.

Maddie glanced at Jana. "What did we learn?"

"That something changes during Gen 7. They will have more babies – girls." Jana looked toward Rex for confirmation.

"More babies?" Kendra seemed startled. "How will we feed them?"

Rex replied with a playful smile, "It won't be us."

Zack inserted quickly, "It will be us ... sort of. Our atoms."

Kendra was more attentive than usual because there was no one at any of the Gen 3 tables to serve as a distraction. Captain Cesar and Doctor Katherine were eating at the far table with Premier Paul and Chief Gail. "Our gardens can only produce a certain amount of food. There's no more growing room."

Rex nodded, "I know. I was joking. Space is another problem that extra births would create. But - there are plans to create more room — in a sense."

"How can that be done?" Maddie asked.

"Remove walls, eliminate halls and create communal living areas." Rex motioned around the Mess Hall. "Imagine if everyone had their own kitchen and eating area. More space would be required than we currently use. More people can be housed if we eliminate private quarters and build barracks for sleeping. No walls, no halls."

"They can't do that!" Maddie exclaimed. "That would take away our privacy."

"The changes are going to happen after Gen 8 is born, or most of them. Gen 7 will begin the preparations for Stasis revival. Humanity One will be less than a decade removed from settling Earth Two when the work begins. Space for the additional people will be more valuable than privacy."

Maddie relaxed. "Well, at least it won't affect us."

"Those are the secrets?" Kendra asked, moderately disappointed. A normally serious eater, she picked at her food. "Doesn't sound like much for us to worry about."

Jana glared at Kendra. "That's not all the secrets. Unless Rex was able to hack into a Menu choice called SEVENTH, there are a lot of secrets we still don't know. Besides, did you not hear me? Gen 7 will have extra babies, at least four per woman." She paused to make sure everyone was listening before she whispered, "Only girls."

"Only girls?" Zack asked, suddenly cognizant of the statement.

"Yes, I heard you," Kendra responded to Jana. "That doesn't mean it makes sense."

Zack was still wanting an answer. "Why only girls?"

"You tell me," Jana responded to Zack.

"I ... I don't know." Zack slumped into his chair, intimidated by Jana.

Maddie cocked her head and glanced toward Marly. "That makes no sense. If Gen 8 is all girls, how will there ever be a Gen 9? Marly, what do you think it means?"

Marly avoided eye contact with Sean as she tried to answer. "I really don't know ... unless they want more women to have babies when we get to Earth Two."

"But – without men?" Maddie quizzed.

Marly blushed and timidly replied, "Maybe the men in Stasis will be the sires."

"Yuk!" Maddie exclaimed. "Two-hundred-year-old men with their great granddaughters. That's sick."

Zack said cautiously, softly, "Not granddaughters. The Crew members are not necessarily blood kin to the people in Stasis."

Maddie scowled. "Maybe so, but it still sounds wrong."

"Still, it sounds like Gen 8 will be expected to have lots of babies for Earth Two, regardless of who sires them. It would be hard to regulate genetics using Gen 7 men. It has to be Stasis sires," Marly said pensively. "Zack, are there more men than women in Stasis?"

"I don't know for sure, but I don't think so. My room is equal men and women." Zack noticed Marly and Sean were separated. Maybe that meant Marly was available. He smiled at her. She did not respond as he hoped.

"Maybe there are some things we shouldn't know," Marly offered. "Look at us now. All of us are repulsed by the thought of the age difference."

"It is repulsive," Maddie countered.

"*We* think so. And thinking about it is a distraction from our duties. The rules of society are in place to help us survive." Marly held Maddie's glare while she spoke, then returned to spearing vegetables with her fork.

"Secrets! If we know what is expected of us, we can better tend to our duties. Rules are in place to control us, not help us."

Rex leaned forward and spoke with urgency in a hushed tone, "Shush! Rules are important. Even if we know all the secrets, we must still follow the rules."

Maddie's nostrils flared and her chest heaved as she stared at Rex. Their matching blue eyes did not waver. She saw the set of his jaw. She knew he was right. She still did not like it. She relaxed and glanced toward Captain Cesar's table. Doctor Katherine's eyes frequently cut toward the Gen 4 table. With a softer voice, Maddie replied, "I'm not so sure that's right. If we knew the secrets, the rules might change."

"Maybe," Rex said, also more relaxed. "Regardless, we have to follow rules. Comply with societal mores to survive. There are very few of us to accomplish a huge undertaking. We are in this as one."

"Then, treat us as one. No secrets. Did I understand that there are more secret Menu choices?" Maddie was still undeterred from her quest.

Jana looked toward Rex, "I wasn't able to open SEVENTH. Were you?"

"No. It requires codes from the Captain, the Premier and the Chief Medical Officer. The three codes must be combined. If each has only six characters, that makes it eighteen." Rex shook his head. "Even with my code hacker, it would take more years than the Mission is long to stumble on the passcode. Without the three codes ..." his voice trailed.

"How do we get in?" Maddie asked after several moments of contemplative silence. "There's always a way."

Rex pursed his lips before he spoke. "We have to find the three codes and combine them. Knowing in what order to combine eighteen characters will still be a daunting challenge – maybe insurmountable."

"How many ways can three numbers be combined?" Maddie challenged.

"If it were that easy, to use each part as a single number, I could do it without my code breaker. But it may require a specific sequence for shuffling the combined numbers. Billions … trillions even."

"So, we just give up and let them win?"

"It's not about winning," Rex replied.

"How can you say that? If they keep the secrets from us, we lose." Maddie's anger was still with her.

Rex was losing patience. The challenge of getting the secrets was an enjoyable distraction from routine but learning them would be a victory that could not be shared. "The only way we lose is if the Mission is a failure – and those secrets are less likely to be the cause of failure than our current course change."

"Don't brain it up," Maddie said curtly. "What do we have to do to get the passcodes?"

Rex knew there was nothing to be gained by arguing with Maddie. Her mind was set, and Maddie's mindset established the Group think. He slowly spoke. "The passcode for SEVENTH was set by the Innovators. The Captain, the Premier and the Chief Medical Officer inherit their portion of the code when they assume their positions. The codes are written so they won't be forgotten. My guess is that they are on an indestructible personal object or on their personal computers."

"So, we know where to look. Right?"

"Maybe. I think I found the Premier's code. It was a string of six characters at the bottom of his computer's Menu screen."

"Are you sure?" Jana almost jumped forward with eagerness.

"No, but I memorized them just in case. If we could gain access to Doctor Katherine's and Captain Cesar's personal computers, maybe theirs is kept the same way. It's actually quite ingenious. No one really looks at small type on the bottom of computer screens."

Jana replied, "I can get into Cesar's quarters easily enough. No one notices whether I'm in the Con-Sys Room or not. It's like I'm invisible. This will be easy. Marly, can you get into Doctor Katherine's quarters."

Marly's eyes widened and her already pale face paled further. She blurted, "No! I can't do that."

Jana scowled. "Why not?"

"I'm already under scrutiny." Marly hung her head and blushed.

"She can't do it," Sean said defensively. "Maybe I can."

"No. Let's get the Captain's code first. Then we can plan how to access Doctor Katherine's quarters. She lives alone, doesn't she?" Rex interceded. There was no way Sean could explain his involvement in the Chief Medical Officer's business. He saw growing aggravation on Maddie's face.

"I think so," Marly sheepishly replied to Rex's question. The physically mature thirteen-year-old appeared younger than normal.

Rex smiled. "Okay. We'll wait for Jana."

CHAPTER 17

DISCOVERY

Jana watched Cesar and Joseph. Both men were engaged in their duties. Cesar was in the over-seeing Captain's Chair, his above-average height magnified by the Chair's height and the low ceiling. Joseph was in the lesser Trainee Chair. She knew Cesar was still focused on the course alteration. His eyes were glazed over as often as not, a sign that his Communicator was activated – engaged in private conversation. More secrets. She was there, breathing oxygen and trying to maintain an air of importance befitting a future Captain even though she was not privy to the Captain's secrets. If she became Captain that day, she would not have the knowledge she needed to have. She smiled at Maddie. Maddie was finally allowed to shadow Della in the Con-Sys Room, her chance to prove her viability. Jana would prove hers by finding the Captain's code.

The day progressed from one status update to another without incident. Finally, the time seemed opportune. Jana wandered around the Con-Sys Room until she was near the doorway. After a quick look to see if anyone noticed, she slipped through the door and into the hall. The hall was narrow and dimly lit. No waste of space or energy for a mere passageway. She knew the assumption would be that she was away on a bathroom break.

Jana glanced around before she entered Cesar's quarters. The place was familiar. She had been there before, mostly before her Grandma passed into recycling. Not very much after that. Cesar was a private person. Remote and unreachable, only alive when Humanity One required his attention. After her Grandmother recycled, when she got to see Cesar as he was, she wondered why her Grandmother chose him as her mate. She scanned the quarters. She was surprised that his bed was perfectly made, the top blanket smooth and tight. Her heart almost stopped when she did not immediately see his computer screen. She was relieved when she found it. It was built into the wall in front of a small desk. She had never noticed it when she went to visit her Grandma. There was no need at her young age. The Captain's computer was a touch screen with a physical keyboard, probably not as robust as the console computer's virtual keyboards, but easy to use. Someday, hopefully, those would be her quarters. That would be her computer. She would change keyboards.

Almost afraid to do so, Jana approached the darkened screen. She touched the smooth synthetic surface, half expecting it to send out an alarm, to warn of her unfamiliar touch. If the computer required facial or biometric recognition to activate it, she would be stymied before she started. It did not. The passcode line blinked in anticipation of an entry. Cesar's mate's name and birthdate were easy to enter. As dark and brooding as Cesar could be, he was unimaginative when it came to passcodes. He was generally unimaginative about anything. He simply relied on the MGR to do his thinking. The Menu screen popped into view. Her heart stopped. No characters at the bottom of the screen.

Jana stood and stared at the screen as she gathered her thoughts. The code could be anywhere in the quarters, written on any object. Writing was not common. Paper was not readily available, not a good use of limited resources. Neither were any practical writing instruments. The code could be etched into a flat surface, horizontal or vertical, anywhere in the quarters. No matter where, it had to be intuitive for the next Captain to find in case the Captain recycled suddenly. It dawned on her that even when Joseph recycled and she assumed her rightful place, if he did not hand her the code, she would have to find it on her own. She began searching frantically, using her eyes and her fingertips.

Unsure how much time had passed, other than it was more than she had planned, Jana activated her Communicator and anxiously waited for Rex to acknowledge her. His presence in her mind was an overwhelming relief. She was not alone. "I don't know where it is!"

Rex unease matched Jana's. It was not a conversation he wanted to be having, especially via Communicator. "Where have you looked? Was it not on the screen?"

"No! I've looked everywhere. I even looked under the mattress. All the furniture and door facings. It's not in here!"

"Calm down. Did you open any of the Menu items? It could be on the cover page of any one of them." Rex visualized opening Menu options and scanning the bottoms of every initial screen. "I'm sure it's there."

"Okay," Jana mind acquiesced, happy to have someone in charge of her emotions, particularly Rex. The Captain's Log opened on the last entry page, a standard condition of the file to avoid search time to make daily entries. Jana scrolled it back to the very first page, the page predicating her great-grandsire's first entry the day Humanity One was propelled from the surface of Earth One's moon, Luna. "Yes!" she exclaimed vocally, then informed Rex that she had found the code on the Log cover page. Her mind's eye captured everything and formed pictures of the Group as she told Rex that everyone would be happy with her discovery. They could now learn the secrets that were being hidden from them. In her elation, she forgot that they still needed the Chief Medical Officer's contribution to the passcode. "See you at dinner." She could barely suppress her excitement as she closed the Communicator.

"What are you doing here?"

Jana's blood froze in her veins. Cesar's always tough voice was harder and more demanding than she had ever heard. She looked toward the Captain framed by the doorway of his quarters. His dark face was even darker than normal. He looked taller than life, the top of his head scant inches from the top of the opening. She felt smaller than she had felt since she was a baby. She wished she could disappear - but wishing did not make it so.

"I asked you a question," Cesar demanded.

"I ... I ... nothing. Just looking for some of Grandma's memories." Jana said the only thing she could think of that might soften Cesar's tone.

Cesar glared at her while she trembled uncontrollably. "Get back to Con-Sys. Joseph will be waiting for you."

"Aye, Captain," Jana could not look at Cesar's face. She could not bear the anger and disappointment she glimpsed before she averted her eyes and bowed her head. She knew Joseph would be fully aware of everything Cesar knew. Cesar barely gave her enough room to pass through the doorway. She could not avoid brushing against his body as she left. She was sure she felt the electricity of his anger.

Five harsh words followed her, cut into her brain, and filled her eyes with tears and her heart with dread as she walked away from the Captain's doorway. "Don't take the Trainee Chair." Cesar left no question of his authority to give the command.

Captain Cesar and Premier Paul stood before the seated Group in the Premier's Decision Room. The room was not designed to hold that many people comfortably. That fact was a moot point; that particular meeting was anything but comfortable. Cesar towered over everyone in the room, even Jana whose back was pressed against a wall rather than being seated.. Paul stood frail and pale at the Captain's side, a contrast of skin tones and fitness. Except for a slight lean to one side, the Captain appeared the epitome of health compared to the Premier. And power. The Captain was the undisputed power in the small room.

Cesar looked from face to face, from eyes to eyes until he settled on Maddie. He snarled, "I suppose *you* are the ringleader. What do you have to say for yourself and your little gang?"

Maddie gulped. She knew her fate - and the fate of her friends - rested with the answer she gave. She wondered why the Captain focused on her. She wondered who told him she was the de facto leader. She wondered how he came to consider them anything other than a group of friends. She reckoned it was Jana. It did not matter. He *was* focused on her. She wondered how much he knew about their quest. She forced herself to meet Cesar's dark glare with resolve. She could not admit guilt or unsolicited contrition, but she had to be as truthful as possible. "Captain Cesar, we are merely trying to learn all we can so we can better perform our duties. We share our learning. The fate of the mission requires that we know all we can know." She waited.

Cesar's glare did not lessen in intensity. If he liked or disliked Maddie's response, no one could tell. Every one of the Gen 4s averted their eyes except Maddie and Rex. "Are you accusing Della of not providing sufficient training?"

Maddie felt the accusation. She blinked. "No! Not at all. Della is an excellent trainer."

"If so, why are you compelled to seek information elsewhere? The wiser option would be to seek Della's replacement as your trainer."

Maddie wondered if Cesar ever blinked. His dark eyes left her no room to hide. Her mother was the object of Cesar's condemnation. She blinked back tears. She could not show weakness. She could not allow Della to become the subject of the meeting. "Della teaches everything prescribed by the MGR." She paused to make sure her words were right. "There is a sense that some information that would be helpful is not available to Trainees ... outside their training. Information other Trainees might have."

Cesar blinked and shook his head with disgust. "Not available to Trainees," he contemptuously repeated Maddie's words. "Young Woman, did you and your gang of thieves ever consider that you are not ready for all information? That you are not mature enough to properly process all the knowledge provided to Technicians by the Innovators? Do you suppose that you are wiser than the Innovators?"

Maddie cringed at the address used by Cesar. She knew he chose those words for effect. She could not help herself when she replied angrily, "I am almost an adult, old enough to make decisions and understand everything I need to understand. The Innovators chose to assume Gen 4 lacked the ability to learn."

Cesar leaned toward Maddie and hissed, "The Innovators knew exactly what they were doing. You do lack the ability to learn properly. You are unwilling to accept your duties, your role in the Mission. The age of adulthood was changed from eighteen to sixteen, a decision that may have been ill-advised considering the lack of mental maturity in a sixteen-year-old." He stopped and waited for her to speak.

Maddie knew she was not going to win. Contrition was in order, but it hurt to think the Gen 4 Trainees were not going to receive the respect they deserved. It was clear that Cesar would not change the training. Cesar would not accept Gen 4s as his equal. There was nothing she could do about that – not at the moment. Her voice softened to hide her feelings. She glanced around to include the Group. "We all know how critical the Mission is for the security of humanity. We simply wanted to know what more we could do. We know there is knowledge not yet shared with us. We wondered what and why."

"Pilfering through personal quarters, private information files, ignoring your duties to seek that which is not for you to know is no way to prove yourself worthy of viability status, let alone adulthood." Cesar turned to glare at every one of the Group. He held his glare until each member was near tears – except Jana. He ignored Jana. "As of today, your personal Communicators will be restricted. None of you will be able to contact the other via Communicator. You will not be allowed to meet independent of a Gen 3's presence. The self-proclaimed *Group* is no more. Your viability as a Crew member is dependent on your ability to abide by these conditions between now and adulthood."

Maddie knew, as the Group's leading influence, they had no choice. "We will abide by the conditions, Captain Cesar."

"Maddison Si Qi-Wu, you cannot answer for the others. Despite your self-appointed role as their leader, you are nothing more than a single Trainee – one of questionable dedication. Each of you is responsible and accountable for your own behavior, for your own viability. Do you want to risk your viability on the behaviors of others?" Cesar's voice remained harsh and direct as he panned the Group.

Maddie knew his words were directed toward her influence on the others. She replied, "I accept the conditions." She wanted to look at the others, to encourage the others to accept, but she knew her action would be taken as defiance of Cesar's edict. She wondered why Premier Paul was not saying anything.

Cesar turned his eyes toward Sean, Rex, Zack, Ying, Kendra and Marly in turn. Ying was confused, unsure, but he responded affirmatively. After receiving assurance from each of them, Cesar said, "Now, go tell your Trainers what has transpired, what you have done. Your Trainers will deal with you as they deem fit. They may consider recycling as their only option." After a pause to allow movement toward the door, he said almost as an afterthought, "Maddison, wait a moment."

Maddie's knees were weak. The call to stay was unexpected. Cesar's reference to recycling froze her blood. The only thing that gave Maddie comfort was the fact that Jana was still in the room, standing sullenly alone in a corner, as she had been when the rest of the Group arrived. The blonde teenager griped her hands tightly together behind her hips to stop them from trembling and bit her lower lip to prevent it from quivering.

As soon as the released members of the Group left the room, Cesar turned his angry eyes to Maddie. "No more rebelliousness. Cut your hair to comply with norms. Take it to Recycle. Now, go tell your Trainer what has transpired."

Maddie's eyes filled with tears. Cutting her hair meant losing her identity, her uniqueness. It meant she was compliant, an immediate visual affirmation of her acquiescence to the monotony of conformity. She had no choice but do as Cesar commanded. "Aye, Captain."

Maddie could barely see through her tear-blurred eyes. Fortunately, Della was the only person standing in the dimly lit hallway, easy to find. She did not mention everything that transpired inside the Decision Room. She knew Della was already aware. There was no doubt in her mind that Cesar's Communicator was activated with every Trainer during the meeting. The fact that Della was in the hallway waiting for her confirmed her assessment. She sobbed into Della's shoulder, "Cesar says I have to cut my hair."

Maddie did not notice that Jana did not follow. Joseph was not there to meet his Trainee.

CHAPTER 18

SECRET REVEALED

Maddie was seated at a different table than normal in the Mess Hall. Della was at her side. She felt naked without her hair. The weight of it was greater than she would have ever imagined it to be. She missed the familiarity of it. The frequent requirement to move stray strand from her eyes, her mouth, away from her nipples to stop the tickling, had become part of a habit she did not even know she had. She found herself moving her hands in the same gestures - each time, momentarily confused by her vestigial actions.

Maddie saw Della tense-up when Rex and his mother, Melba, took a seat on the bench across the table from them. She knew the reason for the tension. A shiver ran up her bare nape. She shook it off and smiled weakly at Rex. He returned a bemused smile. It was her first time in public without her hair. She was afraid to verbalize a greeting, or even hold his eyes very long. The Captain made it clear that the Group was disbanded. There could be no more private meetings, no secret conversations, no insolent activities. Focus on their personal job duties only. The young Gen 4 Trainees were expected to prove their viability ... period. She listlessly nibbled at her chow and surreptitiously glanced around the Dining Hall for the others. As much as anything, she wanted to see if they recognized her without her long, golden hair.

Marly was seated with her mother near the table normally used by the VLT. Marly's small body was facing away from the rest of the room. Pamela did not even want Marly to be able to see the others. Verbal communication was not the only means of exchanging thoughts.

Kendra was seated at a table of Gen 3 adults, the same group to which she often devoted attention. Neither of Kendra's parents was with her. One of the women at the table was a Food Processor, probably there as Kendra's chaperone. Kendra casually acknowledged Maddie's surprise-filled eye contact before returning her attention to the conversation at her table. She merely listened without expression.

Zack was seated with his sire and Trainer, Matt. He tried to avoid Maddie's querulous look in his direction. His eyes widened when Maddie's face reacted to words from Della, apparently a warning to mind her own business. Della's agitation was obvious to anyone who bothered to look. It was not a good thing for one's offspring to be on a disciplinary warning. It was not a good thing for the parents. It created questions about their abilities as trainers. He dropped his eyes and focused on his meal.

Ying sat at a table of Mech-Techs and Elect-Techs, slowly eating his meal, generally ignoring the Gen 4s in the Dining Hall, and listening to the more experienced Crew Members talk about their work and things they knew that he did not.

Other than Rex, Kendra was the most visible to Maddie. Jana was not in the Mess Hall. Eating times were staggered into three feedings to allow full use of the kitchen and the facilities, at one-hour intervals. Maddie wondered if Jana was given tighter restrictions. After all, Jana was begin trained to be Captain. Of all positions, the Captain was expected to follow and support the MGR without question. If Jana was to ever be Captain, she had to be purged of her perceived duplicitous ways. Maddie blinked back a tear. She should not have involved Jana, even though Jana chose to be part of the Group.

"How is your training going, Maddie?" Melba asked to make conversation. "If I remember correctly, you're barely a month younger than Rex. You should be nearing adulthood very soon." She made a point of noting that Maddie was younger than her son. "Are you ready to follow in Len's and Della's footsteps?"

Maddie saw Della blush angrily, all the way down to the top of her breasts. The original question could have been asked without additions. Even so, she saw no option other than being polite. "It's going well. I have been allowed to sit with Della in Con-Sys. I have passed all my qualifications. All I need is to achieve adulthood. Con-Sys Tech is pretty easy, unlike Rex's training." She nodded toward Rex and smiled. She saw his face change expression as he readily accepted the praise. She knew he was not shy about his intellect, and he liked to hear others recognize it.

"Every duty is valuable and requires attention." Melba looked toward Rex. "Fortunately, Captain Cesar believes the members of your little group are valuable in those duties, viable if you maintain your focus."

"It wasn't just *Maddie's* group," Della snapped, louder than the relatively quiet room required. Heads turned for a brief moment and the low chatter dissolved into anticipatory quietness for a few seconds. The decorum of privacy dictated that conversations continue after the brief interlude.

Melba seemed pleased with the goaded reaction. "I'm sorry, Della." She reached across the table and touched Della's forearm, which was immediately jerked away. "I didn't mean to imply the whole sordid affair was on Maddie. All the youngsters knew what they were getting into." She looked at Rex who was watching Maddie's facial gymnastics. "Even the brightest can be swayed to question the norm. Maddie is very influential, which is a credit to her leadership abilities. Maybe she should have ventured into some other area of expertise."

Della felt the sting of Melba's needling. "Maddie's training is of no concern of yours. Unlike some, she accepts that which is hers to have and leaves that which belongs to someone else alone."

Maddie knew Della was holding back, more than she probably should, considering Melba's aim. She wished that Rex's trainer, his male parent, Stan, had served as Rex's chaperone during dinner. It would have been much less tense. The Gen 4s only had to be accompanied by a responsible adult. She asked, "Where is Stan? I expected Rex's trainer to be with him." She hoped her interjected topic shift would allow Della to disregard the unforgiveable.

Rex replied. Speaking was not forbidden, as long as it was chaperoned. "Stan is involved in a calculation and was detained by Chief Scientist Gail. I'm unaware of the content, but I have to believe it is important if it kept them from their chow."

Maddie did not smile or allow her expression to change. Rex revealed more than the two adults supposed.

Melba looked straight at Maddie without allowing her eyes to shift toward Della, "There is always so much that those Sci-Techs have to do. They let it consume their lives, leaving little time for family."

Maddie forced a smile. She knew Melba was using the new subject to continue her snide attack against Della. She did not like it but at that point in her life, she also knew that she could not react, no matter how much she wanted to for Della's sake. "We all have a lot to do. As Captain Cesar said very clearly, we all have enough in our own duties that we don't have time to get involved in what others know and do." It was a paraphrase, but she had to end the conversation before Della said something regrettable. It would serve no purpose except to give Melba another victory.

Melba smiled demurely. "Very wise – of you and the Captain. Your leadership is strong. Rex, you're barely eating. We need to finish so you can return to your training. I'm sure Stan could use your help."

"Could, should - but would is probably not to be," Rex replied before he wolfed down the rest of his chow. As soon as his plate was cleared, he rose and nodded to Della and Maddie, "I suppose we need to go. Thank you for allowing us to share the table with you." Rex knew the reason for the discomfort. Some secrets were poorly kept. Knowing secrets was important for future decision making, but they were not necessarily good topics for open conversations.

Maddie watched Della's harsh eyes follow Melba's rear until the woman was out of the Dining Hall.

"You've hardly touched your chow. Eat." Della cut her eyes at Maddie and then turned her attention to her plate.

As she ate, Maddie watched Kendra's facial expressions. Kendra's freckles were normally forced to dance across her nose by a variety of laughs and grins. The red-haired Gen 4 seemed attentive to the conversation among the Gen 3s at her table, but Maddie could tell by the lean of her head that Kendra's auditory focus was on the table of Mech-Techs where Ying was seated.

Kendra wanted to listen to the Gen 3 conversation at her table. Tiffany San Sanshiwu, her friend from Food Processing, agreed to chaperone her during dinner because Jean was unavailable at Kendra's regular eating time. It was no great secret that the rowdy table of Gen 4 Trainees was no more. The details were not general knowledge, but everyone knew something had broken the Group apart, something other than the members of the Group. Kendra found the Mech-Techs' conversation to be more interesting.

"Someone said the meteorite wasn't normal," said a voice from behind.

Kendra strained to eavesdrop and still appear focused in her own world. The conversation had bordered on being conspiratorially interesting for several minutes but had made a definitive turn toward something she was compelled to hear. Something she believed she needed to hear. Cesar's recent warnings were momentarily forgotten.

"Who made the repairs?" another voice asked.

"Ying, weren't you part of the repair crew?"

Ying seemed reticent to respond. "Uh ... yes. It was my first repair assignment."

"So, what did it look like?"

"I don't know for sure. My Sire, Chi, and Mech-Tech Ballard retrieved the meteorite. It was small enough to be held in their palms. I didn't hold it. Besides, I'm not sure how meteorites should look."

Kendra could tell from Ying's tone and hesitancy that he did not want to be involved in the conversation. He was only an occasional participant in the Group but suffered full scrutiny when Jana was caught on Cesar's private computer. Rex Communicated to the Group what happened as soon as Jana was discovered. Her immediate reaction to the discovery was apprehension. She should have worried more. She shuddered as she recalled the meeting with Premier Paul and Captain Cesar. It was mostly Captain Cesar. He is a big, dark, angry man even when he is acting normally. He was an exaggeration of himself during the meeting. They were all convinced that he would declare them unviable, bound for recycle that very day. She strained to listen while pretending to smile at the conversation at her table.

"Rumor has it that it was man-made – or something-made." The voice carried a know-it-all air to validate the claim.

"How could it be something man-made?" was the incredulous response.

"A projectile, fired upon us by an alien craft," came the reply.

Ying interjected, his fear of the conversation heavy in his voice, "No one said it was man-made. Just odd."

"Well, wouldn't a man-made projectile be odd out in the void of space?" The voice expressed disdain for being challenged. "I'm just telling you what I've heard. You Mechanical guys can check it out. You people are the ones who found it."

Kendra knew from the comment that the person who brought up the meteorite was an Elec-Tech, someone who would not have firsthand knowledge of a hull repair. She felt empathy for Ying's hesitancy when he responded to the last challenge.

"Maybe I can ask Chi. He held it in his hand and gave it to Chief Mechanic Donald."

"You do that, Mech-Tech *Trainee* Ying." The voice was disrespectful, almost mocking. To the Gen 3 Mech-Tech, he added, "Can one of you guys find out if there's anything to the rumor?"

Ying was not a charter member of the Group, but he was a Gen 4. The disrespect shown him bothered Kendra more than she expected it would. Too often, the Gen 3s showed little regard for Gen 4's. That became even more apparent after the meeting with the Premier and the Captain. What Maddie had been saying all along made a lot more sense. In her Hydroponics world, Kendra did not face rejection on a regular basis like the others did. Hydroponics was lonely duty most of the time, planting, tending, harvesting vegetables with minimal interaction with other humans. Only Zack functioned in a similar environment, tending the Transport Support Vessels filled with people in Stasis – his crop. The biggest difference between his world and hers was the lighting. Hydroponics required strong light to support photosynthesis. Stasis required no lighting other than that needed by the Sta-Techs to maneuver through the maze of TSVs. Kendra felt her face flush with anger toward the Elec-Tech who slighted Ying. She turned to see his face. His back was to her.

Ying's feelings were hurt. If not for the effects of the recent events involving the Group, he might have ignored the Elec-Tech's comment. He had to prove his viability. The Captain made that clear.

He blurted, "It was a long, shiny object. Not a flattened, dark object like a meteorite. I saw that much."

The Elec-Tech laughed. "Now, Trainee, why didn't you say you saw it? There you have it." His last comment was directed toward the others at his table, confirmation of his superior knowledge. "Even the Trainee recognized the object that hit us was probably a projectile. Someone tried to harm us. We were attacked. It's a poorly kept secret that a course alteration was made. That never happens. Supposedly, it occurred to avoid an uncharted asteroid. Maybe it is an alien vessel that we are evading, one bent on our destruction. We don't have any weapons, you know. Flight is our only defense." The voice was smug.

"I didn't say it was a projectile ..." Ying stammered. He did not want to be involved in any further conspiracy theories.

"You didn't say it wasn't. If it wasn't a meteorite, what else could it be? But - that's based on rumors. Who knows? Maybe it's nothing. But we are far off course."

"Kendra? Kendra, are you listening?"

Kendra was jerked back to her table conversation. Five curious faces stared at her, including Kevin San JiuJiu-Jiushi, 26. "What?" She felt her face heat. "I'm sorry. I was thinking of something." Her stomach churned, worse than it had been doing during the last month.

Kevin worked in Stasis, a young Gen 3. "We just asked if there is any more news about the new wheat strain." He smiled warmly.

Her stomach flipped. Kendra's mind raced. She had to recall whether the wheat was a secret that she would have only shared with her closest, most trusted friends, the Group – and should not have. It was an inopportune time for her to engage in further conversation about a secret. She remembered it was not a dark secret and felt a flush of relief that she did not vomit from the intense rush of anxiety. "Harvest in another couple of days. It looks good – but I'm a root crop Trainee, not grains."

Kevin laughed. "You're being modest. You could grow anything. You may be a Trainee, but you already have adult responsibilities with your own Grow Room. Everyone knows about the extraordinary redhead in Hydroponics."

Kendra blushed and smiled. The heat in her face caused tears to form in her eyes. "You ... the wheat shows great promise. More bread and cereals."

"That's good," replied one of the female Gen 3's. "It would be nice to have more bread with our meals. She reached over and touched Kevin's forearm. "Maybe we could put a little more meat on this one's bones if we had more bread." She laughed and her eyes twinkled.

The woman had a mate. She was in her late thirties. Kendra could not stop her frown from forming. Her topaz eyes darkened. "I think his bones look just fine." Kevin's disarming laughter softened her reaction. She immediately regretted her words when the other three women giggled at her, especially Tiffany. Tiffany knew about her infatuation with Kevin, the youngest Gen 3 – a man without a mate.

"True," the woman said, "but he could be a little more like Len San Wu with big pecs." All the women laughed aloud. The woman added, barely above a whisper, "But then - he might have the same reputation."

Kendra was not sure what the closing comment meant, but she laughed to go along. Across the room, she saw Maddie's curious look. Without further comment, she excused herself from the table. "I need to go to the bathroom. Tiffany, do you need to go with me?"

Tiffany laughed. "I think not. Go pee."

Kendra knew Maddie was still watching her. As she walked toward the doorway, she rolled her eyes to indicate where she was going. Maddie gave a barely noticeable nod.

Other than the outside door, the bathroom was an open room. There was no privacy, no stalls or partitions, no place to hide. And the seats were crowded together. Good manners dictated that you kept your eyes away from anyone else in the room. Kendra was relieved that she was the only person in the room. She squatted on one of the small stools so she would not look suspicious. Within moments, Maddie came into the bathroom and did a quick scan of the area.

Maddie lowered her waistcloth and took a seat near Kendra. She whispered, "What is it?"

"The Mech-Tech's found what's described as a projectile that breached the hull. Ying was part of the repair Crew. The Gen 3s seem to think it was from a weapon used by an alien vessel – the rogue asteroid we changed course to avoid."

Maddie stared at the floor a moment until she finished peeing. She actually had to go. "I haven't heard that. Do you think it's true?"

"Another secret," Kendra replied with an eyebrow raise.

"True." Maddie stood and redressed. "Maybe Rex knows something. He was somewhat involved with the course calculation. Keep listening. By the way, is Jana eating at a different time?"

"I don't know, but I can eat at the first chow time tomorrow to see."

"Good. I'll go at the third chow time. Where's your Trainer?"

"She ate earlier. That was always her preferred schedule. Tiffany accompanied me. I saw Rex's mother was with him."

"Yes. That probably won't happen again," Maddie said curtly. "Della despises Melba."

"That's not fun at mealtime."

"Not at all." Maddie changed subject back to the original. "I can get word to Sean about the projectile. He can pass it along to Rex in the males' room. Maybe Rex knows something."

"It's going to take a while to have that conversation, isn't it?"

"What choice do we have?" Maddie asked.

"Maybe we could ignore it," Kendra replied with a shrug. "By the way, I like your hair."

Maddie ran her fingers through her four-inch hair and felt the strands drop away after a very short run. She skewed her face. "I feel naked without it."

"What prompted you to cut it?"

Maddie paused before answering. Honesty was the only real option. "The Captain said I had to conform." She changed the subject quickly, "You go out first, since you came in first." She watched her buxom, freckled friend leave the bathroom. Kendra's breasts were full, growing as she quickly approached adulthood. Her own breasts were small in comparison to Kendra's. Actually, even compared to Marly's.

⁂

Maddie sat at Della's console. Della sat behind her, to one side, observing. Maddie was monitoring the atmosphere of Humanity One, most of it. It was done under Della's authority as an adult. The console's lights and screen were mesmerizing – and generally boring. Too often, Maddie's eyes diverted to glance around her. There was not a lot of activity and no one seemed concerned even though Humanity One was off the Innovator's course. She wondered about Jana. The Captain Trainee no longer roamed the Con-Sys Room, pretending to be important and busy. She wanted to ask someone, even Della, but was afraid to mention her name, for fear of making things worse for her friend. In all likelihood, the Captain was punishing her by making her continue her training with the Second-in-Command on the other shift. Isolating Jana from her friends. Cesar probably did not want Jana in his sight. He was an old, bitter man, and he always got his way.

Maddie needed to contact Rex, to give him the information that Kendra overheard. Sean was the key, but, because of his age and stage of development as a Con-Sys Tech Trainee, he was still doing his training in the Training Room. She worried about the young teen. He was deeply affected by the Decision Room meeting. Neither he nor

Marly had been acting normally in the days leading up to the meeting. In any case, she hoped Rex could access the information to prove or disprove the rumors.

After two days of creative questioning of Della, Maddie was able to devise a scenario question that required a computer demonstration to answer. The demonstration could not be done at an operational console in the Con-Sys Room. Della took Maddie to the Con-Sys training room at the end of their day. Sean was in the training room with his sire and Trainer, Blake, just as Maddie hoped he would be. Nearly forty-eight hours after the Decision Room meeting, Maddie found herself sitting beside Sean at the same computer screen. The question she devised was intricate enough, and serious enough, that Della and Sean's sire, Baker, decided it would be valuable for both Trainees to learn the lesson together. Maddie knew they would. She also knew the two Trainers would leave them alone to work through the scenario rather than stand over them, coaching them through it. The Trainees would learn better if they found the answers on their own, even if by trial and error.

Finally, alone, Maddie whispered, "Sean, get a message to Rex. Tell him the asteroid is an alien vessel. The proof is in the hull break projectile." She did not want to say too many words. Sean would forget some of them.

Sean was shocked. "I can't do that. The Captain will recycle me."

"No, he won't. That was just a threat," Maddie did not expect resistance. Sean always responded positively to anything a female asked of him.

Sean whispered urgently. "You don't understand. Marly and I were caught ..." he paused, unsure whether to complete the sentence. He did not. "The Captain was very clear."

Maddie did not waste much time on thoughts of the precocious Medical Trainee or what Marly and Sean could have done, other than they were much too young. "Sean, I need you to pass that along to Rex."

"Why don't you do it?"

"I can't go where he goes. You can use the bathroom by the Mess Hall. Simply tell him and leave. He'll know what to do." Maddie felt her frustration building. Fear of discovery was worsened by Sean's reticence.

"I'm afraid to."

They needed to make keystrokes to indicate they were working to solve the scenario all the time they were alone. Maddie keyed quickly and input the solution. "Sean, we have less than half a minute while they verify from their terminal. Will you do it?"

Sean's jaw was set. He reluctantly nodded. "Okay. What was the message?"

"The asteroid may be an alien vessel. The hull breach was a projectile." Maddie stared at Sean's profile. He was afraid to look at her. She heard Della and Blake approaching. "I think we got it, Sean. What do you think?"

Sean kept his eyes on the screen, his neck erect and stiff. "I think so."

The scenario response was critiqued until both Trainers decided the Trainees properly understood how to react in real time. The training session was a success.

~⚉~

Rex was with Stan during the next meal. Della was more at ease, laughing and enjoying the meal break. Two other Gen 3s joined them and engaged in conversation that did not include the Gen 4 components at the table. Maddie nervously watched Sean at his table. The boy was almost afraid to look up from his plate. Finally, he glanced her direction. She made a face that indicated she wanted him to do something. She was sure he knew what it meant. She had to be careful, to not be noticed. Even so, Rex saw her and gave her a questioning look. She used her foot to touch his shin beneath the table and nodded toward Sean who was walking to the bathroom. Rex understood.

Maddie nervously waited to see the two Gen 4s return – singly - from the bathroom. Rex returned first and flashed a smile of acknowledgement as he took his seat. Sean had done his job well. Later, Sean cautiously entered the Mess Hall, paler than normal and apparently expecting to be confronted – or ambushed. Maddie smiled reassurance as he carefully slid onto the bench at his table. He nervously returned the smile and continued eating his meal, visibly relieved now that his deed was done.

Maddie would have to wait for a response from Rex. She hoped it would not take another two full days.

CHAPTER 19

LOST TIME

Cesar could not get comfortable in the Chair. His back ached. His head throbbed, filled with unresolved issues. Joseph sat silently in the Trainee Chair, eyes glazed, either zoned or locked on something straight ahead. Cesar tried to follow his son's eyes, to see what they saw. They led to a single console - Della San Qi and her Trainee, Maddie. Cesar closed his eyes for a moment and slowly shook his head. Joseph had to get past his heartache. Jana made her decision to engage in immature activities. No one influenced her. If Jana was weak enough to allow someone such as a Gen 4 Con-Sys Trainee to influence her to do what she did, she was not worthy to be Captain. Joseph had to understand that ... or Cesar would have to re-evaluate Joseph. The role of Captain was too critical for self-doubt, for second guessing, or for blaming others. Premier Paul did his duty. Doctor Katherine did her duty. They did not like it, but they did it – just like the Captain was required to do.

Cesar watched Maddie. He wanted to blame her, but it was not in him to do that. The Con-Sys Trainee would become an adult within a matter of weeks. Her efficiency reports were stellar. She would make an excellent Con-Sys Tech. She was ready. She had even greater potential. Her rebellious nature was the result of her curious mind. A curious mind was an anathema to a structured society, but he admired those who were curious. They never became lost in the routine. Controlled, they found answers where others did not even recognize the questions. Uncontrolled, they could cause chaos. Maddie just needed controls. She needed parameters. She needed to understand the value of the MGR and learn to use the Innovators' guidance. With that, all her questions would be answered. Without her hair, she seemed more subdued. She was better off under Della's watchful eyes – and his.

His greatest mistake, as yet unconfirmed, might be his seeming disregard for the MGR. He approved the course change, the evasive maneuver. Humanity One was off course, engaged in a maneuver that was calculated to avoid a Mission ending collision with the rogue object. If Chief Scientist Gail were correct, the maneuver would return Humanity One to the correct course, the one calculated and established by the Innovators. The wide arc would require two-hundred-seven hours, fourteen and one-half minutes to complete. If the calculations were correct – any deviation from the Innovators' plan had to be suspect, the vessel carrying the only hope for the survival of humanity was one-hundred hours into the arc. In one-hundred-seven hours and some minutes, Humanity One would be safe, though severely off schedule. Seventy-five hours and fifteen minutes behind schedule to be exact. Humanity One would arrive in Earth Two's stellar system more than three days late. Earth Two and its moons would not be properly aligned to greet Humanity One, to provide the exact gravity neutral positioning required for the final execution of the Mission.

Cesar squirmed as thoughts swirled through his mind. Twenty-five thousand people who trusted the Crew to transport them to Earth Two, to revive them so they could save humanity, might never see the outside of their TSVs. He, Captain Cesar Er Yi, would be responsible for the failure. A future Captain ... maybe Joseph ... and a future

Scientist ... maybe one of the Gen 4 Sci-Techs ... would have to find the correct solution to the delay or to the final orbital insertion – if there was one to find.

Cesar's mind filled with Premier Paul's image. He allowed the Communicator to activate. "It is done." A chill ran though the stoic Captain. An obligatory acknowledgement ended the Communicator link. The young people failed to understand the complexities of life, of duty, and of the Communicators. All Communicator exchanges were recorded, to be deleted at the Captain's discretion – or when the Captain had time. They knew that. It was part of their training. But – they tended to forget that simple fact. Words. Ideas. Thoughts. Images. Everything was there for review if needed. More critically, the inexperienced user would often invoke a connection that was unintended, especially if the mind was concerned about another person's awareness. Jana was worried that Cesar would discover her in his quarters when she opened her Communicator to talk with Rex. Her fears. Her disdain for others. Everything was revealed to Cesar in an instant.

The Gen 4's who identified themselves as the Group were all exemplary Trainees. High IQs. Curious minds. Capable of successfully guiding Humanity One through space for their part of the journey. But – they lacked the discipline that had been imposed upon Gen 2 and Gen 3. Cesar feared the loss of dedicated focus and discipline that exemplified Gen 1. Without it, too many questions would be asked, questions that either did not need to be answered right away or did not pertain to the Mission. Distractions from success. The Innovators, through the MGR, were very clear about Crew creativity. Creativity created untenable risks, risks for which the Innovators could not anticipate solutions. Stop creativity during the journey and limit the risks to those things already known. Yet, Cesar wondered if maybe human nature was unsuited to long space journeys, generations of confined space and confined thinking. To someone less dedicated, the conditions inside Humanity One might seem like a prison or bondage – no allowance for personal choice. That was why Maddie had to cut her hair; to demonstrate the necessity for convention and conformity. To focus her mind on the Mission and her part in it, nothing else. The Mission did not allow anything else.

Cesar touched his computer screen and selected an icon. He settled back in the Chair and closed his eyes. Somewhere within Humanity One's computer core an executable file initiated a programmed action. Three solemn tones were emitted by the vessel's speakers. He did not open his eyes until they were completed. He did not see whether anyone else noticed or reacted. He did not need to know. Haggling with Joseph, convincing Joseph that there was only one option delayed the process, made the end more painful for the both of them.

The seventy-five point two five hours worried him. It worried him more than the fact that Humanity One was not yet back on its programmed course. The calculations were there for returning to the Innovators' course. But - there was nothing in place, no calculations to recapture the time lost. Chief Gail was very clear that Humanity One lacked the ability to regain time. Even so, Cesar knew the decision was the right one. Without it, the vessel that carried the hope of humanity would be lost. The original flight plan would have Humanity One and the rogue scattered across space. Without the change, Humanity One would be a tattered and shattered cluster of twisted metal shards, nothing more than space debris. He wondered if any of the humans in Stasis would have been momentarily awakened, aware long enough to grasp the scope of the failure. He hoped not.

As it was, even with what seemed to be a Mission catastrophe, Humanity One was still viable and filled with humans capable of saving the Mission. Cesar eagerly – though desperately - clung to the belief that his actions, his heresy, had saved not only Humanity One but also the Mission. He also believed he had saved the people most likely to solve the problem. For sanity's sake, he could believe nothing less.

Chief Gail, so eager to replace Gen 2 Chief Scientist Robert and to resolve the rogue collision crisis, was less eager to face the current crisis. She had no solution. She saw no solution. The proton drives were nearly depleted ... or would be ... by the time the collision averting course change was completed. Realignment of the solar sails and the stellar engine parasols would require precise timing and more energy than normal. In effect, there was no energy for propulsion beyond the essential navigational moves. To recoup the lost energy reserve - not that there was ever a large reserve - would require at least another generation. Even if Gen 4 developed a solution to regain the lost time, Gen 5 would be the first generation to have the resources to implement the correction. Or ... it could be Gen 6 if the current life span did not hold steady. Cesar moved his head to relieve tension in his neck.

The energy recovery options were at best a hope. The Innovators calculated every object, from star systems to roving comets, into the course plan of Humanity One. The power of gravity to push and pull for navigation and propulsion. The strength of solar winds to shove against the solar sails and drive the vessel steadily forward. The energy provided by particles ejected by a star system's sun that were captured by the stellar engines and used to power the proton drives, and the vessel's electrical systems. All those calculations, designed to span twenty-four decades, were dependent on proximity – and timing. Timing was critical throughout the calculated journey. Cesar's head pounded as he considered the reality of the situation. He wished he knew more astrophysics. He wished he understood mathematics. There was too much that he did not know. He relied on the Sci-Eng Techs for the answers. He had to face the fact that the Chief of Science and Engineering had no answers.

The screen on the Captain's computer changed background color, from its normal dull gray to off-white. An alarm. A subtle reminder that a routine function was due. Cesar pulled himself upright in the Chair. Business as usual. "Joseph. Status."

As routinely as ever, Joseph elicited an *"All normal"* from each Con-Sys Tech. The only thing out of the ordinary was that Della's Trainee spoke for her. Cesar nodded his approval and made his entry in the Captain's Log.

CHAPTER 20

FINDINGS

Rex was beyond suspicious. He was borderline paranoid. If the meteor that struck Humanity One was in truth a projectile, he wondered why the Captain would suppress that knowledge. Already on a slippery footing with the Captain, the Sci-Eng Trainee knew his investigation could lead to disaster, not just for him, but for anyone remotely associated with him. The Group was at risk. But so, apparently, was Humanity One and the Mission. He had to care about the Mission more than anything else. The Mission was all that mattered in the long run.

Rex's history of delving into arcane data bases, background knowledge of the sciences that drove Humanity One's Mission, was known, understood, and accepted. Few people cared to know the background details, even among the Sci-Eng Technicians. Even Chief Gail glossed over much of the science history. She was good at mathematics. She did not need the history of math to be good at calculations. The MGR gave her all she needed to perform her functions, reason enough to use rote calculations as they were intended. Rex's curiosity drove him to know more, to understand more. No one questioned it when he searched the vessel's computers. That fact helped some, but it did not erase his paranoia. Someone could easily be monitoring his computer activities. Cesar might not have been satisfied to simply keep the Group members separate.

Maddie's message was somewhat unclear. Sean was terrified. His bowels released while he was stammering the message. It was a good thing the young Trainee was sitting on the toilet. Rex saw the hidden smile on Maddie's face when he returned to the Mess Hall before Sean. He could read Maddie's face better than anyone – even her own mother. The two of them were privy to a secret that might never be revealed; would not have to be revealed because they already knew it. If Ying had not made his cryptic comments earlier, Rex might not have grasped Sean's message. The projectile posed an entirely different potential for Mission risk. Sean did not say it, but if the meteor was truly a weaponized projectile, the course change might be a futile endeavor. His curiosity, his need to know, overcame his paranoia for the moment.

Chief Gail's mathematical smugness was her weakness. Her common passcode was *pi* to the fourth decimal – with the ellipsis at the end. Rex could access her personal files from any Sci-Eng computer terminal. His skills with computers assured that. He searched for any passcode protected files that Chief Gail might have. One file caught his attention, $E=MC2$. A basic equation known to any scientist. The basis of understanding most physics principles. Same passcode as her system passcode. Not very creative for someone who had deposed her Chief for lack of viable creativity.

Rex read the file with interest. A convoluted attempt to understand energy sources available in space. Interstellar space offered fewer opportunities than the space within the grasp of a star system. Stars emit tremendous amounts of energy, most of it projected unimpededly outward until it seemed to dissipate. Chief Gail's file was several years old but showed recent activity. Her work was predicated on the notion that there was insignificant available energy beyond the heliopause, after the point of terminal shock. Even the Innovators knew the interstellar medium offered opportunities. The stellar engines relied upon capturing the energy of particles within the void. He smiled to himself. At least he was not the only one trying to understand energy options.

Rex found a protected file named *pir2h*. After a moment, his brain separated the characters into a readable name, *pi r2 h* – the volume of a cylinder. The projectile was described as a cylinder with a tapered end. The formula Chief Gail used to name the file was probably not complete, but it was understandable. He opened the file. Chief Gail included measurements and a variety of metallurgical notations. She determined the object as an unknown crafted alloy ejected at extremely high velocity from a projectile weapon. She was open with her interpretations and beliefs regarding the reason for what she described as an attack, as well as her thoughts about how to counter the attack. The file was, after all, protected, only to be read by her. Rex found her thought processes for Humanity One's defense to be unsupported by facts, largely emotional and speculative. Humanity One had no weapons, no defensive capabilities. In her writing, he saw some of the same arrogant attitude that she exhibited the day she replaced Chief Robert.

Rex did not know where Maddie's suspicions about the hull breach and its possible connection to the rogue came from, but her concerns were valid. Humanity One ... humanity ... faced a doubly dangerous problem. The vessel would be – already was - days behind schedule which put it at risk of failing to safely make its rendezvous with Earth Two, plus it might be in the crosshairs of an alien enemy. From what he could determine, Mission failure was more than likely. He had ideas that could alleviate one, but not the other. He had no secret weapon on hand. His paranoia was replaced by a sense of urgency.

A full day passed before Rex was able to surreptitiously nod to

Maddie in the Mess Hall. He saw her eyes widen with understanding. They needed to talk, to compare what they knew and try to comprehend what it meant. Knowing the projectile secret did not answer anything; it only created more questions.

Stan was busy at a computer terminal. It was his assignment to recalculate the course based upon Humanity One's current position. Within that calculation was a precise measurement of energy resources available. Rex moved a chair close to his trainer's side, careful to not disturb Stan's thought processes. Finally, Stan looked up at Rex who was taller than him even when seated. He smiled. "Have you been learning from the archives?"

Rex nodded and replied, "I have." His first thought was driven by paranoia, whether that was Stan's way of letting him know that he was monitoring his research. His second thought was that he needed Stan to continue the conversation. He did not want to drive the topic too much. He had an idea that Stan needed to hear, to support. He knew not to push the matter too hard. His sire might not be supportive of what he had to suggest.

Stan glanced back at the screen, "I just don't understand what you see in those old files. Too much information, a distraction from our Mission. But enjoy it while you can." He chuckled. "In a very short time, when you reach adulthood and are assigned adult responsibilities, you won't have time for idle research." He shook his head as he continued to look at the work he was doing on the computer. "Whew! This course alteration is going to be tight on energy. We missed something in our original calculation."

Rex leaned forward to look at a line of data Stan indicated with an index finger. It provided him the perfect segue. "There is something we haven't considered."

"What would that be?" Stan leaned closer to the screen, searching for an error in his input data. "I'm sure I've captured all the available data."

"You have. But – there is more data that can be used." Rex watched Stan's slow-to-develop reaction. Past discussions such as he was about to introduce had always ended with a stern warning. "We can capture more energy from the interstellar medium. The Innovators restricted their focus to protons. By focusing on protons, they ignored the other particles and their energy equivalent."

Stan's face darkened into a scowl. "We've had this discussion. Your thoughts border on heresy. Haven't you created enough trouble for yourself already? There will be no forgiveness the next time."

Rex controlled his body language, remaining visibly subservient and inquisitive while he verbally challenged his sire. "I don't mean to question the Innovators. I am using their knowledge from the archives. They focused on protons only because that is all they needed to support the course they calculated."

"And that is why we remain committed to their calculations, to the plans they made for us." Stan glanced around nervously, as if afraid someone would overhear their words. "Keep your mouth shut and prepare for viability as an adult."

Rex's replied with words that spilled faster than he would normally say them, afraid Stan would stop him before he could finish. "Sir, your own calculations show we will be out of energy reserves by the time we return to the correct course. We will also be more than three days behind schedule. That has a tremendous ripple effect on the success of the Mission. One missed rendezvous after another. We need to get back on schedule. We need to increase our speed. For that, we need more energy for the proton drives. I know how to get more energy without significant change."

Stan shook his head and held up one hand. "Stop it! Stop making crazy claims. I don't mind conversations about this in our quarters, but I won't tolerate that behavior in public. The Innovators considered every possibility in their calculations. They put the best solutions in the MGR. Don't you think they would have provided for more energy if it were possible? Just stop it!"

"But, Stan, it's not a failure on the part of the Innovators. They simply didn't need to do it. We do," Rex pleaded.

"No! Don't you think that if it were possible, the Innovators would have done it, or at least mentioned it? Enough wasting my time and yours."

Rex's heart hurt as he watched Stan close the conversation with a telling shift closer to the computer. Stan physically blocked any further discussion. Rex knew he had the answer, the solution. He could not just give up. "Stan, you don't understand. If we don't do something quickly, even before we complete the alteration, Humanity One ... all of us ... are at risk of being destroyed. That rogue is an alien vessel. They've fired upon us once. They will probably do it again."

Stan's face was twisted with anger when he turned to face Rex. "Stop it before I have to report your heresy to Chief Gail. There is no place for speculative, inciteful comments like that. You are being distracted by your own imagination ... and that of Maddison Si Wu-Qi. Go to quarters and let me work."

Rex was dismissed ... and heart broken. Ash-faced, he walked away from Stan's workspace and to his room in the family quarters.

CHAPTER 21

CLANDESTINE MEETING

Maddie recognized Rex's nod as affirmation of Kendra's overheard conversation. During the next chow time, she signaled Kendra to meet her in the restroom. The two friends managed to get time alone together without creating suspicion. "It's true," she whispered, even though no one else was in the room with them.

"How did you find out?" Kendra asked from her position on a toilet.

"Rex told me."

Kendra perked up. "You talked to Rex?"

"Not exactly, but I was able to get a message to him. He checked and got back to me."

"What did he say?"

Maddie realized her enthusiasm was overstated. "He nodded to let me know it was true."

"That's it?" Kendra was disappointed.

"Well, it's kind of hard to actually talk, you know," Maddie replied defensively. "Maybe we all need to meet."

"How? We're under a microscope."

"I'll think of something," Maddie resolutely said. "You want to go out first, or me?"

"Go ahead. My stomach is bothering me. I think I ate something that isn't agreeing with me." Kendra was pale. She showed signs of whatever was ailing her.

Maddie "accidently" walked into the Con-Sys training room. Sean's sire, Blake, smiled and greeted her.

"Hello Maddie. Do you have another scenario?"

"Oh, no. Not really. I was wondering if Della was in here. I didn't see her in the Con-Sys Room. Our day is over. I'm surprised you and Sean are still in here."

Blake laughed. "Sean is practicing another pump failure response. You know how many times those response sessions have to be done before they become second nature."

Maddie grinned and nodded her head. "Yes. Yes, I do. Well – I'll look elsewhere for Della. Do you need a drink or anything – since you're going to be here a while?"

Blake was caught off guard by the question. "Ah ... actually, I do need to go to the restroom. If you don't mind, can you answer Sean's questions ... if he has any ... while I go?"

Maddie's ruse to distract Blake so she could set Sean up with a message for Rex did not even have to be used. Blake momentarily forgot the restrictions. As soon as Blake left the room, Maddie whispered to Sean, "Tell Rex we're going to meet in Sanitation tomorrow night – after everyone is asleep."

"I ..."

Maddie scowled, "Don't argue. Tell Rex and Zack during our late meal. I'll tell Kendra, Jana and Marly."

Sean blushed red and kept his eyes on his computer screen. "Okay."

Maddie was standing nonchalantly by the door when Blake returned. "Thank you, Maddie. I forgot I wasn't supposed to leave Sean alone with non-adult females. I'm sorry I put you in that position."

Maddie appeared nonchalant about Blake's faux pas. "That's okay. I just stood here by the door. Sean didn't have any questions. See you tomorrow – or maybe in the Mess Hall." She left bemusedly wondering what had transpired in Sean's life besides the Group break-up. Blake's reference to non-adult females was odd to say the least. Sean's angst was deeply rooted.

❧

Maddie was the first to arrive in Sanitation. It was an area filled with smells, most of them objectionable in nature. The machinery was automatic, only requiring human intervention when something went awry or when loading recyclables. After the point of entry into the recycle equipment, the San-Re Techs generally waited for the final output. Maddie saw one San-Re Tech, the "night shift" attendant, Gen 3 San-Re Technician, Bill San Liushi-Liuliu. Most recycling activities that required humans took place during the first twelve hours of the day. At night, the equipment that was in use ran with minimal oversight required. Sanitary Recycling was probably the only section that did not require around-the-clock staffing.

Kendra was the next to arrive. "Where are the others?"

"I haven't seen anyone else yet. I couldn't get close to Marly to tell her. Did you?"

Kendra's nose wriggled. "Whew! I like the smell of Hydroponics better. No. I couldn't either. Either Pamela or Doctor Katherine was glued to her side all the time. I suppose they really don't want her to have anything to do with us."

Maddie shook her head slowly. "That's sad. It's not like we were doing something that was going to hurt anyone. She's a brilliant girl. She's going to make a wonderful doctor. I suppose we've lost her as a friend until adulthood."

"Is Jana coming too?"

Maddie shook her head. "I haven't seen her since our meeting with the Captain. She's training on Second's shift, I suppose. That would be the best way to keep her away from us – from our bad influence."

Kendra shook her head in unison with Maddie. "Sad. Jana is already unhappy about her chances of becoming Captain anytime soon. That has to be hard for her. And – I'm not sure we influenced her one way or the other."

Maddie nodded. "She knew what she was doing as much as we did. Ah ... there's Rex. Hello Rex."

Rex smiled greeting to both females.

Maddie loved his smile. It felt familiar. She returned the smile. She was eager to hear what he had to say about the projectile.

Kendra grinned; her freckles less noticeable in the dimly lit Sanitary Recycling Room.

Zack hesitantly entered the Sanitation Room. With a tentative smile, he approached the others. "Why are we meeting here?" He looked nervously at the humming machines that were running through programmed cycles. His room was crypt-like silent. Sanitary Recycling was noisier than any other area. After the Captain's meeting with the Group, Recycling had unsavory connotations to the young Sta-Tech.

"Limited Crew. It's the only place we can meet and not be discovered," Maddie responded quickly. "As soon as Sean gets here, Rex can tell us what he's learned."

Zack shook his head, "Should we be meeting at all?"

"Of course not," Maddie replied sternly, "but how else are we going to update one another on all these secrets that are being kept from us?"

Zack's eyes widened. "We almost got recycled for our meetings. I don't want to go through that again. We will get recycled if we're caught. I'm not sure knowing their secrets is worth the risk."

"Then, let's don't get caught," Maddie said. She looked toward the door. "Where's Sean?" She was impatient.

"Maybe we shouldn't wait for Sean," Rex replied. "He's worried about getting caught. Too much so. He has something else in his mind. He's terrified. Is Jana coming?"

"I haven't seen her since the meeting," Maddie answered, unhappy that she was responding to the same question again. "Go ahead, Rex. Tell us what you discovered. We can't stay here too long – or we will be discovered."

"Okay. I'll make it brief." Rex looked around to make sure no one else was nearby. "The rogue is not an asteroid, at least, the Captain doesn't think so. It's an alien vessel that fired a projectile weapon at us at least once." He paused to allow the others to ponder what he had told them. The questions came rapidly.

Zack asked, "Are they going to attack again? What can we do?"

Kendra asked, "Do we even have weapons? Did we really change course to avoid collision, or are we trying to outrun them?"

Rex held up his hand, "I don't know a lot more than what I just told you. I don't know if they are going to attack again. I do know we don't have weapons. Yes, we really did change course to avoid collision – because we can't outrun them. Humanity One is not equipped to increase speed."

"So, there is nothing we can do?" Maddie asked.

"Not if we continue our blind adherence to the MGR," Rex replied.

"What does the MGR have to do with it?" Kendra asked.

"If we accept the fact that the Innovators made a mistake ... or two, maybe we can assume there are options other than what is written in the MGR. For one thing, I know we can make changes that will increase our available energy, that will give us more power to run our proton drives at a higher output. That could give us greater speed. But I don't think anyone is willing to think the Innovators made an error."

Kendra seemed to shrug off the comment about the Innovators.

"How will increased energy help anything? Can we go faster? Can we outrun the aliens?"

"We can go faster if we have enough energy and make some changes to the drives. Maybe we can outrun them. Better than that, we can get back on schedule, so we don't miss Earth Two."

"Miss Earth Two? What schedule?" Maddie asked.

"The course change to avoid collision will cause us to be more than three days behind schedule. That's a massive difference for our mission. In fact, it's a failure difference."

"So, we traded one problem for another?"

"Better late than never ... to a certain extent," Rex replied with a shrug. "We can overcome the schedule – if the Captain will allow me to do it. We could not overcome a collision."

"So, what do we do about the aliens? What if they come after us?"

"I'm not sure what that answer is. It will all come down to energy availability. With enough energy, we can go faster. I know how to get the needed energy, but blind adherence to the MGR won't allow it. With the extra energy, maybe we can enhance the proton drives to work as a weapon."

Kendra subtly motioned for silence. Bill was approaching the Group. Everyone grew silent and looked toward Bill. Their fear grew.

"What are you doing in Sanitation?" Bill asked. "No one ever comes down here. The smells can be disgusting at times."

Maddie was a quick thinker. "We're looking for a friend of ours."

Bill grinned. "Funny place to look for a friend. Like I said, no one comes here – not intentionally. Who's your friend?"

"Gen 4 Captain Trainee, Jana Si Yu-Liu." Maddie knew Jana was not in the area, but her name would carry some weight and, hopefully, stop any suspicions.

Bill's eyes dropped and his grin disappeared. "I'm sorry. I thought her friends would have known."

"Known what?" Maddie asked, shocked by Bill's tone.

"Like I said, I'm sorry. It's tragic. So young. She appeared outwardly healthy, but that doesn't mean much. She recycled."

"When?" Rex asked. The others were agape at the news.

"Two days ago, I think."

"What happened?" Rex challenged.

Bill resisted the challenge. "I don't know what happens to people that causes them to be recycled. I just perform my recycle duties."

"I'm sorry. I didn't mean to sound pushy," Rex apologized. He fought to keep his emotions in check. "It's just that we didn't know anything was wrong with her. Don't they tell you anything?"

Bill nodded acceptance of Rex's apology. "I was the one who entered the body into recycle. She passed in Medical. Heart malformity is what the records said. It should have been caught when she was a baby. There's a lot of heart issues, especially among young Gen 4s and Gen 5s."

"Gen 5?" Maddie regained her senses. "I didn't know there were any Gen 5 babies."

Bill smiled ruefully, "More than you would think, considering Gen 4's aren't much more than babies themselves."

Kendra's face reddened, noticeable even in the dim lighting, "We're almost adults."

Bill shook his head, unyieldingly, "Only because the age of adulthood was lowered to allow time for training before demise. We will all recycle before we reach forty-five. There's nothing that can be done to stop it."

Rex controlled his emotions. Jana was volatile, but she was a friend — a healthy friend. "I don't expect us to stop it, but I also don't expect someone to do anything to accelerate it." He caught Maddie's eyes and cut his toward the door.

Bill's face twisted querulously. "Accelerate it? You think something bad happened."

Rex shook his head. He realized he had allowed his emotions to seep through. "No. Not at all. It's just that Jana was a close friend to all of us."

Bill nodded understanding. "We will all lose close friends. But, after recycling, they are still with us. Their molecules and atoms live on in following generations." Pragmatic, conditioned words.

Maddie, still shaken, said, "Well, I suppose we found Jana. Just not what we expected. Thank you, Bill. We need to go now. We have our duties." She wanted out of Sanitation, away from the recycling machines that they all would enter eventually.

Outside Sanitation, Maddie whispered to the Group, "Let's meet again in two days. We need to tell Sean and Marly – if they will come."

"Here?" Kendra asked with a shudder.

Maddie nodded. "It's the safest place."

CHAPTER 22

MEDICAL

Maddie could not focus. From her chair in front of the Con-Sys console, with Della nearby, her eyes occasionally strayed toward the Captain. It was not hard to see the tension on his face. It was not hard to tell there was a darkness surrounding Cesar and Joseph – and a division. They seldom interacted, not in the same way they did before the meeting. Businesslike was the best way to explain their interactions. No emotion, at least no emotions that were allowed to come to the surface. Jana was gone. Passed to recycle. Congenital heart malformation. Maddie tried to rationalize what her mind declared was irrational. She could not make sense of a teenager recycling because of heart failure. Not Jana. Jana was hale and hardy as far as anyone could see. The thought that Jana's health – the health of every Crew member – was another of the secrets angered her. Marly, in one of her open moments, had revealed things that seemed farfetched at the time, but the thought that the precocious girl's words were more accurate than anyone could imagine crossed Maddie's mind. Cryptic if not secret.

The night visit to Sanitation left Maddie struggling emotionally. In her world, the world of Humanity One and Crew duty, the only thing that should cause fear was Mission failure. From her earliest memories, from her earliest lessons, Mission success was primary – the reason for human existence on Humanity One. Even the inevitability of recycling was not something to fear. A good life lived, one that furthered Humanity One's safe journey toward the 8th Generation, did not simply end at recycle. In the end, every atom in each generation along the journey would be there for colonization of Earth Two. Eternal existence promised by the success of the Mission. Jana would still be there, was still here – molecularly, atomically. But – it was not as simple as that. Until that moment, until learning of Jana's recycling, Maddie believed it *was* as simple as that. Jana's recycling caused her to question her beliefs. It caused her to lose focus.

"Maddie!" Della's urgent whisper to get her Trainee's attention filled the silence of the Control System Room.

Maddie felt her mother's hand shove her bare shoulder, where her blond hair used to hang. Her mind regained focus. She turned her head to look askance, fully aware of the silence and of eyes. Everyone within line of sight was looking at her. She jumped to her feet and turned to face Joseph. Her vocal cords felt frozen. Her voice cracked when she blurted, "All normal." She plopped into her chair as soon as Joseph acknowledged her response, aware that the questioning eyes slowly turned away, all except Della's.

"What's wrong with you?" Della whispered as the status update continued.

"I ... uh ... nothing. I was just thinking of something." Maddie was embarrassed.

The status update culminated in Joseph's declaration to Cesar, "All normal."

Della spoke softly. "Maddie, are you not feeling well? You haven't been yourself today." The mother's face showed concern. A nearby Gen 3 Con-Sys Tech nodded and smiled understanding.

Maddie wanted to open her heart, to share her emotions regarding the loss of her friend. She knew adults did not do that. Only a few weeks from adulthood, she could not display any weaknesses. To do so might cause her to be deemed unviable, and she knew where that would lead. "I'm tired. I didn't sleep well last night." That was not a lie. After the meeting in Sanitation. She barely slept at all. The information about the likelihood that an alien vessel had attacked Humanity One, the knowledge that it could happen again, roiled her mind. While she understood why the knowledge should not be bandied about as gossip, she did not understand why the Crew would not be allowed to know it, to prepare for another attack, to steel themselves for the potential of non-recyclable doom. The information regarding the course schedule and the energy depletion worried her. It should be shared. Rex said he could solve the problem, but the MGR would not allow it. Jana's heart malformation death should be known. Bill stated that there were several heart malformity deaths among Gen 4s at an early age ... and Gen 5 babies that should not even be conceived yet. If there was a heart malformation epidemic, everyone should know. Jana was her friend. Jana was her first close friend who recycled. Her heart and mind ached over Jana.

"I think you should go to Medical, to make sure you're not ill," Della said. "Now is the best time to do it. Go." There was no room for argument. The mother's words were heavy with concern.

Maddie thought a moment and realized the opportunity a Medical visit could offer. She could talk to Marly, invite her to the next meeting, make sure the young Trainee was okay.

~⚭~

Gen 3 Doctor Aaron San Shisi-Shiwu greeted Maddie when she arrived at Medical. Doctor Aaron was 38 with a bald spot. The baldness would not have been noticed except for the fact that he had not shaved his head for a couple of days. He had a two-day-old 5 o'clock shadow that formed a dark halo around the top of his head. "Why are you here today? Menstrual cramps?"

Maddie was taken aback by the question. "No. I'm just not feeling well."

"Is it your time of month?"

"No!" Maddie answered abruptly. "I'm worried about my heart."

Doctor Aaron pursed his lips. He appeared disappointed. "Maybe you're pregnant. Remove your waistcloth and hop up on the exam table."

"I will not!" Maddie glared at the Doctor. "I am not pregnant! I want my heart checked."

Doctor Aaron paused momentarily. "Very well. Let me pull your records." A nearby console screen came to life as he touched icons. A virtual keyboard allowed him to query the core computer. He studied images of an infant's body scans and read medical summaries attached to the file. He smiled as he returned his attention to Maddie. "Take a seat on the table," he said as he positioned his stethoscope for use. "Let's have a listen to your heart."

Maddie was uncomfortable with Doctor Aaron's hands on her torso during an exam that involved listening to her heart and lungs, taking her temperature, and reading her blood pressure and heart rate. She sighed relief when he stepped away and pointed toward the screen. "Everything sounds good and looks good. Blood pressure is a little high. Your birth records indicate a normal heart and good health. You are as healthy as any woman your age should be. Do you have any other symptoms? Upset stomach? Indigestion? You really could be pregnant."

"I'm NOT pregnant!" Maddie adamantly stated. "I was just worried about my heart. Couldn't it have gone bad after birth?"

Doctor Aaron shook his head. "Anything is possible. Every Gen 4 baby has a thorough medical screening, especially their hearts. Babies with malformed hearts don't live very long. Most pass to recycling within three days."

"That's awful. What about Gen 3 ... and Gen 5?"

"Gen 5 receives the same attention as Gen 4."

Maddie relaxed slightly but remained wary of the overly eager Doctor's interest. "You said Gen 5 receives the same attention. Are there Gen 5 babies?"

"More than there should be," Doctor Aaron replied. "Close quarters. Opportunities abound," he said with a smile. "What is your training?"

"Con-Sys Tech. I'm already qualified and filling a console." Maddie embellished only slightly.

"The tension and stress level has to be high, working that closely with Captain Cesar. He is demanding. Your heart issues are likely nothing more than stress in your new role. I see you're not yet an adult. You probably feel obligated to prove your capabilities to the Captain. To prove you are viable. Learn to relax."

Maddie focused on Doctor Aaron's eyes. They were roving, admiring, as he talked. He did not notice her attention at first. When he did, she smiled demurely. He reacted as she expected he would. "You mentioned Gen 3 but said nothing about them. Are Gen 3s at risk of heart failure?"

"Generation 3 was the first to demonstrate a noticeable increase in cardiovascular issues. The Doctor shrugged lightly, to minimize the severity of the conversation. "Once it was determined that they were prone to heart issues, protocol changed. Every Gen 3 has had a heart risk assessment."

"So, they will live regular lives?"

The Doctor was pleased that the young woman was attentive. "A few have recycled already as a result of heart malformities. That's how it came to the attention of the Medical Office. A number of our Gen 3s are walking timebombs, with cardiovascular systems that are on the verge of collapse. But the remaining members of that generation are as healthy as we could expect inside a space vessel biosphere."

"What does that mean?"

"Most of them should get their 45 years."

Maddie noticed Doctor Aaron was not inclined to include himself in the Gen 3 grouping, probably because he did not want her to focus on his age. His answer did not match the intent of her question. "Are heart issues natural to humans?"

Doctor Aaron moved closer to the exam table. He leaned forward and spoke confidentially, "Not to the extent they are now."

Maddie saw the swagger. The man was going to impress her with his knowledge, and with his willingness to share. That suited her just fine. "What does that mean? Sounds secretive."

Doctor Aaron smiled. "Not exactly secretive. Just not discussed a lot. No need to distract the Crew with unnecessary information. Our gravity on Humanity One is about a third of Earth normal. Our bodies, especially circulatory and skeletal systems, depend on gravity to function properly. Our hearts are forced to work differently under low gravity conditions, hence high blood pressure. Bone density is also affected."

"So, how does that affect us?" Maddie forced herself to not draw back when Doctor Aaron placed a cool hand on her shoulder, a move meant to appear as one of comfort and reassurance. Instead, his action disturbed her.

"More heart problems, even failure after a few years if there are even minor congenital malformities. Shorter bodies because the bones don't develop the same. Weaker bones that would be a problem in Earth normal gravity. Painful osteoarthritis for some as they age."

"The Innovators didn't know about these problems?" Maddie asked.

"Of course, they did. Medical is trained to observe for and prepare to treat known problems associated with space travel. Eyesight. Cardio-vascular – high blood pressure, arrhythmia. Bone weakness. Muscular atrophy. White blood cell count. Even genetic mutations and increased cancer. But – we know what to do."

"Really? My friend recycled a few days ago. It was said to be because of a heart malformity. She was fifteen, almost sixteen." Maddie knew she could shake Aaron's smugness.

As expected, the Doctor's hand dropped away, and he drew back slightly. "That can't be. We haven't had any heart issues that caused recycling in almost a year."

Maddie knew not to press. She got the answer. "Maybe the rumor was wrong." She wondered about the 12-year-old Recycle Trainee that Marly said died of a heart problem. She needed to see Marly. "You know how rumors are when there are secrets. People are compelled to say something about everything."

Aaron laughed lightly. "That is true. So, what secrets do you have to share? I wouldn't want rumors to spread about you."

"All my secrets will pass into recycle with me," Maddie said with a laugh as she slid off the exam table. Her waistcloth slid and bound in her crotch. Rather than unbind it and draw his attention, she ignored it and said, "Thank you, Doctor Aaron. You've made me feel better. Is Marly Si Shiyi-SanShier around? I'd like to tell her hello."

Doctor Aaron was aggravated at being dismissed. It showed. "She should be in the ward, but no one can get near her without Katherine or Pamela standing guard." His tone expressed more emotion than his words.

Maddie found Marly. Marly's eyes darted left and right with fear. She was alone.

"What are you doing here?" Marly whispered urgently. "We can't meet without a chaperone."

"I had my heart checked by Doctor Aaron. I didn't want to pass to recycling like that 12-year-old Recycle Trainee ... or Jana."

Marly averted her eyes. They filled with tears. "I'm sorry, Maddie. I couldn't tell you."

"Secrets, Marly? Really?" Maddie scowled her disapproval.

"Doctors are sworn to secrecy," Marly protested. "We can't discuss medical issues."

Maddie intensely said, "We need to meet alone. Tell me more of your secrets. Our lives depend on it." Maddie looked around. Someone could approach unseen. She did not want to risk exposing either of them to further scrutiny.

⁓⁓⁓

Maddie was compelled to share what she had learned. If nothing more than to serve as a warning for her friends to be cautious. During the late meal, she was able to meet with Kendra in the restroom. The meeting was very short, barely long enough to whisper what Doctor Aaron had inadvertently blurted that put serious doubt about the reason for Jana's passing. She worried about Kendra. The normally cheerful teenager appeared drawn, emotionally and physically.

Fortunately, Rex and his sire sat at a table with Maddie and Della. Without being obvious to the adults, Maddie nudged Rex beneath the table during a conversation she directed toward her duties monitoring the atmosphere and how Sanitary Recycling contributed to scrubbing the air of particulates. Rex understood her message for a clandestine meeting.

Sanitation was unusually quiet. Only one machine was running, humming softly on the far side of the Sanitary Recycling Room. San-Re Tech Bill was nowhere to be seen, which suited Maddie.

As soon as Rex arrived, Maddie grabbed his forearm. "Rex, the

Captain recycled Jana as punishment. She didn't have a heart problem. Marly knew about it. That's why she's terrified."

Rex's face twisted from disbelieve to disgust. He angrily whispered, "This vessel is facing disaster, yet protecting their precious secrets is more important than our lives. I need to talk to the Captain."

"You can't do that! You'll be recycled!"

Rex knew she was right. "Probably, but there are bigger problems than that. The course schedule delay. The rogue ... the alien vessel. And I have a solution. We can't worry about recycling when Humanity One is facing annihilation. If we don't do something, there will be no one to recycle."

Maddie's brow furrowed. "Rex, be careful. The Captain hasn't left his Chair since this began. The course change is serious."

Rex scowled. "I know it's serious. I helped with the calculations. The real issue in all of this is the depletion of our energy resources."

"What does that mean?"

"When we get back on course, not only are we behind schedule and facing a potential attack without a defense, we'll barely be able to sustain Humanity One's environment. Planned course corrections for the next generation or longer will be at risk because of it." Rex paused to allow Maddie to process his message. "Stan and Chief Gail aren't willing to hear me. I have to tell the Captain."

"No, you can't. I think the first thing we need to learn is why Jana was recycled ... and not the rest of us."

"What difference does that make?"

"If Jana was recycled, the Captain – the VLT – must be afraid of something she learned. Something they wanted to make sure no one else learned."

"Bigger secrets." Rex fumed as he considered the loss of a friend, of a valuable Crew member, all to prevent disclosing some secret information. No one was safe if the Captain was willing to recycle his own granddaughter to protect secrets. Too many secrets and unshared information. He wondered if the secret Jana recycled to protect was about Humanity One's current situation – that Mission failure and total destruction was imminent. Rather than tell the Crew, the Captain preferred to maintain the secret because that was the culture of Humanity One. Maybe the Captain decided recycling Jana would be less painful for her than being vented out into space. Maybe the Captain did it out of love for his granddaughter. In reality, Rex knew there was nothing he could do to change the secretive culture aboard Humanity One. But - there was one thing he *could* change. He had information that could save Humanity One; that would save humanity if he was allowed to share it. He would be heard; he would make sure his information did not become a protected secret; or he would be recycled. All the lives on Humanity One depended on him, whether they knew it or not.

If the Captain thought he was protecting Jana, his granddaughter, from the final disaster by recycling her, Rex was willing to take the risk. If his words were heard, his warnings heeded, Humanity One and its Mission could be saved. He knew what he had to do, but that was his secret for the moment.

CHAPTER 23

HEAR ME

Rex normally was able to set his mind at ease, relax and rest, when he was in his quarters, in his small sleeping space – the only reasonably private space inside the vessel. No more. Too many thoughts raced through his mind. He knew the course insertion point was near. He was privy to the calculated alteration. His – the Group's – indiscretions had not removed him from normal, planned activities. He was still part of the small group of Sci-Techs that maintained the calculations to ensure the maneuver went as planned. Those same calculations provided him the uneasy knowledge of Humanity One's survival chances. Add to that a Captain who was more inclined to protect the Innovators' MGR than his own progeny. Or a Captain who was willing to provide an easy demise to his granddaughter to save her from the pain of a cataclysmic end. He slept fitfully. It was only two nights in a row, but he was tired – and cranky.

Rex was driven by feelings of desperation. The Mission schedule delay, the possibility that an alien life form was bent on the destruction of the human race, the repeated angry rebuke by Stan of his plan to remedy one of those problems – if not both – fed his resolve. He envisioned himself taking the much bigger Captain by the nape of the neck and shaking sense into the wizened, grayed head. But the Captain was unapproachable.

Maddie was right. The Captain did not wander the vessel. His movements were restricted to the passageway between Con-Sys and quarters. Apparently, the Captain's food was brought to him, eaten while sitting in the Chair or in his quarters. Bathroom breaks and brief naps were the only times he left his post. Try as he might, Rex could not find an opportunity to speak with the Captain. Stan made sure of it.

Course insertion was completed successfully. The ad hoc Sci-Tech group essentially disbanded. Even knowing the schedule was three days behind, Chief Gail and her charges were relieved and elated that the alteration was a success. Rex was not. As far as he was concerned, as far as the fate of Humanity One was concerned, the alteration was not a success until they were back on schedule. He was cranky and out-of-sorts. Tired and disgusted to the point of recklessness. He was determined to present his plan for enhanced energy harvest to Captain Cesar.

For more than twenty-four hours after insertion, the Captain was in his quarters, no doubt recouping sleep. Totally inaccessible. That only served to feed Rex's frustration and further embolden him. The salvation of Humanity One was at stake. The salvation of everyone he knew was at stake. The future of humankind was at stake.

Stan led them to a mess table apart from Maddie and Della. Not out of any desire to avoid them, rather he chose to sit with other Sci-Techs for a change. Even though the alteration was not a closely guarded secret, it was not a subject for open discussion while in progress. To avoid temptation to discuss it, Stan used his role in the Group's chaperone restrictions as an excuse to sit at a different mess table. From a general Crew perspective, everything was back to normal now that Humanity One was back on course. The relief was palpable throughout the vessel. The entire episode had become a gentle buzz of rumor in the Mess Hall, accompanied by the usual good spirits of dedicated Crew members.

Rex's back was to the entry door. He felt the Captain's arrival long before he saw him. First, Premier Paul shuffled to the VLT table with a plate of chow. Rex's heart rate increased with anticipation as he watched the aged Premier. Doctor Katherine followed not far behind him. Then, Captain Cesar. The three were greeted with nods and smiles from the Gen 3s positioned to make eye contact. Rex felt his face flush when he saw the Captain.

Maddie was disappointed that Stan did not join her and Della. After the clandestine meeting in Sanitation, she had not had a chance to speak with Rex. She saw that his normally fresh and eager eyes were changed. Haggard and glazed. The anger of that night was stronger. She ate her chow and watched her friend, unminding of the conversation at her own table. Rex was not facing her as he ate, but she could see his body tense as he watched the VLT take their table, the first time in more than a week. All of them were there. Probably fresh from a VLT meeting. She was sure they were freshly updated on the current status of Humanity One's course alteration and the impending dangers. Rex's neck stiffened when the Captain came into his view. She watched him, fearful of what he might do.

"I really need to go to the restroom," Stan said abruptly, as he carefully extricated himself from the table bench without disrupting the people on either side of him.

Rex poised himself. He looked over his shoulder to watch Stan leave the Mess Hall. He ignored Maddie's worried eyes. He rose without saying a word. He walked the short distance to the VLT table. He gathered his thoughts, as he moved, words that were already burned into his brain. He drew himself to his full height and spoke with as much confidence as he could muster. "Captain, I have the solution to our lost schedule hours – days. We can harvest more energy, increase the efficiency of our stellar engines. We can have the process operational within a week, maybe two."

Captain Cesar raised his eyes at the sound of his name. He slowly chewed a mouthful of food – and appeared to listen.

Chief Gail scowled and started to speak. Premier Paul placed a hand on her forearm to silence her.

"Captain, with the energy I can generate, we can increase our speed and regain the lost time on our schedule." Rex looked for a sign that the Captain was hearing him, heeding his words. The man sat and ate, barely disturbed by his presence. "Captain, with the extra energy, we can travel faster – maybe overcome the shortened life spans of the generations. That way, we can still arrive at Earth Two during the Eighth Generation, like the Innovators planned."

A slight change of expression crossed the Captain's face. Doctor Katherine stopped eating; her interest piqued, torn between listening to Rex and watching the Captain's stoic features for a sign. Premier Paul remained vigilant of Chief Gail's and the Captain's reaction. His hand was still on Gail's forearm.

"Captain, I know you don't have to listen to me. I'm just a lowly Gen 4 Trainee, but I assure you that I have a solution to our problems. Even for the danger of an alien attack." Rex saw a reaction in the Captain's eyes.

The Captain set his utensil on his plate and glared at Rex. "Rex Si Wu-Ershiliu, why are you alone? You were warned."

Rex gulped. The reaction was not the one he expected. "Sir, I was warned that I could not be alone with other Trainees. I am with Gen 3 Sci-Techs." He motioned toward his table. Everyone at the table squirmed, unhappy to be in the limelight.

Maddie shuddered. She wanted to yell at Rex to sit down. She wanted to scream at the Captain to listen. She wanted to say something, but she was frozen. The Captain was capable of recycling his own granddaughter because she displeased him. Anyone else would be easier for him. Her eyes filled with tears. She saw Stan return to the Mess Hall. Even with blurred vision, she saw the shock on his face.

"REX!" Stan commanded in a voice no one expected from the normally mild-mannered Sci-Tech. "Back to your table this instant!" He strode to his Trainee and harshly grabbed Rex's left bicep. He yanked Rex away from the VLT table, a surprising move considering Rex's more physical stature. "Now, sit and finish your chow." Stan, still showing his anger, turned to the Captain, "Captain, I apologize for my Trainee's behavior. He has yet to learn that his dreams are not the same as true knowledge."

Captain Cesar scowled at Stan for a moment, then made a small head nod that dismissed the subject.

CHAPTER 24

CRISIS

Maddie struggled to concentrate on the screen at her console. Monitoring atmosphere seemed insignificant at the moment, as it had for all the moments since the day before - since Rex's outburst in the Mess Hall. Her mind screamed for answers. She dreaded the possibility of hearing the tones, the death knell, the indication of the Captain's response to her closest friend. Her mind needed to know. Her heart did not want to know. To not know meant everything was okay. Some secrets were good.

Maddie's lack of concentration on her own screen allowed her to notice a sudden shift in the dimly lit Control Room. She heard a soft alarm emanating from another Con-Sys console. Della's head was turned. That helped Maddie find a place to focus, a point at which the room's energy seemed to be the highest. At first, she feared it was the beginning of the recycle intonation. By following Della's lead, she saw Captain Trainee Joseph walking toward a Con-Sys Tech whose face was intermittently awash by an amber strobe.

A yellow light was not good. Maddie tried to recall what that particular Con-Sys Tech was monitoring. It was not atmosphere. She had atmosphere for most of the vessel. Her mind raced to thoughts of hull integrity. It could be another meteor – or worse, a projectile – bound for impact. An impact that would catastrophically vent atmosphere. Her eyes returned to her console as she awaited the onset of alarms that would soon be vying for her attention. Rex said he could provide sufficient energy to escape another attack, but no one wanted to hear from a non-adult. She could not maintain focus on her screen. The tension was too thick near the amber light. She watched as Joseph's eyes followed the pointing fingers of the Con-Sys Tech. The room was almost tomb silent. Her training finally pulled her mind back to her console, to the impending warning she would receive when the hull was breached and atmosphere began venting. Her mouth was suddenly dry.

"There," said the Con-Sys Tech.

Even focused on her console, Maddie's ears could not help but hear the words spoken in the otherwise silent room.

"Are you sure?" questioned the Captain-To-Be.

"Yes. It's the same signature," confirmed the Con-Sys Tech.

"Okay. Cancel the alarm. The Captain will respond." Joseph walked back to the Chair. A zoned look on his face indicated that he was activating his Communicator.

The Captain's face twitched as he and Joseph discussed the alarm via Communicators. Maddie's curiosity divided her attention between the two men and her console. The Chair and its occupant were illuminated for effect at all times, a tangible reminder of the power of that position. It was not hard to see the subject matter was tense. Both men stared at one another, though it was not necessary for their Communicators. Not hearing, not knowing made her want to scream for answers. She did not notice Della drift toward the Con-Sys Tech with the alarm, but she was fully aware when Della returned and slid into the offset chair beside her.

"What is it?" Maddie whispered; afraid someone would hear her ask.

Della's facial lines, the lines that were normally barely noticeable, were deep with concern. "The rogue. It has changed course."

"What?" Maddie's voice was too loud. Several Techs turned to look toward the source of the sound. She lowered her voice and whispered, "What?" as if by doing so, no one would notice her previous outburst.

"The rogue that we changed course to avoid, it has changed course. It's following us." Della's voice was strained with fear. She made it clear that she did not want to talk further, not there, maybe never.

"What are we going to do?" Maddie was afraid.

Della patted her daughter's arm. "Don't worry. The Captain will take care of it." The message to Maddie was to go on about her duties.

From that point, the Con-Sys Tech with the alarm was locked in Communication with the Captain and Joseph via Communicator. No one in the Control Room knew what was taking place – at least not officially.

Della, like other curious Con-Sys Techs, touched the assigned screen in front of Maddie and selected from the drop-down MENU. The screen filled with new data - the data available to the alarmed console. Neither the Captain nor the Con-Sys Tech had blocked the data.

Maddie was unable to sort it out as fast as Della, but she grasp the crux of the information. The object identified as the original rogue asteroid was on the same course as Humanity One, one-hundred million meters behind and tracking at the same speed. Humanity One was being followed. Maddie vainly tried to swallow, to moisten the inside of her throat.

The Captain filled Maddie's mind. She barely noticed that every Con-Sys Tech reacted the same as she did. The Captain opened his Communicator to everyone in the room. "We believe an object, an asteroid, is on the same course as Humanity One. It is traveling the same speed; therefore, it is not a danger to us. We will monitor it and take whatever actions may be necessary to ensure it does not pose a danger in the future. I recommend that if you speak of this, you do not present it as a danger. That information would distract others from their duties and jeopardize the Mission."

Maddie wanted to feel reassured. She could not. Too many secrets. The Captain wanted her ... and the others ... to keep a secret. It was not just an object. The Captain knew that. It was the same object that previously was on a collision course, a course that Humanity One avoided by expending its entire propulsion reserve energy. The object changed courses too. The object was not an asteroid. But Cesar kept that secret by not admitting it was an alien vessel.

Another flurry of activity erupted two hours after the object's behavior was first noted. Maddie only noticed it because Della suddenly rose from the improvised Trainer chair. "You need to return to quarters." Della's voice was tight, her face drawn.

"What?" Maddie was shocked by Della's sudden action.

"Don't argue. You are free until I call you back. No one in Con-Sys but adults. Now go." Della's sense of urgency was unmistakable.

Maddie knew to not argue. Two other Gen 4 Trainees left. Premier Paul hustled in through the door as they were leaving. For the first time since the Group was disbanded, Maddie found herself truly unattended, alone without chaperone – without need for extra precautions to avoid detection. She knew she should go to her quarters, avoid the appearance of violating the Captain's orders. Her mind still screamed for answers about Rex. Sanitary Recycling would have the answer – if anyone there would answer.

Maddie did not know what was happening in the Con-Sys Room, but she knew it was a secret – maybe the biggest secret of all. And only adults were allowed to know it. Her fear was replaced by anger.

CHAPTER 25

REUNION

Maddie walked from the Control Room toward her quarters. She had to go there. Her fellow Trainees might be asked about her later. She chatted with them about what they knew, aware that more was happening. They were all aware that they might never know the whole truth. Two of the three were unconcerned about that. Maddie waited inside her quarters for a few minutes then slipped into the passageway, unseen, unnoticed.

Her progress toward Sanitary Recycling slowed abruptly. Ahead in the dim passage, someone was approaching. She lowered her head. For the first time, she was glad she did not have her trademark long hair to broadcast her identity. Technically, she was not in violation of Cesar's orders. She was not with another member of the Group unchaperoned. Still, questions would be asked, and after Rex's confrontation, there would be no leniency. She kept moving with her head down, planning how to pass the person in the narrow hall without showing her face.

"Maddie! What are you doing here?"

Maddie's head jerked up as she stopped in her tracks. "Rex? Rex? It's really you." Without thought, Maddie rushed to Rex and embraced him. Tears of joy filled her eyes as she pressed herself against him and received his returned embrace. She pulled back and beamed a smile. "I hadn't heard anything. I thought ... I thought ... what did the Captain say?"

Rex was somewhat puzzled at Maddie's reaction. "Nothing. He said nothing. Just ate and scowled until Stan yanked me away. Chief Gail is aggravated, but she hasn't really said anything about it. Why are you here?"

Maddie hugged him again then answered. "I was told to leave Con-Sys. All the Trainees were." She glanced around and whispered conspiratorially, "We need to talk. I was going to San-Re ... to ... to check on you."

"On me?" Rex paused, and then grimaced. "Oh. I understand." He pulled her to him, her head against his shoulder. "I'm sorry I caused you pain. I'm fine ... but I was just told to leave Sci-Eng by Chief Gail also. Do you know what's going on?"

Maddie looked around again, nervously. "I think so. Let's go someplace where we can talk." She took his hand and hurried down the passageway toward Sanitary Recycling.

Sanitary Recycling was much noisier than Maddie remembered. And more odiferous. Smells joined the noise to make the air heavy. Across the room, a few San-Re Techs were visible working around various machines. Maddie looked toward a wall with several pedestrian doors. She nodded to indicate they should move that direction. In her mind, she knew they should have waited until night shift, when only Bill was there. He was usually there alone, and he would not ask too many questions - if he saw them at all. Their chances of being discovered were much higher when the full Crew was on duty.

"Maybe one of those is empty," Maddie whispered above the din.

Rex nodded approval and followed.

Sanitation Chief Kara San Luishiyi-Qishiqi, stepped around a machine to face the two teenagers. She was as startled to see them as they were to see her. Sanitary Recycling did not get many visitors. In reality, none of the work centers were tourist attractions. No one had time to visit. There was always work to be done, a mission to accomplish. "Lost?" was the only thing she could muster.

Maddie and Rex stopped dead in their tracks.

Rex did not miss a beat. He flashed his most charming smile. He remembered Chief Kara's reaction when he spoke to the Captain. She was attentive, sitting at the table watching the event unfold. He probably would not have noticed her, except that she seemed more interested in watching him than hearing his words. It was disconcerting at the time. He knew he had an effect on women, even women as old as his mother. He found a use for it. "Oops! You caught us," he said, his voice filled with more suggestion than apology. As he spoke, he grasped Maddie's hand, pulled her closer to him and looked lustfully into her eyes. "We were just looking for a quiet place."

Kara's face softened; a slight touch of jealousy passed before she smiled with a twinkle. "Not too many consider San-Re to be a quiet place."

Rex smiled and squeezed Maddie to his side. "Do you know of a better place?" Roguishly, he let his eyes move up and down Kara's torso, teasing her as he spoke.

Kara blushed and smiled knowingly. "Time and place. If you've got the time, there's always a place." Her eyes toyed with Rex's for a moment, then she looked at Maddie and whispered with a smile. "Lucky girl." She looked over her shoulder to see if anyone else was near. She nodded toward one of the doors. "There's nothing scheduled for that sorting room today. I probably won't be looking in there for an hour or two. Maybe ..." she let her voice trail off as she turned and walked away.

Maddie was shaking against Rex's chest. She had never seen Rex intentionally use his raw sensuality to influence a female. She was not sure whether to be jealous or grateful. "Hurry," she whispered. The two of them rushed through the small door.

The sorting room was small, barely six feet square. A compact, wall mounted shelf held a computer screen and offered a chest-high workspace. There were no chairs. The room smelled of past occupation, whatever manner of recyclables required hand sorting before final processing.

Maddie freed her hand from Rex's. "Well, that was a disgusting display," she said.

Rex laughed, "Sex erodes the strongest will. Now, what's going on? You were sent out of Con-Sys and I was sent out of Sci-Eng."

"Right. All Gen 4 Trainees were sent out of Con-Sys," Maddie stated.

"Hmm. Come to think of it, the other two Sci-Eng Trainees were sent out before me. I wasn't singled out. Neither were you. Something is definitely ..."

"I know what's happening," Maddie interrupted Rex's comment. "The big secret is that the rogue ... the alien vessel is following us."

Rex stared at Maddie in shock for a moment. "Are you sure?"

"I'm positive," she replied, upset that he questioned her statement.

Rex thought a moment. "How much do you know about it?"

Maddie returned to her whisper, wary of ears. "It was noticed about two or three hours ago. At that time, it was matching our speed from about one-hundred million meters. The Captain told us it was not a danger and that we should not discuss it with anyone else. Then about half-hour ago, the Trainees were told to leave, and the Premier went into Con-Sys."

Rex looked toward the floor and spoke his thoughts aloud. "Another secret to keep. I wonder what changed. Maybe the rogue gained speed. Maybe it's closing on us." He looked up to Maddie's expectant face, "He knows there is nothing we can do, but I'd bet he's called upon Sci-Eng to come up with a solution. That's probably why I was ordered to leave."

"Will your ideas work? Can you help? Shouldn't you be there?"

"It may be too late." Rex shook his head. "If the aliens are determined to attack us, there is nothing that we can do to stop them. My plan requires at least a week to put in place, then it will still be weeks, maybe months, before we can harvest enough energy to use for increased propulsion."

Maddie was frightened by Rex words, more so by the look or resignation in his eyes. "There has to be something we can do."

Rex glanced around the small sorting room. His eyes settled on the computer terminal. "First, we make sure that what we think matches what we know. No need to stress if it's not necessary. I'll see if I can access Science One."

"What is Science One?"

"It's the Focus Room computer that would be used for secretive calculations. If Chief Gail is working on the problem, that's the most likely place she will be."

Rex opened the computer and slowly began his search of the system with a series of administrative moves and queries. His face twisted in puzzlement. Undeterred, he continued to query the system. Finally, an active screen replaced the one on the San-Re computer. "Got it!" he exclaimed; his eyes wide with excitement. "They're in the Premier's Decision Room. Let's see what they have for conditions."

"Why in there? Is it safe to look at it?"

"Cesar is probably updating the Premier and telling the other Chiefs. It's safe enough."

Maddie moved closer, shoulder against Rex's upper bicep. Numbers and words were magically adding to the jumble of information already on the screen. The concept was not completely foreign to her, but it created palpitating excitement to watch the display surreptitiously.

"There!" Rex pointed to the screen, to a line of data on the screen. "They are calculating the speed and distance of the rogue. There's no doubt it's a vessel, or at least an object under someone's control. That's got to be Chief Gail on the computer. You're right. It's approximately one-hundred million meters away, pacing us."

"How did it get on our course without anyone noticing it before now? The Con-sys Tech on Tracking should have seen it altering course. It had to turn." Maddie's mind filled with questions.

"I don't know," Rex replied. "Maybe everyone was too focused on Humanity One's travel, its return to course. That kept the Captain preoccupied, I imagine."

Maddie nodded. "True. He pretty much stayed in that Chair until we were back on course. We all knew how important it was to him."

"Group Think. When the entire group focuses on one thing, one solution, everything else is invisible to the group and the individuals in it. It turned at some point. If it truly is an alien vessel, I'm sure it's designed for navigational moves."

"You mean turns and speed changes?"

"Exactly. Humanity One was designed to travel a relatively straight path on a single mission. It wasn't designed to fly around objects. We can only make minor moves or, like the alteration, wide and arcing moves. Much less energy is expended using gentle nudges that don't require massive battles with inertia. Apparently, the Rogue can move with more flexibility." Rex watched the numbers unfold on the screen as someone entered data to submit for calculation. He scowled and shook his head. "They're going over the same calculations they always do. Chief Gail is no different than Chief Robert. Textbook stuff. Nothing innovative. The old data will only yield the same results. I wonder what else they have."

Rex touched the screen and guided toward the initial data, the criteria that identified the total problem. He wanted to see ... he needed to see ... what problem they were trying to solve. "Look! That's what changed. They received a signal."

"What kind of signal?"

"Alien," Rex said flatly. "The Captain wants to know what the signal means. The calculations they are performing have nothing to do with the signals. What are they doing?" What he saw made him angry. He stopped and looked at Maddie. "Who monitors for signals in Con-Sys? Which Menu selection?"

Maddie closed her eyes and visualized the Con-Sys Menu. She trained on all of them. She knew the function of each Menu Item. "RadOpt. Radio Optics."

"Good." Rex quickly left the Decision Room screen and returned to Admin. He searched for and found the Con-Sys Menu. He opened RadOpt. He watched carefully for a few seconds. "Do you understand what it's telling us?"

Maddie raised her hand slightly to indicate she was studying the screen. "Yes! There. The signals are still coming. They are coming from the area of space behind us. From the direction of the alien vessel."

"What are they saying?"

"I don't know. It just shows that electromagnetic signals are being intercepted. The same patterns, repeated every six minutes or so."

"I wonder if we are replying. Never mind. We probably lack the capability. The Innovators didn't provide us with a wide range communication system," Rex snorted derisively, "because there are no other sentient beings in the universe."

"Are the Chiefs working on the signal? You said they weren't."

"They are not. I think they're stymied, so they're double checking course and speed. Rearranging furniture, so to speak. They don't know what else to do. They're not focused. Let's look at the signals. Maybe we can decipher them."

Maddie stared at the line of code that represented the alien signal, that interpreted as waves on the screen. She stared until everything around her, including the screen, abruptly darkened. Maddie wanted to scream, but she knew it would do no good. Instead, she quickly recalled the door in relation to where the two of them were standing. She bumped against Rex as she turned to the remembered direction. Rex's hand flailed against her until it grasped onto her waistcloth.

"Maddie, are you alright?" Rex's voice was strained.

"I'm fine. I'm headed toward the door. Raise your hand higher. Hold my shoulder. Not my rear."

"Sorry. I just grabbed the biggest target," Rex replied with a nervous laugh.

"Sick," Maddie replied. Any other time, she might have laughed with him ... and swatted his hand. "The door is this way. Stay close." Her bare toe hit something solid. She stopped and Rex ran into her, mashing her warm skin against the cool barrier. She felt the door handle on her abdomen. "We're there. Back up just a little. I've got it."

The door came open. The noise and light, seemingly brighter than earlier, from the Recycling equipment welcomed them.

"What just happened?" Maddie urgently asked.

"The system detected an unauthorized intrusion."

"I thought you knew what you were doing."

"I do, but that doesn't mean I'm authorized to do it."

"Are we caught?" Maddie's vocal cords tightened and she felt her face pale.

"No. The system is designed to prevent accidental intrusions. It just eliminates the source of the intrusion by killing power to that area. The power supply and the lights just happened to be on the same circuit in this small room."

"Will they come looking for the problem?"

"Probably not right away, but no need to wait around to find out. San-Re will have to contact Elec-Tech to re-establish power."

"Chief Kara will know we did it."

At that moment, Kara came into view across the large room. Rex winked at her and waved goodbye. He nudged Maddie forward. "And she won't tell anyone. She will think we knocked into something while we were in there. She won't want to explain her part in our little tryst."

CHAPTER 26

GET REX

Cesar saw Paul's reaction to the face-to-face revelation of the Rogue's behavior. Once again, the Premier was going to offer indecision. Paul held the status of Premier, but he only made the decisions that were suggested and supported by the MGR. The presence of a sentient-alien vessel was not considered by the Innovators. There was no stock answer, no programed decision. Again ... or as usual ... Cesar would be called upon to determine Humanity One's course of action. Resigned to that fact, the Captain said, "Paul, let's convene the VLT. They need to be aware of everything that is happening. Maybe they can offer input."

Paul stammered. "Uh ... sure. I think that would be appropriate. If the object is something other than an asteroid, the Chiefs need to be aware." He looked expectantly at the taller, more confident Captain.

Cesar waited for Paul to connect his Communicator to the other seven VLT members. After a brief moment watching the Premier's blank stare, Cesar realized Paul was unsure what to Communicate. He took charge and initiated the Communicator. He told all the Chiefs to gather in the Premier's Decision Room. He pushed himself away from the Chair and told Joseph to take it until he returned.

The top half of the computer screen in the Decision Room displayed a graphic representation of Humanity One's course with Humanity One followed by a blinking red dot. Cesar downloaded speed and distance data from Con-Sys tracking onto the split screen. He also displayed an active reading of a two-second spurt of low frequency electromagnetic radiation waves along a central line. Chief Gail, still enamored with her newfound status, sat close to the Captain, close to the screen.

Premier Paul stood and softly opened the meeting, "Chief Kara is unable to join us immediately, but Captain Cesar has some information that bears sharing." He lowered himself into his chair, and avoided the puzzled looks of the other VLT members.

Cesar contained his feelings. The Premier's words and actions were de facto deferral of everything involving leadership of the meeting to him. "We are being followed." He paused to allow a slow ripple of nervous reactions to pass. "The Rogue object that we altered course to avoid collision with appears to have changed course. It is now matching our speed one-hundred million meters directly behind us."

Medical Chief Katherine's eyes widened. "It's chasing us? Why?"

"I didn't say it was chasing us. It appears to be following us."

"How can an asteroid change course?" asked Stasis Chief Deanna.

"It can't - except when pulled by gravity or knocked off course by another object. Asteroid can't make the change that has been made; not naturally."

"What do we do to protect ourselves?" Chief Deanna asked.

"There's not much we can do," Cesar responded flatly. "But that's not the entire reason we called this meeting. We are receiving a radio signal."

"From the Rogue object?" Elec-Tech Chief Bernie asked. "Is that it on the screen? What does it say?"

Cesar scowled, a gesture that always quieted those around him.

"We can only assume the signal is coming from the Rogue. Yes, that is the signal on the screen, and we are here to determine what it says."

"Are we the right people to determine that?" asked Mech-Tech Chief Donald.

"Of course, we are," replied Sci-Eng Chief Gail.

Cesar cut his eyes toward the novice Chief. "Some of us may be the right people. Others of us are not. When we do decipher the message, we need to agree upon a response."

"Can we respond?" asked the Elec-Tech Chief. "I don't think our radio capabilities are up to the task."

"First question then; can you upgrade our radio capabilities quickly? We can detect radio signals. Surely, emitting understandable radio signals should be easy enough to achieve." Cesar leaned toward Bernie, to isolate the answer from interference.

Bernie shook his head sideways as he rolled his eyes up in thought. Finally, he nodded and looked straight at the Captain. "I'm fairly sure we can. There are some references, some work instructions, in the Electrical MGR. I can start that work immediately. I may need some Hard Fab and Soft Fab assistance for parts." He glanced toward Chief Donald.

"No problem," replied Chief Donald. "Tell me what you need. Some specs would help ... if you can provide them."

Chief Gail was about to explode, eager to be involved. "I'd like to check those figures, the speed and distance. Is the Rogue gaining on us? We have to have a plan of action in case they are." Without being invited, she moved to the computer and began manipulating the speed and distance data. She input data for calculation, determining Humanity One's course compared to the projected course of the Rogue. She calculated Humanity One's speed compared to the Rogue's projected speed. The others sat and watched.

Cesar interrupted her after a couple of minutes of hurried

calculations. "I believe the data we have is directionally correct. We are being followed. What we need now is to decipher the signal. It's repeating at six-minute intervals. If they are trying to talk to us, we need to know that. We need to know what they are saying, AND ... we need to have a response."

Gail thought the screen flickered, paused a moment, just as Cesar got her attention. "Who's working on the decipher?"

Cesar leaned toward Gail. "I was thinking that finding a solution is a Sci-Eng chore." He stared at Gail until she gulped and nodded.

"That makes sense, though I'm not a linguist."

"Neither am I, but I think between you and Bernie, you should have people who are good at identifying patterns. This signal repeats exactly. It means something. We need to know what it means so we can react - either respond or get away."

Gail was puzzled. "How do we get away? We don't have the capability."

"Sometimes, the best way to get away from a fight is to negotiate. Maybe we can talk our way out of trouble."

"What – exactly – is our current capability?" Chief Deanna asked. As the oldest living Crew Member, she knew the answer to her own question as well as anyone on the vessel, even though the knowledge within the answer had nothing to do with her Stasis duties. Airing the obvious sometimes creates an opportunity to expose something less obvious.

Cesar answered solemnly. "After our alteration to avoid collision, our capabilities are limited. Our energy reserve is essentially depleted. We have no power to maneuver. And - as we all know, Humanity One is traveling at its maximum design speed."

Chief Deanna nodded pensively for a moment while the others allowed her the respect she deserved. "So, there is nothing we can do. What if their message is that we stop and surrender?"

Gail interrupted, "Humanity One doesn't have brakes. Slowing is achieved by furling the solar sails to stop the forward pressure. A full stop would take years to achieve ... if at all. A significant portion of our momentum is gravitational pull – and we can't stop that."

Cesar cut his eyes toward Gail. The novice might require serious training to understand VLT protocol. "Bernie, you and Gail get your most trusted people on the signal. I want to know what it means within the hour. And this is top secret. We can't distract the Crew."

Gail glared at Bernie, disturbed by the obvious slight.

Bernie nodded and rose from his chair. With a poorly hidden smile, he replied, "Aye, Captain. Gail, have your team meet me in my conference room. I'll have the scopes and wave analyzers ready." He did not wait for affirmation before he left the Decision Room.

As soon as the two left the room, Cesar turned to Chief Donald, "Can you do an analysis of the Rogue? So far, it's been a blip on our screens. A dot of light. I'd like to know what it looks like."

"I can. I'll need to pull in a couple of my people and at least one Con-Sys Tech."

"Do it. Use Della if she's up to it." Cesar glanced toward Doctor Katherine questioningly.

Doctor Katherine nodded approval.

Cesar knew Della's health was perilous. The seemingly healthy woman's immune system was on the verge of collapse, another malady associated with space travel. Della's daughter was spared recycling because Della was genetically predisposed to be among the Gen 3s who were projected to recycle early. Fortunately, that genetic malformity was not passed to her offspring. She would not have time to bear another child and train a replacement. Della was unaware of her condition. It was a condition that would descend upon her rapidly when it worsened. No need to worry her with distracting information. Doctor Katherine tracked and studied everyone aboard Humanity

One. When life expectancies were found to be less than the Innovators' original calculations, knowledge of each Crew Member's health had to be part of decisions such as the one Cesar had to make regarding the Group. Every decision he made was made to cause the least harm to the Mission. Maddie did not inherit her mother's faulty genes and promised to be a top Con-Sys Tech with a keenly interpretive mind. Rex's mental prowess saved him, as did Marly's and Kendra's. All four were the jewels of Gen 4. The others in the Group were baguettes, accent pieces that complemented the collection and made it cohesive. Except Jana. Jana was to be a leader, *the* Leader. Joseph had time. Jana did not.

After Chief Donald left, Cesar Communicated with Joseph to free Della for a duty assignment in Mechanical. Questions about a Con-Sys Tech working in Mechanical would be asked eventually. As much as he wanted the subject to remain secret, he knew secret status was doomed to be short lived – another malady associated with space travel inside a small vessel.

Chief Deanna waited until she was sure Cesar was finished with his Communications. "Cesar, what more do we know? Our STVs must be protected, in the event aliens are demanding surrender."

Cesar understood the aging Chief's concerns. He did not understand why she thought there would be something he could do for the STVs that he could not do for the Crew Members. "Deanna, everything must be protected. Without the Crew, the STVs are of no value."

Deanna snapped, "Without the STVs, the Mission is a failure."

Cesar responded wearily. Everyone had an agenda they believed superseded all others. "I know that. But - until we know what we are facing, we can't develop a plan."

"How big is the Rogue?"

"Hopefully, that will be determined by Chief Donald." Cesar wanted a moment of silence so he could think. In the back of his mind, he felt a thought forming. Too many distractions prevented it. "Remember, originally the blip was interpreted to be an asteroid. That was all we considered until we discovered a fashioned projectile, but it was only conjecture until the latest movement of the object. It remains to be seen what it actually is, especially its size and shape. Regardless, any species capable of traveling through space in a fully controlled vessel is capable of much more than we are." He knew his statement was not entirely accurate. Humankind had controllable vessels that were used within the Solar System. Humanity One was specifically designed for operational efficiency and payload – no frills.

Hydroponics Chief Kellie had silently listened. She mused, "So, we could be facing a foe so advanced that we aren't a match for them physically or intellectually?"

Cesar shook his head. The conversation was becoming too speculative, too distracting from the known. "I don't know. All I know is that we need to know two things; what they want and how big their vessel is. They may simply be saying hello. They could be space pirates demanding treasure. I won't speculate. It does us no good to idly postulate without facts."

"Understood," replied Kellie. "What can we do to help?"

"Go about your business without creating a distraction until called upon. Until we know what we can do, what we need to do, not creating distractions is the best thing anyone can do." Cesar turned toward the Premier. "Unless you have something more to add, the meeting is adjourned."

Paul cleared his throat, "Thank all of you for coming. Remember, no distractions. I will keep you informed as we learn more. Thank you."

Cesar moved his body in an attempt to lessen the pain in his back. Without relief, he settled back and grimaced. The job of Captain, leader of Humanity One, was always stressful. The weight of the

Mission rested firmly on the Captain's shoulders, but that weight had never been so great as it was at that moment. Avoiding the collision with a rogue asteroid was stressful. Regaining the course and knowing Humanity One was seventy-five hours off schedule was stressful. Neither compared to the knowledge that another sentient race was following Humanity One across the void of space with unknown intentions and there was nothing that he could do in response.

The idea finally formed in the silence that surrounded Cesar and Paul after the other VLT members left. "I want Rex Si Wu-Ershiliu!"

CHAPTER 27

SOUNDS

"Where do we go?" Maddie asked.

"I'm not sure. I want to see those signals. Maybe we can find a computer and a quiet place in Hydroponics. Someplace where I can study them," Rex replied. The disruption in Sanitary Recycling left him more curious than frightened.

"Why there?"

"Most of the Grow Rooms are unattended, filled only with vegetables left alone to grow. There's no need for a steady Crew presence at all times. Maybe we can access a computer without being seen."

Maddie scowled. "And cause another one to crash?"

"Not this time. I touched the screen and changed it to see what else was on view. My mistake. The system detected dual access and reacted. Besides, I know what I'm looking for now, and where to find it. RadOpt. Also, I'm sure others are remotely monitoring that screen, trying to solve the puzzle. The authorization protocol will likely be temporarily disabled."

Maddie was less than enthusiastic. She was not sure the protocol could be disabled. Rex could be telling her that just to calm her, to give her false hope. Her desire to know the message in the signal was tempered by the fear of discovery. Chief Kara might be inclined to not mention the tryst of two Gen 4s, but that did not mean the next person would be willing to look the other way. "Let's see if we can find Kendra's room. Maybe she can help us," she said with cautious acceptance.

"Okay. Let's." Rex grinned rakishly and darted down a passageway that would take them to the Hydroponics section of the vessel. It was not uncommon for young lovers to wander through the garden rooms, smelling the fresh air and chatting – developing a relationship. If the two of them did not meet someone face to face, their presence should not raise too much suspicion.

In the first Grow Room, the two quickly developed a sense of euphoria. The air was fresh and heady. Higher CO_2, above 5.3%, has the tendency to expand arteries and capillaries throughout the body. The increased blood flow causes muscles to relax and creates mild euphoria. It was not the same effect as a drug, but it was a break from norm without the side effects of drug enhancement. That was one the reasons young lovers strolled the gardens.

A Gen 3 performing routine tasks in the room cast a knowing smile their way. Rex grinned and clasped Maddie's hand, even though she instinctively tried to pull it away from him. An attended Grow Room. Without speaking, Rex continued on his way with Maddie in tow and moved into another Grow Room. They saw Kendra before she saw them, the red flame of her short hair easily identifiable, even from behind.

Kendra was facing Sta-Tech Kevin JiuJiu-Jiushi, an enamored smile on her face as she listened to him talk. His eyes were locked on her face. Her hand was held against his chest by his hands. Kevin's mother was Stasis Chief Deanna. His was a late-in-life birth for the Gen 2 Deanna. An older sibling passed to recycling long before achieving adulthood. Heart attack at an early age. Deanna gave birth to a second child to train as her replacement. It was generally unclear whether Kevin's father was the same as that of his recycled sibling. Doctor Katherine knew. That was all that mattered.

Kevin saw the two approaching from behind Kendra. His mouth twitched. His eyes darted nervously, as if searching for an avenue of escape.

"Hi, Kendra," Maddie said, barely louder than a whisper.

Kendra's head jerked to look toward Maddie and Rex. Her face flushed. The redness spread from freckle to freckle, then down her neck until it reached her areolas. Her hand dropped free of Kevin's chest. She stammered. "Hello." Her startled, topaz eyes were locked on her two friends. She bemusedly watched as Maddie freed her hand from Rex's. "What are you doing here?" She furtively searched the garden for other eyes, someone who might reveal everything.

Maddie knew to not divulge their mission in front of the Gen 3, even if he did appear to be a friend of Kendra's. "Just getting some fresh air and ultraviolet. Some vitamin D enhancement is always good." Maddie could not take her eyes off Kevin. She knew who he was. She simply did not understand why he would be in the Grow Room ... alone with Kendra. He was a long way from Stasis.

Kendra noticed Maddie's point of attention. She scrambled, talking faster than normal, "Do you know Kevin? He's a Sta-Tech, next in line to be Chief. He's here for fresh air too."

Rex grinned. "Aren't we all. Does it help to do chest compressions?"

Kevin blushed. "I ... ah ... I need to leave. It's almost duty time." He tried to hide his interest in Kendra. "I'll see you ... later ... sometime. Nice Garden. Thank you for giving me the tour. I'll return the favor sometime."

Kendra waited until Kevin disappeared through the doorway before she suspiciously asked, "Now, what are you really doing here?"

Rex replied with a question. "Is your computer nearby?"

Kendra pointed toward a small door. "It's in the tool room, away from the high moisture in the garden. Why?"

"I need to check something."

Kendra's face was flushed, frightened. She spoke in a loud whisper. "This is dangerous. Someone could come in here. Even Kevin knows we shouldn't be together without a chaperone."

Maddie pushed aside a considered comment about chaperones and touched Kendra's forearm. There was more important business than teasing her friend. "This is important, Kendra. The VLT is keeping another secret."

Kendra blanched. Her hand pressed against her lower belly. She whispered forcefully. "Maddie, if they catch us here in daylight ..." Her voice trailed off. She knew Maddie was not concerned about the risk. For whatever reason, Maddie was fearless. Kendra was less certain of her future.

Rex said reassuringly, "Kendra, I'll hurry. That asteroid we changed course for the one we thought ... the one we now know is an alien vessel ... it's following us."

Kendra's eyes glazed in thought momentarily. "Following us?"

"Yes."

Still holding one hand over her belly protectively, Kendra asked hesitantly, "Is it going to attack us again?"

"We don't know that, but it is signaling us. If I can get on the computer, maybe I can determine what it's saying."

After a moment's thought, Kendra nodded vigorously and pointed, "There. It's in there. But hurry."

Rex and Maddie barely fit in the tool room, more of a closet. The computer file Rex sought was easy to access. He was in RadOpt within a minute. Both faces jutted close to the screen, as if the proximity would make interpretation easier.

Kendra's head was inside the tool room, peering around the two bodies in an effort to see the screen. After a few minutes, she asked, "Does that represent sounds?"

Rex raised up and grinned. "Absolutely! I should have thought of that, Kendra. Does this computer have speakers?" He hurriedly searched the computer even as he asked. His face dropped. "No. No speakers. We need access to speakers so we can hear the signal."

"Where do we find a computer with speakers?" Maddie asked, perplexed. Even Con-Sys did not rely on sounds for normal monitoring. The only sounds that mattered were the alarms. The alarms only emitted sounds if ignored too long. Incoming sounds were interpreted as waves on a screen. That arrangement was less disruptive in a crowded room full of monitoring consoles. Until the alien vessel made its communication attempt, sounds were of no real value.

"Entertainment computers have speakers," Kendra offered.

"Yeah," Rex mused. "How do we get this onto an entertainment computer without being caught?"

"Copy chip?" Maddie asked.

Rex nodded. "Why not? Kendra, do you have any copy chips in here?"

Kendra's face scrunched in thought. The action made her face appear more heavily freckled. "I think there are some in that small drawer. Old records of growth. I'm not sure why they are saved there rather than on the computer."

"Preserve core memory probably," Rex responded. "Eight human generations is a long time to save chow growth records. A lot of data. I bet they won't miss one." He found the small metal chips. He inserted one into the computer's access port and directed it to save the data he selected from the RadOpt file. "I hope that's it. Now, to find a way to access the entertainment computers ... probably in the music room."

"It shouldn't be difficult. Anyone who hears it will just think it is a corrupted file," said Maddie with a sense of relief. Even though the sounds would be alien created, they should make more sense than the oscilloscope tracings. Sounds would better lend themselves to deciphering.

CHAPTER 28

KEVIN

Maddie missed being with her friends. Their concerns about secrets was not the common interest that held them together. Common need was the glue that bonded them. Kendra's outlook was closest to Maddie's in curiosity and drive. Kendra was more open to opposing views than Maddie. She was able to calm Maddie when no one else could, even Rex. And the two could talk. Despite the urgency to decipher the alien signal and the concern about being caught in violation of the Captain's orders, Maddie was curious. She grinned mischievously. "Okay, tell me the truth. What was Kevin doing here?"

Kendra did not want to blush, but she could not stop the crimson coloring that spread from her red hairline to her breasts. "It's like he said. He wanted a tour of the gardens."

Maddie laughed while Rex impatiently observed the exchange. "Just like you take tours of Stasis?"

Kendra responded indignantly. "I've toured Stasis. Kevin is next in line for Chief and he knows a lot about Stasis, more than most people." Despite her tendencies to do otherwise, she found herself blurting to cover her nerves. "Zack can't uncover secrets from Stasis for us, but I'm sure that Kevin knows them." She knew she was being too defensive, but she could not help herself.

"Really," Maddie's tone changed. "What secrets does he know?"

Kendra blinked. "Lots of things. He took me into places not very many Crew members get to see." She blushed again.

Maddie glanced toward Rex. She knew he wanted to pursue the signal interpretation. Even so, Kendra's comment deserved a challenge. "Like where? To see all the TSVs? Not very many of the Crew care to see that."

"Stasis in not just TSVs with adults. There are several storage areas with other things in stasis." Kendra was torn between not revealing everything Kevin had shown her and being honest with her friends.

"What other things?" Maddie turned to Rex. "Did you know that?"

Rex replied, "No. What are they?" He was not happy to be distracted from the original mission, no matter how momentary.

Kendra inhaled deeply. She was now committed to speak. "Kevin showed me the TSVs, some of them. There are thousands. He said twenty-five thousand. He showed me things about them. How they are monitored."

Rex nodded dismissively, impatiently. "We are aware of that. What did he show you about them that we don't already know?"

"The people in the TSVs are different than us."

"What?" Maddie was surprised by the statement. "How are they different?"

"Darker skin. They don't look the same."

"How dark. Darker than the Captain ... or Jana?"

"Not so much that kind of darkness. They aren't pale like us. And Kevin said they are mostly in their thirties, the same age as Gen 3."

"That's because that's how old they were when put in Stasis on Earth One," Rex stated, still not hiding his impatience. "The Innovator had good reasons to select people in that age range for the journey. They are healthy. They are fully educated with experience. They are still young enough to bear children to populate Earth Two."

"But Crew members don't procreate after thirty," Kendra protested.

"Because life expectancy is shorter aboard Humanity One. That's why we are allowed adulthood status at sixteen. That's why we can begin procreating earlier, to give us time to train our children."

Kendra was slightly miffed that Rex took the mystery out of her information. But ... she knew that was what he usually did – brain things up until it drained the mystery and, sometimes, the fun. "But why are there thousands of embryos," she challenged and waited for a response.

"Embryos? Human embryos?" Maddie asked. "Are you sure?"

"Positive. So, Rex, why are their human embryos?" Kendra was still upset with Rex's pedantic dismissal. She wanted to see how he would respond to her revelation.

Rex was stumped. "I can't answer that factually. How many are in Stasis?"

"Thousands. More than there are people in TSVs."

Rex thought a moment. "Maybe the Innovators decided the extra embryos could be used to increase genetic diversity. The embryos can be implanted if couples have difficulty procreating – or in addition to their own children. That would provide more bloodlines without the resource cost of transporting more people."

"Is that for sure?" Maddie asked, puzzled.

"No. Not for sure. Just speculation," Rex replied with a shrug.

"And there were creatures. All kinds of creatures, plus embryos of those same creatures." Kendra continued recounting what she had seen.

"What do you mean creatures?" Maddie was eagerly curious, her concerns about being discovered were pushed into the recesses of her mind.

"Some with four legs. Some with no legs. Some appeared to be hairy. Others seemed hairless, especially the legless ones."

"Was there anything to describe what they are?"

"A lot, but I don't remember it all. Bovinae. Caninae. Pisces. They were in groups, sorted by legs and hair mostly."

"What are they for?"

Rex intruded and answered more overbearingly than he intended, "Earth One was home to more than humans. The planet was inhabited by a diverse population of creatures and plants. Some of the creatures were food and fiber sources for humans."

Both young women stared at Rex. The idea he presented was foreign. Finally, Maddie asked, "How do you know this?"

"Reading old archive files." Rex shrugged. "I'm curious. Everyone should try it. You learn things."

"They ate those creatures?" Kendra's face reflected disgust. "They looked ugly. Some were very large. We're not going to eat them, are we?"

Rex shook his head. "I'm sure we won't, but the children of Earth Two might. That is probably why they are included, to breed and provide additional chow sources, especially if Earth Two doesn't have biological diversity that's suitable to humans."

"We have plenty of chow from our gardens to feed us," Maddie stated angrily. "We don't need anything else."

Kendra saw Maddie's growing ire with Rex. She did not want them to degrade into a point-counterpoint. She hesitantly continued, "I also saw a huge seed bank in stasis. Seeds of plants we don't grow in Hydroponics. Kevin said he's read the history of the seeds that Stasis protects. He said some of them are for plants that are taller than ten humans stacked atop one another."

"What are they for?"

"I don't know, but Kevin said everything in Stasis was important, maybe as important as the people in Stasis. The Innovators thought of everything."

"Well," Rex said pragmatically, "they didn't think of everything. We need to determine what the aliens are saying to us." He opened his clenched hand to emphasis the small data chip. "If you two want to continue talking, continue. In the meantime, I'm going to go listen to this."

Maddie was torn between following Rex and staying with Kendra. She opted to stay with Kendra. Less chance of being discovered. There would be too many people around the entertainment area. If they kept pressing their luck, someone would report them for being together without a Gen 3 chaperone. As she watched Rex disappear into a passageway, she turned to Kendra and grinned. "Okay, Rex is gone. Is there something between you and Kevin?"

Kendra blushed. She averted her eyes and smiled sheepishly. "Something."

"I knew it. Tell me about him." Maddie was eager to hear her friend's story. She had always thought Rex would mate with Kendra or Jana. With Jana gone, the obvious choice was Kendra. Maybe Kendra's options were wider than anyone imagined. Mating between Generations was not considered an option because the age difference was still too great after only four generations of elapsed time and controlled procreation.

"He's nice," Kendra replied. Unsure, she continued. "We began talking in the Mess Hall a few months ago."

"What about?"

"Just stuff. I knew he worked in Stasis. I hoped I could learn something more. I didn't know he was the son of Chief Deanna."

"Chief Deanna? How old is he? He looks young for a Gen 3."

"He's only twenty-six." Kendra's voice softened. "His older sibling,

Chief Deanna's first born, recycled before achieving adulthood. Heart failure."

"Heart failure?" Maddie winced. The phenomenon was too frequent. Too convenient.

"Yes. Chief Deanna was allowed to have another child to train as her replacement."

Maddie thought about the chain of events that would have led to Kevin's eventual birth. Chief Medical Officer Katherine would have made the decision to allow it. Births were tightly controlled. Population control was a fact of life, a matter of continuation within the finite confines of Humanity One. To maintain the four hundred plus inhabitants, very few couples were allowed more than one child. She thought about what she had learned from Doctor Aaron. That era would have been when Gen 3's health issues were coming to light, when Medical procreation decisions were made in hopes of protecting life expectancy. She wondered why a parent whose child recycled because of heart failure would be allowed to have another child. Her thoughts formed verbally, to Kendra's shock, "Why was Chief Deanna allowed to have another child if her first one was defective?"

Kendra stared at Maddie. She wondered how her friend could ask such a question about Kevin. "Why shouldn't Chief Deanna be allowed to have a replacement?"

Maddie was shocked by her own brashness. She should not have asked the question so bluntly, if at all. She stammered her response. "I'm not saying she shouldn't have, but I hope ... for Kevin's sake ... that Medical studied the issue. Is Kevin medically sound?"

"Of course!" Kendra snapped. "The problem was with Deanna's mate. He wasn't allowed to sire her second child."

Maddie wanted to ask who Kevin's sire was but chose to avoid that and to change subjects. "Has Kevin mentioned any secret knowledge from Stasis? Zack apparently doesn't have access as a Trainee. Surely, Kevin ... as Chief-To-Be ... knows something more."

Kendra looked away from Maddie. A slight movement of air fluttered the turnip greens. The motion caught her eye, striking immediate fear in her heart. Satisfied the movement was not a danger, her topaz eyes returned to Maddie's face. Anxiously awaiting face. Maddie's curiosity, her relentless desire to know secret knowledge caused the Group to be dissolved. And Jana to be recycled. Kendra was good at keeping secrets – but not all of them. "He explained that when Humanity One's Crew reaches Gen 7 and Gen 8; changes will take place in Hydroponics to allow room for more plant varieties. Taller plants called trees. The trees will be used on Earth Two."

"Why grow them on Humanity One? Just plant the seeds on Earth Two."

"Apparently, the trees require decades to mature. To be successful, they need to be at least half a decade old to transplant."

"That's a long time."

"He said the trees don't mature for years, and that they keep growing for decades."

"That's amazing." Maddie was fascinated by the trees, but they were not her interest. "Did he say anything about the people in Stasis? Anything we don't already know."

"Not really."

"What did you do in Stasis, when you weren't learning the secrets?" Maddie's question was teasing.

Kendra blushed.

CHAPTER 29

DECISION TIME

No one was using the music player. Rex was filled with relief at his good fortune. A group of Gen 4s and a few Gen 3s were watching a movie stored in the entertainment computer. The colorful action was displayed on a screen that was one wall of a sloped-deck room with utilitarian seating, The Theater, as it was known. The sound was always louder than it needed to be. No one ever adjusted it, though most would complain about the volume at one time or another. The cinematic offerings were other-worldly. It was difficult to relate to the movies for the inhabitants of the known world of Humanity One. A world – Earth One – with various modes of powered transportation that traveled along seemingly unending roadways, across vast expanses of water, or through endless open skies was the setting for all the stories. Each story had a protagonist and an antagonist of some nature that moved from one crisis to another – accented by mood altering music – until an ending arrived. Rex wondered if everyone thought it odd that all the people, the actors, in the movies wore full body clothing – most of the time. Of course, the environment portrayed by the movies was not controlled like that inside Humanity One. Also, each movie was prefaced by a voice-over that encouraged all viewers to regale in the fact that a successful Mission to Earth Two could once again make all the wonders shown in the movies a reality for humankind. Rex learned early that being the protagonist, the hero, was the only choice. He seldom watched them after his twelfth year. Reading and viewing the knowledge in the ship's archives provided more entertainment and made more sense because it was not contrived. The archives even explained the penchant for clothing as protection against the elements and as adornments. He wondered if the Gen 1s had watched those same movies; their hearts and minds filled with nostalgia and regret for a way of life lost. No other Generation would feel the same.

The small chip did not go into the music player easily. It was slightly curved, bent from poor storage. His fingers trembled with anticipation and nervous fear of discovery. It required two tries before it seated properly in the reader slot. Rex commanded the data to play. He was able to distinguish a pattern of syllabification that resulted in three distinct sound patterns. After listening repeatedly, he believed the sounds were definitely words of an unknown language. He varied the play speed. Each version a different octave and cadence, but decidedly the same words. He could only assume that the original speed and pitch on the chip was the natural sound. The voice used to make the sounds was not exactly the same as a human voice, but it was not unpleasant to hear. Context meant everything in interpretation. Rex was forced to make assumptions about context because there was none.

"Sci-Tech Trainee Rex Si Wu-Ershiliu."

The commanding sound of the voice cut through Rex's mind, interrupting his concentration on the other sound, the alien voice. Startled, he jerked around to see who called his name. He recognized the man as a member of a small security team that roamed the vessel and reported to Captain Cesar. "Yes. I'm Rex Si Wu-Ershiliu." He responded automatically, fearfully.

"Come with me. The Captain has ordered that you be escorted to the Premier's Decision Room."

Rex gulped. The man's face was steady and emotionless. He could not discern a reason by reading the man's expression. He was afraid that Cesar was finally reacting to the Mess Hall confrontation. "Why does Captain Cesar want me?"

The security man answered flatly, "I didn't ask. Follow me."

Rex knew he had no choice. He resolved to not tremble, to not show fear. If his fate were to be the same as Jana's, it was a fate that he would have to face alone, like she did. If he could avoid it, it was his to avoid. With thoughts of the future on his mind, he pulled the chip from the computer port and tucked it into a conveniently designed fold in his waistcloth.

The walk from the Entertainment Room to the Premier's Decision Room was silent. Rex was not pushed or rushed along the passageway. He followed. The security man trusted that Rex would do so willingly and calmly. In truth, even if he chose to flee, there was no way to avoid discovery if a serious search was underway. Humanity One had few hiding places.

After opening the Decision Room door, the security man motioned for Rex to enter, then closed the door behind him.

Rex was on his own. Stan was not there, nor was his mother. No one to defend him, to plead his case, to plead for his life. The lighting was even throughout the room. No stark difference from one end to the other. The dour faces of Premier Paul, Chief Doctor Katherine and Captain Cesar stared at him expectantly from across a large table. His mind reeled with a loud thought, *"The Triumvirate awaits."* He had no idea what that meant, but it was what he thought in that moment. Rex was not sure if being called before only three of the VLT was a good or bad thing. The "secret" Menu Items he read before the Group was disbanded clearly defined those three as the powers who would lead the final phases of the Mission. He could only wonder if they would lead the final phases of his life. He waited; his hands clinched against the waistcloth around his hips to control his trembles. His last visit to that room did not end well.

Premier Paul sat in a central chair on the opposite side of the long, oval conference table. With chairs enough for the entire VLT surrounding it, there was only enough extra space for a computer table inside the room. Typical space saving in Humanity One's design. Without smiling, his gnarled hand motioned toward a chair across the table and directly in front of Rex.

Rex complied by clumsily seating himself in the chair. Captain Cesar watched him closely from a chair immediately to the Premier's right, as did Doctor Katherine from a chair on the left. His throat was tight. He was sure it was just heavy mucus, but he did not want to break the silence by clearing it. He held his hands in his lap rather than expose his nervousness by placing them on the table.

"Rex Si Wu-Ershiliu," Premier Paul's voice was stronger than he appeared to be physically, "your continued heretic ranting has brought you before us today." His gray eyes barely blinked as he assessed Rex's reaction. "You defy the Innovators by claiming you can increase the speed of Humanity One. You denounce the greatness of the Innovators by promising energy resources that only you can deliver. Why do you insist that you know more than the Innovators?"

Rex was sure his throat was closed. He could not muster enough saliva to swallow. He was sure he would suffocate. Cesar's dark eyes glared between Rex and the Premier. If Rex were not more worried about the precariousness of his position, he would have wondered whether he or the Premier was the object of the dark looks. Doctor Katherine simply stared emotionlessly. His voice cracked. He had to restart his response because the sounds that came out of his mouth were not legible words. "I am not denouncing the greatness of the Innovators. I am offering their science."

Premier Paul scoffed. "Their science? Do you not think they would have shared their science if it were so?"

Rex blinked. It was obvious that Premier Paul, that most of the Gen 2s and Gen 3s, did not know about the Innovators' science. They only knew the contents of the MGR. The MGR was their science, the foundation of their reasoning, the answer to everything. He pulled himself upright and placed his hands and forearms on the table, an automatic response to present his confidence. "Just the opposite, Premier Paul. They *do* share their science. It is in the archives. Their science is the basis of my idea for harvesting more energy."

Premier Paul's face reddened. "Are you so immature that you think we don't know the science of the Innovators? The heresy of increasing speed is tantamount to declaring everything the Innovators provided us as inconsequential. Greater speed, if it were possible, would have already been available. The Innovators would have seen to that. You are declaring the Innovators to be fallible – or worse, fools."

Rex was compelled to defend himself. No one else would. "In no way did I imply that the Innovators' science was fallible. I would never say they were fools. Their science is valid. Very valid. Under the circumstance they faced, they used the science the best way possible."

"And yet you declare you can do it better?"

"The conditions of our journey have changed from what the Innovators predicted. We are now behind schedule. We have encountered aliens, non-humans, that we didn't expect, that the Innovators believed did not exist – at least not to be a threat to our Mission."

"Rumors!" Premier Paul's eyes became slits.

Rex jerked back from the Premier's angry retort. "You know and I know it is not a rumor. The aliens are attempting to communicate with us even as we sit here." He revealed what he knew, knowledge that he also knew was not shared beyond a very small group that did not include him.

Doctor Katherine's eyes widened. Captain Cesar's eyes fixed on Rex, the center of his undivided attention. Premier Paul was duly startled, as Rex hoped – or feared. The Leaders of Humanity One could react badly toward the one who dared to know a secret. That fact was not a secret.

Paul started to speak. Cesar held up his hand without taking his eyes off Rex. "Sci-Eng Trainee Rex, what do you know of alien communication?"

"Only that we are receiving a repeated message. More importantly, I know that we have to do something different than is covered by the MGR if we want to complete the Mission successfully. To avoid failure, we must first acquire more energy resources."

Cesar's dark-skinned-hand held Premier Paul at bay with a simple gesture. The conversation was now his to lead. "Do you really believe Humanity One can go faster?"

Rex relaxed. The Captain's tone was less accusative than the Premier's. The Captain sounded genuinely inquisitive. "With the proper modifications."

"What kind of modifications?"

"Software changes within the energy harvesting system. At present, we capture only the proton particles that bombard our stellar engine parasols. We can capture more of the available particle energy if we change our process."

"Heresy!" The Premier sounded enraged. "The MGR does not provide for changes."

Cesar raised himself to his full seated height, almost a head higher than Paul. "The MRG also does not provide for other sentient beings.

We must find a solution. We brought Sci-Eng Tech Rex here to hear what he has to offer. Let's listen to what he has to say."

"I didn't bring him. You did," Paul snapped.

Cesar's brow furrowed. He replied slowly and deliberately, "Yes ... I did, because unless we do something, our Mission is a failure and Humanity One is lost."

Paul calmed, "But the MGR ..."

Cesar interrupted Paul and added his own ending to the sentence, "The MGR demands that we complete the Mission successfully. *That* is the primary objective of all of it." He turned to Rex. "What makes you think you can improve energy harvesting? How will that increase speed?"

Rex studied his fingers as he entwined them. "In simple terms, space contains more than just protons. Because of planned need, only protons are currently harvested because they are easier to contain. By adjusting the stellar parasols' capabilities, we can harvest other particles for use. With that, we will have more particles for the proton drives to expel."

Cesar thought about Rex's response for a moment. "Would the increased number of particles allow us to use the proton drives to defend ourselves."

"I haven't given that much thought, though in principle it might work that way. But I must clarify, even if we make the upgrade to the software, it will take time to achieve sufficient energy reserve to begin the speed increase."

"How much time?"

"Depends on how much speed increase you want."

"Enough to demonstrate we can control our speed, that we aren't helpless, and that we are leaving the alien's territory."

Rex met the Captain's eyes for the first time. "Are we in their territory?"

"I can only assume that is the reason they are following us."

"And the reason they are trying to communicate with us?"

Cesar slowly nodded. "Probably."

"What are they saying?"

"We don't know. That is why Chief Gail is not present to hear your seemingly heretic ideas. She and others are working to decipher the signals."

Rex thought a moment before he spoke. "Has she converted the electromagnetic signals into auditory?"

"You mean sounds?" Doctor Katherine finally spoke, almost startling everyone else in the room.

"Aye, Doctor. They sound like words, three distinct words."

Katherine was puzzled. "How do you know that? We didn't even know that. Did we Captain?"

"No, we didn't. It makes sense though. Sounds might be easier to identify. But the question now is, how do you know they are sounds?"

Rex knew he had said too much. The Captain approved Jana's recycle because she dug into information not hers to know. The alien communication was not his to see – or hear. Exposing secrets can lead to recycling. "It's part of Humanity One's record – unless it's quarantined from general access." He made up a cover story. "When I study in the archives, if I come across data that makes no sense to me, I sometimes convert it to sound to help decipher it. I converted what I found to sound."

Cesar was not satisfied with Rex's response, but he chose to not pursue the explanation. "Why do you waste time from your duties to pursue random data? If you are remiss in performing your duties, you are no longer viable."

The weight of the Captain's words was clear. "I study the archives to enhance my knowledge," Rex quickly responded. He hurried his answer. "I learn the basis of the knowledge, of the science used by the Innovators. That makes it more meaningful, more usable. I believe it makes me even more viable. There is much more to their knowledge than that revealed in the MGR. I believe they expected us to use their knowledge, all of it, not just the MGR, if we encountered unplanned problems. Success of the Mission depends on our use of their knowledge, all of it."

Cesar smirked, "You're talking too fast. That makes me suspicious." He nodded toward the computer screen. "Show me your plan for the improved energy harvest."

Rex squirmed. "I don't have a prepared plan."

"What? I thought you knew what to do."

"Aye Captain. I do know what to do. I have thought about it for a long time. It can be done."

"You come to me with nothing more than an idea, a scheme?" Cesar shook his head.

"It's called a thought experiment," Rex scrambled.

Cesar leaned back. "Thought experiment? Maybe you *have* been neglecting your duties."

"No Captain. I did that work on my time away from my training. In my free time. I study the archives, the mathematic basics that support the calculations used for Humanity One's creation and journey. Very often, great mathematicians used thought experiments to develop theories. From that, they could test them before putting them into practical use."

Cesar looked toward Paul and Katherine, not for approval or support, but for emphasis. "How soon can this thought experiment become reality?"

"It will require two, maybe three days, to complete the software changes." Rex doubted he could complete the recoding in that time, but he did not think an answer of a week or two would be accepted favorably.

"Who do you need to help you make it faster?"

"It's code writing. I have to reset the acceptance parameters for the particle harvest within the original software. I also need to recode some of the parasol positioning parameters. No one I know understands both coding *and* particle science."

"Are you saying no one in Science Engineering knows what you know?" Doctor Katherine interjected skeptically.

"No, Doctor. That is not what I'm saying. Many Sci-Eng Techs understand particle science, but coding is done by Elec-Techs. I know of no one who knows both."

"And you do? Why are you privy to what no one else is?"

"Like I said. I study the archives. I have Elect-Tech friends who share what they know. Anyone who wants to learn it can do so. I wanted to learn it."

"Everyone else is concerned about their duties. Avoiding distractions." Katherine scolded.

"A greater depth of knowledge, an understanding of the underlying principles that form that knowledge, helps everyone perform their duties."

"A Hy-Tech would be distracted by computer coding knowledge," the Doctor argued, "which would reduce her ability to produce maximum crops to feed the Crew."

"Possibly, but as a Sci-Eng Tech, a broader, more in-depth knowledge helps me consider options for problem solving – options not always presented in the MGR. I believe the Captain has knowledge that does not pertain to being Captain, but it helps him address a variety of issues more quickly."

Cesar raised his hand, once again taking control of the conversation. "Regardless of the distraction or value, you say you can provide more energy, more speed. I want that completed ASAP. Now, what do the three words sound like?"

Rex paused before he reached into the fold in his waistcloth and withdrew the small data chip as he nodded toward the computer. "Does that computer have audio capability?"

All eyes turned to Premier Paul. After a moment of panicked reaction, he replied, "I'm unsure, but the computer in my quarters is capable. Chief Robert likes …," he paused embarrassedly, "… liked to listen to music while he relaxed.

"May we use your computer to hear the words sent by the aliens?" Cesar asked of the Premier.

Paul glanced toward Rex. "Of course. It would be good to hear this voice from the supposed alien. Maybe we can put this all to rest and not violate the MGR."

Cesar ignored the comment as he rose from his chair and moved cautiously around the chairs toward the door that led to the Premier's quarters. Rex followed the older people and waited for the Premier to offer his computer. He noticed the Captain's struggle to walk when he first arose.

The sound from the speakers filled the room. Rex played and replayed it, happy for the opportunity to continue what he had started before being interrupted by the security man.

"That doesn't sound like any words I've ever heard," Premier Paul finally stated. "What makes you think it's words?"

Rex answered, "The file is electromagnetic waves which are essentially sound waves. They began as sound when the aliens transmitted them and were converted to electromagnetic signals. This is simply converting them back to the original sounds."

"The MGR says nothing about that."

"Listen," Cesar admonished the Premier. "Just listen."

Again, the four listened for several minutes. Finally, Cesar sat back and looked at Rex. "Can you tell what they are saying?"

"No. In the assumed context, I could make some conjectures."

"Let's hear some of your ideas."

Rex scrambled to backtrack. "I don't know that I'm right. Just guesses. Probably wrong."

"Say it," Cesar commanded.

Rex gulped. "Their tonal inflections aren't harsh, or don't seem to be. It doesn't sound like they are angry. But ... they are challenging."

"Understood. Tell me." Cesar glared.

"They may be telling us to stop. Or maybe they are asking why we are here."

"In three words?" Paul asked.

"Their sentences may be structured differently. I don't know. They may have intentionally used fewer words, like Cesar just did with "Tell me." There are not enough sounds, enough words to understand their language, to know for sure." Rex felt trapped. He was not a linguist, and his natural self-confidence had put him in the limelight on a subject he did not understand. The meaning of the message was a guessing game.

Cesar's face softened imperceptibly, and his eyes glazed momentarily. Rex recognized the subtle signs of Communicator initialization. Paul and Katherine were apparently engaged as well. He accepted the reprieve that came with their distraction.

After a few minutes, Cesar focused on Rex. "I have instructed Chief Gail and Chief Bernie to allow you access to the energy harvest computer systems immediately. Also, they both said they have not considered converting the signals to sounds. They will do that now. Attend to your energy plan." The last words were a command and dismissal.

Rex turned to leave and froze when Doctor Katherine effusively said, "Why don't we connect the incoming transmission to a Communicator?"

"What?" Cesar and Paul both asked simultaneously.

Cesar continued, "What are you suggesting?"

"The Communicators function in a totally different way than

auditory communication. It relies upon the entire body of meanings associated with messages, including the potential to share the surroundings of the people in Communication, whereas normal auditory communication merely relies upon sound patterns."

"I generally understand the concept," Cesar said, dismissively puzzled. He wanted the answer, not the explanation. "What are you suggesting? That the Communicators could interpret the signals we are receiving?"

"Possibly. The Communicators utilize our brains' electromagnetic impulses, readable in an EEG, which are transmitted to other Communicators and converted back into electromagnetic impulses via TMS, transcranial magnetic stimulation. Sights, sounds, emotions, even physical pain can be transmitted and understood by the receiving Communicators."

"So, you believe those radio signals can be synthesized through a Communicator?"

Rex watched Doctor Katherine's face as she formed an answer. The idea was pure genius as far as he was concerned. He developed a new respect for the Gen 2 Medical Officer. Her suggestion was bold and not from the MGR.

"The Communicator will have to be an implant. It can't function on its own. Someone will have to receive the signal." Katherine paused pensively before adding, "It could be damaging."

"I'll do it," Rex volunteered eagerly. The prospect of Communicating with an alien life form was exciting.

Cesar scowled. "You'll do no such thing. You have a task. Get to it."

As Rex left the room, he overheard Doctor Katherine cautiously offer, "It will come with some risk. It has to be someone intelligent enough to understand but willing to risk recycling if it fails badly. Someone who has very little remaining life to lose and a viable replacement available. I know who that person should be."

Rex did not hear the name offered by Doctor Katherine.

CHAPTER 30

NEW LIFE

The opportunity to learn more secrets intrigues Maddie. "Do you think Kevin will give me a tour of Stasis?" She grinned at Kendra. "I promise that's all I will ask of him."

Kendra laughed. "We can't get caught together."

"So, you want me to go see him alone," Maddie teased.

"Not what I said," Kendra slapped Maddie's forearm playfully. "Maybe I can go for a short time. I'm caught up for the day. After all, we were told we couldn't be together without a Gen 3 chaperone. Kevin is Gen 3." She paused and her brow tensed with strained focused. The Communicator required effort, especially for the less experienced. She finally relaxed. "Okay. Kevin will meet us at the entrance. Let's go."

The narrow passageways crowded the two friends together as they hurried toward Stasis. They only met one person along the way, a Gen 3 Hy-Tech woman who smiled and greeted Kendra warmly. "You look radiant today, Kendra. Even more than usual."

Maddie bemusedly watched the exchange as the three of them carefully passed in the tight space. She noticed Kendra wince slightly as the two Hy-Techs passed and brushed against one another. Kendra rubbed her breast as they continued on their way. "Are you okay?"

Kendra quickly dropped her hand to her side. "I'm fine. Mandy accidentally hit me with her shoulder."

Kevin met the two of them as promised. His face beamed at Kendra. "Follow me and I will show you my world."

Kendra blushed and smiled. "Kevin, Maddie has never been in Stasis. We thought today would be a good day to tour."

Maddie grinned, "It has to be a quick tour. Captain Cesar excused the Con-Sys Trainees for the rest of the day, so I thought I could use it to learn something new. Maybe we could see some of the TSVs. Kendra was telling me that you also have garden seeds in Stasis. Maybe you could show us that area. All we ever hear about is the people in Stasis." She did not want to openly ask to see everything, but figured a general request would get the tour started outside the normally expected areas.

Kevin's eyes lit with excitement. People like to share what they know, prove their worth with their knowledge. A future Chief is no different. "Absolutely. How much time do you have? My day is almost over, so I've got all night if you want."

Maddie laughed. "Maybe an hour. The Captain might call us back before our day is done." She did not want to spend too long unchaperoned with Kendra and risk being caught, though Kevin's presence would be acceptable as a chaperone. She was not sure if each had to have a Gen 3 present, or if one Gen 3 was sufficient. She also wondered if the restrictions would end when they achieved adulthood. Rex was mere days away and she was not far behind him.

"Then the short tour it is. Let's go to the Training Room first. I can introduce you to our people in that room and you can see how the TSVs are tended on a small scale." Kevin led the way.

Zack was startled. He looked up to see who had entered his normally lonely room. Kevin seldom came into the Training Room. As an adult Sta-Tech, he monitored the larger rooms with hundreds of

TSVs. Kendra and Maddie were a bigger shock. He averted his eyes, afraid that by looking at them he was subject to recycling.

"Sta-Tech Trainee Zack," Kevin said with a grin, "I think you know Kendra and Maddie." He did not wait for confirmation. "They want a tour of Stasis. I'll try to not disturb your charges while I show them around."

Kevin explained how the TSVs maintained the individuals within them. He pointed out the control and monitor panels and computer screens that helped the Sta-Tech ensure the safety of each individual in each TSV. He closed his explanation with, "The loss of even one of our TSV inhabitants could seriously affect the success of our Mission. Each person in Stasis holds knowledge and skills that will be necessary to establishing humanity on Earth Two ..." he paused then added, "and reestablishing human civilization."

"I thought the archives held all the knowledge accumulated by the humans on Earth One," Maddie challenged.

Kevin was not swayed. "Reading the knowledge and actually knowing how to use the knowledge are two vastly different things. That's why all our training, yours and mine, is a combination of study and practice. Within these vessels are human beings, contemporaries of the Innovators, who can process that knowledge and transform Earth Two into the civilization that existed on Earth One. They will be the Founders of Earth Two's civilization. They have used their knowledge while on Earth One. There's more to knowledge than just knowing." He grinned to soften the urgency of his tone.

"Is that why some knowledge is kept secret?"

Kendra's brow furrowed. She was not expecting Maddie to approach the secrecy subject that bluntly, especially not with Kevin. Her stomach knotted.

Kevin did not appear to be affected by Maddie's question. He grinned. "I'm not aware of knowledge that is being kept secret, but some knowledge that we could access would be useless to us at this point in our journey toward Earth Two."

"But should it be kept secret? Why can't we know it? As you said, there's more to knowledge than just knowing. Someone should be allowed to practice the use of that knowledge."

Kevin remained calm and engaged, even though Maddie was increasingly insistent. "That makes sense to a degree. The Innovators realized the importance of practical application, or practice as you call it. That is the primary reason for the people in Stasis. So much of what they know can't be practiced inside a vessel like Humanity One."

"But, if something happens to the people in the vessels, even one – like you said, - something important could be lost. We should know everything there is to know." Maddie was on her soapbox.

"As I said, it would be useless. If it's useless, it's a distraction from the journey." Kevin motioned with his hand, "These vessels and the vessel we travel in demand our focus and undivided attention. A minor mistake by one of us today could easily compound into a major mistake by journey's end. It is better to let that knowledge bide its time until its time has come."

Maddie felt as though Kevin was dancing well-choreographed steps of an adult dance, the dance of a Chief-To-Be. His kind reaction to her was likely because of his affection for Kendra – and it was apparent that there was affection. She decided to allow the subject to rest for the moment. "Okay. Where do we go to see Kendra's garden seeds?"

Kevin laughed, a disguised sign of relief to change subjects. "Oh! You really do want to learn the secrets. Not many people even care about the seed Stasis Room. The people in the TSVs are more interesting to the average visitor." He familiarly placed his hand on the small of Kendra's back to gently guide her forward. "The Agronomy Stasis Room is down this passageway."

Maddie was surprised at the size of the Agronomy Room. Rows

of drawered shelves left little room for a person to navigate among them. The shelves were cold. The room was dark until they entered. Automatic lighting slowly brightened to allow visibility. A LED monitor panel was mounted to each section of shelves. Temperature and humidity were primary readings, with additional measurements that Maddie did not understand. "What does agronomy mean?" The word meant nothing to her.

Kevin replied, "Good question. Agronomy is the study, or science, of plant growing. In Hydroponics, the growing conditions are designed to support our chow crops in a soilless environment. We don't expect to produce our edibles in rooms when we settle Earth Two. We will use the native soil to grow our crops."

"Why would we not simply build Hydroponics on Earth Two?" Maddie asked. "Kendra and the Hy-Tech's know how to do it that way."

Kevin motioned around the huge room. "As you might imagine from the size of this seed storage room, with wide open space – and more of it – we will grow many more varieties of plants."

"What more could we need?"

Kevin smiled and walked to a shelf of drawers and touched the monitor. The monitor screen became a computer screen. "In drawer 07-98 is two-hundred pounds of seeds, cotton seeds. This is how cotton is grown on Earth One." The screen showed an inset of a cotton plant against a seemingly endless field of cotton plants.

"What is cotton?"

Kendra interjected. "We grow a small amount of cotton. It's used, along with recycled cotton, to make waistcloths." She was eager to share what she knew.

Maddie pointed to the screen, "But that makes it look like we will need a lot of cotton."

Kevin nodded. "We will. Even more than these few seeds can provide. It will take a few years to reach full productivity on Earth

271

Two. Inside our controlled environment, we don't require full body cover – except for some specialized tasks. In the open space of a planet's atmosphere, we will be exposed to temperature changes that could make us uncomfortably hot or cold, rough surfaces that could abrade or cut us, solar radiation that could burn our skin. A lot of potential hazards. Full body covering will protect us. We will even need coverings for our feet because the surface of the planet will be rough and uneven, capable of harming the soles of our feet."

Maddie stepped closer to the screen and studied the cotton plant and field. She looked at Kendra. "I didn't know we grew cotton. I guess that was a secret too."

Kendra blushed. She took Maddie's words as an insult. "No. Anyone who wanted to know could have known it. If you want to see how cotton is grown, we can go see it."

Maddie turned to Kevin, "You kind of make it sound like growing chow on Earth Two will be different than on Humanity One."

"Oh, definitely. Gravity. Natural rainwater. Soil nutrients. There are many factors. Even the conditions of the soil. We have starts for fungi, enzymes, microscopic organisms, and other things to add to Earth Two's soil if it lacks any of those things necessary for plants to grow properly. Agronomy is a vast science, but not one that we need to know in its entirety on Humanity One." Kevin grinned mischievously, his eyes twinkled teasingly, "That's another one of those secrets."

Maddie ignored his side comment, though it did register in her mind. "What other kinds of plants will we have? Will we need something different than we already grow – other than just more of them?"

"Of course. Over here are our tree seeds." Kevin led the two females to another shelf of drawers. He touched the monitor to reveal a screen. He input using a touch menu. "The seeds in 04-22 are a variety of apple tree." He moved aside so Maddie could get closer. An inset of a red apple with yellow streaks was surrounded by a leafy tree with heavy fruit hanging from every limb. "This tree grows up to twenty-five feet tall and can produce as many as 5 bushels of apples per growing season."

Maddie studied the pictures. She looked at Kendra. "Do you have any of these secretly growing?"

Kendra shook her head and scowled at her friend. "No. We don't have any rooms big enough for those trees ... or any trees."

"What are they - the apples?"

Kevin replied, "They are an edible fruit. I don't know how they are eaten, but I do know we have more than fifty varieties of apple trees. We have seeds of hundreds of edible fruits, including different varieties of each. Growing them will require large expanses of land."

"What do they taste like?" Maddie asked.

Kevin laughed. "I don't know that any more than you do. I'm sure they must be tasty if the Innovators decided to take up space for them."

"What other seeds do you have in here?"

"Grass seeds. Shrubs. Flowers. And other vegetables that offer variety for consumption."

"What is grass?" Maddie knew that if she asked, Kevin would take them to a monitor that would show grass growing. It was green. "What is it used for? Food?"

Kevin shook his head. "Some of it is used to feed animals. I'm not sure what all its uses are."

"What are animals?" Maddie was not going to allow unknown words discourage her curiosity.

"That's in another room. We have some animals in stasis and more in embryonic form. And ... before you ask, I know very little about the animals other than some were used for food. They require vast amounts of space to grow and reproduce. The people in the TSVs know what to do with them."

"What would it hurt for us to know?"

Kevin thought a moment, collecting his thoughts, gathering memories of learned knowledge. "That is knowledge that has no value, a mere distraction. If you knew how to grow, slaughter, and process a bovine into chow, what good would that knowledge do inside Humanity One? We've never seen chow harvested from a bovine and we will never see it. There is no need to know that knowledge. It would be a distraction."

"So, you think the secret knowledge should remain a secret?"

"I don't think of it as secret knowledge. I consider it as knowledge that has no value. I know some of these things because I expect to become Chief of Stasis someday, so I studied some of the archives. None of what I learned in the archives has helped me do my duties of caring for all the people, creatures, and seeds in Stasis. Caring for them in Stasis is nothing like caring for them on Earth Two will be."

"But did it distract you?"

"It would have if I had pursued more than the precursory amount I did. I learned very quickly that there is more knowledge available than I can absorb and little of it helps me make our Mission a success. Do you want to see the Zoology Stasis Room?"

"What is that?"

"The animal room."

Maddie glanced toward Kendra who was swaying nervously. "Not today. Thank you for giving me the tour. I think Kendra needs to return to her Grow Room."

Kevin smiled warmly. "If you have time sometime, I can give you a longer tour. See the animals and introduce you to some of the people in the TSVs."

Maddie perked up. "They can communicate?"

Kevin laughed. "No, not like you are thinking. But each has a story and if you have the time and inclination, you can learn their stories."

After Maddie and Kendra returned to Kendra's Grow Room,

Maddie said, "I forgot to ask about the human embryos. What are the human embryos for?"

Kendra responded, "I thought we agreed it might be in case the people in Stasis have difficulty procreating."

"We speculated that to be the reason, that and additional genetic diversity, but we don't know for sure."

"You should have asked Kevin. He might know."

"I should have, but ..." Maddie grinned, "I reckon you will be visiting with Kevin before too long. You can ask him when you do."

Kendra blushed. "If I can find out without creating suspicion, I will."

"Good. Maybe we will at least learn that secret knowledge."

CHAPTER 31

EMBRYOS

Maddie saw Jean San Sanshier, Kendra's mother, enter the opposite end of the Grow room as she exited. She shivered at the thought of getting caught. She knew the Gen 3 Hy-Tech would have no choice but to report the two Trainees if they were seen together unchaperoned. Again, she was glad she was not sporting her long hair, a dead giveaway even at a fleeting glance. Jana was held to a different standard for reasons unknown to Maddie. Recycled as punishment for digging into the secret knowledge they all sought. Maddie shivered again. She knew Cesar would not give her a second chance. Rex crossed her mind. She thought about the young man she considered her best friend, her male friend so close to adulthood, mating age. He should have completed his investigation into the sound of the alien signal. He and she were taking a risk by pursuing that information. It was not their knowledge to have. She wondered if he had interpreted the signal. She wondered if his duplicity had been discovered, hers soon to follow. His Communicator was still blocked to her.

Maddie's thoughts of Rex and concerns about their safety were not enough to stifle renewed curiosity brought about by her Stasis tour. The visit to Stasis provided too much information to fully assimilate. The new knowledge she held was still like a secret to her. She found herself knowing more than she could understand. The unfamiliar plants and animals held within the Stasis rooms created more questions than Kevin provided answers. Maddie was unable to ask all the questions that the information created. Worse, she knew the answers would lead to further questions. Knowing secret information was not helpful if that knowledge only led to more mysteries, more secrets.

Aside from not knowing enough to be able to form precise, logically progressed questions, Maddie was also afraid to press Kevin too hard. She had to be careful to not create suspicion in his mind. Though his Gen 3 adult status might be considered chaperone for the two Gen 4s, continued inquiries into areas outside their training assignments could easily bring the two back before Captain Cesar and Premier Paul.

As Maddie walked through the passageway, she wondered how close Kendra and Kevin were. Kendra was still a few weeks shy of becoming an adult. She would be old enough to choose a mate soon. The thought of a Gen 3 mating a Gen 4 did not mesh with the paradigms of Maddie's world. What would their child - or children, if more than one was allowed - be? Gen 3.5 or Gen 4.5? Doctor Katherine and the Medical Office would probably have a hard time tracking cross generation procreation. Gen 8 was to be the final generation, the Generation that would colonize and begin terraforming Earth Two. The finality of Gen 8 in the Mission to Earth Two was not a secret. The general knowledge of that was in the MGR for anyone to read. That fact was almost pounded into their heads. Duty demanded that Humanity One arrive at Earth Two with Gen 8 mature and intact, ready for colonization and the salvation of humanity.

Maddie realized the embryos were a twist, an addition that did not fit the MGR as she knew it. The secret knowledge, those things she did not know, by its very nature must be designed to address the embryos. Whatever the secret knowledge might be, it would definitely be distracting – especially for Gen 7 as they prepared for the birth of Gen 8. It was distracting enough for her, three generations removed.

Maddie saw the entrance to the Medical Offices. She thought of Marly. Marly could answer questions - if she would. Marly's fear was greater than all the others. The young Doctor Trainee had knowledge, by nature secretive – or at least, closely held. Marly probably knew how early recycling decisions were made. Knowing too much could cause apprehension, even revulsion, like knowing how tofu was made. With a forced air of confidence, Maddie pushed through the doorway and entered Medical. Almost immediately, she heard a familiar voice wafting down a hallway. Della. She did not comprehend what was said, but Della's voice was followed by a voice she easily recognized as Captain Cesar's. He thanked her for having the courage to help the Mission.

Maddie blanched. If she had arrived earlier, or if she had not recognized the voices, she could have been caught trying to talk with Marly. She quickly left Medical and hurried along the passageway toward her quarters. She worried about Della, about what her mother could have done that required courage and a visit to Medical. She could not think of anything about a Medical visit that could be good for Della, even if it did help the Mission. Handsy Doctor Aaron's words were not ambiguous in his description of Gen 3 life-shortening ailments.

She was so involved in her own thoughts that she did not notice Marly until they brushed against one another in the passageway. "Marly!" Maddie gasped with surprise.

The young medical prodigy froze, her bare back instantly pressed against the cool wall to put as much space as possible between her and Maddie. "Maddie?"

Maddie quickly looked around. A nearby storage closet door caught her attention. She grabbed the teenaged female's upper arm and all but dragged her into the tiny space, physically overcoming the young Doctor Trainee's resistance. Until her eyes adjusted, it was too dark to see. The reveals at the top and the bottom of the door was wide enough to allow light to filter inside the small room. "Marly, I need to know why Della is in Medical."

Even in the dim light, Marly's eyes showed nervous fear. "We can't be together."

"Marly! Why is Della in Medical? Is something wrong?" Maddie whispered insistently. She was sure she could smell the younger teenager's fear in the tight quarters.

"I don't know. I didn't know she was in Medical, Maddie." Marly replied confusedly, frightened by Maddie's presence and by the older female's intensity. She scrambled for words that would extricate her from her situation. "I will find out for you if I can. Please, we can't be caught." Her voice was shaking along with her trembling body.

"Please do." Maddie relaxed. She realized she was scaring the precocious thirteen-year old. "I do have another question for you, because you know medicine."

Marly was hooked. Maddie had appealed to her pride. She relaxed slightly and whispered, "What is it?"

"Embryos."

"Simple. Gametes – male sperm and female ovum – fuse. A single cell zygote results after fertilization. Rapid cleavage follows with creates a blastula, a ball of cells awaiting further division. At that point, the cells undergo gastrulation, a process where they form layers that begin the specialization processes that create the embryos various functional parts." Reciting data, a litany of cold facts, helped calm the Doctor Trainee.

"Marly," Maddie said sharply to stop the brilliant girl's regurgitation of medical knowledge. "I know what an embryo is. What I want to know is why there are thousands upon thousands of embryos stored in Stasis."

Marly's face froze in thought as she processed Maddie's query. "Embryos in Stasis? I thought there were people in Stasis."

Maddie smiled knowingly. For some reason, she delighted in telling the young medical prodigy something unknown. "There are, but there are as many or more embryos as people. Why would the Innovators secretly store embryos?"

Marly's voice tightened. "Fear of radiation outside of Stasis." It was almost a question rather than an answer.

"What does that mean?"

"Stasis is shielded against most extra-terrestrial radiation, almost as well as Earth One. Maybe better."

"And?"

"And ... maybe the Innovators feared the Crew might suffer genetic mutations after eight generations." Marly's childlike face contorted with concern. "Maybe they were afraid we might not be healthy enough to bear children by the time we arrive at Earth Two, or ..."

Maddie waited for Marly to complete her statement. When it did not come, she asked, "Or what, Marly?"

Marly barely whispered loud enough to be heard, "Or we would not be the kind of humans they want us to be."

"What? What are you suggesting?"

"Maybe the radiation will change us, we won't be the same." Marly's tone was ominous.

Maddie's throat tightened and a chill washed over her. She immediately remembered Kendra's comment about the people in the TSVs being different. "We would still be human. That won't change." She was more hopeful than adamant; hoping that saying it would make it so.

"We've already changed," Marly replied. "We don't live as long as the Innovators. We have more cancers and health issues. Still human but not very hardy."

"What does that mean, not very hardy? How hardy do we have to be?"

Marly felt the sting of Maddie's questions. The young girl, proud of her intellect, her grasp of medical knowledge, was still a young girl. Maddie was her idol. The one non-adult female that she admired. Her admiration sprang from the fact that Maddie was ruthless when pursuing the revelations of secrecy. She felt like her idol was attacking her with the relentless questioning. Her eyes teared. "Maddie, I'm just telling you what I know to be true. Don't be angry with me." She sniffed.

Maddie leaned back. "I'm sorry Marly. I'm not angry with you. Not at all. I just think that what you know is important." She found herself with more information that did not seem to congeal into an understandable body of facts. She was no closer to knowing all the secrets than she was earlier. "The secret knowledge we want to know may be about the embryos. How many people even know about them? Few, I imagine." She pressed Marly, "Why do you think we are not hardy? How hardy do we have to be? I'm healthy. So are you."

Marly sniffed and cowed, still not convinced Maddie was calmed. "We have been raised in a low gravity vessel. Less than a third the gravity of Earth One, or Earth Two for that matter. Everything about us that makes us physically human depends on gravity."

Doctor Aaron had described problems related to Earth's gravity, or the lack thereof on Humanity One. Maddie reckoned she should have pursued it with him, but his behavior toward her made her uncomfortable. "Gravity? How?"

"Our musculoskeletal system was defined by the gravity of Earth One. Without gravity to challenge our muscles and force strength into our bones, we cannot survive on Earth Two."

Maddie protested, "We can survive, even if it is difficult."

Marly glared through tear-filled eyes in the dimly lit closet.

"Survive? Maybe. Thrive? No. The people in Stasis still have solid musculoskeletal systems. When they awaken, they will prepare to move to Earth Two, to return to the same kind of gravity they enjoyed on Earth One. They will thrive."

"But, what about the embryos?"

Marly shook her head angrily. "I told you. I didn't know about embryos until you told me when you pulled me into this closet. I'm through speculating. I don't know."

"Can you find out? You have access to Doctor Katherine's knowledge."

Marly stared at Maddie, dumbfounded by the request. "Jana was recycled for accessing the Captain's private knowledge. We barely avoided recycle for being a part of Jana's crime. I won't repeat that mistake again." She reached for the door handle.

Maddie grabbed Marly's wrist. "Wait. About the embryos. You say we have been altered – mutated – by radiation. What if the embryos are mutated?"

Marly tried to shake her wrist free of Maddie's stronger hands. "If there are embryos in Stasis, they are protected by additional radiation barriers in that part of the vessel. I told you that already. Besides, all of this quest for secret knowledge is useless. We will be long recycled before Humanity One reaches Earth Two."

Maddie loosened her grip. "It's probably more likely that we won't reach Earth Two."

Marly paused her escape. "What do you mean?"

"More secrets. Humanity One is being chased by an alien vessel. Our power reserves were spent avoiding the collision. Now we can't elude the aliens. Rex knows how to escape them, but the Captain and the others ignore him."

"Aliens? I haven't heard that."

"Of course not. It's secret knowledge." Maddie exhaled. She had the impact on Marly she needed. "Go on back to Medical where you're safe ... for now." She paused for effect before adding, "But please, see if you can find out why Della's in Medical. I'll be in the Mess Hall at first chow."

Maddie watched the smaller female scurry out of the closet door and disappear through another doorway.

CHAPTER 32

VOICES

Della's heart was beating rapidly. Doctor Katherine repeatedly explained the potential dangers, providing more graphic detail with each iteration. The added information did nothing to allay Della's fears. The input of direct radio waves could cause her Communicator to malfunction. The malfunction could be as benign as a tingling sensation that lasted as long as the signal, or as critical as an aneurism caused by overstimulation of the language conceptualizing areas of her brain. The Chief Medical Officer did not simply say either/or of those two extremes. Doctor Katherine was compelled to explain in detail how the brain functions to process language input signals and to develop responses.

Doctor Katherine meticulously explained the dangers. "If the direct signal input is not accepted by your brain, it could cause a series of misfired electrical spasms inside your language centers. Wernicke's Area will be the primary portion affected, but language comprehension involves several areas of the inferior parietal lobe and the left temporal. The posterior superior temporal gyrus, the middle temporal gyrus, the inferior temporal gyrus, the supramarginal gyrus and the angular gyrus will all be affected. You might experience a brain tingle, a feeling of "what's that?", or the impact may be so severe that it leaves you unable to understand any communication. Worst case, it could overload your parietal lobe and cause a fatal aneurism. Do you understand the risks?"

Della did not completely understand. Processing the language that the Doctor used increased Della's anxiety, though it did not lessen her resolve to help Humanity One. Most of the words used by the Doctor were unfamiliar, rendered meaningless by their novelty. The only words she needed to understand were "could ... cause a fatal aneurism." Those were the words that had her heart pounding. The entire experiment might result in immediate recycling. But ... the safety of the Crew was at stake. She could not say no. "Yes. I understand," she replied with a dry throat.

Captain Cesar placed a huge hand on her shoulder and soothingly asked, "Con-Sys Technician Della, are you sure you want to do this? If you say no, I will understand. Everyone will understand."

Della smiled nervously. Even though she was already committed to the task, she knew everyone would not understand if she backed out at that late stage of the task. She only regretted not being able to tell Maddie, to see her one last time – if that was to be. Doctor Katherine had already attached the electrodes that were supposed to send the alien signals directly to her Communicator. One of the thin wires tickled her left ear when she nodded vigorously. "I'm sure. Tell me what to do." No one would ever question her commitment to the Mission's success. Duty demanded she do it. Duty was her life, her reason for being.

Cesar looked toward Premier Paul and then Doctor Katherine. He nodded gently to each of them. He patted Della's shoulder encouragingly before withdrawing his hand. "Doctor Katherine, tell Con-Sys Tech Della what to do."

The wizened Doctor's face did not smile. Her pale gray eyes calmly watched her patient. "Della, lie back on the table, place your hands across your abdomen with your dominant hand on top, and close your eyes. You must relax and focus on the signal, on your Communicator. I will tell you when it starts. If you notice anything unusual, raise your hand immediately and I will stop."

"I don't want to stop," Della replied with as much courage as she could muster.

"We will stop and analyze where we are before we continue. A pause to make sure we are doing it correctly. We want to do it correctly. We will do this." Doctor Katherine patted Della's hands and smiled. "Now, close your eyes and relax."

Katherine looked at Cesar querulously. He nodded final approval. "Okay, Della, I am starting the signal.

Della tensed. The examination light was directly overhead. Even with her eyes closed, she could feel the pressure of the light on her eyeballs. She was sure she could see the veins in her eyelids, dark against a scarlet background. She was not sure what she saw. The Doctor's warning pulled her mind away from her eyes and brought her focus to her Communicator. A thousand thoughts ran through her mind, none of them significant enough to be remembered. She felt a message within her mind. It did not linger.

"Anything?"

Della refocused on her ears, searching for something audible. Doctor Katherine had asked a question that deserved an answer. "What?"

Doctor Katherine repeated, "Are you sensing anything?"

"Something. I'm not sure. Was that it?"

"I sent the signal to your Communicator. Did it mean anything? Did it make sense?"

Della did not open her eyes. "Not really, but it was brief. Succinct. Can you do it again? Maybe I can concentrate more."

A brief pause was followed by the Doctor's voice. "Okay. The signal starts *now.*"

"*Why are you here?*"

"Do it again," Della said urgently, breathlessly.

"Okay. The signal starts *now.*"

"*Why are you here?*" The message was clear. Short and sweet. Mechanically pure. A detectable tone of wary urgency. Della's eyes popped open, and immediately squinted against the examination light. "I heard it. *Why are you here?* That's what they are asking."

Cesar leaned forward. "Are you sure?"

"Positive. I can do it again to make sure." Della was unnerved by Cesar's challenge. She wanted to sit upright, but Cesar was in the way.

Cesar leaned back and looked at Doctor Katherine. "Can we repeat it, but with the other recording? The one with several iterations of the signal. To see if every message is the same."

Katherine leaned closer to Della, placidly empathetic. "Della, did you feel anything? Pain? Confusion? Anything out of the ordinary?"

"No," Della replied. "I can listen to the other recording." She glanced toward Cesar and smiled bravely, seeking his reassurance.

"The other one contains a dozen different signal intercepts," Cesar said. "We think they all say the same thing, but we're not sure. It would be helpful to know if there are any threats in their signals." He looked expectantly into Della's eyes.

Della nodded. "Their tone is questioning – sort of demanding. I can do it. It didn't hurt. It doesn't feel any different than when my Communicator is activated."

"Doctor?" Cesar nodded to Katherine.

"Very well. Della, close your eyes and relax. I will tell you when the signal starts."

Della waited for the Doctor's words. As soon as she heard them, her mind was filled by a repeated string of communications, "*Why are you here?"* They each carried the same wary urgency, with an increasing impatience as the messages repeated. When the signals stopped, she was jolted back to the confines of the examination room. She said breathlessly, "It's all the same message. They want to know why we are here. Do you have more signals?"

Cesar patted her shoulder. "Con-Sys Tech Della, you have done a brave thing. That's all we have. Everything is the same. Thank you for your courage."

"Are we through?" Della asked of Doctor Katherine.

"I think so. Stay still. You can sit up as soon as I take those electrodes off."

Cesar held up his hand. "Not just yet. Give me minute." With a familiar zoned look, the Captain stared straight ahead.

Electrical Chief Bernie stopped the work he was doing with Chief Scientist Gail. He understood Cesar's Communication and responded, "I think we can have something operational within a couple of hours. I assigned two of my brightest Elec-Techs before Chief Gail and I started on the decipher. They were confident they could have a radio transmitter working very soon. Are you ready to try to communicate with the aliens?"

"I am. We used the Communicator system," Cesar did not go into detail, "to interpret the signal. You and Chief Gail can cease your work. We now know what they are saying."

Without filter, Chief Bernie sent feelings of relief and disappointment, with a tone of annoyance, along with his responding Communication. "That's good. What are they saying?"

"Why are you here?" Cesar responded. "No threats, at least not now. As soon as you can provide a transmitter, we will try to send a Communication back."

"That's four words. We only hear three distinct sounds. How will you communicate with them?"

"The Communicator shares meanings, not individual sounds." Cesar knew Chief Bernie knew that. He continued by answering Bernie's question. "By connecting a Communicator to your enhance radio transmitter."

Chief Bernie's initial response was a wave of doubt. "Interesting. Will that work?"

"We'll see. Go help your Elec-Techs and expedite their task. I'll Communicate with Chief Gail so she knows she can release from the interpretation task." Without waiting for a response, Cesar switched his Communicator to Chief Gail. "Chief Gail, we have interpreted the signal. Chief Bernie has been reassigned to developing and installing a radio transmitter. In the meantime, see if Trainee Rex can use assistance. Don't interfere but be available if he needs anything."

Chief Gail was not pleased with the "assistance" directive. Cesar did not care about her new status. She was technically equal to him; the Captain was merely a Chief just like she was. She would have to make him understand her value and claim her place as Chief Robert's replacement.

Cesar shook his head and smiled wryly. Chief Gail did not hide her emotions very well. He had more important matters to attend to than her feelings. He patted Della's forearm and smiled. His face seldom smiled. It was an unfamiliar look, especially for Della who only saw his Captain's Chair face. "Della, I would like to try to Communicate with the aliens. Chief Bernie will have a transmitter set up shortly. Would you be willing to try to connect to the transmitter?"

Della did not hesitate to nod. Tentatively, she asked, "Yes. I'll do it. Will that work?"

"I don't know. As far as I know, this will be the first time something like this has been tried with a Communicator. The MGR does not mention it. I need to return to Con-Sys. In the meantime, Chief Katherine, can you coordinate with Chief Bernie for a system monitor to be moved into this room? We will need to connect the electrodes for Della. Chief Bernie is already focused on making an improved radio transmitter a reality."

⁓

Marly's face felt flushed. Outside the examination room door, she was able to overhear most of the conversation. Some parts were missed - the initial connection of the electrodes – but she arrived soon enough after her meeting with Maddie to understand why Della was in Medical. She was enthralled by what she was hearing. So much so that the door began to open before she realized she needed to move from her eavesdropping spot. She would have been caught if the door had not paused when Cesar stopped to tell Doctor Katherine to arrange a monitor for the room. She rapidly wheeled and walked away from the doorway. Before she was able to disappear into an empty examination room, the Captain's distinctive voice called her by name.

"Hello, Doctor Trainee Marly. How are you today?"

Marly stopped and turned to face the much larger man. In her agitated state, he appeared even more imposing. She gulped and forced a greeting smile, with faked surprise. "Hello Captain Cesar." She clinched her fists to keep her hands from trembling. If the Captain had not paused to speak to Doctor Katherine, she would have been caught. She was cognizant of the dangers of her risky behaviors on that day. She already had two marks against her. She was not sure she could survive a third. Recycling would have been her fate. "I am doing well. I have a patient that requires my attention." It was a lie. She was a Trainee, not an intern with patient responsibilities. She did not know if she could maintain her composure against the Captain's greater presence.

"Carry on," Cesar said. The Captain did not know the details of

Marly's duties, nor did he have reason to care at that moment. He was simply being polite.

"Aye, Captain." Marly stepped into the empty examination room and closed the door. She leaned against the door, closed her eyes, and trembled. She remained in the room until her nerves were settled. Her indiscretion with Sean compounded by her association with Maddie's and Jana's pursuit of secret knowledge caused her to doubt her own judgement, a dangerous mental state for someone who chose to become a doctor – especially if that someone was destined to be the youngest doctor ever. And her risky behavior was not over. After spying on the Captain and the Chief Medical Officer, she still had one more thing to do. She felt obligated to tell Maddie that Della was okay – and what Della was doing. She owed her friend that much. After a few minutes, she stepped from the room and headed to the Mess Hall. It was an hour early for her meal, but no one would care.

The early chow line was busy. That was good. Marly simply slipped into line with her tray and slowly chose chow servings that suited her. Maddie, without a food tray, was watching from a mixed table of Gen 3s and Gen 4s, none of them former members of the Group.

As soon as Marly entered, Maddie joined the chow line with a tray behind the young Doctor Trainee. She was not able to stand next to Marly, but they were only separated by two people. With a well-executed skip over chow choices rather than waiting for the two to get servings, Maddie was behind Marly. They were not in violation technically. They were not alone. "Hi Marly." A simple greeting that escaped scrutiny.

"Hello Maddie." Marly did not want to engage publicly. She already had her message prepared. She said cheerfully, "I saw Della earlier. I was glad to see she is doing well, as usual.

Maddie smiled. "I'm sure she was glad to see you as well."

Marly glanced furtively to either side before she whispered

hurriedly, "She's interpreting some kind of signal for the Captain." Before Maddie could ask more, Marly took her tray and sought a safe table where she could eat and regain control of her trembling body.

⁓≋⁓

"This should work," Chief Bernie said as he checked the connecting wires a third time. "I don't see anything loose." His statement was directed toward no one in particular, toward everyone in the room. Captain Cesar nodded approvingly but said nothing.

Della sat on the edge of the examination table, relieved after Doctor Katherine relented and allowed her to go to the restroom. Even though Chief Bernie and the Elec-Techs created the radio transmitter much sooner than they had promised Captain Cesar, the wait with the electrodes dangling from several points on her head was long and boring — and nerve wracking. Doctor Katherine had to shave spots in Della's blonde hair to secure the electrode pads. Della was not worried about it. Her hair would regrow quickly enough. She was hungry though; but Doctor Katherine warned her against eating before the experiment. If it did not go well, she might puke what she ate; strangle on her own vomit.

Chief Bernie grinned guardedly. "Now, we see if it will work correctly. Della, do you want to do the honors and access the Con-Sys electromagnetic scanning system, since you were helping with it before Doctor Katherine took you away?"

Della eagerly and nimbly opened the Rad-Opt menu on the computer monitor. The act gave her something to do other than wait. The device controls were not identical to the Con-Sys Room consoles, but they were easily interpreted. At least the Elec-Techs realized the need to be user friendly. The Elec-Techs had created their radio tuner/transmitter from spare parts with a LAN connection to the Control System computers. They opted for a hardwire connection rather than a Wi-Fi connection to avoid the possibility of leakage to other Communicators. Caution was key. The radio used specially created software to connect to the same external antenna used by the vessel to intercept electromagnetic signals. "It's ready to activate reception." She studied the unfamiliar screen options a moment. "And ... it would appear ... transmission is available by touching this icon." She pointed to the screen.

Chief Bernie grinned again. "We were hoping it would be intuitive. You certainly figured it out quickly enough."

Captain Cesar watched quietly until Chief Bernie and Della were finished. "Are we ready, Doctor Katherine?"

"Della is properly attached, according to what Chief Bernie has told us."

"My concern is are we ready to help Della if something goes wrong?"

Doctor Katherine scowled. She knew the Captain's words, though sincere, were spoken to put Della at ease even though his primary concern was whether or not it would work. "Della knows the risks. I have Med-Techs ready if needed."

"Good. Then let's be ready for the next signal intercept. Con-Sys says they are still on a six-minute repetition."

"Aye Captain." Katherine moved toward the examination table. "Della, let's make you comfortable."

"Why do I need to be on the table?" The larger group in the examination room made Della feel vulnerable lying on the table. Chief Bernie and an Elec-Tech had joined the Captain, Premier Paul, and Doctor Katherine.

"Too many unknowns. If live reception or transmission causes problems, you are much better presented for treatment if you are on the table. Besides, I think we need to repeat the same process we used before, eyes closed, body and mind relaxed."

Della nodded and reluctantly settled on the table. She closed her eyes and waited for Doctor Katherine to make the final connection, to activate the computer switch that connected the incoming signal to Della's Communicator. Within seconds of Doctor Katherine's notification of connection, a wave of nausea swept over Della. At first, she thought her hunger was the cause, then she realized her Communicator was trying to transfer signals to her brain. Static. Illegible input that confused her brain and disrupted her equilibrium even though she was flat on her back. She opened her eyes and stared at a point on the ceiling away from the overhead light until she overcame the vertigo and the feeling passed. Then sounds and visions. She closed her eyes to concentrate.

Della heard the words *"Why are you here?"* clearly. Familiar words in a familiar format. But the words were wrapped inside other information. A savory stew of inputs. Sounds, of course. That was expected. Sights that were not anticipated. An unfamiliar console and a gray hand with a thumb on each side activating a control, the SEND control. She muttered the word, "Transmit." That was the Elec-Tech's command to touch the screen icon.

Della focused to remember the exact words the Captain wanted her to send. "We are travelers bound for a distant planet. We are passing through. We apologize for the intrusion." She exhaled heavily when she finished. Chief Bernie had told her the response would not be instantaneous. The distance was too great for that. There was also no guarantee that her Communication would actually transmit. Plus, there was no guarantee that the alien's electronics would accept the transmission from her Communicator. They could only hope that the alien mind on the other end could accept the Communication. She kept her eyes closed and focused on her Communicator. She waited an indeterminate time, alone in her own mind.

Without warning, a feeling of shocked amazement swept over her.

A frantic reaction ensued. Thoughts interpreted as a call for someone of greater authority, searching for help. Surprise and a loss for what to do. The console blurred as the eyes seeing it swiveled at dizzying speed to one side. Humanoid forms were blurred as the eyes moved rapidly around a room filled with control screens staffed by those forms. Finally, a face appeared, apparently the greater authority, the sought-after help. Size was relative. Without a point of reference, the form that filled the mind of the someone connected to Della via the radio seemed tall.

The thin gray form scowled and barked a question, "What is wrong?"

Della felt the fear within the person – she could only think of the entity to whom she was connected via her Communicator as a person. The person was frightened that the Commander was angry with him – or her. The person responded verbally for Della to hear. "Commander, I am receiving a response."

"Well, Specialist Atny, what is the response?" The voice was strong and blunt, and instantly attentive.

Della observed the exchange, momentarily relegated to the role of eavesdropper. She controlled her Communicator to avoid extraneous thoughts from transmitting ... not an easy task under the circumstance. Most Communicator connections allowed bleed-through of feelings, even visual interpretations of surroundings. Specialist Atny was receiving the Communication through a neural connection similar to the Communicator. Della barely breathed, afraid that simple bodily function would be transmitted, as she waited.

"They are travelers from afar. They are passing through our territory. They apologize for the intrusion." Specialist Atny did not add or detract from the message from Della.

"Travelers? How far? Why did they come this way? What kind of creatures are they?"

Della saw the concerned and untrusting face of the alien vessel's Commander as it barked out the questions. She was sure she heard Specialist Atny gulp before he – that gender became clear in the thoughts and feelings that flowed – responded.

"None of that was transmitted, Commander Schnt. The Communication was only those few sentences. They responded to our question."

"Then ask them where they are from. Where they are going. Why did they invade our sovereign space? What kind of creatures are they, carbon, silicone or something else?"

Della saw the field of vision shift from the fully clothed Commander back to the console. She wanted to wonder about the aliens' exact physique, but she squelched the thought before it could filter into her Communicator stream. Gray fingers pressed buttons and touched screen icons, all marked with unfamiliar symbols. She still felt as though she could understand the use and purpose of each control feature. Her mind filled with the questions already posed by the Commander.

The Communicator Communications lagged, the same as any long-distance radio transmission. To Della, the lag was only obvious after she transmitted and waited for a response. A matter of seconds, but noticeable. She knew Specialist Atny would experience the same effect. She muttered, "Stop send," and waited until she heard Doctor Katherine's voice.

Della opened her eyes, "Captain, Commander Schnt wants to know where we are from, why we came through their territory and ..." she smiled, "what kind of creatures we are."

Cesar could not control his reaction. His eyes were wide open, a large dark pupil centered in a white orb that stood in contrast to the darkness of his face. "It worked?"

"Yes. I saw them. Specialist Atny must use a neural interface, something like my Communicator. He has controls, but in his excitement, he failed to shut down the connection. I saw the inside of the vessel's control room and the face of Commander Schnt when they talked."

"You actually saw them?" Cesar asked incredulously. "What do they look like? Are they human?"

Della swallowed. "Yes. I saw Commander Schnt clearly. The others were a blur because Specialist Atny's head was turning to look for the Commander. They're almost human. Thin bodies. Large heads. Flat noses. Thumbs on both sides of their hands. Large mouths with small teeth. Gray skin. No hair." She paused, then added, "Fully clothed, from neck as far down as I could see."

Premier Paul spoke, "Humanoid. I suppose that's good. At least they aren't reptilian - or some other grotesque form."

Cesar scowled, "Regardless. They have an advanced technical advantage ... and an offensive advantage. We need to answer them. I refuse to divulge the location of Earth One or Earth Two."

"If we aren't reasonably honest with them, they might detect that and become aggressive," Premier Paul said hesitantly. "The Communicator won't hide deception.

"We can be reasonably honest without being totally open. Our home planet has entered a climatic cycle that will not support our species. We have located another planet many light years away that will become our new home. We are simply following the most direct route." Cesar looked to the others in the room for input – or daring them to refute his idea.

Katherine and Bernie nodded without comment. Neither was willing to commit to the conversation between the Captain and the Premier. Paul replied, "what you just said makes sense. I'm sure their science should support that explanation."

Chief Bernie was puzzled. "What science?"

Paul answered, "Their science should include the study of planets and the evolution of planetary climate."

"Maybe their planet doesn't have serious climate changes."

"I think planetary climate may be a common feature for all solar systems. Nothing in nature is stagnant."

Katherine cleared her throat to stop the discussion. "Tell them we are carbon based, water dependent, oxygen breathing humanoids. If they are different, they will likely Communicate that."

Cesar looked at Della, "Can you remember all of that?"

"I think so. I could allow them to see what I see when I connect."

Cesar lowered his head. "No! Let's keep that a secret. Ask them what kind of creatures they are. Ask them if their home planet is nearby. That should test their openness."

After a few minutes rehearsing what she would Communicate, Della laid back on the table and closed her eyes. "Our home world's climate changed. We are traveling in a straight line to another planet with survivable climate several light years from here. We are carbon based, water dependent, oxygen breathing humanoids. What kind of creatures are you? Is your home planet nearby?"

Della remained still with her eyes closed, focused entirely on her Communicator. She waited for the two-way time lag.

Specialist Atny either did not possess the ability to shut down the neural connection that allowed Della access to his emotions and perceptions, or he was too excited to think to do so. Commander Schnt was hovering over the Specialist's shoulder, close enough that his warm breath washed across the subordinate's face. A recent meal was heavily spiced, savory and pungent. Della noticed the smell even as she was overwhelmed by the sense of excitement when her message was received.

"Their planet's climate changed. They are traveling to a new planet on a straight line from their home planet. They say they are carbon-based humanoids, dependent on water and oxygen. They want to know what we are and where Bntl is."

Della felt Specialist Atny's excitement ebb as he watched the Commander's face darken. The pale ash-gray color of the Commander's face actually became darker in shade, almost charcoal-gray. "They must be fools if they think we will reveal the location of Bntl. Did they ask for it by name?"

"No, Commander." Specialist Atny was suddenly apologetic. "They did not. They asked if our home planet was nearby."

The Commander's face paled back to what seemed normal. "Repeat what they said. Not what you interpret. I will do the interpretation. How did they ask what we are?"

"The same wording as we used, Commander. What kind of creatures are you?"

Della watched the Commander's wide mouth twisted thoughtfully for almost a minute. "Tell them we are carbon-based humanoids as well. No. I will tell them. I don't want to miss anything."

A headphone that connected Specialist Atny to the console was transferred between the two humanoids. The Commander adjusted it to cover his small ears and connect to his neural interface. Della anticipated the chance to be inside the Commander's mind. She knew she needed more air in her lungs. She exhaled heavily to make room for a fresh lungful. She was connected to a strong mind, much stronger than the mind of Specialist Atny. Every bit as strong as Captain Cesar's mind. She resisted being overwhelmed. She knew that if she did not resist, the Commander would interpret her emotions, her thoughts. The sound of a snarling voice filled her mind.

"You have this set to share sensory!"

Della lost the unfiltered information. Dead silence. No input. She opened her eyes wide long enough to catch a retina full of bright light. She turned her head sideways to avoid the light and to look at Captain

Cesar through the dark spot created by the examination light. "The Commander cut Communication. Apparently, their Communication device's range of Communication is dependent on their console equipment and Specialist Atny failed to severe the sensory transfer."

"What did they say?"

"Nothing, other than when the Commander scolded Specialist Atny for not severing the sensory transfer. It just went dead." Della blinked nervously while Cesar absorbed what she had said. "What do you want me to do?"

Captain Cesar worried. Probably more than he should have. But worry was all he could do. Humanity One was not designed to interact with aliens, let alone defend against them. The Innovators were confident that there were no aliens to encounter; or at least confident that there would be no chance of an encounter along the chosen route. Commander Schnt did not reconnect with Della, even though Cesar had Della reach out to the aliens for more than an hour after the severed connection. Cesar could only assume that the alien Commander's anger toward his subordinate was now being directed toward Humanity One, the invaders. The signals stopped. The aliens had their answer. No need to continue broadcasting the same question over and over. They had no need to communicate further. What would come next was anybody's guess ... except it was the Captain's duty to know that, to make that guess. So ... Cesar worried.

CHAPTER 33

PREPARATION

In only three days, Rex was ready to share his solution. Cesar received a message from Chief Gail via Communicator in the midst of a status report. He withdrew from the Communicator to see Joseph waiting for a response. "Duly noted. Continue on the Mission," Cesar said dismissively as he pushed himself out of the Chair. "Captain Trainee Joseph, take the Chair. I will be attending a meeting in the Premier's Decision Room." Mindful of the lean caused by the pain in his back, the Captain pulled his shoulders back to maintain his posture as he walked from the Control System Room.

Alone in the dimly lit hallway, Cesar allowed his back to slump to a less painful posture. The pain was worse than normal, added to by tightened muscles at the base of his skull. The anticipation of Rex's promised improvements, of the advantages those improvements offered, did not relieve his tension. Considering the recent Communication with the aliens – and the affirmation of the existence of aliens, Rex's promises needed to be a reality. Every passing hour without knowing if the youngster's ideas were valid or mere heresy, heresy to which he had subscribed, made the pain worse. Fortunately, he would not be attending the update meeting with Rex without some understanding of the status of the work to harvest more energy. Chief

Gail made sure that she delivered an update every time Rex made an advancement. He did not ask for it, but he appreciated it even though he knew it was her attempts to remain relevant as a Chief. He would have preferred to hear it from Rex, the one who truly understood what each advancement represented, could answer questions accurately. At least, there would be no surprises ... he hoped.

Rex sat nervously in a chair with easy access to the Decision Room's computer console. Captain Cesar normally sat in that chair, but Premier Paul had directed Rex to sit there while they waited for the Captain. He quickly rose to his feet when Cesar entered the room. For three days, his whole world was a computer console - inputting data, rewriting code, and making software changes. He genuinely believed he was right, that he could improve the energy harvesting and storage system. He did wish he had not been quite as brazen, as adamant when he declared he could do it. A less harried pace would have better served his sense of confidence. His only breaks were for short naps in his quarters and toilet breaks. The work was too important, too critical to even allow time for meals in the Mess Hall. Chow was brought to him on request. He was eager to show the results of his efforts ... and afraid they were not enough to please the Captain. His viability was on the line, put there by no one other than him and he knew it.

Cesar surveyed the room. Chief Gail sat close to Rex. She knew Rex would be the center of attention. Chief Bernie and Chief Donald bookended Premier Paul on one side of the long oval table. A lone chair close to the entry door was vacant and ready to be filled. He waved for Rex to sit and nodded greetings to everyone before he sat. "Sci-Eng Technician Rex, have you finished the software changes?" He knew the answer, thanks to Chief Gail.

Before Rex could respond, Chief Gail corrected Captain Cesar. "Sci-Eng Trainee."

Cesar lowered his head and looked hard toward the novice Chief.

"A matter of age, not ability. Besides, as I recall, Rex is less than a week from adult status." Without shifting his eyes away from Gail, he said, "Rex, give us an update." He held the eye challenge until Rex started to speak.

"Aye Captain. The Stellar Engine software has been successfully reconfigured. We have prepared the specifications for mechanical changes to the parasol control mechanisms and its harvester." Rex waited. The bravado that pushed him to challenge Cesar in the Mess Hall was gone. Three feverish days of effort would be for naught if his theories were incorrect. Matter-of-fact discussion without embellishments was all that mattered. And he was exhausted.

"How long will the mechanical changes take?" Cesar's brow furrowed. He knew he would have to ask to get information. Nothing volunteered. The subdued Rex sitting in the Decision Room was much different than the brash young Rex who confronted him in the Mess Hall. He worried that the reduced confidence might bode poorly for success.

Rex's eyes momentarily shifted toward Chiefs Bernie and Donald. "I am uncertain. Though I would think no more than two days."

Chief Donald spoke up as soon as Rex's words were said. "This is not a simple task. My people are fabricating parts we designed based on Sci-Eng Technician Rex's recommendations, but the final install will require a walk outside the vessel."

Cesar was not surprised by Chief Donald's comment. He knew a simple software code change would not be enough to make everything better. He had only hoped differently. He knew the reality of it all was that the only simple things were those written into the MGR. "What does that entail, Chief?"

"The parts for extra-vehicle installation will be ready before morning – tomorrow."

Cesar nodded, "Hence, two days. Sounds reasonable. That's

quicker than the original guesstimate." He glanced toward Rex and grinned approvingly. "Promise small. Deliver big."

"Captain, it's not that simple," Chief Donald protested. "We are not equipped for extra-vessel-activities. There is nothing in the MRG regarding EVAs. We're in new territory – figuratively and literally. The team that goes out to do the retrofit could fly away into space with no way back."

Cesar scowled. "What's the plan? We have no other options." He looked back to Rex. "This is your plan. What are your thoughts?"

Before Rex could respond, Chief Donald replied, "Trainee Rex said there are archive files that cover EVAs by the Innovators. Cable attachments of some sort. We are already reviewing those files. We have to design umbilical systems and test them."

"So ... how long will that take? You don't have cables available?"

"We do, but we don't know how to attach them to Humanity One. There's no indication that the outer surface is anything other than smooth plate. The EVA archives we have found don't pertain to Humanity One, only to other types of spacecraft; spacecraft designed for EVAs. We don't even know if our pressure suits are capable of protecting the Mech-Techs assigned to the retrofit. This is completely new to us, outside our training."

"Rex can help," Cesar said.

Rex cleared his throat. He heard his name used too many times. He recognized the reactions of the Chiefs. Suspicion and resentment. He wanted to be duly recognized but he did not want to be considered the Captain's favorite – not openly. "Captain, I still have work to do to fully implement and integrate the new software. The connection between the parasol and energy storage will require another day at least."

"I thought the software was configured." Cesar said suspiciously.

"It is up to the point of installation. We still need some hardware changes within the internal system – so the changes I've made don't interfere with routine performance of the vessel's control systems. But that work can be done concurrent with the external work." Rex waited expectantly.

Cesar nodded and contemplated what he had been told. He saw the concern and hesitation in Rex. Politics always found its way into every project. "It's still quicker than your original estimate. Make this one happen. Chief Donald, I know your Mech-Techs are fully capable. Between you and Chief Gail, I'm sure you will come up with something. Chief Bernie, I assume you will still be supporting Rex?"

Bernie nodded. "With some assistance from Hard Fabrication, no doubt. The new system may require some rewiring and mechanical switches."

"Don't waste any time. We need to know if the alien vessel is intent on stalking us. The only way to know that for sure is to increase speed and see how Commander Schnt reacts."

⌇

Della smiled at Maddie. Her daughter's expression showed concern. For three days, Della's routine as a Con-Sys Technician was broken. Cesar insisted that she report to Medical frequently for further attempts to Communicate with the alien vessel. All to no avail. She knew Cesar was worried, and that worried her. She kept her knowledge to herself. Her activities kept her away from her daughter. It was the first time she had seen Maddie awake during that time. "What have you been doing?"

Maddie relaxed. "Nothing. I haven't been allowed to return to the Con-Sys Room. What's going on?"

Della knew the youngster was fishing for information. The Captain's warning to the Gen 4s was being observed with exception. Youthful curiosity cannot be dictated into submission. "I went to Medical for a check-up." She lied – mostly. Doctor Katherine did check her heart rate, blood pressure and EEG throughout the connection to the alien's broadcast.

"Are you okay?" Maddie knew the answer, though the follow-up visits after Marly reported back to her were cause for continued concerns. Marly offered no real information during her hurried comments, not enough to make the daughter feel comfortable, especially with Della's further secret visits. Always more secrets. And Marly was intentionally avoiding Maddie.

"Fine. I should get all my years before recycling. So why have you been doing nothing? There are always simulations to run, to practice your skills. We have some practice scenarios ready for Technicians and Trainees."

Maddie cringed. She hated practice. She wanted reality. She changed the subject. "Have you seen Rex?"

Della briefly froze.

Maddie caught Della's momentary reaction to her question. It chilled her. "Did you see Rex in Medical?"

Della recovered. She scowled. "No, and you don't need to be seen with Rex. You have been warned." She wanted to tell Maddie the more important reason, but she preferred to allow that to remain unspoken. That information was not hers to share.

Maddie scowled in return. "I haven't seen him for three days. I usually see him in the Mess Hall … and the other Gen 4s. I wasn't trying to meet with him. I'm just wondering – considering what happened to Jana."

Della felt the anguish in Maddie's voice. "Maddie, Rex is fine." She only knew that the young Sci-Eng Trainee was deeply involved in a secret project for Cesar. He was not in the same danger as was Jana. He was critically viable. Potentially the most viable person on Humanity One at that moment.

"You've seen him?"

"Not exactly, but I've heard that he is honing his skills in preparation for adulthood. As you should be." A little lie would do no harm.

"His skills are not in need of honing," Maddie protested.

"Maddie. Rex is fine. You - on the other hand – are attracting too much attention ... not all good. The training scenarios are important. You need to go to the Training Room. I am surprised no one has ordered you to go." Della was concerned. Len should have made sure Maddie knew about the new training. She would have a word with him before he fell asleep.

Maddie sat with Della and Len in the Mess Hall. Della was more talkative than usual. Nervous energy. She would not afford Maddie time to engage with anyone else in the large room.

Kendra tried to signal Maddie for a meeting. Even though Maddie was not viably occupied during the three days that Della was making unprecedented visits to Medical, she was also not available for Kendra. No reason. Just happenstance. Maddie saw Kendra's freckled face flushed red with urgency. The Hy-Tech had something to tell. Maddie wanted to hear it. Della prevented it. Maddie could only smile apologetically when Della led her from the Mess Hall and deposited her in the Training Room.

Maddie saw Con-Sys Trainee Sean at a console, intensely monitoring a scenario. He did not look up from the screen. On either side of the young Trainee sat seasoned Con-Sys Techs. They were just as focused on their screens, often using the virtual keyboards or icon selections to interact.

Con-Sys Tech Connie saw Maddie enter the room. She smiled and motioned the Trainee toward an empty console. "I've been wondering when you would be here." Her voice was low so she would not disturb the others in training.

"No one told me," Maddie replied. "I was available." She knew her comments were lame attempts to shunt blame. She should have remained in touch with seasoned Con-Sys Technicians even while not allowed into the Con-Sys Room.

"Well, you're here now. You have some catching up to do. I'll initiate the scenario. We'll start from the beginning. Remember, this is a live practice in Con-Sys. Behave accordingly."

Maddie nodded understanding. All Communication would be on screen or through Communicator with Connie. She could not assist others or ask for their help. She was on her own. She hated scenarios. Hull breaches. Atmosphere issues in different sections of the vessel. Power disruptions. There was only so much that could go wrong in her finite world.

Maddie's head jerked back in mild shock. The screen graphics noted that a strange object was hurtling toward Humanity One at a high rate of speed. Its projected impact zone was over Crew quarters and the Mess Hall. Its impetus and accumulated inertial energy could easily penetrate the external hull and the secondary hull. Nothing below those two were resistant enough to keep it from creating a major atmosphere venting event. She had three seconds to initiate a response to mitigate the damage and loss of life.

The console screen immediately offered optional actions. Maddie frantically reacted. They were actions not normally offered in scenarios. By touching three visible icons, she isolated the impact zone from the rest of the vessel. Lives would be lost. Atmosphere would be lost. But in neither case would those loses be Mission ending. She then informed Sci-Eng and Mechanical of the hull breach. The scenario ended and a review began to flood onto her screen.

Maddie did not blink as she read the review. Her actions were commended as accurate, but slow. She had mitigated lives lost to only forty. The volume of atmosphere vented was less than one percent of the vessel's total. Very few atoms lost. The vessel was saved. Her hesitation increased the atoms lost by ten percent. She did not see Connie nod when she Communicated her surprise, "That was different!" Maddie did not have time to bask in what she considered a success. Another scenario began.

Initially, the scenario was almost identical to the first event. Maddie anticipated her actions and touched the appropriate icons to mitigate the damage much more quickly. An easy lesson for someone with her aptitude. The results were the same – or appeared to be. Except the scenario did not end and the screen did not fill with a review that told her of her successes. Instead, another object was detected. Its trajectory put the Control Systems Room in jeopardy. Maddie faltered. The screen displayed options, actions that horrified her. Isolating the Con-Sys Room meant her own non-recyclable end, and the end of everyone in the Con-Sys Room. Even the Captain. She touched the suggested icons. The screen turned red. The scenario ended with an alarm and a screen filled with two words. *Mission Failure.*

Maddie stared at the screen in disbelief. Past training offered a variety of scenarios, most of which required quick reaction, planned actions that could be repeated automatically in the correct sequence to avoid Mission failure. Alarms and flashing lights attracted the attention of the Trainee and the Trainer. The screen's flashing and the alarm's embarrassing wail continued until Connie overrode it.

"Startlingly real, isn't it?" Connie's voice was calming, without recrimination. She did not use the Communicator.

Maddie stammered, "I ... I froze. I didn't respond quickly enough to save Humanity One."

"What caused you to freeze?" Connie asked in a quiet voice.

"Ah ... I ... I don't know. Making the decision to sacrifice everyone in Con-Sys, I suppose."

"It was easy enough for you to sacrifice people in quarters. What made it different for Con-Sys?"

Maddie knew where Connie was leading her. She had to face the truth. She tried to rationalize. "Humanity One would be lost either way."

"No. Con-Sys does not actually control Humanity One's course. It monitors the internal and external environment. Based upon those observations, decisions are made. Those decisions are input into the vessel's control computers and the limited options available are put into effect. The core computers are deep within the vessel, far from potential external damage."

"If that area vents ... is exposed to space ... the Captain and his Trainee will be lost. There will be no one to lead the Crew, to make the decisions for Humanity One." Maddie did not think of her responses as being argumentative. She was trying to cover her mistake with excuses. Besides, she did not recall any training that told of the core computers buried inside Humanity One. Secrets.

"Not true. Second and his Trainee will be in quarters. Their quarters were not involved in the initial point of attack. They are ready to assume command immediately."

"Why didn't we know about the core computers? And – what about the Con-Sys Room?"

"You didn't remember the core computers because your mind froze. The Elec-Techs can quickly erect a secondary Control Systems Room, probably closer to the computers. The Mission can continue as long as the parasols and sails remain intact. Given time, the breaches can be repaired – but not if a majority of the atmosphere is vented into space. Without atmosphere, nothing else matters."

"I guess I placed too much value on the Captain," Maddie said lamely.

"No. You placed too much value on yourself. The appropriate

action was to seal off Con-Sys – to assure the integrity of Humanity One. Unfortunately, that action would eliminate any possibility of survival for anyone inside the room. In effect, the proper action would seal your fate as well as the fate of everyone else in the room."

Maddie hung her head. Self-preservation impacted her decision, her viability as a Con-Sys Technician. "I'm sorry. There was so much …"

Connie placed her hand on Maddie's bare shoulder. "Shush! That's why we train. We have to take our personal feelings out of our work. The success of the Mission must always override any other thoughts. Now, let's go again. Back to Communicators." She quickly touched a reset icon on Maddie's screen.

The training scenarios were designed to be real, at least to the mind of the Trainee. For the first time in the history of Humanity One, Con-Sys Technicians were being trained to act and react within a directed conflict scenario. Random, stray objects in space were always a risk to cause damage, most of it minimal. Guided projectiles were designed to create as much damage as possible and to neutralize the vessel. In the scenarios, the aliens would not relent until Humanity One was destroyed. Maddie felt the tension of impending doom as she strained her eyes to avoid missing a single signal from her console. She knew she could not afford to miss anything. The Captain and the VLT apparently knew something would happen. She had to be ready. She obliquely understood why Sean and the others were so intently focused that they did not acknowledge her arrival. The reality of her duties, of her required dedication to the success of the Mission, became more tangible.

⸺⸺

Captain Cesar adjusted his position in the Chair. The status update was the last thing on his mind, but it was necessary to maintain routine. No one in the Control System Room thought things were routine. As a matter of fact, everyone knew better. The status update forced them to not dwell on the extraordinary circumstances Humanity One faced. A nonroutine response brought him to attention.

"Visual attained on the Rogue." Captain Trainee Joseph repeated the statement for the Captain.

The blip recognized days before, the electronically created spot of light on a console screen that put Captain Cesar on notice that everything was not right in his world, had been captured as a visual. The improvements made by Chief Bernie and is team were paying dividends. Cesar could see what his adversary looked like. His heart fluttered a little. Seeing would be believing. Not that he did not already believe, but it would make Commander Schnt less ephemeral, less of a ghost. "Display it on the wall," he said with the least emotion he could.

Trainee Joseph repeated the Captain's command.

Cesar pursed his lips as he studied the vessel under the control of the alien Commander. He recalled the description of the aliens offered by Con-Sys Technician Della San Qi. "Magnify," he commanded. He watched as the image grew larger until it completely filled the wall screen that normally displayed space outside Humanity One like a windshield. The vessel was not what he envisioned. Asteroids in general are bulky and odd shaped. Commander Schnt's vessel was comparatively sleek, not that it needed to be aerodynamically designed for space. Along the wider parts, which he assumed to be the top and bottom, there were several extensions. Having never seen the outside of a spacecraft, he could only assume they were sensors, weapons, or propulsion. A bulge at the end away from him was probably the Rogue's primary propulsion system. It had no parasols or sails for energy harvest. He knew Humanity One relied upon expansive, thin, flat surfaces to capture stray protons and feel the effects of stellar winds. The renderings of his vessel without the parasols showed it to be spherical. No streamlining of any kind. Humanity One was an ark.

Nothing more. The vessel on the wall screen was made to maneuver. It was a spaceship.

The image slowly darkened to the point of near invisibility against the blackness of space. The Technician's voice sounded frightened. "Captain, we are losing lighting for visualization."

Cesar knew that space seldom offered good lighting for optics. The nearness of a star provided a fleeting amount of spectrum for Humanity One's optical imagers to discern the Rogue. "Thank you. Save the image and send it to Chiefs Donald, Bernie, and Gail. I will give them instructions."

The image offered no clue as to size, but it was clear that the Rogue was in a different class than Humanity One. Built to maneuver, change speeds and fight, its size was irrelevant if its intentions were to attack.

"Con-Sys is sending an optical image of the alien vessel to the three of you." Cesar's Communicator effortlessly connected to the Mechanical, Electrical and Engineering Chiefs. "Study it as time permits. Understand that we need to determine its capabilities and intentions." He accepted a few moments of discussion without allowing any off the cuff guesses.

CHAPTER 34

GEN 8

Kendra's face was flushed. Whatever Kendra wanted to share was still causing her to stress. Maddie tried to signal for her to calm herself. The Training Room sessions took all of Maddie's time, and her focus. Secrets seemed less important. And she still worried about Rex, even though Della assured her that Rex was working on a project for the Captain. The Captain's focus on the Group members seemed to have abated in light of the more immediate threat. Maddie knew it would still not be a good thing if they were caught meeting unchaperoned.

The Mess Hall table discussion on that day was about the alien craft and the intensive training to mitigate attack damage to the Mission. A new control system was introduced but limited to only two Con-Sys Technicians per duty shift. Maddie's Sire, Len San Wu, was one of those chosen to use navigational controls. Len was explaining what he knew of the work being done by Sci-Eng Trainee Rex that paved the way for the proton drives to provide positive propulsion that would increase Humanity One's speed. It was all whispered and secretive, but at least Maddie – a Trainee – was not pushed away from hearing, even though not welcomed into the discussions.

Maddie's heart skipped when she heard Rex's name attached to a definitive project. He *was* safe. Della had told her the truth. She was elated. Somewhere in Science and Engineering, Rex was studiously implementing his plan with Captain Cesar's approval. She wanted to hear more, to ask questions about Rex, but Kendra's reddened face twisted and scowled to get her attention. She knew that if she delayed much longer, Kendra's behaviors would attract unwanted attention. She nodded agreement to her friend and excused herself to go to the restroom, hating to miss any part of the Con-Sys Techs conversation.

Maddie had barely cleared the Mess Hall doorway when Kendra bustled into the passageway. The two of them entered the restroom one behind the other. Maddie quickly scanned the small room to make sure no one was there. "Kendra, what has you in such a tizzy? Rex is okay. He's working on his plan."

Kendra paused before she spoke, immediately dismissing Maddie's news. "Good. Real good. I found out something! Kevin told me about the embryos."

"Calm down," Maddie whispered. "Someone might come in any minute. What did he tell you?"

"The 8th Generation will carry them."

Maddie blinked as she processed the simple statement. "What do you mean, carry them?"

"Remember when Rex and Jana broke the codes? The 7th Generation will be allowed to have four children – all girls? The 8th Generation is planned to be all female."

"I remember. We didn't know why. It was a big secret." Maddie was attuned to Kendra's pending revelation.

"I know why. Kevin does too. He told me. Probably all the Chiefs know it. Did I mention he's going to be the next Chief of Stasis?" Kendra was not her usual collected self. She was anxious to tell all that she had learned. She hurried her speech and rambled.

"Kendra, tell me what you've learned." Maddie wanted to hear what Kendra had to say. She also did not want to lose the opportunity if someone walked into the restroom while Kendra was prattling excitedly.

"The 8ᵗʰ Generation will be implanted with the embryos. Their purpose will be to give birth to all the embryos."

"Why embryos? Why not just have more babies? That makes no sense."

Kendra looked over her shoulder and lowered her voice to a whisper. "It does. By the 8ᵗʰ Generation, our physiology will have changed. We won't be able to survive on a planet with full gravity. Genetically, the humans on Humanity One will have mutated because of radiation. Our bodies will be altered by lack of Earth gravity. We won't be the same as the Innovators in Stasis."

"What?" Maddie asked a little too loudly. "That's ridiculous." Marly had already explained what was happening. So had handsy Doctor Aaron. Maddie had chosen to not grasp its significance, to extrapolate it into a coherent understanding of human life aboard a space vessel. She did not want to know that information because it did not fit everything else she held to be truth.

"No, not really. We know the life expectancy of Gen 3 is much less than Gen 1. That could worsen. Heart disease and immunity disorders are the main issues. Gen 8 will not be any stronger. Definitely not strong enough to survive on the surface of a planet."

"So, the Mission is doomed to be a failure?"

"No. That's why Humanity Ones has humans in Stasis and lots of embryos."

"What difference does that make? They are suffering the same issues, the radiation and gravity."

"Not really. Stasis is super insulated against radiation. The people in Stasis are generally immune to the effect of gravity. The same with the embryos. The bodies of the people in Stasis are not growing under the effects of low gravity. Their bones and muscles are still strong. Genetically, the embryos will still be like they were on Earth One."

"But the embryos will get some genetics from their mothers," Maddie grasped for a point of argument.

"No. That's not how it works. Gen 8 will simply be the vessels to bring them to birth, providing nothing more than nourishment and warmth. The embryos' genetics are the same as the Innovators. When the babies are born, they will be transferred to Earth Two to be raised there by the people from Stasis, and the Gen 8 will be re-implanted with another embryo."

"That's horrible!" Maddie's anger grew as she came to understand the future of her progeny. "Our atoms will never live on Earth Two."

Kendra's anxious desire to reveal what she had learned was abated. Her level of adamancy was lessened. "That's what it seems. That is the secret that has been kept from us."

Maddie fumed. "All work with no reward. I'm not having a baby. I'll not be a part of this."

Kendra touched Maddie's arm. "As Kevin told me this, he also pointed out that our sacred Mission is to save humanity. Without us performing our duty, humans will cease to exist in the universe. And I'm having a baby."

"What? You accept this? You accept being lied to?"

Kendra averted her eyes. "It's not about this. I'm having a baby."

Maddie started to vocalize her next retort but noticed Kendra's topaz eyes were filled with tears. She instinctively looked down at Kendra's belly. Kendra's hands were covering her belly protectively. She asked incredulously, "You mean you're pregnant now?"

Kendra nodded and bit her lip.

"Kevin?"

"Yes."

"I thought so." Maddie embraced her friend. "Does he know?"

"I need to tell him."

"Maybe. Maybe not," Maddie said as she pushed Kendra back while still holding onto her shoulders. "He could lose his step to Chief."

"We could be mated."

"You're not an adult yet."

"Less than a month away."

"Wait until you're an adult. Officially mate and hope no one notices. Have you asked Medical for approval?"

Kendra sniffed snot. "Not yet."

"Do it. You can ask for approval before you become an adult. I assume Kevin wants to mate with you. Right?"

"We've talked some."

"Well, it's time to talk a lot." Maddie hugged Kendra again, thoughts of her recent training and the Gen 8 revelation momentarily lost. "And do it quickly." She pulled away from her friend and noticed a coolness where Kendra had smeared fluid, tears maybe, on her shoulder. "I'm going to tell the Group what you've learned. I won't use your name if you don't want me to."

Kendra sniffed more as she looked at the floor. She then looked into Maddie's eyes. "I'm the one who told you. I will not deny it. But we still have to do our duty."

Maddie scowled. "All our lives we have been told that in the end, after recycle, we have one thing to look forward to: our atoms will live on when we reach Earth Two. It's a lie. We end here, in this vessel ... or vented into space. That's the secret that they have been keeping from us."

CHAPTER 35

ALTERCATIONS

Rex shrunk lower in his chair. The Premier's Decision Room was crowded with the VLT members. The modification work was done. The energy harvesters were working as he theorized. In fact, the energy harvest was even better than he could have hoped. His original projection was that it would require six months or more to accumulate sufficient energy to activate the proton drives and increase Humanity One's speed. After implementation, a recalculation based upon real data indicated that accumulation period would be less than a month. His improvement provided Humanity One the option to travel faster and to reach Earth Two as much as twenty years sooner. That was the reason for the meeting. Captain Cesar offered that option to the VLT. Rex was there to explain the math and science behind the proposal. Cesar trusted the newly anointed adult Science Engineering Technician to be non-political – and more credible. But some VLT members still wanted to believe in the infallibility of the Innovators, of the MGR.

Cesar scowled at Premier Paul. "Why are you waffling on the subject? We have had this discussion. I thought we settled the matter."

Paul tried to hold Cesar's gaze. Cesar's resolve was strong. He cleared his throat. "Captain Cesar, we have discussed it but only as a means to recoup the lost time. We have not discussed maintaining higher speed in defiance of the MGR."

"It would not be defiance of the MGR," Cesar snapped.

Chief of Stasis Deanna spoke in her unmistakably soft and resolute style, "Captain, we have yielded to your desire to implement young Rex's theories as a means to return Humanity One to its original course schedule. We even accepted the side benefit of more energy for life support efforts. We do not wish to arbitrarily yield the truths that the Innovators put in the MGR."

"What truths? The MGR contains instructions and operating procedures to guide us to our destination, to Earth Two." Cesar's scowl should have been enough to stop any argument, but MGR was too deeply imbedded in the minds of many, especially the Gen 2 VLT members.

"And those instructions are designed to ensure our Mission is a success. Failing to abide by them will surely result in failure," replied the Premier. His frail appearance was belied by his strong voice.

While Sci-Eng Trainee Rex worked to implement his recommendations, Cesar had re-evaluated his beliefs. The MGR was easy to follow, easy to serve as the final answer to many questions. The words in it were clear and precise, not subject to interpretation. During his time of self-evaluation, he also faced the possibility of an attack by the Commander of the alien vessel. Even though nothing was detected, there was the possibility that other alien vessels were coming to Commander Schnt's aid. The MGR had no instructions or procedures for addressing aliens or alien attacks. Rote training - and blind obedience to the supporting source of that training - had elevated the MGR to the status of an infallible derivation of the Innovators' infallibility. Cesar questioned that. "Those instructions provide no guidance for alien encounters. We are now without Innovator assistance. The Mission faces a humanity erasing end if we don't step away from what we know and reach for the answers that we don't know."

Chief Deanna protested softly, yet pointedly. "Captain, what you are suggesting exposes more questions than we can possibly find answers to resolve. The MGR for Stasis defines the timeline for awakening our charges in stasis."

Cesar shook his head. He looked toward Doctor Katherine. "Chief Katherine, can you offer some enlightenment on the timeline for arrival at Earth Two orbit and the status of the Generations?"

Premier Paul protested, "That is something we have discussed. We concluded that we already know there will be some issues that future generations will need to resolve. It is not ours to solve."

Cesar barked, "Just like we decided a future Captain would have to find the solution for the time we lost? No. It is our duty to solve as many problems, to answer as many questions as we can so future Chiefs don't have to sit in this room and frantically resolve the issues we ignored."

"Maybe that is so, but what you are proposing will create additional questions. Who will have to answer those?"

Cesar glared at Paul for a moment, then looked to Chief Medical Officer Katherine, "Doctor, would you answer my question?"

Doctor Katherine leaned forward and looked from face to face around the oval table. "It is no secret among us that the shorter life span of the generations will likely cause the need for an additional Generation before we reach Earth Two orbit."

Chief Gail perked. Her eyes widened and she leaned forward. "I didn't know this. What do you mean, an additional Generation?"

Doctor Katherine nodded understanding. "Your rapid ascension to Chief did not allow time to complete your training. I'm sorry for that. The fact is that we strongly suspect that the changes we have made to accommodate the shorter life span, reducing adulthood from eighteen to sixteen and encouraging births before the age of eighteen, will result in target Gen 8 being born too soon."

Chief Gail was not pleased. "Why wasn't I told?"

"Again, I apologize for that. Your ascension was not orderly as we anticipated."

"It had to be done," Chief Gail snapped.

"Possibly so," replied Doctor Katherine, "but you missed some of the leadership training."

"So – you're saying we will have to go until Gen 9 before we reach Earth Two?" Chief Gail's face was clouded with anger.

"Enough!" said Cesar. "We need to increase speed, not just to regain our lost time, but to reach Earth Two earlier than the Innovators planned – when the 8th Generation is ready."

"Earth Two will not be in alignment with its moons," Chief Bernie countered.

Cesar was exasperated. He knew what had to be done. As he looked at the faces of the VLT, he saw some resistance. But he saw more anxious hesitancy than anything. They would all prefer to allow the decision to be deferred to a future generation. Unless the decision was clearly defined by the MGR, none of the Chiefs were willing to speak in favor of it. Even novice Chief Gail, who was more upset over not knowing all there was to know, was hesitant to go against the others – to completely abandon the Innovators' time schedule. Sci-Eng Tech Rex was the only one whose face did not show resistance or hesitancy. Mildly watching, the youngster's eyes met his and seemed to telegraph approval. "Sci-Eng Technician Rex, provide calculations and timing for increased speed."

Rex's face flushed lightly at the sudden notice thrown his direction. He had expected to hear a vote or an arrival at consensus. "Aye Captain. It can't occur until sufficient energy has been harvested."

"I understand that. That is why I want the exact timing. I also need to know how much energy will be required to maintain that speed and how soon Humanity One will arrive at Earth Two."

Premier Paul sputtered, "But Chief Bernie stated the obvious. The moons will not be properly aligned for static orbit. And Chief Gail should lead the calculations."

Without looking at the Premier, Cesar asked Chief Bernie, "Are you suggesting that the proper alignment of Earth Two and its two moons is a once in forever event?"

Chief Bernie reddened. "No. I'm sure that alignment repeats itself cyclically. We just don't know what that cycle is."

"There. Another answer for us to find." Cesar immediately turned to Chief Gail whose face was twisted with anger. "Chief Gail, I expect you to lead the calculations since Rex is within your department ... but remember to do as Chief Scientist Robert did with you – defer to the one with the proper skills and knowledge."

Chief Gail's face softened. She knew further protests or indignations would lead to questions of her own viability. She had already proven how easily it could be done.

Premier Paul knew there was nothing more he could say. Years of deferral to Captain Cesar had led to that moment. "What of the alien vessel?"

"What of it?" Cesar asked curtly.

"Are we in danger of attack?"

"We will know that when we increase speed, if it accelerates to match our pace, then we must have a plan of defense."

"What would that plan be?"

"Let's discuss our options. Now is as good a time as any," Cesar replied as he adjusted his position in the chair to relieve the pains in his back. He had the discussion going his way. Without a vote, the Chiefs had abdicated the decision about speed and timing to him.

"We have the proton drive," Chief Gail suggested quickly. "We should be able to convert it to a cannon of sorts."

Cesar saw Rex nod once. That subtle gesture was enough to relax his mind. "I'm not sure if that is feasible, but it sounds like we have options. The proton drive can deliver speed or maybe perform as a weapon. How would the drive work as a weapon?"

Chief Gail leaned forward, eager to be recognized, to be heard. "The stream of protons create an "opposite but equal reaction" which forces Humanity One forward. But, along with that is the matter stream, the protons, that are ejected. Of course," she nodded toward Rex, "the changes made to the energy harvesting system provides more than just protons. Each of those particles collected has natural energy. That stream possesses energy. The heavier the stream, the more energy. With enough particles, we should have sufficient energy to strike the alien vessel if it is trailing behind us."

Cesar allowed the Chief to talk, express herself. A simpler explanation would have sufficed, but he did not want to interfere with her thought processes. Some of the others likely needed the details. "How soon before we know if that is feasible? And will it interfere with our goal of increasing speed?"

"No. It might actually improve our velocity ... if they are behind us," Chief Gail replied. She glanced toward Rex. "I'm sure we can have some idea of a time frame for the weapon as soon as the current issues are addressed."

"Very well," Premier Paul said authoritatively, almost frightening himself with the boldness of his voice. "We have work to do. Is there anyone who does not think this will work?"

Cesar smiled to himself and adjusted his back once again. The pain lessened. In the end, Paul had to present himself as the Leader. Despite everything he had been taught to be true, Cesar believed there was hope in face of the current dangers ... and it did not come directly from the Innovators.

⬿⬿⬿

Maddie trained. One intense, seemingly unbeatable scenario after the other. She trained until her reactions were as automatic as all the other duties she was trained to perform as a Con-Sys Technician. Her actions became instinctive in that she did not have to dwell on her responses. Failure would not come from delayed reactions. But ... she was bored by the unrelenting repetition, the preparation for the unknown. Somewhere out in the silver speckled vastness of space that surrounded Humanity One was an alien vessel. Somewhere in the dark recesses of Humanity One, a group of Sci-Eng Technicians was working to develop a defense. She wondered if Rex was a part of that group. She had not seen him in the Mess Hall for more days than she cared to remember. He was an adult now. She would be in a matter of a few more days.

Maddie knew too much. Her mind would not ... could not ... settle. The embryos, the plan for their use; the aliens, the danger they presented; Rex, the part he played; the big secret of their existence. What she did not know for a fact, her creative mind backfilled. The Crew would never see Earth Two. Not in person. An attack by the alien vessel was imminent. No one was safe. Mission failure was imminent. Rex, her confidant and probably closest friend, was being exploited to develop a solution to Humanity One's plight. And the secrets continued. She shuddered as if the motion would rid her of the fears – and anger – that plagued her mind. She needed her friends around her, The Group. They should all know what she knew. They deserved to know. Every Crew member deserved to know what fate had in store for the vessel that carried the future of humanity.

The Chiefs were decidedly preoccupied. Working on the problems that faced Humanity One. Ignoring the possibility that Maddie and other Gen 4s might be able to contribute to the solution. Except for Rex. At least Cesar recognized Rex's abilities. Their preoccupation provided an opportunity that had not been available for weeks. The Group could meet without being noticed. Maddie had to make that happen.

Zack was afraid. The fear of early recycling was real. There was no fear in Stasis. All he had to do was prove his viability as a Sta-Tech and he could enjoy a full life. Unexpectedly, in the dimly lit passageway between Stasis and his quarters, Maddie appeared with an urgent request for the Group to meet. There was no way he could muster the courage to agree, to say yes. Not under normal circumstances. But Maddie's blue eyes and inviting smile tantalized his salacious mind. Without Jana's statuesque figure as an alternative, he believed his choice for a mate should be Maddie ... if she would choose him over Rex. There were other Gen 3 females, some nearer his age, but Maddie fascinated him, even without her teasing hair. He glanced around to see if anyone was within hearing or line of sight. He whispered nervously, unsure if the sweat in his armpits was because of fear or fascination, "Okay. If you're sure it will be safe."

Maddie smiled as she left Zack perspiring in the hallway between quarters and Stasis where she found him. She hoped Sean, Marly and Ying would be as easily persuaded to meet. She knew Rex would not be able to join them. A pity. He could provide much more information.

Sean was easier to access but harder to convince. His flimsy body trembled when Maddie whispered her idea for The Group to meet. His eyes flitted side-to-side as she coaxed him. Only after several minutes and a reminder that he and she were privy to information about the alien vessel and the practiced responses to an attack, information that should not be kept secret from anyone, did he relent and agree to meet.

Ying argued against the riskiness of a full meeting. Maddie saw his adolescent eyes drift toward her breasts and loincloth. He did not perspire like Zack. He was unashamed of his interest in her as a potential mate. His behaviors made her aware of her maturity, an awareness that was not as unsettling as it was under Doctor Aaron's lingering eyes. "Ying, Kendra and I have secret information that we need to share. Are you interested in knowing the secrets or not?" She decided to be blunt.

Ying scowled slightly. The visible effects of the facial gesture was enhanced by his epicanthic folds. "I'm not interested in becoming victim of recycling – like Jana. Cesar's warning was clear."

"Then don't join us. But in case you change your mind, we will meet in San-Re after the work shift ends. There won't be but one, maybe two San-Re Techs in the entire room. There are several small sorting rooms along the left wall. We'll meet in the third one from the front end." Maddie skillfully turned away, letting her hips draw his attention ... and his response.

"Okay. I'll be there."

Maddie smiled without turning to look back at Ying. She knew what he was doing.

Marly tried to ignore Maddie. Pretending to be late for a task. Maddie persisted. She knew Marly, physically mature, was still a thirteen-year old at heart. The young girl was dedicated to her medical training. Becoming a doctor, the youngest doctor ever, was all that mattered to Marly. That and avoiding early recycling.

Maddie also knew that Marly and Sean were keenly interested in one another, though Marly would often flirt with Rex. Maddie was sure Marly understood her pubescent attraction to Rex was misplaced adulation. Rex would be long mated by the time Marly was old enough to mate. After that, assignations would be what they would be. "Sean will be there. He wants to know what is happening. Don't you?"

Marly's soft brown cheeks reddened. She pressed her lips between her teeth. Her brown eyes blinked as tears tried to form. She stared at the floor for a moment. "Okay. If I can." She hurried toward Medical.

Maddie had only Kendra to confirm. She walked to Hydroponics and found her red-haired friend. Kendra was bent over while tending a bed of her plants, unaware of Maddie's approach. Maddie sneakily tapped the small of Kendra's back. Kendra squealed with fright and jerked upright. Maddie laughed. Kendra scowled.

"You almost caused me to pee myself," Kendra chided.

"I'm sorry," Maddie laughed. "It was too inviting. Did you talk to Kevin?"

Kendra blushed, something that her pale complexion seemed to invite. "Yes. He said he will talk to Doctor Katherine, to start the approval process."

"Is he going to tell her that you're pregnant if she doesn't approve?"

Kendra averted her eyes momentarily. "I don't think so. Why shouldn't she approve? Our trailing numbers indicate we have no common ancestors."

"True. I guess I was actually just wondering how you're feeling."

"I'm feeling fine, other than some nausea from time to time. I think it is normal. At least that's what the archives say. What are you doing, besides frightening your friends and risking exposure?"

Maddie laughed again. "I told you I was sorry. The VLT is too focused on the alien vessel and Rex's project to increase speed to notice us." She glanced around before she continued. "I have the Group ready to meet tonight. In Sanitation in a small sorting room that Rex and I found. You need to be there so we can share what we have learned about the embryos."

Kendra was puzzled. "You and Rex?"

"We met there to try to decode the alien message. No one will be in those rooms at night."

"Oh. Do you think that's wise, meeting like that?"

"We won't be caught."

"Not that. Do you think it's wise to tell them about the embryos and everything?"

"They deserve to know. We promised to share all information when we first formed the Group. I don't think it would be fair to not share after all we've been through."

Zack was shocked. His long-held belief that his atoms would enjoy Earth Two at the end of the journey was shattered. "That can't be true," he protested. "Everything ... everyone is recycled. What becomes of us?"

"That is why we are sharing this," Maddie replied. "We ... our atoms ... become part of the universe, not part of the human colony on Earth Two."

Kendra watched each member of the Group, mindful of the fact that what was being shared could have an undesirable effect. That was her agreed upon role since Rex was not available. If anyone became too emotional, it was her task to help keep them grounded.

Marly cleared her throat and tried to make her immature voice sound authoritative, "Maddie, it is not as dire as you make it sound. There has never been a direct atom for atom recycling of humans."

As soon as the door to the small room closed, Sean maneuvered himself close to Marly. He basked in the warmth of her body cramped against his, even though the room was not so small as to force them as close as he was. Her words startled him. "What does that mean?" he asked with a crack in his voice.

Marly smiled and pressed closer. "The recycled atoms are retained as specific elements, but they are not reformed into a human being."

Sean blushed. "Oh. I knew that. But those atoms are used and absorbed by future Crew members ... future humans."

"In a sense, yes," Marly responded.

Maddie was impatient. There was much to tell and limited time to do so. "Let me finish. Gen 8 will never go to Earth Two. They will recycle inside Humanity One. Their atoms will not go to Earth Two because they will not be needed there. Gen 8 will be all females and they will give birth to the frozen embryos, all of them. Gen 8 will have no children of their own." She paused to make sure her friends were listening. "Our grandchildren will never set foot on Earth Two. Do you comprehend that?"

Ying was baffled. He understood mechanical things. Human things were less clear to him. "Why? Why will our grandchildren not be allowed to go to Earth Two?"

Maddie appreciated his question. "Because generations of living inside Humanity One with low gravity and space radiation will make them unable to live on a planet with full gravity."

"Why?" The answer did not resolve the questions in Ying's mind.

"Mutations. We have mutated already. Our live span is shorter than Gen 1, or even Gen 2. That is why we can be considered adults at sixteen." Maddie glanced at Kendra, "That is why we can bear our children as soon as sixteen."

Marly chimed in, unwilling to allow someone else to answer questions that seemed medically related, "The Innovators predicted some amount of mutation was possible."

Maddie looked down at the smaller girl, "Yes, some. They failed to predict the shortened life expectancy. Gen 8 will be born too early. Humanity One will not be anywhere near Earth Two when Gen 8 is old enough to be implanted with the embryos. The Mission will fail unless something is changed."

Marly tried to defend her position. "But the embryos can be born and be more mature when Humanity One arrives at Earth Two."

Kendra interjected, "Hydroponics will not be able to sustain as many as are supposed to be born. Stasis will also be reviving some of the Gen 1s in the TSVs. If we are not in Earth Two orbit by that time, the Mission will fail." She found herself saying "we", as if they would be the ones crewing the vessel at the time. But the belief that their atoms would live on in following generations made that make sense.

Maddie nodded agreement, then said gravely, "But that may not even come to be." She paused to make sure the Group was listening attentively. "At this very moment," she nodded toward Sean, "we are preparing for a possible attack by the rogue vessel, the alien vessel. We have no weapons. If they do attack, our mission is doomed. Maybe we are doomed."

"I thought Rex had an idea that would help us," Zack plaintively said.

"His idea was to increase energy harvest and help us increase speed so we can get back on our original schedule, the one set by the Innovators. He didn't have plans for weapons," Maddie answered.

"So ..." Ying struggled to form his question, "why are you telling us all of this? Can we change it?"

Maddie's face flushed. Her purpose was to expose secrets. That had always been her goal. She was perturbed that Ying did not understand the value of knowing the truth. "We have the right to know what is happening ... what is going to happen to us, to Humanity One. That's why I'm telling you this."

Ying smirked and glanced around the small room at the attentive faces of his friends. "We are risking our lives, the risk of being recycled early, just so we can know we are doomed? Why don't we try to change it? Is Captain Cesar simply sitting in his chair awaiting our doom?"

Maddie had no response. She did not know what was being done other than last ditch measures, response reactions designed to prevent a single attack from completely destroying Humanity One. Reactions that would hopefully save the vessel that carried the last humans to their new home. "I think we need to talk to Premier Paul, offer our help."

"How can we help?" Marly asked. "Do you have any ideas about how to change the mutations? Do you know how to extend our lifespan, so Gen 8 is not born too soon? Do you know how to fight against the aliens?"

Maddie glared at the younger girl. Marly asked the questions for which Maddie had no answers. "And that is the same thought process used by the Captain and the other Chiefs. We are too young to know the answers, but we are not too young to help them find the answers. We aren't bound by tradition. That's why Rex had his ideas about how to make Humanity One go faster. His thoughts are not restricted. Maybe Humanity One can go fast enough to escape the alien vessel and, just maybe, Humanity One can go fast enough to reach Earth Two before we have mutated to the point that we can't survive the planet's gravity."

Marly bowed up. She knew she was being dismissed. She did not like it anymore from Maddie than she did from adults. Less, in fact. "We have already mutated to that point. Our bones and muscles are too weak. Our hearts couldn't pump our blood under the gravitational force of a planet."

Maddie knew Marly was probably right. Marly knew more about human physiology than she did. "Well, even so, I bet they haven't considered traveling faster and arriving earlier, early enough that Gen 8 won't be born too soon." She looked into the eyes of each of her friends. "Are you willing to go with me to speak with the Premier, to offer our help?"

Reluctantly, each member of the Group nodded agreement.

CHAPTER 36

REVELATION

Across the table from Premier Paul, Maddie looked straight ahead. Then, an eye check that was intended to gain support from her friends, from the Group, was met with averted looks and nervous twitching. Even Kendra. Angrily, she wished Rex were present. Or Jana. They were the only two who could stand firm under Premier Paul's critical gaze. She missed Jana. Jana paid the price for being a part of the Group. She worried about Rex. Would her meeting with the Premier jeopardize her best friend? She worried even more about what she knew, about the secrets that their incessant searching had revealed. She knew the older Generations relied upon the MGR as the only source of solutions to the Mission threatening problems that faced Humanity One. Especially the Gen 2s. She knew someone had to listen. She also knew that of all the VLT members, Premier Paul was the most approachable. Their hope was that the Premier would allow them to speak. Maddie realized that "they" might be her alone. The others were withdrawn in fear. The Group had been warned against meeting without chaperones. Recycling was on their minds, made more certain by the presence of the absolute leader of Humanity One's occupants.

Premier Paul met Maddie's gaze. A quick survey of the Group made it clear that she would be the spokesperson, at least in the beginning. "Why are you here?" he asked harshly.

Maddie did not expect the conversation to start with a strong challenge. It was apparent that the Premier would have preferred to not be talking with them. "We requested this meeting so we could express some concerns we have about the success of our Mission."

"No. Why are you here as a group? Did Cesar's warning not resonate with the lot of you?"

Maddie tried to not show her nervousness as she lamely covered, "We are here with you. We thought that was acceptable, Premier."

"But you have met before in preparation for this meeting. You have violated the conditions set for you."

Maddie scrambled and hoped her response would not be pursued too deeply. "It is unfair for you to assume we met without someone nearby, without a Gen 3 chaperone. Are we required to have one chaperone each?" Challenge a challenge with a challenge. Ask a question to avoid answering directly - or lying. Those were her options at that moment. Her voice had to be heard.

Premier Paul pondered Maddie's response. He looked from one member of the group to the other. Zack fidgeted but never raised his eyes. Marly's pretty smile was forced, practiced like a physician's. Sean was properly distanced from the young teen, the object of his pubescent adulation. His hands were below the table. Ying looked ill, as did Kendra. Kendra's freckled face had a green tint. She definitely was not feeling well. He knew the question he should ask to put the Group in its place. Maddie was deflecting. If the youngsters - two of them fast approaching adulthood – felt the need to ignore the warnings against meeting, they might have something important to say. They knew the consequences. Apparently, their words were worth the risk. He also was pleased that they trusted him. "I suggest I am neither unfair nor wrong in my assumption. But - be that as it may, what do you have to say that is so important?"

Maddie felt relief that the Premier chose to allow her to speak rather than pursue the Group's reckless disregard for their constraints. "Premier Paul, we each," she motioned toward the others, "are concerned about the Mission. We have learned," she wanted to say "secrets," but she knew better, "a lot in our training ... and through our curiosity. We believe ... from what we've learned ... that our Mission is doomed to failure."

Paul heard Maddie's fumbling words as she struggled to express her thoughts. He knew the Con-Sys Technicians, probably the Trainee's as well, were being trained to respond to the possibilities of an alien attack. He anticipated what might be the cause of the Group's concerns. It was the cause of his concerns about the Mission as well. And the Captain's. "Captain Cesar has a plan to save the Mission. I understand your fear of the alien vessel, but I assure you that the Captain will protect Humanity One and the Mission."

Maddie blinked. The Premier was calm and reassuring. No accusations. He was wrong, but he was listening. "It's not that. We are aware of the alien vessel. That is not a secret to us. We are also aware that Rex Si Wu-Ershiliu is working to improve energy harvesting. Rumor has it that the work is almost completed."

"It is," Paul lowered his head, stared pointedly into Maddie's eye to add, "and that is no secret either. It may not be discussed openly yet, but that is largely because there are still doubts whether or not it will work. Yes, young Rex is proving himself to be quite proficient as a Sci-Eng Tech. If I remember correctly, he achieved adulthood a week or two before you will, Maddie."

"Uh ... yes. In three more weeks." Maddie shook her head. The Premier was never to the point. His conversations often wandered around the periphery of a subject. It was disconcerting. She knew that much about the man. "Premier Paul, that is not why we are here."

"That may be so, but the most immediate threat to our Mission *is* the potential for alien attack. We have no defensive capabilities."

Maddie inhaled and held her breath as she slowed her mind. Talking to the Premier about the Group's concerns would not be as easy as she had hoped. She wished Rex were with her. Maybe the Premier would take the discussion more seriously. "I understand that, Premier Paul. I have been training, as has Sean, on responses to any attack. I don't know everything about what Rex is doing. I haven't seen him in days, but I believe the ability to increase speed will allow us to escape the aliens. Everything that can be done about the aliens is probably being done."

Paul studied the young woman. He remembered her rebellious nature as personified by her long hair. He preferred conformance. Easier to lead when everyone complies without qualms or selfish agendas. He had seen more noncompliance during the last few weeks than he had seen in his life prior to that. It bothered him deeply. He was unsure how to deal with it. He reluctantly asked, "Then why are you here?"

Maddie spoke rapidly, afraid the Premier would skirt the subject if she did not say everything at once. "We have always been taught that Gen 8, our grandchildren and the atoms of our bodies, will colonize Earth Two. We have learned that is not true. It was never true. We have learned that the Gen 8 will be all females. They will be used to give birth to embryos stored in Stasis, not to have babies of their own. There was never supposed to be a Gen 9. Those embryos are the children of the Innovators, the same as Gen 2. The Innovators' children will live on Earth Two. We are being used to save the Innovators while our atoms are condemned to never colonize Earth Two." Her face was flushed. She felt the heat of it. She paused to catch her breath; afraid the Premier would respond while she sucked more air into her lungs. "But all that doesn't even matter now because Gen 8 will be born too soon. We are recycling too soon. The Innovators' children will be born too soon. The Innovators' children will have to have their own children and grandchildren while still in space. They will suffer from lack of gravity and radiation just like we have. They won't be able to colonize Earth Two. No one will."

Maddie watched Premier Paul's face twist and contort as she spoke. He wanted to stop her. She could tell, but she kept talking as fast as she could, to say as much as she could before he stopped her by jutting his open hand toward her. She caught her breath and waited for his response.

"Again, you pose to know more than the Innovators. You were warned of heresy, all of you." Paul's eyes were hardened as he purposely looked at each member of the Group, assuring himself that he had their full attention.

Maddie wanted to scream her frustration. Again, her words were being ignored. Her youth was all that mattered to the elders who led Humanity One. Her anger made her tremble.

"But ..." Premier Paul's tone shifted, "we are aware that the radiation of space and the lack of gravity has caused our lifespans to be less than originally planned. That is why you can achieve the status of adulthood at age sixteen. It originally was older. If you are insistent on spouting against the Innovators, maybe you need to gain a better understanding of why our Mission is so important."

Maddie watched carefully as the Premier spoke. His words seemed less ominous because his face softened. "We understand ..."

Premier Paul raised his hand again to silence Maddie, and any of the others who might find their tongues. "I doubt you understand the entirety of our Mission. You only understand the rote training about the Mission. That should be sufficient for viable performance by most Crew members in their support of the Mission, but since you have decided the Innovators' plan may have some areas that need to be addressed, I will provide a better understanding." Paul crossed his arms on the table and leaned forward. "You are correct that it will be the children of the Innovators who will be transported to Earth Two for colonization, along with the revived people in Stasis. The Innovators knew long space travel would have a detrimental effect on our bodies." He nodded toward Marly. "Doctor Trainee Marly can probably better explain how low gravity makes planet life untenable for us. She probably already has, considering what you have said. That information is not secret. It is simply not a subject of normal conversation. It is a hard fact. Discussing it, dwelling on it is nothing more than a distraction from the Mission. It is why the Chief Medical Officer and Cesar changed the age of adulthood with the onset of Generation 3.

"Humankind, our ancestors, which includes the Innovators, determined that Earth One would soon become climatically hostile to human life. Survival of the species was in doubt. There was no doubt that the civilization formed by humanity would not survive. The people we call the Innovators ... they did not call themselves that ..., a group of scientists and leaders, worked hard to save the civilization they knew and humanity as a species. Humanity One is the result of their work, of their efforts to avoid extinction.

"Sitting here today, we don't know what has become of Earth One, of the humans Humanity One left behind. Enough time may not have passed for the full effects of the climate shift to have reduced humans to subsistence living in small groups scattered across the planet, but it will before very many generations have passed." Paul paused and sighed. "In all likelihood, by the time Humanity One reaches Earth Two, humans will be struggling to survive on Earth One as their civilization tumbles around them. All that remains of our species and the many varieties of other Earth species will be inside Humanity One, ready to spring forth and revive humanity's greatness on another planet.

Eventually, humans will grow in sufficient number and technology on Earth Two that vessels not unlike Humanity One can return to Earth One and provide technology to replenish the humans who survived, if any survive. Humankind will then inhabit two Earths." Paul leaned back in his chair, "But that will be hundreds of years in the future. Probably thousands or more while Earth One phases through its climatic cycle and returns to one more conducive to humans. That is the reason for our Mission."

"We know that," Maddie replied impatiently. "But we ... our atoms ... were never meant to be a part of that. Only the children of the Innovators will be allowed to live on Earth Two and return to Earth One. We are nothing to the Innovators."

"We are all children of the Innovators," Paul snapped. "We are all humans. The survival of humanity is our Mission. It would serve you well to remember that simple truth."

"But our atoms won't go to Earth Two," protested Zack. The timid teen found the courage and a cause to speak.

"Atoms are just that," replied the Premier. "They are atoms with no knowledge or memory of their existence. No one knows the origin of any single atom."

Maddie watched as Zack's face reddened angrily. She wanted to intervene, but he needed to participate.

"No! We know our atoms are recycled. We live on inside Humanity One. We were supposed to live on as atoms on Earth Two."

Premier Paul's brow wrinkled, barely noticeable among the wrinkles that lived on his brow. "Atoms don't live. Not in the sense of you or me."

"Why then are we told recycling is a good thing because our atoms are reused? They live on after we are recycled," Zack protested, still upset.

"Recycling *is* a good thing. All the atoms contained within Humanity One constitute our small universe. We have access to no new atoms for the creation of things, including growing our own bodies. That is why we limit our population. Our resources are limited. That is why we recycle even our own bodies. Without all the original atoms, we cannot survive."

"I want my atoms to see Earth Two! To live on Earth Two!"

"Zack!" Maddie commanded. "This is not why we are here. We are here to warn Premier Paul of Mission failure. As important as our atoms are, they will mean nothing if the Mission fails." She turned to the Premier. "The Mission is doomed to failure. As you just said, the number of atoms available determines our population, yet it is planned that Gen 8 will be larger than all previous generations and will give birth to as many embryos as possible after we enter the orbit of Earth Two. That will not happen as planned."

Paul's mouth twitched. "Explain."

"Because our lifespans are shorter and births are happening sooner, Gen 8 will be born probably fifty years before we reach Earth Two. That means the Mission will fail unless we do something."

"What do you suggest we do?"

Maddie was startled by the question. "Find another planet that is closer."

"I hardly think that is possible. The Innovators would have chosen a closer planet if one existed."

"The Innovators were wrong about aliens." Maddie regretted her phraseology almost instantly.

Paul's face reddened. "Again, your heretic thoughts expose you."

"It is not heresy. You know the Innovators did not believe there would be alien encounters. Maybe they missed a planet. If we look, maybe we can find one nearby. If the aliens can find one, why can't we?"

"The aliens have shown themselves to not be cordial or inviting. We cannot live near them."

"Have we tried to explain why we are here? Maybe they will be friendly if we explain things."

"We have had Communications with them. Your own mother risked recycling to make contact. They are not friendly. We are in danger from them."

Maddie blanched as she considered Premier Paul's comment about Della. "I ... I ... she did? I didn't know."

Paul smirked. "I'm sorry we didn't get your approval."

Maddie realized the message the Premier was trying to deliver. She regrouped her thoughts around the reason for the meeting. "I didn't mean that. But - the aliens ... their danger to us ... should not keep us from finding another planet, a few years further away. Surely the universe has many planets." Maddie really thought her idea had merit. The Group seemed to think it did. It was starting to wither under the Premier's visible displeasure.

"A planet capable of supporting human life has to be a near perfect match to the planet that spawned us. Water. Climate. Temperature. Solar radiation. Gravity. Earth Two was likely selected because of where it is in its climatic cycle. I doubt we possess the expertise to consider all the variables necessary. Besides, Humanity One lacks the equipment to search for viable planets. That was not part of the Mission."

Maddie was disheartened. What Premier Paul said made sense. Finding another planet was not an option. She had only one more idea. "Then we need to reconsider how many generations will be required to complete the Mission. Gen 8 should not be forced to become all female. A later generation will have to do that."

"Maddie, I understand your concern." The Premier glanced around the table. "All of you. I assure you the Vessel Leadership Team is developing plans to address the very issues you have raised. I thank you for sharing your thoughts with me. In closing, do I need to remind you that you are under strict directives to avoid private meetings among yourselves?"

Maddie knew the Premier's patience was at its end for the day. "No, Premier Paul. We understand."

"Good. No matter what you may think about the Innovators' plans, the primary Mission of Humanity One is the preservation of humanity. Whereas Humanity One is the vessel that carries the human body and human technology to Earth Two, we are each a vessel to carry the human spirit to Earth Two. That is so for each generation that has been entrusted with humanity's preservation. Thank you for trusting me. You may return to your duties; and please leave one at a time to avoid further issues."

Premier Paul watched the Group leave in single file, reasonably spaced. He suspected more than one of them would engage in conversation before they separated completely. Maddie was curious. Her curiosity had to be controlled. It created distractions from the Mission for her and everyone around her. He found himself distracted by the thoughts she planted in his mind. The Innovators warned of distractions and wrote the MGR to help avoid thinking that was not germane to the Mission. In all his years as Premier, he had been able to avoid distractive thoughts within himself. He had also been able to prevent distractive thinking from corrupting the Crew. He was tired.

CHAPTER 37

EVASIVE ACTIONS

Cesar adjusted himself in the Chair. Joseph expectantly, and silently, sat in the Trainee chair. The dimly lit room was quiet. Quieter than normal. Seldom was there much sound other than the continuous flow of air through ducts, the background sound of fans that circulated fresh air throughout the vessel and pulled away the carbon dioxide laden air for scrubbing. It was eerily quiet. The air was thick with anticipation. Maybe some fear.

Rex stood by Premier Paul's side an arm's length away from the Chair. Rex's invitation to be in the Control System Room was an honor, though the newly realized adult probably did not grasp the idea. His mind was on other things – on one other thing. That moment in time, that point in Humanity One's journey, that instant in human history would forever be remembered as the day the Mission's success was assured. Or it would not be remembered at all because the Mission was doomed to ultimate failure. Neither Chief Gail, nor any of the other Chiefs, were offered the option to be witness to the event. Rex would probably have to bear the wrath of his slighted section Chief, but that was not Cesar's worry, especially not at that moment.

The energy harvesting improvements created by Rex were a success, even more than Rex had imagined. Within a matter of weeks,

Humanity One possessed enough power reserve to test the proton drive, to see if a steady stream of particles could create a significant increase in velocity.

From the moment it was first detected following Humanity One, Commander Schnt kept his vessel perfectly spaced, pacing Humanity One as both vessels plowed through space in that part of the Milky Way galaxy. The alien vessel had not deviated from its trailing course. Commander Schnt also continued to ignore attempts at Communicator contact. Cesar often tossed in his bed at night, unable to sleep because his mind tried to visualize what the alien Commander was thinking. What were his plans? Was he awaiting additional resources, more vessels, from his home world? Was he overly cautious, studying Humanity One for signs of weaponry? Cesar even tried to put himself into Commander Schnt's position and imagine what he would do under the same circumstances if their roles were reversed. Without an understanding of the alien's intentions, all those questions were mere distractions.

The one thing missing from Cesar's imagination was battle. War. He knew nothing of armed conflict. His sire, the first Captain, August Yi, might have known about battle, but he did not share it. August only taught the lessons of the MGR. Battle was not necessary on a voyage that had zero chance of encounter with aliens. The Innovators were sure of it. That was what Cesar learned. That was all Joseph knew also. Thoughts - even knowledge - of war would only be a distraction for the Crew. Cesar was leaving his heir unprepared to serve as Captain in the universe recently unveiled by reality. Once again, Cesar found himself facing problems that were never imagined by those he trusted most – The Innovators. The beleaguered Captain cursed their lack of foresight. And maybe his own blind allegiance.

It was time to see if young Rex's theory was right, if young Rex's vision of the universe was the *real* reality. "Joseph, initiate the proton drive."

"Aye Captain. Initiate proton drive."

An unpretentious command. Few words. All it would take was a simple stroke of a keyboard, or a touch of an icon on a screen. Cesar did not know how exactly the command would be executed. He did not need to know. He only needed to know that Rex had properly programed the system to properly respond to the input. He only needed to know that an obedient Con-Sys Technician would do as told. He only needed to know how to wait for the results of his simple command, of Rex's complex work. He waited, trying not to show his impatience. Humanity One's response to the command would not be immediate. There would be no sensation of speed change. Young Rex calculated that any difference in velocity would only be measurable after at least an hour, maybe two. Proton drives are not rocket engines, not in the classic sense. They emit a steady stream of subatomic particles. The emission was the action. Forward motion was the reaction. Speed and velocity were cumulative effects of continued proton ejection through the drive. Inertia played an important part in velocity increase. Once inertia was overcome, speed and velocity could be maintained with minimal added energy. That first step to change velocity was the most critical ... and telling.

Cesar's back muscles tightened. Stress and nerves. His arthritic vertebrae did not like tightened muscles. The pain increased faster than Humanity One's velocity. He squirmed to ease the pain. It did not work. It got a few moments respite while he focused on making an entry in the Captain's Log. Once completed, the pain returned in force. He pushed himself up from the Chair. Joseph leapt to his feet. Cesar waved him down and half-smiled as he began to pace in the small amount of space available. The wait would be what it would be. There was nothing that could be done to change it. Not even one of

Rex Si Wu-Ershiliu's brilliant ideas. He smiled at Premier Paul as he passed near him. Paul seemed as deep in thought as he was. He knew his lifelong friend Paul feared repercussions ... voodoo-like reprisals from ghosts of the past ... for ignoring the MGR, for choosing a path not covered in detail by the Innovators, for being distracted by things not worthy.

An hour elapsed without conversation. There was nothing to be said. Cesar returned to the Chair and settled in for the status report. "Status," he said authoritatively.

Joseph stood and began his routine status request from the Con-Sys Technicians, one primary function at a time. Stellar engine and solar wind panels were reported to be *"All normal."* Normal was different than prior to Rex's changes. Those functions were operating at the new normal. Proton drive response was different, but as expected. *"Proton drive active."* Joseph called for the velocity update as the last status request. That was as Cesar had requested as part of the day's event.

The entire room waited to hear the response. Everyone knew it should be different, but there was no guarantee. It was a theory, only a theory. Though the Con-Sys Technician did not abnormally delay his response, the wait seemed interminable. *"Velocity plus 2% of normal."*

Joseph turned toward the Chair and declared, "Status all normal except proton drives and velocity. Proton drives are active, and velocity is 2% above normal."

"Thank you, Captain Trainee Joseph." Cesar relaxed. Two percent was a significant increase from normal. Rex assured him that a yield of five percent was possible. "Trainee Rex, does that velocity match your calculations?"

Rex tensed as all available eyes turned to him. His mouth was dry. He struggled to make words for a moment. "Aye, Captain. Very closely."

"How much more velocity do you anticipate?"

"Velocity should increase an additional two percent with the same elapsed time from this point."

"The velocity will be a total of 4% greater after another hour?"

"No, Captain. Velocity will be 4.04% greater than normal."

"How long before we regain the hours lost?"

"Approximately one-thousand eight-hundred fifty hours, Captain."

"Is that when we initiate deceleration to maintain schedule?"

"No Captain. That is the time required at achieved velocity to regain the lost time." Rex was nervous. He made no calculations regarding deceleration. His personal goal was to increase the vessel's velocity and then maintain speed for the duration of the journey.

Cesar's momentary delight evaporated. "How long to reduce velocity to MGR rate? We need to return to schedule." Ignoring the MGR to avoid the rogue was necessary. Ignoring the MGR to regain the time and distance lost was necessary. There was no rationale for ignoring the MGR further. It was within the realm of possibility that Premier Paul and the other Chiefs might find him to be unviable if he continued to ignore the MGR.

"I'll have to make those calculations, Captain. That was not in my plan."

Cesar stared at Rex. A quick glance toward Premier Paul indicated the Premier was following the conversation carefully. Not a surprise. Cesar knew his viability was on the line. "You need to make those calculations. I'm not sure what your plan is, but mine is to regain the time lost and return to schedule. Nothing more."

"Aye, Captain." Rex gulped. "Deceleration will have to begin sooner than eighteen hundred hours. Deceleration requires more time than does acceleration." He hoped the Captain would understand.

"Then get to it. Our objective is to return to the schedule calculated by the Innovators. Understood?"

Rex had other ideas. It was now or never to present them for consideration. "Why?"

Cesar was startled by the question. The conversation was not loud. No one other than the four people in the area of the Chair needed to be involved. His reaction was loud enough to turn a few heads. "What do you mean why?" Question asked, he followed with his own answer to reiterate his position, "Because it's the Innovators' plan."

Rex inhaled deeply and held his breath for a moment before he replied, "Why do we need to match the schedule? What if the alien vessel accelerates to match our speed – or worse, catches us? I think it would be better if we continue at a higher velocity."

Cesar was angered by the youngster's insolence. Subordinates followed orders obediently. They did not argue with or second guess their superiors. "I suppose you also think you are better trained to Captain this vessel as well?" he snapped.

"No, Captain. Not at all, Captain." Rex did not expect the reaction he got. "I merely meant we might be better prepared to elude the alien vessel if we are traveling at a faster rate. Our only hope is flight."

Cesar calmed himself. Over the prior weeks, he had come to realize that Rex's mind was a creative one. The young man was not satisfied to accept easy answers or to ignore hard questions. Still, Premier Paul, the old line, MGR only, leader of Humanity One, was observing the interaction with piqued interest. The Premier's interest was disconcerting. The Innovators could not be ignored completely. It was a moment during which Cesar could not show weakness or doubt. "Make the calculations for deceleration. I will Communicate with Chief Gail to assign a team. Chief Gail will lead the team." As brilliant as Rex was, he was a novice adult and needed to understand his role, his place. Besides, the assignment might serve to narrow the rift that had grown between Chief Gail and her charge. Balance the power. "In the meantime, I will monitor the alien vessel's response."

Cesar watched Rex leave the Control System Room. He felt some small remorse because of Rex's dejected posture. He did not want to discourage the young man. Rex was destined to become a Chief. Even if Gail lived a long life, Rex would become the titular Chief of Science and Engineering – just as Cesar had become the titular Premier. Premier Paul remained near the side of Cesar's chair. Cesar made additional entries in the Captain's Log and waited.

"Status," Cesar commanded. An hour had slowly passed. He patiently awaited the status reports he truly wanted to hear. Finally, he knew. Everyone in the room knew. Velocity was at 4.04% of normal as predicted by Rex. A rough calculation in his mind indicated that by maintaining the achieved velocity for the duration, Humanity One would arrive more than a decade earlier than the Innovators planned. He had no idea what that would do to the Mission. Uncertainty could only portend failure. The proton drive was still active. Velocity would continue to increase if the proton drive continued to spew the particle stream. *If* the drive had access to a steady particle energy source.

The moment of truth was at hand. Cesar cleared his throat. "Status of alien vessel," he commanded.

"Alien vessel status," Joseph repeated more loudly.

Con-Sys Technician Len San Wu reported evenly, "Alien vessel tracked for an hour into the increase then veered port to travel perpendicular to our course. Alien vessel is receding in that direction."

Cesar accepted Joseph's repetition of the report. "Any further communications from the alien vessel?"

"No Captain."

"Then I would say we are lucky."

"How so?" Premier Paul interjected.

"Apparently we are not moving toward their home world." Cesar smiled his relief to Paul. The two of them had lived a lot of years as leaders of the vessel that carried the known remnants of humankind into the future. They had faced the unknown challenge of aliens without guidance from the Innovators. Their world had been upended. Cesar knew the vessel would be at risk of Mission failure if he had not pushed Paul to accept a solution that did not involve the MGR. Even so, he was not in a mood to gloat or brag about his creative thinking. All he had done was rely on the strengths of someone else. He had Rex to thank for the success. The solution was Rex's idea. The push to implement the solution was Rex's persistence and courage to face whatever fate awaited him. At least, in Rex he saw hope for the spoiled generations to come.

"Captain Trainee Joseph, disengage the proton drive. Then take the Chair. I need to retire to my quarters." Cesar lifted himself from the Chair as he was speaking.

"Aye, Captain," Before Joseph could relay the command or rise from the trainee chair, he was interrupted by Premier Paul's hand on his forearm.

"Is that really what you want to do?" Paul asked of Cesar.

"We have achieved our goal. The alien vessel has left us, and we will be on schedule with our course after we fully execute Rex's calculations."

"But - will what we've accomplished ensure Mission success?"

"We have managed to regain the schedule provided by the Innovators. That is calculated to lead to Mission success."

"I wonder," mused Paul.

Cesar saw the consternation on the Premier's face. With only a slight pause, he said, "Trainee Joseph, belay the order to disengage the drive. Take the Chair. Premier, maybe we can continue this in my quarters."

CHAPTER 38

MISSION REBOOT

Cesar invited Paul into the room he and his mate once shared. After Robert was recycled, he gave a brief thought to joining Paul in the Premier's quarters to free up the space, but there was no immediate need for the area. It was, after all, the Captain's quarters. "Something is on your mind, Paul. What is it?" He sat in a contoured chair; a design approved by the Innovators. It helped ease his back pain somewhat. One of Doctor Katherine's powders would help even more, but he could not take the dose until he was free to sleep. First, he had to deal with the Premier, no doubt a harangue for operating outside the MGR ... again. That had happened a lot lately.

After a moment of indecision, Premier Paul bluntly said, "Maybe we should reconsider our speed."

"You mean velocity?" Cesar made the distinction to throw Paul off balance. A desperate attempt to lessen the impact of Paul's initial arguments against increasing Humanity One's rate of travel. The agreement was already made, and the deed was done.

Paul did not react. "Whatever. Maybe we should consider going faster."

"What? Why?" Cesar realized that Paul was focused on the thoughts in his own mind, probably the same thoughts that seemed to have distracted him in the Control Systems Room. He leaned forward in his chair, fully attentive.

"Because we must plan for as many as three or four additional generations at our current speed ... velocity."

Still puzzled, Cesar responded warily, "That's a problem for a future Premier." He feared the Premier was leading him into a discussion he did not want to have.

"So was correcting our course schedule," Paul said earnestly.

Cesar was taken aback by the prescience of the Premier's cautious conversation. He marveled at the determination in Paul's pale eyes. Paul was never afraid to say what he thought, but the man was easily swayed after saying it. He did not like to be held to task later. "True, but I had the solution handed to me by Rex. There was no need to leave the decision to the future if we have the solution in hand."

"And maybe we have been handed the solution to further problems that are destined to face our progeny," Paul replied wistfully.

"Such as?" Curiosity replaced Cesar's wariness.

"The generations. For some time, we have known the problems caused by shorter lifespans. The generations require fewer years than the Innovators reckoned."

Cesar closed his eyes in thought before he said, "Agreed. The shorter lifespans seem to indicate that the MGR regarding Gen 8 might be premature. Paul, you have always been a stickler for the MGR, the one who holds us all to the standards set by the Innovators. What's changed?"

"Let's just say that my eyes have been opened to reality. The reality is that strict adherence to the MGR will doom our Mission."

"What makes you say that?"

"I'm no scientist, but I believe we will implement the Innovators colonization plan three generations too early ... long before arrival at

Earth Two ... if we don't make changes. If we follow the MGR to the letter."

The pain in Cesar's back returned with a vengeance. He grimaced.

Paul misinterpreted Cesar's expression of pain. In a resolute voice, he said without a hint of hesitancy, "I'm serious Cesar, and you know it. If we revive the Innovators in Stasis as Generation 8 is being born ... as the MGR tells us ... they will be dead before we reach Earth Two, before they can colonize Earth Two with their children. The Mission will fail."

"I know," Cesar slumped his shoulders and exhaled. "What do you suggest?"

"Again ... I'm no scientist, but I think the Gen 4 malcontents ... the Group, as they call themselves ... may have answers."

"Does that include young Rex?" Cesar wanted to be angry, instead he felt a growing knot of realization in the pit of his stomach.

"No. I suppose Rex was doing your bidding. It was the others, mostly Maddison Si Wu-Qi." After saying the words and realizing how they could be interpreted, Paul quickly added, "They asked if I would meet with them. They were not alone."

Cesar tried to ignore the knot that threatened to push the bile up from his guts. "What did young Maddison have to offer?"

Paul was puzzled by Cesar's suddenly ashen face and sad eyes. He answered pensively, He feared what the Captain's reactions might portend. "Thoughts. Distracting thoughts by definition. But valid thoughts."

Cesar groaned lightly. "What kind of thoughts could be powerful enough to open a man's eyes?"

"We ... you and I and the others are too close to the Innovators."

"What does that mean?"

"Our parents were the same generation as the Innovators. They *were* the Innovators."

"Maddison had to tell you that?" Cesar asked incredulously, the knot in his stomach momentarily forgotten ... though the cause of it was not ... as he wondered why the comment was made.

"No. But her words gave me pause to consider how we think. We are very linear in our thoughts."

Cesar moved in his chair in hopes the movement would lessen the pain in his guts. "If that means we allow one thought to logically follow another, I suppose that is true."

Paul shook his head lightly, "No. It means we're narrow minded. Tied to what our parents taught us."

"I think we are more open minded than not."

"In our own way, maybe, but not as open as these young people are."

"They don't have the experience we have. They have not had to face the reality of ensuring the success of the primary Mission. They don't fully comprehend what failure means. Their minds are not open to that possibility."

Paul's eyes danced nervously, barely able to look onto Cesar's. "They *are* young. They lack life experience. But ... they *do not* lack comprehension. As a matter of fact, their youth and lack of paradigms may enhance their ability to solve problems. They have fewer established notions."

Cesar's gut wrenched. The pain was great enough to replace that of his back, a gut punch. "We have already determined that they have violated the MGR, disregarded time-honored protocols ... not to mention violations of privacy." He tried to use anger to force rueful thoughts from his mind.

"WE determined that. WE didn't want to hear them ... or understand them."

"They were spying, digging in places not for them to be. They were neglecting their duties, becoming unviable. Delving into things that only served to distract them from their duties. Apparently, nothing has changed."

"One thing has changed, Cesar," Paul replied softly, but not timidly.

"What would that be?" Cesar snapped. "The fact that they spoke directly to you? Tell me what has changed, Premier." He wanted to rid his mind of regrets. Anger toward the Premier might help purge the thoughts that plagued him.

"Our willingness to act rationally even if it means turning loose of that which we have always held dear and ..." Paul paused reflectively, "and maybe sacred. We are learning to not hide behind the MGR."

Cesar fought against the urge to puke. The conversation was not one he wanted to have. Not now. Not after what had transpired. The decision – the solution – was final. Forever final. It could not be undone. But he had to finish, he had to hear what Paul was suggesting. "Quit beating around the bush. This is not about Maddie and her Group. What are you trying to say?"

"Increase Humanity One's speed ... velocity ... so it arrives as defined in the MGR, when Gen 8 is readily available."

Cesar felt the bile in the back of his throat. He closed his eyes and fought to control his regurgitation reflex. "We don't even know if that is possible."

"We don't know that it isn't. We wouldn't even consider it as possible, but the youngsters have shown us they do."

"They don't know enough."

"Maybe we don't either. The difference between them and us is that they aren't afraid to search for answers wherever the questions lead them, while we depend on the MGR to answer all things."

Cesar eyes filled with tears. Jana was not afraid to dig for answers. She sacrificed her atoms to find those answers, to go where the questions led her. He stared at the floor for an eternity before he looked into Paul's eyes and asked with a broken voice, "How did she act?"

"I sensed that she was afraid, but she knew the time to speak was now. She recognized that if we do not do something now, it will be too late – if it isn't already."

"Not Maddison. Jana."

Realization hit Paul. He pursed his dry lips and carefully formed an answer. "Frightened. Confused. Alone."

Cesar sobbed softly for several minutes. He did not think about his audience as he relived that day when he met with the Group and gave them each a warning – except for Jana. She did not get a warning. As the Captain's granddaughter, she did not get a warning. She was the example for all to remember, of the lesson to be learned – that the MGR was the law of the vessel. He knew nothing else. What he did was done to preserve the Mission, to protect the Crew Members from distracting thoughts that would render them unviable and risk Mission failure. Distracting thoughts that now might prove to be the salvation of the Mission.

Slowly, Cesar raised his head to look at Paul. "I will talk to Rex."

"I would like to be part of that conversation," Premier Paul stated. It was not a request.

Rex frowned defensively. He was not expecting anyone to interfere with his calculations. Cesar was adamant regarding the deceleration of Humanity One, upset that Rex did not have the answer at the moment the question was asked. Chief Scientist Gail led a small entourage toward his workspace. Captain Cesar and Doctor Katherine were the most prominent among them. Stan tagged along with Premier Paul. Rex could not imagine how anything good was going to come of the meeting that was heading toward him.

To set the record straight, maybe deflect some of the angst he saw on the approaching faces, Rex said, "I don't have the deceleration schedule completed."

Chief Gail waved away Rex's words. "That's not why we're here. We have something more important."

Rex saw a wave of annoyance cross Cesar's face. He was relieved to see that Cesar's eyes were on Chief Gail. He hoped that would bode well for him. He had heard a rumor that Maddie and the Group met with Premier Paul. Thoughts of the potential fallout from that meeting had proved distracting as he forced himself to focus on Cesar's new orders. He could not help but wonder if Cesar's presence was the result of that meeting.

"Rex, what if we don't decelerate?" Cesar asked abruptly, his facial expression daring Chief Gail to interrupt again.

Rex's eyes danced between the expectant faces that now encircled him. He felt vulnerable seated in front of his computer terminal. The faces towered over him. Physically, he was accustomed to being above all of them except Cesar's. "We arrive ahead of schedule." He gave a concise answer, fearful of adding to it.

"How far ahead?" Chief Gail interrupted crudely.

Before Rex could respond, Cesar raised his hand to silence the novice Chief. She cringed as if the hand had struck her. "Technician Rex, how many years sooner will we arrive at our current velocity?"

Rex squinted away his surroundings as he focused on the data available in his mind. Finally, he opened his eyes and answered, "About seventeen years sooner."

"That's not enough." Cesar turned to Doctor Katherine. "How soon do we need to arrive to support the MGR generation plan?"

Doctor Katherine's mouth twisted wryly. "Whatever we do will violate the MGR."

"Not my question."

Doctor Katherine nodded. "To achieve the MGR of the Eighth Generation providing support for Earth Two colonization, we need to arrive no later than 90 years. Even that will require some careful birth planning for the next four generations – and no surprises in longevity."

Rex listened intently, performing calculations as the conversation unfolded and their quest became clear. He felt the eyes focused on him rather than Cesar. The eyes were asking the obvious question. He gulped and answered, "We can't achieve the velocity to arrive in ninety years. If ... and that is a big IF ... we can achieve ninety percent of the speed of light, we can arrive in a century. But that velocity may *not* be achievable for Humanity One even with our modifications."

Gail refused to be stifled, "But if we are traveling near the speed of light, time passes more slowly for us." She beamed with pride.

Rex hesitated long enough for her to bask in a few approving nods for her brilliant revelation, then gently contradicted, "Not for us. Only for the world outside our vessel. Time is relative to the observer. For us, a year at ninety percent of the speed of light is a year of aging."

The corners of Cesar's lips curled upwards slightly as he cast a sideways glance at Gail. "Rex, how soon before we can know if ninety percent is possible?"

"Maybe a week of continued acceleration. Maybe more. I'm guessing at this moment. Acceleration to that speed cannot be calculated exactly because we do not know the potential of our proton drive. All we have is my data for improving the harvesting system to allow more particles for use in the drives."

Premier Paul hesitantly asked, "Are you saying we may achieve ninety percent in a week?"

Rex shook his head. "No. I'm saying I may know more about our potential after a week of continued proton drive use. To make that happen, the solar and stellar parasols will have to harvest a lot of energy particles. A lot of ifs and maybes."

"Are the parasols capable?" Paul asked.

"The parasols can only harvest what is available. In some areas of space, the harvest is meager. To get the most particles, we have to be near star systems. I don't know what's ahead of us."

Stan interjected, "That is a problem too. The Innovators calculated all space objects along the route when they plotted our course. Those calculations are time factored. If we arrive early, we may put ourselves in harm's way or miss energy gathering opportunities."

Cesar nodded. "You're right. We need to increase our observation capabilities so we can account for objects and alter course as necessary. But it sounds like we may still arrive too late for Gen 8 to provide the required assistance to the Stasis colonists. Suggestions?"

Rex waited for one of his superiors to respond. None of the elders spoke and all eyes eventually settled on him. He suggested, "Add one generation. Push Gen 8's duties onto Gen 9."

"That violates ..." Premier Paul began automatically, stopped and restarted, "that sounds no worse than anything I can think of. Cesar, what do you think?"

"I think I'm the one who asked the question. Rex is the only one who has provided an answer."

"We need to figure the ramifications of adding a generation. What more must we factor into such a decision?" Doctor Katherine asked.

"What issues do you anticipate?" Cesar asked.

"None in particular. More degradation of human physiology. There is so much we do not know. The Innovators put too much thought into each phase of this Mission for us to be cavalier about changing it."

Cesar snorted. "And there was so much they didn't know when they wrote the MGR. We've abided by the MGR without question for more than sixty years."

"And they have kept us safe," Katherine argued.

"They have gotten us to this point, but we and our Mission are far from safe," Cesar retorted. "We are not being cavalier by engaging everything we have learned. It's time we used the knowledge we have gained and that which they left for us. We need to solve problems with it." He glanced toward Paul with a twisted smile. "Maybe it's time we quit being so linear in our thinking."

"You would throw away everything you know to be true? To not follow the MGR is heresy." Katherine scowled a warning to Cesar by glancing around the circle of faces. "This is too much of a public venue to express such thoughts – even for the Captain."

Cesar stood erect. His face reflected a deep sadness and an underlying determination. "The MGR offers guidelines for achieving a successful Mission. The Innovators wrote the MGR expressly to assure a successful Mission. They used all the knowledge available to them at the time. We know they did not know everything there was to know. Following the MGR means doing the right things to ensure the Mission is a success. Nothing more."

Rex watched the two VLT members face off at his workstation. A larger battle was brewing. Something was tearing at Cesar's soul, something other than the thought of a failed Mission. All he could do was wait for directions from the VLT.

Premier Paul intervened. "As Captain Cesar said, maybe it is time we become less linear in our thinking. What is happening is greater than even the Innovators imagined. We are their children. We must not fail them. We cannot hide behind the MGR. We must embrace some creative solutions. Do what they would do if they were here with us."

Rex was shocked at the Premier's tone as much as his words. He knew the Premier was not customarily forceful, but this time he was passionate. Still, he waited for the outcome.

"Very well," Doctor Katherine acquiesced. "But - expect further problems. If we do not set the example, how can we expect Gen 3 and Gen 4 to follow the teachings?"

Cesar first looked at Rex then addressed Katherine's concern, "We can expect them, and subsequent generations, to do the right things to ensure the success of the Mission to save humanity. That was always our Mission. It will be theirs. We all know that is all Humanity One offers. Humankind cannot survive for long inside a vessel such as this one."

Katherine shrugged. "You're the Captain. I know the MGR for Medical is infallible."

"Well that may be," replied Cesar, "but I have my doubts. Did the Medical MGR tell us that lifespans would be reduced from seventy years to fifty within a single generation? Did it tell us we would have to reduce adulthood to a mere sixteen years of age to ensure time for training replacements? I was called upon to change that definition while still too young to be cast in that role."

"Heresy," Katherine stated.

"Is it heresy to follow the truth? The Innovators ... your parents and mine ... wanted us to know the truth and follow it. For them, the truth was within the MGR. For us, the truth is what it has become. The MGR still offer guidance for how to use the truth as we find it."

Rex watched, waited for the disagreement to escalate. It did not. Doctor Katherine shook her head disapprovingly and remained silent. He anticipated Cesar's next words.

"Rex, is there any reason we shouldn't continue use of the proton drive to accelerate Humanity One?

"None that I know, Captain."

"I'll issue the order," Cesar paused and looked at the small, assembled group, "if there are no viable objections."

There were none. Chief Gail stood over Rex's shoulder as the others left the Science and Engineering Department. He nervously began inputting data for calculations of velocity over time and of energy requirements to accelerate to and sustain ninety percent of the speed of light. The Innovators had established a course and velocity that relied upon inertia and gravity to maintain it with minimal assistance from solar, stellar and proton drives. That would not be the same for the new velocity. The MGR offered no guidance. He was on his own. His viability was at risk and he knew it.

CHAPTER 39

ANALYSIS

"We must make deviations from the Innovators' course to capture more energy." Rex practiced the words in his mind long before he said them aloud to Captain Cesar and Premier Paul.

"Won't that lengthen the journey? Require more time?"

"We don't think so," chimed in Chief Gail. "I've had a team of Techs studying the course coding in the navigation system. Our course was never a direct one. It appears to be a wandering path with planned deviations from a straight line to approach specific star systems and to avoid others."

"There must be a reason," Cesar said with a scowl.

"We think it is to capture necessary energy to sustain Humanity One and avoid gravity wells or potential asteroid belts."

"Think? If you are suggesting adding kilometers to the journey, you better have a good explanation. Not just "we think.""

Gail stammered and pleaded for help with her eyes.

Rex replied, "Aye, Captain. I have recalculated the course out as far as our enhanced monitoring allows, about one third of a parsec ... about a year and a half ahead."

"Are you sure that's correct? The monitoring system is new and virtually untested."

"I believe it is very close ... on an astronomical scale. I have measured as much as has been available and done the calculations. As our velocity increases, our tunnel of visibility narrows, but we still have the ability to see objects in the distance of space. There are star systems along the Innovators' course that can provide needed energy if we deviate slightly to move close enough to them."

"But will that put us off course, lose our way?"

"No. Any deviations correct back to the original course, plus ..." Rex added deliberately, "we will gather the energy to complete our acceleration and to maintain velocity. If we do not make the moves, our velocity will drop, and our energy reserves will be depleted. We will simply drift at an ever-decreasing velocity until we reach the next star system on the Innovators' course."

"And Humanity One will suffer Mission failure," Cesar exhaled heavily. He mulled the new information and the new request for a moment before he responded. "Do it. Both of you personally deliver the course changes to Captain Trainee Joseph. Thank you, Rex. Thank you, Chief Gail."

Cesar smiled through his pain at Rex and Chief Gail. He waited until they were out of the Premier's Decision Room. "Paul, have you spoken with Maddie and her friends?"

Paul's face contorted momentarily before he responded. "You've had Maddie involved in the training and implementation of the new Forward Scanning Telemetrics System. I would think you had opportunity to talk with her."

"Not so much. She has been busy. Her and her protégé, Sean. Since acquiring adulthood and given extra privileges with the new system, she's taken to her assignment with a vigor I've never seen in a Con-Sys Technician." Cesar's smile reappeared. "Not a distracting thought in her head."

"Sean Si Sanshier-Juisi? Is he covering a control system?"

"He's covering the FST console on the other shift."

"He's a long way from adulthood. Maddie is barely an adult in her own right."

"Yes, but he's trained and needed. Adding systems has put a strain on our resources."

"The Innovators didn't design Humanity One to support the new tasks and duties we have created."

Cesar rubbed his face with a huge hand in an attempt to wipe away the persistent tiredness that was new to him. "Premier, we need to call the VLT into session. We have decisions to make."

Paul saw the Captain's pain. He knew about the arthritis. He knew about the unease caused by a series of violations of the MGR. Neither of those was the source of the pain. He knew that also. "We have met once this week. Is it not something that can wait? Everyone is busy."

Cesar stared across the small meeting room. The wall was not interesting. "I think not. Something Sci-Eng Tech Rex said earlier - in another conversation - has given me an idea."

"Do you want to share it with me before hand?"

"Rex said the energy harvest could provide more energy for everything. I wonder if that would apply to Hydroponics."

"We can simply ask Chief Kellie."

"No. I think that will require input from several of the Chiefs, especially Donald and Katherine. It's not just about Hydroponics. It's a major shift in thinking ... and doing."

"I can bring them in now, if it's that urgent."

Cesar pulled himself upright in his chair. "Allow a few minutes so I can go to the head. Maybe get a snack from the Mess Hall." His eyes lit with a thought. "As a matter of fact, call them to the Mess Hall. We can take Mess with the early group. What I have to discuss should not be kept secret. Maybe someone in the Mess Hall will have thoughts to add." He pushed himself away from the conference table and rose. "I'll meet everyone there." He Communicated to Joseph that he would be delayed until after Mess.

Maddie slid her tray along the chow line. She was hungry, but she was mostly tired. The FST console required constant attention twelve hours every day. She spent at least half an hour with Sean on either end of her shift to reassure him – and herself – that the system was functioning properly. The system was new, and it lacked automatic sensors. Monitoring the incoming data required intense focus. No daydreaming. She wondered what she had done wrong to warrant that arduous assignment. She reckoned it was because of her Group meeting with Premier Paul. A small price to pay in the scheme of things. Premier Paul had convinced Captain Cesar to increase Humanity One's speed. Rex said the new velocity would allow Humanity One to arrive several decades earlier. He also said the MGR colonization protocol was modified to allow Gen 9 to replace Gen 8 as the final generation on Humanity One. It did not change the fact that their atoms - her atoms - would never see Earth Two.

Rex nudged her from behind and smiled when she turned to see who was crowding her. She smiled in return. It was good to be able to talk to her friends in public without fear. "What are you working on today, Genius?" she asked kiddingly.

"Solutions to save humanity," Rex chuckled. "And you?"

"Getting chow. I'm starved. Right now, I'm focused on saving myself." Maddie ladled a bowl of vegetable soup with tofu bits. She hoped they were seasoned with some of Kendra's pepper spices. Kendra was assigned to a larger Grow Room when she reached adulthood. The crops in her new room were more diverse than her root crops. She nodded toward the tables, "I see Kendra and Kevin are sitting at our table with Zack."

"Good. I haven't had the opportunity to visit with Zack for a while. Nor Kendra. Actually, I've only spoken with you ... and not very often, at that. A lot has happened since we sneaked into that little room in San-Re to decipher the alien message."

Maddie finished filling her tray and shuddered. "At least they started listening to us, even though the Captain did punish me by putting me on the FST console."

Rex laughed. "That isn't punishment. It's an honor. You should be proud. He wanted you and your open mind on FST to help develop the system. He even worked it so Sean could be your Trainee. That's unheard of to change training mentors. Haven't the Elec-Techs been coming around with questions?"

"Yes, and Chief Bernie. I thought they were keeping an eye on me because the Captain didn't trust me."

Rex continued laughing as the two sat side-by-side across from Kendra, Kevin, and Zack. Zack's eyes dropped embarrassedly after staring at Maddie's hair. She quit cutting it as soon as she achieved adulthood. It was still shorter than she wanted it to be, but its blonde luster was returning as it grew longer.

"What's so funny?" Kendra asked, infected by Rex's good humor.

Rex put his arm around Maddie's shoulders and drew her to him. "This silly girl thinks the Captain doesn't like her."

Kevin grinned as Maddie playfully slapped Rex and pulled away from him. "Tell me who he does like."

They all fell silent when Captain Cesar entered the Mess Hall and began filling a tray. He was earlier than usual for his midday chow. Frequently, especially during the last few months, Joseph carried a tray to the Captain's Chair. They tried to not look toward him, but he caught at least one of them watching and smiled acknowledgement. As he walked past their table on his way to the VLT table at the far reaches of the Mess Hall, he paused and softly said, "I encourage you to listen to our conversation today."

Maddie's stomach fluttered. She felt as though she might have blushed. Kendra certainly did. Even her breasts reddened. "I wonder what that means."

"No telling," Rex replied. We'll listen when they talk." He turned his attention to Kendra. "Kendra, Kevin when is your baby due?"

Kendra's redness had barely subsided when the question recolored her skin. "How did you find out?" She glared at Maddie, with a poorly disguised smile.

"I see what you're eating. Extra cranberries, for one. A good source of iodine. Tofu, chickpeas plus beans, and a big pile of cooked cabbage. Extra protein, vitamins, and essential elements for fetal development. That's a Medical approved diet if I ever saw one."

Kevin helped his new mate. "Not soon enough to cause too many questions," he answered with a laugh and a squeeze around Kendra's waist.

"Congratulations," mumbled Zack. His disappointment was real. Kendra was mated and it was clear that Maddie was choosing Rex.

The remainder of the VLT entered the Mess Hall in single file with Doctor Katherine in the lead and Premier Paul at the rear. The Group ate silently and warily watched until Premier Paul completed filling his tray.

Maddie finished her chow as she watched the VLT members take their seats and cautiously begin eating. Every member except Cesar seemed on edge, worried about something. Kendra interrupted her concentration.

"Rex, when are you and Maddie going to mate? Everyone is waiting for it." Kendra grinned impishly at the fact that she put Rex on the spot in retaliation for his question about her pregnancy.

Maddie scowled and stopped the conversation with a wave of her hand. Her focus was on the VLT. She wanted to hear anything they might say. Something was different.

Premier Paul paused eating and loudly cleared his throat. The small chatter that normally filled the Mess Hall faded into near silence. "Let's call this Vessel Leadership Team meeting to order." He nervously glanced around the room and spoke in a voice loud enough for everyone to hear, "In a break from tradition, the Captain has asked that we hold a public meeting to discuss matters that relate to the Mission, the Vessel and the Crew. Are there any objections to holding a public meeting?"

Chief Gail unhappily responded, "Oftentimes we express personal thoughts and ideas that are not for public scrutiny. Those thoughts could seem offensive to some people."

Captain Cesar replied in a voice that was loud and direct, "Then I suggest everyone be on their best behavior. May we begin?" He nodded toward the other tables. "I see some have finished eating their chow. Let's not detain them from their duties any more than necessary."

Gail dropped her head and returned to eating.

Premier Paul cocked his head and nodded toward Cesar.

"Good," Cesar said. "Chief Kellie, if additional energy resources were available to Hydroponics, could you increase production?"

Kendra gasped. Maddie's eyes darted toward her before returning to Cesar.

Chief Kellie thoughtfully replied, "It is possible that if we had more intense lighting, we could increase photosynthesis. There would still be the matter of water and growth medium nutrients."

"Explain what that means."

"Humanity One has a finite amount of water for use. The same with the nutrients. They are replenished, and the total volume sustained by Sanitary Recycling ... by recycling all solids and liquids."

Maddie glanced down at her empty water glass. She knew, as did everyone, that every drop of water on Humanity One had been processed through a human body several times. She shook off the thought.

Cesar turned to San-Re Chief Kara. "Chief Kara, with additional energy resources, can Sanitary Recycling support increases in Hydroponics requirements?"

Chief Kara seemed to anticipate the question. "Aye, Captain. The extra energy would be helpful, though our current recycling capacity exceeds the demand. We basically run only half of an Earth day with a skeleton crew on the off shift."

Cesar glanced knowingly around the VLT mess table. "Let me make sure I understand this right. If we increase the amount of recycling needed, we are not in danger of exceeding capacity?"

"Not at all," Chief Kara responded. "It's as if the Innovators designed Sanitary Recycling to meet a higher demand."

Premier Paul cleared his throat to get the attention of the others. Then he spoke in his soft voice. "I'm sure that is in anticipation of the final approach to Earth Two when the residents of Stasis will be revived and living among us."

Chief Gail blurted, "But, the revived people will be available to assist with Crew duties. We don't have the luxury of additional Crew. We are already stretched beyond our limit with new systems and new duties."

"We won't be if we increase the birthrate," Cesar stated.

Chief Deanna chimed in. "If we increase the number of Crew above the current four-hundred twenty or so, we risk exceeding the total molecular resources, the atoms available."

Cesar nodded partial agreement. "On the surface, that seems correct. Doctor Katherine, can you add to this line of reasoning?"

Doctor Katherine shook her head, not to refuse but to display her chagrin. "Of course, I can." She carefully looked around the Mess Hall at the faces eager to hear her response. "It may not seem so, to look at the Gen 2 members of the VLT, but the Generations are becoming smaller in stature. We can only hope that the current stature of Gen 4 will be the space norm of humankind."

Maddie glanced at her fellow Gen 4s. They were younger. Some not yet mature. She knew that. Everyone knew that. Even so, there was a physiological difference between Gen 2 and Gen 3. Gen 3s were not as bulky, not as muscular. Gen 4 promised to be no more than Gen 3 ... if as much ... though Rex was an exception.

Doctor Katherine continued. "Muscle mass, bone mass, both are affected by the lower gravity of Humanity One versus the gravity of our home world. Humans on this vessel will predictably continue to be of smaller mass." She paused before she reluctantly added, "To create and sustain the smaller mass humans requires fewer resources – fewer atoms. That was predicted by the Innovators – to a certain extent. Our available resources are to sustain full-mass humans; therefore, it is no surprise that we might be showing a surplus. That surplus could increase slightly before the mass of our progeny stabilizes."

Maddie felt overwhelmed with the information Doctor Katherine revealed. Another secret. Her anger grew as she wondered why something such as that would be kept secret.

Captain Cesar held up his hand to quell a sudden increase in murmured reactions in the Mess Hall. "Doctor Katherine, in view of the fact that we have added duties for the Crew in support of our velocity increase, is there any viable reason we should not increase the number of Crew members through birth?"

Exasperated, Doctor Katherine responded, "We can't allow two births per mated pair."

"I don't expect that to happen. We can allow some additional births to support the vessel and complete the Mission. Right?"

Reluctantly, Doctor Katherine said, "Aye, Captain. Under Medical constraints."

"As always," Cesar smiled as he nodded understanding and acceptance. "With that, Premier Paul, I yield to you."

Premier Paul looked toward the people in the Mess Hall. "Are there any thoughts further to add?"

Maddie rose. She noticed a smile curl the corners of the Captain's lips. The Premier waved his arm to invite her to speak. "Why has this been kept from us?"

"To what do you refer?" Paul asked.

"The fact that we are of smaller mass and that it was predicted."

Doctor Katherine spoke in response, "It was not so much kept from you as it was simply a part of the Medical Department's duties to understand it. Would knowing that you and your children would be smaller than the Innovators have changed your life, affected your duties and viability?"

"No, but ..." Maddie began, momentarily rebuffed.

"But nothing," replied Doctor Katherine. "I know very little of your duties, the knowledge you were taught, the skills you developed. It does not affect my viability and success as a Medical Doctor. Just because we don't know a particular thing does not make it secret."

"But there's more we should know," Maddie protested.

"Then, by all means, learn it when you are not on duty," Doctor Katherine responded dismissively, "if you can find someone with time away from duty long enough to teach you knowledge that you will never use."

The response did not appease Maddie. If anything, it made her angrier. She felt Rex's hand on the side of her thigh, patting caution. She glared at him momentarily before she said, "Thank you, Doctor Katherine," and took her seat. She had questions and it appeared Doctor Katherine might be willing to provide answers.

CHAPTER 40

JUSTIFICATION

Maddie left the Mess Hall leading the Group with Rex at her side. She, or Rex, owed Kendra a response. In the passageway as soon as Crew members not part of the Group were out of hearing range, Maddie stopped abruptly and turned to face the others. The others were barely able to avoid collision. "Kendra, in case you didn't know, Rex and I carry a common trailing number. We share the same Sire. We can't mate." She turned and continued on her way without expecting a response.

As the week passed, Maddie accepted her role as user-developer of the FST system. Without the nagging feeling that the duty was punishment, the task became easier and more gratifying. After Sean relieved her on the console for the off-shift, Maddie went to the Mess Hall for her final mess of the day. Marly was sitting at a table with Doctor Katherine. Maddie smiled and hurried to the table, fearful someone else would strike up a conversation with Katherine before she got there.

"Doctor Katherine, Marly, may I join you?"

Marly smiled nervously. Doctor Katherine nodded but continued eating without display of emotion.

Maddie sat across the table from the two of them. "Marly, you must be as busy as I am. I haven't seen you for several days."

"Oh yes. I am learning so much that I sometimes think my head will burst." The petite girl grinned nervously and looked toward Doctor Katherine for validation.

Katherine finished chewing a mouthful of chow. "Absolutely. Learning the things necessary to be a Doctor requires commitment. There is no easy way. Doctor Trainee Marly certainly has commitment. How is your new assignment progressing, Maddison? Is the new system performing as expected?"

Maddie was frustrated by Katherine's stiffness. It felt like a challenge. She had no doubt that the Chief Medical Officer was aware of everything pertaining to what was perceived as a deviation from the MGR. "We have made improvements in data interpretation. From that, Sci-Eng Technicians can make better calculations and adjustments to Humanity One's course."

Katherine shook her head and looked at her fork as she loaded it with another mouthful. "I hope we aren't making a mistake." She ate.

Maddie waited until the older woman swallowed before she asked her next question. "Doctor Katherine, why are our progeny not going to be allowed to colonize Earth Two?" It was blunt, slightly accusative. She was sure she knew the answer, probably the correct answer, but she wanted to hear it from Doctor Katherine's lips.

Doctor Katherine considered the question as she chewed another mouthful. "Maddie, it's not a matter of allowing or not allowing. As I noted before, the Crew of Humanity One has predictably lost body mass. The Innovators believed this would happen. Without musculoskeletal strength capable of withstanding the gravitational pull of a planet, we would be unable to function. In all likelihood, we couldn't even breathe on our own."

"Then, why are we doing all of this?" Maddie waved her arms to encompass her surroundings and imply the entire vessel. "If we can't get something in return, why don't we simply travel through space and live for generations inside Humanity One? Our grandchildren deserve a future as well."

Katherine winced painfully. "Maddie, that would not be much of a future. Our purpose – our future, as you call it - is greater than survival of our grandchildren. Our purpose, and the purpose of our grandchildren, is to save humanity – humankind and its untold generations of accumulated knowledge. Aside from the fact that Humanity One will not endure forever, humans are not predisposed to living inside the confines of a vessel. Physically, our bodies are subject to degradation. Mentally, we are too inquisitive to be confined. We are adventurers and conquerors by nature."

"What adventure is this? What will we conquer?"

Katherine finally smiled, "The adventure is to travel across space as no other human has ever done. And we will conquer the natural forces that work against sustained civilization. Human history is replete with risen and fallen civilizations, destroyed by an environment that constantly changes – a characteristic of all celestial bodies. We will conquer the need to start over after every climatic epoch. We can take control of our destiny by carrying humanity forward in this vessel ..." she paused, then added, "... by being the vessels of humanity."

Maddie considered Katherine's explanation. It made sense in principle, but in practice – not so much. "If we humans are adventurers and conquerors, why would we sacrifice our atoms in such a cavalier manner?"

"It's not cavalier. Not in any sense of the word. Adventurers and conquerors have yielded their personal atoms ... their genetic lines is a better description ... in favor of the greater good of humanity. Exploring new territory to add to the knowledge of humankind. Providing for the survival of the species is a noble endeavor. A notable cause. That is what we are doing. In the end, we will sacrifice our genetic lines so that humanity can prevail."

"Are our genetic lines not worthy of saving? Aren't we the same genetic line as the Innovators?"

"Yes, we are. For that reason, our genetic lines are not truly sacrificed. I have no offspring, by choice. I leave nothing of myself behind when I recycle."

"You will leave your atoms."

Katherine smiled knowingly; her wrinkled face further creased by the motion. "Our atoms are indistinguishable from all other atoms in the universe. Our atoms are the universe. Our deeds are our legacy."

"But there will be nothing of us, our genetic lines as you call it, left behind," Maddie protested.

"Those who sired and birthed us have sired and birthed the same genetic lines that will colonize Earth Two. The people and the embryos in Stasis are the start of our lines, the same as our lines." Katherine returned to her chow.

Maddie knew the discussion would go no further as it was framed. She asked a personal question. "Why did you not have a child, someone to be your replacement?"

Katherine looked Maddie straight in the eyes. "Maybe because I knew too much. I am not selfless - at least, I was not when I was younger. I suffered some of the same distractions as do you and your Group. I did not want to see my progeny forced to become vessels to grow the Innovators' embryos for colonization. I'm a good Doctor, but I'm not heroic." Her eyes dropped and she returned her attention to the chow tray on the cold table before her.

Maddie saw the pain in Doctor Katherine's eyes. More, she saw the puzzled shock in Marly's. She was unsure how to continue the conversation. She turned her attention to her chow and remained silent. Questions still remained, but someone else at some other time would have to provide the answers.

Premier Paul was startled by the presence that appeared in his mind. His Communicator was activated externally. He responded to the presence he recognized. "Maddison Si Wu-Qi, what have you to say?" The mental language provided by the Communicator was graphic, including presentation of names including numeric trailers. Always all inclusive.

"I wish to meet with you ... privately."

Paul felt the urgency that was not covered by the simple words that Maddie tried to use in her transferred thoughts. He looked in a small wall mirror automatically, a vain attempt at reassuring himself that he was presentable. The pale, withered face that looked back at him showed fatigue. The changes, the deviations from the MGR, took a toll on a man whose previous fifty-six years had been choreographed by infallible entities. The outcomes of those deviations had disproved the infallibility of the Innovators. His entire world was in a shamble, at least his psychological world. "I am in my quarters. How soon?"

"I'm outside your quarters."

"Enter."

Paul watched the door slide open to reveal the young blonde-haired woman nervously waiting to enter. Maddie was one of the most attractive women in Humanity One. He wondered if she had chosen a Gen 4 male for mating.

Maddie nervously grinned and spoke aloud, "I have not, Premier. I'm not sure I will."

Paul felt his face tinge. He should have known better than leave his Communicator in active contact while he pondered. "I'm sorry. I did not mean to offend you by Communicating my indiscreet thoughts."

Maddie smiled and waved her hand to dismiss the subject. "It didn't offend me. It is a question that is on my mind often enough. I may do as Doctor Katherine has done and forego bearing a child."

"That would be a shame," Paul replied, then added, "but I'm sure that is not the reason for your request."

"No, it isn't. I am afraid for the future of the Crew."

"The survival of humanity is our future. The Crew's duty is to make sure humanity survives."

Maddie responded, "Doctor Katherine explained all that to me. I understand why we ... our children's children ... cannot physically colonize Earth Two. I do question whether the Innovators could have designed Humanity One to maintain our mass and strength so we could go to Earth Two, but it's too late for that. It's not too late to make sure we don't fail the Mission they handed to us."

Paul motioned to a small chair and waited for Maddie to sit before he sat on a more comfortable chair. "We have made significant changes to ensure our success. Changes, I might add, that go against the MGR."

"I understand that. Those changes weren't made easily. Rex had to risk his viability to even get the Captain's attention."

Paul nodded understanding. "Yes. Rex saw something wrong and provided a solution."

Maddie replied heatedly, "But he had to scream to be heard."

Paul's fatigue tried to overwhelm him. No one ... especially the neo-adult sitting in his quarters ... understood the toll the last few months had taken on him. "True. But was it that he had to *scream*, or that he had to *demonstrate* belief and commitment?"

"What does that mean?"

"Do you not think the Captain, all the Chiefs, hear voices all the time? Voices of those around them ... along with the persistent voices of the Innovators. They ... we ... have to sift through all the sounds."

"Still, if Rex hadn't risked recycling, nothing would have been done."

"Belief and commitment. Everyone questions the decisions of others. If the Captain reacted to every complaint and followed every suggestion he heard, he would be criticized for vacillation ... rightly so. He is committed to the Mission and Humanity One's success. He can ill afford to lose focus on a whim from one of the many voices in his ears. He can only listen to those that are committed."

Unconvinced, Maddie argued, "But Rex wouldn't have said something if he wasn't committed."

"Why should the Captain listen more to Rex than any other voice?" Paul's voice softened, "But this comes down to your voice, doesn't it?"

Maddie was caught off guard. "No! I am concerned about everyone's voice. Not just mine."

"You have not demonstrated commitment to that. Your words sound selfish."

"That's not true!"

"Your petulance at this moment belies what you declare. Yet, in the final analysis, your voice was heard when it needed to be heard. And the Captain acted on your voice. In truth, he was more committed to your words than you were. If your voice were wrong, it could have resulted in Mission failure and most certainly would have resulted in a declaration of his non-viability because he listened to you. He believed your voice at risk of his own viability. That is commitment."

"I was committed when I suggested we should change our velocity."

"Were you willing to go to Recycle with those words still on your lips? Rex committed. But he did not *only* seek a change. He sought change within the system without seeking to destroy the vessel. Humanity One is all we have. We cannot risk it. It carries the seeds of humanity. Any threat to it must be dealt with adamantly."

"Like Jana?"

Paul paled. His frail hands began to tremble. He remembered the young, frightened face of Jana Si Yi-Liu as Doctor Katherine administered the dose that caused the young girl's face to relax and her soft brown eyes to stare without light. He knew Captain Cesar thought about the offspring of his son and the loss of her life in light of what had been learned since her recycling. He wondered if he should try to enumerate the defensive recyclings in his lifetime. They were done to preserve the value of the MGR. Now, the value of the MGR as an infallible document was in question. Maybe it was being proven wrong so the world that was Humanity One and its Mission could evolve. "That could be." His eyes dropped to stare at Maddie's feet. Smooth skin unmarked by wrinkles and dark spots that Katherine assured him were melanin accumulations as a result of aging and the constant exposure to the vessel's Vitamin D encouraging ultraviolet lights, few though they were. "That could be," he repeated barely audibly.

"We deserve to be heard," Maddie continued, "not recycled for violating some old guideline."

Paul leaned back against his chair and crossed his hands in his lap. "And you were."

"Would we have been if we weren't in danger of attack by the alien vessel?"

"Probably not, but without the presence of the alien vessel and the dangers it represented, there was no need for your voice to be heard." Paul was sure his statement would end the discussion that was adding to his weariness.

"That's not true, Premier Paul. If we had not done anything ... if Rex had not spoken ... if the Group had not demanded to be heard, we would still be on path to arrive at least four generations too late. And, even if later generations realized the need to defer the plans for Gen 8 until Gen 12 or 13, Humanity One's resources might not have been able to support that."

"Maddie, it's important to note that each Generation is a step along the pathway to the final Mission. If a step is shorter than previously planned, that merely means more steps, but the length of the path is the same. Humanity One's resources were calculated to be sufficient to carry the Crew and those in Stasis to Earth Two for colonization. The Mission was not entirely at risk if we did not adopt the higher velocity and all that comes with it."

"Humanity One would have arrived too late. The people in Stasis would have..."

"Maddie, hear me above your voice," Paul interrupted wearily. "You, or the Generation after yours, would have made the necessary decisions to extend the Generations and revive the Innovators in Stasis at the correct time on the original timeline. If you read the MGR for the final phases, you will see that the timing is for the twenty-fourth decade as much as it is for the Eighth Generation. That inconsistency would have been managed within the MGR's constrains, if we had not encountered the alien vessel."

"You say that, but if we were all recycled for heresy, no one would ever speak up again." Maddie was not willing to let go of her moment.

"Maddie, youth is never afraid to speak;" Paul smiled wryly. "though the elderly are often deaf to the sound. Your ears will become immune to sounds before your recycling day."

"If voices are not heard, speaking out becomes futile. Eventually, there will be no voices. Without voices, there is no autonomy. If the voices are silenced, only blind subjugation to the MGR will exist."

"Maddie, you are arguing that we should ignore the very laws that have sustained us for three generations. How can we turn our backs on that?"

"We don't turn our backs on the MGR. We share the reasons they were written."

"We know why they were written. To provide a blueprint for the generations to follow, to ensure the success of the Mission. Did the MGR not help you learn everything you needed to know to become a Con-Sys Technician?"

"By rote, yes. But I don't know why it's important to know what I know. Except, the FST System. Because I am participating in its implementation, I understand the importance. I know why it's important."

"I understand your thoughts regarding the Forward Scanning Telemetry System. You are a developer, not unlike the Innovators were with all the other systems. Does *not knowing* the inner workings of the Environmental Monitoring System make it less valuable to know how to use the system?"

"No, but there is no need for all the secrecy. Too much is kept from the Crew. We could contribute more if we knew more."

Paul stared at the young blonde-haired woman, slowly nodding. "That is probably the most salient point of your argument. I have come to see that there is a difference between distracting information and necessary understanding. We need to strike a balance."

"But still keep secrets?" Maddie asked with a petulant scowl.

"No. Not secrets. All the information known to humanity is in the archives, available for access. One only needs to view it."

"But we have no time because of our duties. We are automatons inside human flesh. I wonder why the Innovators didn't simple program robots to mind their vessel and tend to their own in Stasis."

Paul thought before he responded. "Probably because there were two needs. One, the obvious need for vessels to give birth to the embryos stored in Stasis. Without those newborn humans, there would not be enough humans to quickly colonize Earth Two. Second, unforeseen circumstances such as the alien vessel and the reduction of life span presented problems that only a creative mind could solve."

"And that required information and voices," Maddie replied smugly.

"It did. That is why I have come to see a need for changes. I do not yet know what those changes should be. I daresay neither do you. Have you thought about the fact that during the generations yet to be born, further changes could occur that would jeopardize the Mission? Even shorter life spans. Disabling diseases. Sterility. Even with the additions of Crew that we now have planned, the risk remains because none of the unknowns have been addressed."

"Then go faster. Arrive even earlier," Maddie said in a tone that implied the solution was simple.

"Were it possible. As Rex and Chief Gail have explained it, we are tempting fate by traveling at ninety percent of the speed of light. Going faster exposes us to unpredictable circumstances. We cannot go faster than the velocity we will achieve when young Rex's efforts are completed. Maddie, I fear that I must rest. It has been a trying few weeks, and they have caught up with me." Paul watched the young woman's face twitch as she fought to suppress her thoughts and the desire to verbalize them. "Don't worry. I assure you that we will have opportunity to speak further," he said.

"Thank you. One last thing," Maddie paused as she gathered her thoughts to complete her request, "may we hold a requiem for Jana? She was our friend."

⌁

Premier Paul stood outside Cesar's quarters, unsure how to begin the conversation. He knew Cesar had forgone late Mess in favor of rest. Like him, the Captain showed physical signs of strain. Humanity One was almost at the velocity Chief Gail and Rex assured them the enhanced propulsion system could achieve. More importantly, Humanity One was almost at the rate required to reach Earth Two early enough to avoid Mission failure – if everything else remained on plan.

The Captain attended the off-shift requiem for Jana two weeks earlier. Paul wondered if he would. The Captain's presence was noted by all in attendance, though he remained on the periphery. Joseph did not attend. For whatever reason, the Captain Trainee chose to remain in his quarters with his mate. The Group commanded the attention of diners in the Mess Hall to say their words, to deliver their eulogies in honor of Jana Si Yi-Liu. Paul listened somberly and wondered if the event was the same as an Earth One funeral. Ever since that day, the Captain had behaved differently, often distracted by his own thoughts – but never failing his duties of caring for Humanity One and of training Joseph.

Paul engaged his Communicator to get the Captain's attention. In response, the door slid open. Cesar was hunched in front of his computer screen, finalizing entries in the Captain's Log.

"What brings you calling this time of day?" Cesar asked as he straightened his back and twisted it in an effort to relieve the pain.

Paul saw the motion. More, he saw the pain ripple across the Captain's wrinkled face. The Captain's recent weight loss increased the definition of those wrinkles. "Just checking on you. You seem near the point of exhaustion."

"So do you, Paul. Trying times. But everything seems to be working because of Rex's solutions."

"I suppose. How is Joseph?"

Cesar looked at Paul quizzically. "Finalizing his qualification. I've been letting him take the Chair more each day. I sit in the Trainee Chair and observe. Not much more to teach him. Let him practice what he knows."

Paul knew what the Captain was doing, but the conversation needed to be had. Cesar's faith in the MGR was shaken to the core. Decades of following the MGR to the letter abruptly came to an end. The man had endured more than the Innovators had anticipated, more than they expected anyone would have to endure. Maybe the entire Crew had. While the Captain would not live to what was once considered old age, he had served as Captain longer than seemed humanly possible under the circumstances. Because of his Sire's early passing, Cesar's role as Captain was almost twice the span of a generation as it was calculated by the Innovators. Cesar had every right to be tired. "Cesar, I'm concerned about Joseph's emerging offspring." Joseph's mate would not deliver for several more months.

"What's your concern?" Cesar's eyes darkened quizzically.

"Will Joseph have time to raise and to train his offspring, his replacement? There is no certainty of life-span for any individual — even a Captain."

Cesar glared at Paul for several moments. His eyes softened. "There is no need to worry."

"What?" Paul was startled by the answer.

"Why repeat the past? Joseph will not train his child to be Captain. Rex will make a suitable Captain after Joseph. He will be different. Joseph will be another me, just like I have been another August. Humanity One can no longer depend on the MGR to provide all the answers. Our current state might abide another generation of blind obedience, but problems don't get solved with obedience."

"Have you spoken with Chief Gail? I'm sure she has plans for Sci-Eng Technician Rex."

"Chief Gail has plans for Chief Gail. Just like with Chief Robert, she will destroy anyone who seems a threat to her within her domain. I am requesting a VLT meeting tomorrow to officially place Rex Si Wu-Ershiliu in Captain training. He will learn it fast. He'll provide assistance to Joseph rather than parrot back his Trainer's training, like Joseph has always done for me."

"How will Joseph react to a Trainee not of his choosing at his side? Won't he feel threatened? Is that fair to him?"

Cesar drew himself up straight in the chair and looked firmly into Paul's eyes. "He won't be threatened because he won't have another Trainee at his side, standing in his shadow, learning only what he has to teach. Rex will seek training from the archives to enhance the MGR training for Captain."

"It will still be a threat to Joseph. He will see the attention paid to Rex. The child he sires will lose status." Paul protested.

"Status doesn't save the Mission," Cesar snapped. Then more calmly, he said, "He'll be too busy in the Chair. There's enough to being Captain to prevent any thoughts of threats."

"What does that mean?"

"Joseph will soon find that the duties of Captain far exceed the simple functions associated with guiding the vessel through space."

Paul could not ignore the intensity of Cesar's eyes. He averted his eyes momentarily; contemplating what he understood to be the meaning of Cesar's words. "Maybe Mia San Ba-Qi will do a better job as Premier than I."

"Maybe. Maybe not. That really should not matter to Joseph. He will be fully occupied with the interactive navigation of Humanity One. I spent my entire life watching this vessel follow the trajectory set for it by dead people. Joseph will not have that luxury. He will need someone like Rex to help him. No, Rex will be a blessing, not a threat to Captain Joseph."

"Are you sure this is the right thing to do?"

"I'm sure we can't repeat the mistakes of the past."

"Our past is a good one, established by men and women smarter than us."

"Were they? Sure, they were smart enough to lay the foundation for us. But if they were truly smart, they would have expected us to build on their foundation; conditioned us to do so rather than rely upon them for future decisions."

Paul saw the weary determination in Cesar's face. "I often wonder if we could have succeeded without the MGR."

"We could not have. The MGR are necessary to the Mission. They have proven that, but the likes of Rex and Maddison will succeed because they refuse to simply follow the MGR without question." Cesar paused and finished with moist eyes. "Like Jana might have."

Paul uncomfortably shifted from foot to foot for a moment. "I suppose that is the way it must be," he said with a sigh. His intended conversation with Captain Cesar, to budge the stronger willed man from his bully stance, was settled by Cesar. "I think I should let you rest."

"I need rest more than you can imagine. I'm sure you need rest as well, Paul." Cesar offered a seldom seen smile of friendship.

Paul returned the smile and turned to go.

"One more thing, Premier," Cesar said, "I will cede the Chair to Joseph in one month if Rex's calculations continue to prove successful. Will you accompany me to see Doctor Katherine?"